WHISPERING

A Chagford tale **GRASS**

Why do you whisper, green grass?
Why tell the trees what ain't so?
Whispering grass, the trees don't have to know
Oh no…
A song made popular by The Inkspots in 1939

RICHARD WILLIAMSON

EDGEMOOR PUBLISHING

First published 2011
Published by Edgemoor Publishing Limited
Wykeham House, Station Road, Okehampton, Devon EX20 1DY

© Richard G. Williamson 2011

The right of Richard G. Williamson to be identified as Author of this work has been
asserted in accordance with the Copyrights, Designs and Patents Act 1988.

Edited by Sue Viccars
Designed by Simon Lloyd
Cover photographs by Dave Cutts and Mark Frost

British Library Cataloguing in Publication Data
A catalogue record for this book is available from the British Library

ISBN 978-0-9564246-1-7

Typesetting and origination by Edgemoor Publishing Limited
Printed in Great Britain by Short Run Press Limited

*This is a work of fiction and except in the case of historical fact,
and some names and events, any resemblance
to actual persons, living or dead, is purely coincidental.*

—◦◦◦—

For Bet and in memory of Lindy

PROLOGUE

In 1759 the highly regarded cabinetmakers Ince and Mayhew of
Broad Street, Golden Square, Soho, London, completed a display
cabinet – 'A China Case in the Chinese Manner'– on the instructions
of Nathan Alfred Fulford Esq of Cranmere in the County of Devon.
This fine example of the cabinetmaker's craft stood eight feet in
height and over nine feet in width, and was made in sections for ease
of transport. The long journey to West Devon by horse-drawn wagon
– trundling at walking pace and with many halts to ensure that the
lambswool and hessian packing had not become displaced – took
three weeks. On arrival and installation in the long gallery at
Cranmere, Nathan Alfred Fulford Esq was so overwhelmed by the
beauty and presence of his purchase that he immediately ordered
another identical cabinet to be constructed. This was delivered in the
spring of 1761. From time to time over the following two centuries,
the cabinets required minor overhaul – bits of veneer and mouldings
detached by the flick of a housemaid's duster – these delicate repairs
to be carried out, on the instructions of a succession of Fulfords, by
one firm and none other: Wesson's of Lynchcombe in the County of
Gloucestershire. The arrangement worked well until one of the
cabinets disappeared. Soon it would be the turn of Henry (Hal)
Wesson to wait upon the Fulford family – and their cabinets.

—◈—

PART 1

CHAPTER 1
SPRING 1992

——⟨∿∿⟩——

There was no ceremony when Jane left Cranmere for the last time, no long, drawn-out parting – that would have been the very last thing she wanted. This was as good a time as any. David was in London for a few days and the boys away at school while Catherine, her daughter-in-law, was most likely hunched over her computer with her perpetual cigarette, or in a meeting with her architect and builder who would very soon begin to tear the old house apart in the 'first phase' – Catherine's term – of its partial conversion into luxury apartments. These to be sold on 99-year leases so that they could revert back. To whom? she wondered. Would Fulford's still exist in 99 years' time? And, if so, would they even be aware of a one-time Jane Fulford? She very much doubted it. She would be remembered with affection, she hoped, by David, her son; the two boys, Richard and Thomas; possibly but less so by Catherine; and a few friends. But after a generation, the screen would go blank.

Since Roger's death had left her a dowager – a word she detested – it had taken her a very long time to finally relinquish the last shreds of her term of office. David and Catherine's takeover had been gradual and gentle, but the finality had come as a shock, like an expected death. After fifty-odd years of her stewardship, Cranmere had a new mistress with new ideas and a computer and mobile phone, and was now a limited company. So no longer for her the role of shadowy background figure like Marie, her mother-in-law, now long dead. She would leave. Earlier in the day she had encountered Catherine on the stairs.

'When are you off, Jane?'

'Don't worry, I'll soon be out of your way.'

'I'm not trying to rush you!' Catherine looked hurt.

'No, no, I know you're not.' Jane shook her head in annoyance. 'Please forgive me.' She was immediately sorry for snapping at her daughter-in-law: so thoughtless and unnecessary, and not at all like her. Truth was, she felt tense and unsettled after that telephone call earlier in the morning.

'Stressed out,' as the boys would say. 'Pay no attention, Catherine,' she said with what she hoped was a bright smile. 'When do your builders arrive?'

'Tomorrow morning, they said.'

'Then I will leave this afternoon.' The thought of heavy footsteps on the stairs, raised voices and transistor radios filled her with horror. The tranquillity of the old house was to be destroyed once more, this time possibly for ever. A new chapter on Cranmere was to be written in which she would not feature. It was time to go.

She left by the glazed door onto the terrace, symbolically, the same way she had first entered the house on a similarly perfect spring day, and down the wide steps to the gravelled drive. Keeping to the springy turf beside the hard surface, she walked slowly; there was no urgency, and she wanted to savour the new life all around her, the lush greens of the grasses, the infant beech leaves on the tall trees that lined the drive and, of course, the daffodils. She carried nothing but the walking stick she had taken to only recently, not yet a necessity but an aid. Beside her Tansy, her spaniel and constant companion, trotted contentedly. The Dower House stood facing her a little further down the drive, a miniature version of Cranmere, complete with pediment and its own tiny terrace from where generations of dowagers had kept a critical eye – one, by all accounts, through a telescope – on the fortunes of their children. Would she continue to do so, not forgetting the proud owners of the luxury apartments, with their luxury cars? She thought not.

Looking at her new home, the front now shaded from the afternoon sun, she felt yes, she would be content there for the little time she had left; and, far from any sense of loss or sadness, she felt a certain elation. For the first time in years, she was free. She could arrange her timetable to suit herself without having to take others into consideration, fill her rooms with flowers and plants, snack when she felt like it, watch old films on TV, even stay in bed! Would she be lonely? No, David would be close by and she could talk for hours on the telephone without fear on interruption. Like this morning…

'Mrs Jane Fulford?' A vaguely familiar voice that she could not quite place.

'Yes, who is this?'

'Jane, this is Edward.'

'Oh, Edward!' she exclaimed. 'How lovely to hear from you after all this time.'

'That is not the correct reply,' the voice said severely.

'No, I'm sorry,' Jane said, remembering the rules. She lowered her voice and said, 'Edward, this is Jane,' a procedure they had had to observe during the war years when Captain Edward Channon had been the only contact for news of a husband who was beyond reach in enemy territory. Now, it seemed childish.

'That's better,' he laughed. 'How are you keeping, Jane?'

'I am well, thank you. And moving into my new home this afternoon. I'll give you my number.'

'Away from Cranmere?'

'Good heavens no – the Dower House awaits. I am to be put to grass.'

'Will you enjoy that, Jane?'

'Do you know, I rather think I will.'

The door behind her opened and Catherine looked into the room, said 'Sorry, I didn't know you were on the phone,' and withdrew.

Jane frowned at the closing door. 'What were you saying, Edward?'

'I was saying, we still haven't met.'

'No, I know. Left it a bit late, haven't we? But I still have my mental picture.'

'Mental picture? Do tell me.'

Jane smiled, knowing a little more than Edward realised. 'Oh, let's see: dark haired, clean cut, military moustache and a pipe.'

She remembered the deep laugh. 'I'm sorry, Jane, you are wrong on all counts. And I have the advantage over you: your photograph brightened our office wall for years.'

'You mean you took it down?'

'Had to. It was a calendar, years out of date.'

'What year was it?'

'I'm not sure, it was the year you won the cup at the Devon County Show.'

'Edward, that was in 1938!'

'Was it, really?'

'...perhaps it is better that we do not meet.'

'Don't say that, Jane. One lives in hope.'

'Why did you phone me, Edward?'

'Ah yes. Are you sitting down?'

'I am.'

'I think we may have found your missing cabinet. I'm not entirely sure yet, but it sounds likely.'

'Have you? Where is it?'

'New York.'

'How did it get there?'

'That is what I mean to find out. And hopefully, get it back for you.'

'Can you do that?'

'I can try. But I will have to send someone down to take a good look at your cabinet before he goes to New York. We have to be certain before making any moves.'

'Yes, I suppose you do, but how exciting! When do you want your man to come?'

'As soon as possible, this week if you can manage it.'

'Yes, all right.'

'Jane, he is Henry Wesson, Charles' son.'

She caught her breath.

'Are you there, Jane?'

'Yes, I'm here. I'd heard Charles had a boy but… how old is he?'

'Twenty-eight or nine, I'm not sure.'

'Is he anything like his father?'

'Not so much in appearance as in mannerisms, although there are similarities of course. He's a very decent young man, and he also happens to be my son-in-law. I think you will like him.'

'Will he come here?'

'I haven't asked him yet but I'm sure he will, if only to see his father's achievement.'

'Yes but, does he know…?'

'He knows his father had a monumental row with Roger, nothing more. And he's too intelligent a man to let old feuds cloud his judgement.'

'I hope you're right, Edward.'

'I'm sure I am, Jane. Trust me.'

'I do.'

Truth is, Edward, Jane thought as she put down the telephone, I am not sure that I can trust myself.

A richly ornamented cast iron seat set in the grass was positioned so that the user faced east, looking down the long valley over Cranmere pasture to the peaks of Dartmoor. Reaching this, Jane rested with gratitude to a long-forgotten Victorian Fulford, and for a while watched David's Friesian cattle contentedly cropping the grass. She should, she thought, be equally content. Roger had been in his family vault these past 20 years, where she sincerely hoped he was at peace. She lacked for nothing and now her time was her own, so why this feeling of disquiet? Because that simple message from Edward Channon – damn you, Edward – had stirred up memories that were best left at rest – like Roger.

—◦◦◦—

1938? Ha! The year her life had changed direction. The year she had allowed Tom Challacombe, her riding instructor and a hard man to please, to persuade her that she was good enough to enter the main show-jumping event at the Devon County Show. And she'd had the bare-faced cheek to beat the County's favourite, Roger Fulford, into second place. Not that she hadn't paid for that effrontery many times over, and just as many times had wondered how her life might have differed had she come in second. Even after the passage of years she could recall that July afternoon in minute detail – the heat, the dust, the smells of sweating horse and newly mown grass as she had guided her little dappled mare through the eliminating rounds and to the final. And Tom Challacombe's voice in her ear. 'Now listen to me, Jane. Are you listening?'

'Yes, Tom.'

'You can win this if you just take 'er gently. Rosie's jumping like a little cat today, so nice an' easy for a clear round. Right?'

'Right, Tom,' she replied with a lot more conviction than she felt. She was shaking, she needed a pee, she needed anything but to go back into the arena again. She was the last of four finalists; the three before her had all had the big triple fence down for four faults. Suddenly she was on, with Tom's voice ringing in her ears, 'Go on, maid. Gently now.' The sunlight blinded her after the gloom of the canvas tenting. 'Nice an' easy,' Tom had said, even if a thousand schoolgirl voices were shrieking 'Rosie, Rosie!'. Rosie responded, dancing a little circle before coming up to the start line. 'She's on her toes,' said the voice over the tannoy, 'prettiest little mare in Devon,' followed by a laugh of approval from the male spectators.

Stung by the inference, Jane leaned forward in the saddle, whispering into a cocked ear, 'Come on then, Rosie, let's show the buggers.' She felt the little mare's flanks quiver, her muscles bunch and they were away, over the first two fences with ease, then the third and on towards the big triple. 'Steady now, Rosie,' she called out and Rosie jumped, her little hooves tucked up tight beneath her – in – two strides – over – two strides – and out – and she sensed, rather than heard, the communal gasp of relief and then complete silence until she had cleared the last fence.

The crowd went wild, almost drowning out the tannoy – 'Jane Bowden... clear on Rosalind... this year's winner... cup.' She was laughing, crying, waving to her supporters as Rosie (Rosalind?) danced her little circle before leaving the arena. Once in the tented area she slid from the saddle, put both arms around Rosie's neck and hugged her, and was mobbed by every stable girl and groom and by some of her rival competitors, even Tom Challacombe. Then came a curious lull as she felt a hand on her shoulder and a familiar voice saying, 'Congratulations, Jane. Well done.' Roger Fulford seemed to tower over her.

She looked up at him and smiled, 'Thank you,' adding, she was not sure why, 'I am so sorry.'

'Sorry? Whatever for?'

'Well, you only had four faults.'

'Sloppy riding. You won fair and square, Jane, you deserved it.'

She was surprised at Roger's magnanimity, had half expected him to be a bad loser, to remark on beginner's luck. She knew him to speak to, of course, but only around the show ring, had always found him a bit unnerving in his immaculate riding kit and on his – yes – his high horse.

They walked their mounts into the arena to more tumultuous applause, Jane convinced that this was all a dream – she, going in to receive the cup with Roger Fulford at her side, in second place! The show officials seemed a long way off, a large and important-looking woman flanked by men in funereal black with bowler hats, dusty in the heat of the afternoon.

'You've done a fair bit of this before, haven't you, Roger?'

'A fair bit, yes. Smile for the Lady Mayoress.'

She accepted the cup and rosette to the sound of more falsetto shrieks from the crowd, vaguely heard the over-dressed and perspiring woman saying, 'Awfully well done, such a change to have a gel winner.' Roger, naturally, charmed the Lady Mayoress who was saying, 'Dreadfully disappointing for you, Roger. We were all rooting for you, you know,' when Rosie chose to emit a well-timed and perfectly pitched fart, reducing both prizewinners to fits of giggles. They cantered around the arena in a lap of honour, Roger, very correctly, keeping his mount slightly behind the winner.

'Were you really sorry?' he called to her.

'In a way, yes,' she called over her shoulder.

'You could make amends.'

'How?'

'Dine with me tonight.'

'Yes, all right,' she heard herself saying.

On the way home in the battered old horsebox Jane sat nursing the cup while Doris, Tom Challacombe's head girl, crunched her way through the gear changes. 'I've got a date tonight,' she announced.

'Don't tell me,' Doris grinned, 'Roger the lodger?'

'That's right.'

'Bloody 'ell. Better keep yer 'and on yer whatnot.'

———

At her home in East Budleigh, Jane was hugged by her father, a tweedy country doctor who had been holding a clinic that afternoon but had heard his daughter's moment of glory on his portable wireless, and very nearly, he said, vaccinated a mother instead of her infant. And again hugged by her mother who had been in one of her many committee meetings. Jane had no doubt that her mother would dine out on her win for weeks to come.

'We are so proud of you, dear. Such a pity that neither of us could have been there, but we're having a few friends in for drinks later on to celebrate. That will be nice, won't it?'

'Sorry, mother, I've a dinner date.'

'But you can't have!' Her mother said, horrified. 'It's all arranged.'

'So is my dinner date,' Jane added before her mother could further protest. 'It's with Roger Fulford. He'll be here at seven so I'd better make haste.'

'Roger Fulford! Coming here! Did you hear that, Douglas?' Mrs Bowden addressed her husband, sitting quietly with the evening paper

'I heard,' he said through a cloud of pipe smoke.

Really, I do think you might have told us.' The ritual of plumping up cushions, straightening pictures and magazines had already commenced.

In her bedroom Jane grinned at her reflection in the mirror as she brushed out her fair hair, tucked cruelly into a riding hat all afternoon, and congratulated herself on having ducked out of being shown off to the neighbours, Ugh! What a pity her mother couldn't have missed a committee meeting, just this once.

Through the open window she saw Roger as he pulled into the short drive in a beautiful pale blue open car, an Alvis. She signalled five minutes. The doorbell's ring was followed by her mother hissing through the bannisters, 'He's here, Jane. Aren't you ready yet?'

They dined in Exeter's most fashionable venue, Jane still bubbling with laughter at the way Roger had deftly avoided her mother's offer of dry sherry with a glance at his wristwatch and, 'Would you mind awfully, we've a table booked at the Clarence in ten minutes?' Her mother would have said 'Royal Clarence'. There was no table booked but, Mr Fulford, sir, was greeted by the head porter as he parked the Alvis right outside the front door, and again by the head waiter who found a vacant table as if by magic in an otherwise crowded dining room. She was impressed – what twenty-two-year-old would not have been? – by Roger's bland acceptance of these small privileges as his right. Her parents would have parked the car and walked, and waited for a table, and thanked the head waiter. His family, Roger told her, had been dining at the Clarence for generations. 'Must have paid for the pub three times over.' Pub?

Afterwards she was to remember smoked salmon, lobster and a wonderful confection of strawberries in season. And an overweight, baby-faced man of about Roger's age who came to their table exclaiming, 'Roger Fulford, as ever was. Heard you got toppled by a young filly.' Their uninvited guest pulled out a chair and sat heavily.

'Jane,' Roger said, 'this is Archie. Archie, this is Jane.' He smiled as to a younger brother in his cups.

Archie beamed at her. 'You the gel who did the toppling?' he slurred. And to Roger,

'Met your match, have you, mate?'

'Archie,' Roger said in a tired voice, 'we are old friends, are we not?'

'Very, very old friends.'

'Then you won't take offence if I ask you to fuck off, will you?'

Jane was astonished! She had heard such language before but usually in stableyards, not in the Royal Clarence.

'Offence?' Archie laughed, 'never, dear boy. Take a hint, all that.' Getting ponderously to his feet, he sketched a little wave and weaved his way dangerously between tables towards a service door, to be fielded expertly by a passing waiter who directed him towards the main entrance. The entire dining room watched with interest until he had reached dry land.

'Who is Archie?' Jane asked.

'Archie Stannard, father owns a brewery. Sorry about that, one has to spell things out for Archie when he's whistled.'

'I rather liked him.'

'He's a very amusing little fellow when he's sober, which isn't often. Damned good pilot, as a matter of fact. I've been up with him a few times.'

'When he was sober?'

'Hard to tell, with Archie.'

Stannard's Brewery, Jane seemed to recall, was a vast empire owned by a Lord Stannard. In which case, she began to laugh, whatever would her mother say if she heard they'd told an Honourable to fuck off?

—*∞*—

They'd laughed a lot in those days, Jane thought, her memories echoed by a sudden cackling of rooks in the tall trees, during what was then known as a 'whirlwind romance'. More than half a century might have passed but the good times, and there had been many, still fresh in her mind. They had announced their engagement at Christmastime with photographs in glossy magazines, and a huge party at Cranmere where Bertie Fulford, Roger's father, had attempted to proposition her mother. Yes, there had been plenty to laugh at then.

—*∞*—

CHAPTER 2

Henry (Hal) Wesson took the phone call in his workshop. Where else would he be mid-morning on a weekday? He had spent the past hour or so cutting mahogany veneers for the side of a pretty little chest of drawers that had been damaged in a house fire, a boring and repetitious job, so the interruption came almost as a relief. It was his Uncle Ted.

'Ah, Hal, I wonder if you would call in some time today. There's something I need to discuss with you, and perhaps ask your advice?'

'Yes, no problem, Uncle. Afternoon all right?'

'That will suit nicely.'

Uncle Ted, also known as Sir Edward Channon – no blood relation but a lifelong friend of his father – had been Uncle Ted from day one. Since his marriage to Bella Channon some two years since, Sir Edward had also become his father-in-law, though it was hard to think of him as anything other than Uncle Ted. But it was unusual for him to summon Hal in this way, almost as though there was some urgency. Maybe, he thought, it was another insurance job, fire damage like the chest he was currently working on, or maybe not: it was hard to tell with Uncle Ted. Not for nothing had he been chairman of one of the oldest insurance companies in the City. On his way up he had encountered fraudsters and smooth operators in every shape and size. And now? He might be semi-retired, but his mind was as keen and incisive as ever, as was his judgement of his fellow men. Anyone who underestimated Sir Edward Channon was in for a big surprise. Returning to his bench, Hal glanced quickly around the workshop. Originally the ground floor of a heavily beamed barn, and one of the few in Lynchcombe that had not suffered in the barn conversion craze, it was a huge room with workbenches fitted around three of its walls. In his grandfather's day ten or twelve men had occupied these benches, but now they numbered only three. Arthur Buckley was a quietly spoken man in his mid-fifties who had, like Hal, served his apprenticeship under Charles Wesson. His son Keith, still in his early twenties, worked by his side and had the makings of a first-rate craftsman. Together with Hal, they made up the workforce of 'Charles Wesson and Son. Wheelwrights, Cabinet Makers and Restorers' as the sign on the front of the building proclaimed to the world. His father had put that sign up on the eve of his nineteenth birthday. It meant that he had completed his apprenticeship and was now a partner in the firm, a milestone in his career. Less than twelve months later both his parents died in a tragic air crash in Italy. That sign, Hal had vowed, would never, ever be changed.

He found his Uncle Ted sitting by the fireside in his study in Lynchcombe House.

'Hal,' he said as the door opened, 'how good of you to come so soon.'

'You called and here I am,' Hal smiled. 'Please don't get up, Uncle.'

Sir Edward subsided gratefully into his leather armchair, nodded his thanks. Now well into his seventies, the small courtesy of rising to receive a guest was not as easy as it once had been.

Hal took the chair on the opposite side of the fireplace. 'Keeping well, Uncle?'

'Not so bad for an old war horse. And you?'

'Never better,' Hal said and waited for the opening pitch. Uncle Ted had never been one to prevaricate if something needed to be said.

'Does this mean anything to you, Hal?' He passed over a large sheet of cartridge paper on which was a detailed drawing of a china display cabinet in eighteenth-century style, and clearly expected a reaction.

Hal's reaction was a low whistle of appreciation, and he immediately recognised both the handwriting and the draughtsmanship. 'This is one of Father's drawings, isn't it?'

'Yes, it is.'

'Then is has to be the cabinet he rebuilt just after the war.'

'That's right.' Sir Edward smiled. 'Did he tell you anything about it?'

'Not a great deal, although I do recall him saying it was in about five hundred pieces. Oh yes, and I think he said he fell out with the owners. I could be wrong.'

'I believe there was some difference of opinion.'

Hal continued to look at the drawing. Hs father had been a very accurate draughtsman. The cabinet was in three sections, each with its own pagoda roof, the corners surmounted by tiny carved wood figures of Chinamen or winged dragons or serpents. Not content with that, its creator had carved every flat surface with a blind fret in the most intricate designs. 'Most probably,' he said with a smile tinged with sadness, 'Father was trying to talk himself out of working on a thing like that. Hardly surprising.'

'Do you know of your family's connection with these cabinets?' Sir Edward asked quietly.

'No, not really. I believe there was some ages-old service contract or agreement, but Father never spoke of it as far as I can remember.'

'That's right, there was,' Sir Edward's gaze was on the logs smouldering in the open hearth, 'and I can tell you how it started. My family firm, Channon Grieves, were the original insurers from the day the cabinets were first delivered to Cranmere in the 1760s. In fact, I believe we were responsible for introducing the Fulfords to the Wessons. We go back a long way, you know.'

'Yes, we do,' Hal smiled, wondering where all this was leading to.

'The Fulfords have lived at Cranmere for centuries; they're very private people almost to the point of eccentricity. They will not allow any photography in the house which means that nothing can be recorded in their insurance inventory except by description, and that drawing you have there, and neither will they allow their inventory to be included in our computer files.'

'I don't blame them,' Hal said. 'Computer files haven't proved to be all that secure, have they?' 'Well no, but their obsession with privacy does present a few problems. Apart from our in-house valuer, who is no longer with us, very few people have set eyes on the cabinets, not even the museums or the Furniture Society.'

'That's the third time you have said "cabinets", Uncle. Do you mean there are more like this?'

'There were two.'

'Were?'

'One of them went missing,' Sir Edward said, and Hal had to suppress a smile. It was almost a standing joke within the family. But the term was a throwback from the war years when, as a young man whose defective eyesight had precluded him from more active service, Captain Edward Channon had served his time in a concrete cell three floors beneath London's Baker Street and directed Special Operations Executive (SOE) operations behind enemy lines. His quick mind and organisational skills had saved many lives at a time when the word 'missing' was not used lightly. Today, if Uncle Ted was unable to find his morning paper or reading glasses, they had gone missing.

'Are you saying this cabinet was stolen?' Hal asked, looking at the dimensions written in the margins of his father's drawing. 'A thing that size?'

'Possibly, or more likely lost in the post-war shambles. Until very recently, I thought it must have been destroyed.'

'You mean it's reappeared?'

'Seems like it, in New York, but we won't know until we've had expert advice.'

'Ah,' Hal said, 'I'm beginning to understand.'

Sir Edward smiled, 'I thought you might.'

'Would this mean a trip to New York?'

'If you agree to take it on, yes. And Dartmoor.'

'Tell me more.'

'Why don't we have a drop of tea first?'

'Good idea,' Hal grinned as he got to his feet. 'I'll get it, Uncle.'

———◦◦◦———

Lynchcombe House had been Hal's second home since childhood, the children of the house, Bella and Toby, now his wife and brother-in-law, their parents his godparents and now his in-laws. When he had needed them, the day the aircraft had gone down with both his mother and father on board, they had come to his aid. To brew a cup of tea for his Uncle Ted was no hardship.

In the kitchen Lady Winifred Channon – Winnie to all her friends – was already boiling a kettle. 'Is the old man's tongue hanging out?' she asked.

'How did you guess.' Hal moved to her side, kissed her cheek.

'Because it's ten to four. Whatever are you talking about in there?'

'A vanishing cabinet, I think.'

'Sounds like a magic act,' she laughed. Only a few years younger than her husband, she had retained a youthful figure and outlook on life. If, Hal had often thought, there was any truth in the adage about taking a good look at your future mother-in-law before marriage, then he should have no problems. 'And how is young Charles today?' she was asking.

'Cutting another tooth.'

'Poor little man. Can I drop in to see him a bit later on?'

'You can drop in any time, Winnie. You know that.'

'Yes, I do.' She gave him a quick smile.

19

Returning to the study, Hal set down the tray and looked around him while his Uncle Ted tinkered with the teapot. The familiar room was warm and comfortable, part panelled, part book-lined and untidy. Fishing rods were propped in one corner, papers and books strewn on the huge desk, old slippers and an even older labrador lay on the hearthrug. Although no one would dare put it into words, Sir Edward Channon had, to all intents, handed over the reins of Channon Grieves to his son Toby, and now spent much of his time in this eighteenth-century room surrounded by mementoes and memories, and the faint smell of wood smoke.

Sir Edward slurped his tea in appreciation, put down his cup and saucer and began, 'As far as we are concerned, Hal, our interest in the Cranmere cabinets starts with the outbreak of war in 1939. The cabinets, and a priceless collection of Chinese porcelain, were housed in the long gallery at Cranmere, a many-windowed room which ran along the south side of the house. It also had a glazed roof, and Roger Fulford thought, very sensibly, that as we were all expecting to be bombed at any moment, these things should be moved to a safer place. Your father and grandfather travelled down to Cranmere and supervised the dismantling of the cabinets and their removal to, and storage in, the tithe barn behind the house. By all accounts it is an ancient building, massively built and virtually bombproof, unless it received a direct hit.'

'Is that what happened?' Hal asked with the innocence of one born twenty years later.

'Good heavens no if it had we wouldn't be discussing it now. I'm not sure of the details – bomb blast, your father said. Jane will be able to tell you. I do know that both the Cranmere cabinets were very badly damaged.'

'There's something I don't understand,' Hal said. 'Why did the Germans bomb a place like Cranmere, a private house right out in the sticks? Or did it have a military value?'

'Very good question, Hal,' Sir Edward smiled. 'As you say, Cranmere is situated on the lower slopes of Dartmoor, miles from the nearest big town. It did have a military value however, naval to be precise. They had a wireless listening station half a mile up the lane and an intelligence unit in the house. As far as we were aware, the enemy knew nothing of its existence. But from reports I was getting it seemed that a deliberate attempt was made to destroy Cranmere. It was a very worrying time for us all.'

Hal said nothing. As a boy he had worshipped his 'Uncle Ted in Intelligence'. When he said he'd been underground, all sorts of exciting scenarios were imagined. It had come as a disappointment to learn that it meant no more than a little office beneath Baker Street.

Neither his father nor his Uncle Ted had spoken much of their wartime activities. Perhaps now he might learn something.

'When Jane Fulford phoned me she was very distressed, wanted my advice on how to deal with two valuable cabinets presently strewn across her barn floor and in a thousand pieces, were the Wessons still in existence and where the hell was her husband? My chief concern was for Roger Fulford, a man of outstanding courage, deep in enemy territory. If he had been taken by the Gestapo and interrogated, he might have spilled the beans, though I doubt it. And if he wasn't telling them what they wanted to hear they were quite capable of bombing his home to demoralise him; and I hadn't heard from him for three nights. We had a wireless schedule, you understand?'

Hal nodded but remained silent. This was an Uncle Ted as yet unseen, part of the inside story.

'I lied to Jane Fulford, as I often had to. Said her husband was safe and well. Thankfully he made contact the following night from a point some fifty miles north of where we had thought him to be; he was continually on the move. But why Cranmere was targeted has remained a mystery. I dare say we were reading too much into it, trying too hard, and there was a far simpler explanation.'

—◈◈◈—

CHAPTER 3

On a spring morning in 1939, on her husband's arm and beneath archways of flowers, she emerged from the gloom of Chagford Parish Church into bright sunlight. She was Mrs Jane Fulford of Cranmere. The months leading up to what was one of the last County weddings of the pre-war years had been, and still seemed, a blur of frenetic activity in which she took little part. Her mother, constantly on the telephone – much to her husband's dismay, to say nothing of his patients' – rushed around, red in the face and flustered, making endless arrangements. She was in her seventh heaven, the more so when she first saw the Fulford crest set in stone over the entrance to Cranmere. Nothing, she vowed, must be allowed to go wrong.

A slightly different view was held at Cranmere. Bertie Fulford, a man of limited intellect who wore bushy side whiskers and spoke in a series of staccato barks, fully approved of any excuse for a real binge. His wife, Marie, half French and with impaired hearing – possibly through living with Bertie – merely shrugged and said the staff would take care of things. There was a dining table that extended to twenty-five feet, regiments of chairs and the terrace if the day was fine; the ballroom, dining room and salon if it should rain. *Pas de problème.*

Surprisingly, the day went without a hitch. Beautiful motor cars lined the drive while their owners, some of the menfolk clad in morning coats turning green with age, quaffed vintage champagne as they toasted – and groped – the bride. Just as soon as was polite, Jane and Roger took to the Alvis and drove off into the sunset. They honeymooned in France, driving due south, the sun growing warmer with every mile, ate in roadside *estaminets* and slept in small hotels with shuttered windows. Roger's French was natural, learned from his mother, and Jane noticed how readily his conversations came around to the possibility of war. '*Non*' came the emphatic reply, usually followed by the word *Maginot* (the line of defences built to prevent any future invasion of France by Germany). But the words *le guerre* were prominent in the local papers, which Roger read closely. It was no different at home, Jane thought, with Neville Chamberlain flying back and forth and declaring 'Peace in our time.' Such things seemed of little importance to a couple of newly-weds in southern France with their beautiful Alvis, in springtime. War? Together they could conquer the world.

———❧———

With their return to Cranmere began the process of creating a new home and, for Jane, an entirely new lifestyle; her previous life at a secretarial college in Exeter now a distant memory. Her father's words, the only pre-marital advice offered, came back to her.

'They're different to us, you know, the County set.'

'How are they different, Dad?'

'In outlook, values, inclined to ride roughshod. That sort of thing.'

'Roger does not ride roughshod,' she laughed, remembering even as she spoke Roger's refusal to dip the headlights on the Alvis for any unfortunate oncoming motorist. 'It's Roger I am marrying, not the County set.'

'Do you really feel in your heart of hearts that you cannot live without him?'

'Yes, Dad, I do.'

'Then you have my blessing, but promise me, if you are really unhappy you will come home.'

'I promise, Dad.' And face her mother's wrath! Not bloody likely: this was a one-way ticket. Not for her the tearful return to East Budleigh with a suitcase in each hand. She would make it work.

———❧———

Cranmere was a beautiful, Palladian house in mellowed stone, huge and less than half occupied. The entire east wing had been used for convalescing troops during what Bertie referred to as 'the last show', since when the upper floors had been left empty and echoing. Jane explored the house with Roger, and then on her own, poking in through little doorways onto long-forgotten stairs, thick with cobwebs. Gradually, she found her way around. From the entrance hall with its wide staircase, a turning to the left took her into the ground floor of the east wing, a succession of cavernous rooms with decorated ceilings high above, the salon, the dining room and the ballroom, all beautifully furnished but rarely used. They felt cold, and old, and slightly damp.

The door to the west side of the hall opened onto a smaller dining room which was used daily. Beyond was the drawing room, morning room, library and thence a passage of rooms now used as bedrooms, two of them occupied by Bertie and Marie. A third was set aside for Marie to practise on her cello, filling the house with its mournful drone in the afternoons. Jane and Roger would occupy a room at the end of the passage until their own suite on the first floor was refurbished, something Jane was looking forward to.

'Take your pick,' Roger said, 'as many rooms as you fancy.'

They settled on three bedrooms – in case they had guests – an antique bathroom and a large sitting room, all overlooking the rich pastures of the Cranmere valley. These to be scrubbed and redecorated in Jane's choice of colours.

'Except pink,' Roger said. 'Can't stand pink.'

Otherwise she was to have a free hand. As to furniture, 'Help yourself from around the place, we've got it in truckloads. Anything else?'

'How about a little kitchen?' Jane suggested.

'Kitchen! Whatever for?'

'Because,' she smiled up at him, put both arms around his waist, 'I am quite a good cook and may just feel like tempting my husband with something succulent from time to time.' And, she thought, it would be an improvement on dining with Bertie and Marie in that dismal room where meals arrived lukewarm from a kitchen nearly half a mile away. 'Succulent, eh?' Roger grinned wolfishly. 'Well in that case, fine. Tell the builders what you want.'

She would enjoy this, a free hand, and had already earmarked one or two nice little bits of furniture for their home. She would go foraging. Eat your heart out, *Homes and Gardens*. Perhaps Roger might have shown a little more interest, but he seemed content so long as he was with her and warm and comfortable. She would guarantee that.

Her life began to settle into a routine, the day starting with an early morning ride. Rosie was now installed in a loosebox in the stable block behind Cranmere where Roger kept his two hunters, one of whom Rosie fell in love with. Surprisingly, Roger did not hunt – thought it a stupid pastime – but they rode together every day, Rosie hurrying along to keep pace with Brutus, her new-found love. They used this form of transport to visit outlying farms and to check on fences and pastures –

the horses needed exercise, didn't they?

It was on one such morning, when Roger found a field gate in poor repair, that she began to understand just how discontented her husband felt over the management of the Cranmere Estate. He had served his time at Cirencester Agricultural College and was itching to get his hands on the helm, to introduce some fresh ideas and more efficient farming practices. Any suggestions, however, were frustrated by Bertie and his estate manager Jack Leverett, an odious man who smelt constantly of drink and spent most of his time in the estate office with his employer, swapping stories from 'the last show'. 'The minute the old man keels over,' Roger said forcefully, 'Leverett's out on his ear, and he knows it.' They were sitting on a hillside overlooking moorland freshly green with new bracken, their horses tethered.

'Will you get another manager?' she asked.

'Doubt it, don't trust 'em. Leverett's had his hand in the till for years. Run the place meself.'

'You will need a good secretary, won't you?'

'Yes, I suppose.' He stared at something in the far distance.

'Well?'

'Well, what?'

'Well, what about me!' she said indignantly. 'I have shorthand and typing, and I've done an accounting and management course. Had quite a bright future at one time.'

'What happened?' A slow smile began to form.

'Oh, I met this young man with quite a nice horse.'

'Christ, Jane, I hadn't given it a thought. You and me together, eh?'

'You and me together,' she said solemnly.

'We'll have to seal this business agreement.'

'With a handshake?'

'No,' he reached for her, 'I had something rather different in mind.'

When both parties are clad in jodhpurs and boots, lovemaking is not easy – but possible.

—◦◦◦—

Less than a month had passed when the first milestone appeared in this, thus far, blissful marriage. Bertie died in his sleep. Roger showed little emotion other than, 'Right, now we'll see some changes around the place.' Bertie's coffin, draped in the Union flag, was carried down into the family crypt in Chagford churchyard to lie with his ancestors going back over four centuries.

Thinking about this in bed on that same night, Jane shuddered and said, 'Roger, if I should die before you, promise you won't put me in that horrible place.' He yawned, 'All right, I promise.'

Apart from wearing a black tie for a few days as an outward sign of respect, Roger seemed unaffected by his loss. The same could be said of Marie who moved silently around the house, as she always had, pale and dreamy, pecked at her food at mealtimes and returned to her cello. Jane was reminded of her father's words – 'They're not the same as us, you know' – and in an odd sort of way it was she who seemed to miss Bertie more than most. He'd been a source of amusement with his bushy whiskers and outrageous remarks. But it was considered 'bad form' to show one's feelings. In fact, now that she came to think of it, never once had she seen Roger give his father an affectionate pat on the arm or shoulder, nor his mother a quick hug or a goodnight kiss on the cheek.

Roger's main concern was that he would have to travel up to London for a couple of days to see the family lawyers and bankers. She was not included.

'In the meantime, partner,' he said with his sideways smile, 'come with me.' Together they entered the estate office at the back of the house. Jack Leverett had returned once for a few personal belongings and gone, leaving no more in his wake than a crate of empties and the smell of stale beer. Roger opened both windows to their fullest extent, and the outer door, then stalked around the room peering at yellowed wall maps, opening dusty cupboard doors and closing them quickly.

'Where does one start?' He held out both arms in a helpless gesture.

'How about with a few buckets of hot water and a scrubbing brush?' Jane ran one finger along a dusty ledge. 'This place hasn't had a spring clean in years.'

'Then what?'

'Then a new typewriter to replace that old monster,' she said, pointing, 'and some new accounts books. One of those ledgers was started in 1892!'

'Can you handle it while I'm away, Jane?'

'What am I then, a scrubber?'

'Very far from it,' he said, neatly sidestepping his gaffe, 'but I thought perhaps you could supervise a band of willing helpers in your own inimitable way.' Jane smiled sweetly, 'Leave it with me, Roger.'

Like most large country houses, until the First World War, Cranmere had boasted a full compliment of staff both inside and out. By 1939 the indoor staff were reduced to a cook, Mrs Kerslake, who with her two part-time assistants rarely fed less than eight inside and outside staff at her kitchen table. And a housekeeper, Miss Underhill, sometimes referred to as Mrs Danvers, although the poor woman bore little resemblance to the sinister character in Daphne du Maurier's latest novel. Miss Underhill also had two assistants and a number of cleaning women who came in from the village – which was not a village but a town, the Jubilee Hall having only recently been completed and dedicated. Jane knew all the staff by name and was slowly, if reluctantly, getting used to being addressed as 'Ma'am', a practice she would seek to change in the near future, bad form or no.

The willing helpers volunteered by Miss Underhill were Alice Lobb, a sturdy soul who cycled up the long hill to Cranmere each day, and Millie Morrish, a constantly cheerful young woman of around Jane's age who lived with her parents in one of the estate cottages. Armed with buckets and mops and brushes, they attacked the estate office like revolutionaries. Two smelly old easy chairs and the equally disgusting carpet were slung out, tall step ladders erected and the ceilings and walls swept clean until the dust nearly choked them and they all three ran outside coughing and spluttering. And so they continued until there was no surface that had not been scrubbed clean, even the chimney was swept by Billy Passmore, one of the estate workers, who was dared upon pain of death not to drop one single grain of soot on the pristine floor.

On the following morning, Jane drove into Exeter in the shooting brake, a Humber of huge proportions. In Whittons, the principal stationers, she bought a Remington typewriter with spare ribbons and carbon papers, reams of typing paper, account books, pencils, blotting paper and ink; and two very smart desk lamps, his and hers (and two boxes of Cadbury's chocolates for Alice and Millie). She spent the afternoon putting the finishing touches to a room where she and her husband would be spending a good deal of their time, re-hung the curtains, now freshly washed and ironed, polished the big, partners' desk in the centre of the room, had the desk lights installed, then looked around her with a certain satisfaction. All the old cupboards and the plan chest shone with a dull gleam and the air smelled, not of stale beer, but furniture polish. She had even persuaded the GPO to come and replace the old candlestick telephone with a shiny new model. By the time Roger entered the estate office in the evening, the fire was lit – mainly for effect – and there were fresh flowers on his desk. He sat in his late father's chair, looked quickly around him and then at her. 'Well,' he smiled, 'and what have you been doing while I was away?'

She shot him a warning glance, raised one finger and said,' Roger! Don't you dare...' He laughed, reached out and pulled her onto his lap, did a quick gyration in the swivel chair. 'I'm pulling your leg, you muggins.' He held her close, nuzzled her ear. 'It's wonderful and I want you to show me everything.'

Later, they took their coffee out onto the terrace and sat catching the last of the sunset over Sittaford Tor. Apart from early morning, this was their favourite time of day, a time for relaxing in the warmth coming up from the old flagstones, with bats flashing in and out of the eaves. Jane stretched luxuriously, making her wicker chair creak.

'And how was London looking?' she asked, still a bit peeved at her exclusion. It was, after all, their first separation if only for one night. She would have been bored stiff, Roger said. Well maybe she would, and maybe, she thought, breathing in the warm evening air, she would not have been able to tear herself away from Cranmere; but she would have liked the choice. Roger did not answer immediately. She thought he had seemed a little preoccupied since his return although, as he had told her in some detail – they were partners – his banking and legal meetings had gone rather better than expected.

'I'm glad you stayed here, Jane,' he said at length.

'Why? I was not asked...'

'They're digging trenches in the parks, filling sandbags, closing the museums and art galleries.'

Jane was horrified. Too young to remember the Great War, she could vaguely recall the tail-end of food shortages, and a man in the village who acted strangely; she was told he had shell-shock.

28

'Do you think there will be war, Roger?'

'I don't see how it can be avoided, they talk about little else up in London.'

'Neville Chamberlain wouldn't agree.'

Roger gave a short laugh, more of a bark reminiscent of Bertie. 'Chamberlain means well, but he's living in a dream world. The Krauts have a huge army and air force, just look at the way they rolled into Czechoslovakia. Who's next, one wonders.'

'But I thought we'd come to some sort of agreement.'

'So we did, for what it's worth. Trouble is, no one believes in it, not any more. You can't trust people like that.'

Jane gave an involuntary shudder, and reached out a hand to her husband who took it in his. 'While I was up in Town,' he said, 'a fellow in a wig read out a Proclamation from the steps of the Mansion House. All men under the age of thirty-six have to register for military service.'

'Will you register, Roger?'

'I already have,' he said quietly.

It was Jane's turn to remain silent. She felt somehow cheated, as though this threat of war – something that had been rumbling in the background for months, had she taken heed – was directed at them personally, to disrupt the future they were planning. Now, looking out over the Cranmere pastures in twilight, hearing the occasional bleat of a lamb separated from its mother, it seemed inconceivable that anyone should wish to disturb the peace again, to go to war, to take young men away from their homes, mothers and sweethearts, husbands from wives. 'What will become of us?' she asked in a small voice.

'We will survive, you and me.'

'And Cranmere?'

'And Cranmere, never doubt it. It may be that we have to throw the doors open to refugees or the military, like we did last time. I was only a youngster but I can remember them quite well, hobbling around the place on their sticks and crutches. Marie was a nurse,' he grinned. 'Surprising what you can do when needs must.' Jane tried hard to picture Marie in a white hat, putting on a brisk authoritative manner. Carrying a bedpan? Would it be expected of her? She was beginning to understand that the name Fulford carried certain responsibilities.

Their war started on the following morning with the arrival of a pile of small cardboard boxes in the entrance hall: gas masks, one for each member of staff. Jane and Roger wasted no time in trying theirs on, looking at each other through misted goggles, making strange farting noises when they breathed out. They tore them off in disgust, vowing they would sooner be gassed than wear things like that for more than ten minutes. And then the arrival by registered post of a letter addressed to Roger in an official envelope marked 'Admiralty'. Jane saw his features tighten as he read it through.

'What is it,' she asked anxiously. 'Call up?'

'Worse,' he said. 'They want Dick Perret's farm. I thought there was something afoot, there were people snooping around up there last week.'

'What would they want it for?'

'I'm not sure, but at a guess I'd say a wireless station. It's the highest point, just under Bittern Hill.'

'Can they do that, Roger?'

'Oh yes, they can do anything they bloody well want to. This is just the start.'

—◦◦◦—

CHAPTER 4

A shaft of late afternoon sunlight through the study window caught one side of Sir Edward's face for a moment, its unflattering light reminding Hal how his Uncle Ted had aged over the past twelve months. He took a sly glance at his watch; he was going to be late home.

'How much do you know about your father's wartime activities, Hal?' The question was put carefully, almost casually.

'He was a patternmaker, wasn't he? There are still a few crates of strange wooden objects in our loft, bits of aircraft. Toby and I used to play with them when we were kids.'

'Yes, that's right. He must have made hundreds of them, and your grandfather – he was usually at his bench whenever I called in.'

'I never met Grandfather. What was he like?'

'Oh a tall, rather forbidding character with a shock of white hair. Always put me in mind of a Methodist Minister.'

Hal smiled but said nothing.

'As I'm sure you know, your father's official trade was that of a wheelwright, which was classified as a reserved occupation. There weren't too many wheelwrights about, even in those days, and someone had to keep the farm wagons in good repair.'

'I think he had to put up with a bit of resentment over that,' Hal said.

'Yes, I've no doubt, but how much did he tell you about his service with the Fire Brigade?'

'Not a great deal.'

'Well I will tell you something about it, Hal, because I think you should know. Your father joined the AFS, the Auxiliary Fire Service, when the blitz started, working as far afield as Gloucester and Bristol. I dare say you have seen some of those old black-and-white films of the blitz, burning buildings, men with long ladders and fire hoses. Well that's where your father was, right in the front line. It must have been an horrendous task. The casualty figures for the AFS were dreadful, and those who survived, they paid the price. The scenes he had to deal with, especially where children were concerned, put years on your father. I didn't learn until years later that he was recommended for a George Medal for outstanding bravery. He refused it on the grounds that he was no more deserving than the rest of his team.'

'He never told me,' Hal said almost in a whisper.

'That doesn't surprise me,' Sir Edward smiled. 'He never told me and I was his closest friend.'

Hal sat almost motionless and listened.

'When I telephoned him on Jane's behalf, I was not expecting your father to be able to help her in any way other than offering advice. But he said he had some leave owing and would be pleased to travel down to Cranmere, just to get away for a few days, provided I could wangle him a drop of petrol, which was severely rationed as I'm sure you know. We were able to get round that one on the grounds that he was going to inspect bomb damage. He had a motorbike and sidecar in those days, draughty old thing. Pre-war we would go for miles on it, fishing, all the tackle stowed in the sidecar. Ross-on-Wye was a favourite haunt.' Sir Edward's eyes rested momentarily on the fishing rods propped in one corner of the room.

'I saw your father briefly before he left,' he continued. 'This break couldn't have come at a better time – he looked well overdue for his leave, grey in the face. I was a little concerned for him travelling all that distance. But the next time I saw him, a couple of weeks later, he seemed a different man, bright and chirpy, colour in his cheeks. Clearly the Dartmoor air had done him a power of good. But the Cranmere cabinets, he told me, were shattered. A bomb had landed in the yard, the blast had blown in the barn doors and flattened both cabinets against the back wall. I believe your father scrounged a couple of huge crates from the Royal Navy, picked up all the bits and packed them away. And there they remained for the next five or six years.

'It was not until late in 1946 that the last of the military junk was cleared from Cranmere, including the barn, part of which had been used for storage. And then only because Roger Fulford had been raising hell. When he discovered that one of the crates was no longer there, he hit the roof, contacted every military and admiralty base in the south of England, threatened to sue, sent off solicitors' letters, pulled rank. But of course, many of the people who would have dealt with stores and supplies had already been discharged, and those who remained were disinterested. He kept it up for twelve months or more, hired private investigators, blamed everybody including his wife, even had a go at me as his insurer. Eventually, he gave it up as a lost cause.'

'What do you think happened to it, Uncle?' Hal stifled a yawn.

'I hope I'm not boring you, Hal.'

'No, no,' Hal smiled. 'We had a disturbed night with Charles Edward.'

'He's all right, is he?'

'Another tooth.'

'Ah yes. Now then, where was I? What do I think happened to the crate? Most likely it was loaded onto one of the many trucks and carted away, there were convoys of them shuttling back and forth. And then slung out as a box of rubbish, or burned. The other cabinet was brought up here to Lynchcombe for your father to deal with, but its pair had gone without trace.'

'And now it's turned up in New York?' Hal said.

'If it is the same one, yes.'

'Why do we think it could be the missing cabinet?'

'I received a phone call from Ralph Carrington. I don't think you've met; he was our staff valuer at Channon Grieves until five years ago. He is now with Sotheby Parke Bernet in New York. I can't pretend I liked the fellow much but I did respect his judgement of furniture, and he is one of the very few men who has actually seen the existing Cranmere cabinet, when he was doing an insurance update five years ago. Carrington was recently called in to see a collection of antique furniture in New York. Included is the cabinet, which he is almost certain is the missing one. In which case it puts him into an embarrassing position; if he were to accept it for one of Sotheby's sales, someone in the furniture world would be sure to recognise it no matter how good the Fulford family's security. He didn't say so in as many words, but I got the feeling he thought the insurers might be willing to cut a deal. In which case he would be disappointed, certainly at the figure he was suggesting.'

'How much was that?' Hal asked.

'Two-and-a-half million.'

'Pounds or dollars?'

'Dollars,' Sir Edward smiled.

'Still a lot of money. What's the current state of play?'

'I am dragging my feet until my expert has examined both cabinets. Carrington is doing the same, but we cannot delay. The vendors will have expected Sotheby's to jump at the chance. They may be wondering why not.'

'Surely,' Hal said, 'there must be some sort of provenance with a thing of that value, a record or a receipt at the very least.'

'There is proof of ownership but Carrington is being a bit cagey about it.'

'In what way?'

'I am not quite sure.' Sir Edward's eyes narrowed as he stared at the smouldering logs in the hearth. 'It was something he was saying, or perhaps, not saying. But,' he became more business-like, 'first things first, Hal. Can you spare the time?'

'I will make time, Uncle. So what was the unholy row about?'

'The unholy row, as you so aptly termed it, occurred almost three years later when your father had finalised the restoration of the cabinet and it was returned to Cranmere. He travelled down with it to supervise the assembly and probably wish it a fond farewell.'

'Did they dispute the bill?' Hal asked

'No, it was nothing like that, Fulford was an honourable man in that sense, and mountainously wealthy. Neither was the quality of the work in question; it was something else.'

'What then?'

'Hal, I want you to understand something of the spirit of those post-war years. We were all sick and tired of the senseless destruction around us, let alone the loss of innocent lives, and we were trying to rebuild and repair what we could. I am sure your father felt that the mammoth task he had taken on was in some way symbolic. One of the Cranmere cabinets had vanished and he was not going to see the second one written off as beyond repair, not if he could help it. He could be a stubborn man.'

'Determined,' Hal smiled.

'Yes,' Sir Edward agreed, 'determined.'

'Gradually, the cabinet began to take shape, your father insisting that as much of the old fabric be preserved although, as he often said, it would have been quicker and easier to replace some of the more badly damaged parts. He didn't work on it continuously, of course, but he became almost obsessed with the thing, worked on it in his spare time – unless I turned up and took him out fishing. When it was finished he called me in to take a final look. All I can say is that it was enormous and quite magnificent, all the tiny pieces of moulding in place, every pane of glass, even the little carved Chinamen and dragons. I remember your father saying at the time that if he'd totted up every hour spent on it the bill would have exceeded the cabinet's value. I could well believe it.'

'So what did they fall out about?' Hal asked again.

Sir Edward looked slightly uneasy, fidgeted with his reading glasses before replying. 'I am not entirely sure, Hal,' he said at length, 'because I have never been told, not by the Fulfords and most certainly not by your father; the subject was taboo. But... it is my belief that Roger Fulford may have suggested, or intimated, that your father knew more about the disappearance of the other cabinet than he was letting on.'

'You mean he accused him of stealing it?' Hal said incredulously.

'Perhaps not in as many words but, I think that must have been the gist of it. Mind you,' he added quickly, 'this is only what I surmise, reading between the lines, as it were.'

'Bloody nerve!'

'I quite agree, especially after all the trouble your father had been to.'

'But whatever gave him the idea Father might have stolen his wretched cabinet?' Hal said indignantly. 'I mean, if it was in similar condition and required as many hours to restore, it wouldn't have been worth stealing, would it? And even if it had, it would have been almost impossible to sell, as we are now finding out.'

'I doubt if Fulford had thought it through quite like that, Hal. His reasoning may have been that as your father was one of the few men capable of such expert work, and he'd had the opportunity, he was the obvious suspect.'

'Yes, maybe, but that doesn't mean...'

Sir Edward held up one hand. 'Just listen for a moment, would you? As I was saying earlier, it was at a time when we were all trying to adjust to civilian life. Some found it harder than others, and Roger Fulford was one. He had been living on his wits for five years or more, had learned to trust no one and take nothing at face value. That is what we taught him in my outfit, so in a way I felt partly responsible – and he had been almost paranoid about his missing cabinet. I imagine when he saw the remaining one in its full plumage, it tipped the balance and he let fly.'

'It's a wonder Father didn't hit him.'

'I'm very glad he didn't, Hal. Fulford was a big man and knew all the dirty tricks. I believe your father may have lashed out verbally – he could do that rather well when the mood was on him.'

'Yes, I remember,' Hal gave a rueful smile. Then after a long silence, said, 'Why are we bothering with these people after the way they treated Father?'

'I thought you might ask that, Hal. The answer has to be partly because at the tail-end of my career I want to tidy up any loose ends, and partly because we now have the opportunity to set the record straight for your father. He was deeply hurt at the time. And we will demand an apology from the Fulfords. What do you say?'

'When do you want me to go?'

'Within the next few days, I'll make an appointment.'

'Make it for tomorrow, Uncle.'

—∿∿—

CHAPTER 5

The lane to Higher Weeke Farm wound its way up the hillside between ancient stone hedges, the surface becoming more rutted with every yard. Roger pulled the Humber into a gateway, climbed out and opened the passenger door for Jane. Together they leaned on the gate and looked down into the wide valley below. The air was still, and high above a skylark trilled its song to them. Roger had been very quiet since opening the letter from the Admiralty, except to say that in his remembrance no tenant had ever been evicted from a Cranmere farm or cottage, and this was the worst job he'd ever had to do.

'Do you want me to come with you?' Jane asked, rather hoping he would prefer to face it on his own.

'Christ, yes! I want you for moral support.'

'Then you shall have it.' Her husband needed her and that was enough.

'It's important you get to know these people, Jane,' he said at length. 'They're going to be looking to you while I'm away.'

Although she had given it some thought, this was the first time Roger had put into words what lay ahead, what was *expected* of her. She felt a moment of apprehension, almost panic, as she had before entering the show ring – where she had beaten her husband at his own game.

'It might not be so bad,' Roger said, coming out of his reverie. 'That's Lower Weeke, Will Perret's place, there on the far side of the valley. The two farms adjoin. If the brothers can come to terms, Dick could take his cattle down there and still farm his own land.'

'Don't they get on then?'

Roger, smiling, turned to look up the hillside where Higher Weeke could be seen surrounded by bracken. 'When I was a boy, Lower Weeke was farmed by Dan and Mary Wollacott, who had a daughter named Betty. Both the Perret boys made a bid for Betty, Will came out on top – if you'll pardon the term. So he got Betty and the farm while Dick took over his father's tenancy, forgot about Betty and married an Okehampton girl.'

Jane laughed, 'And they all lived happily ever after?'

'I wouldn't say that. I doubt the brothers have exchanged a dozen words since.'

'Do you think they will now?'

'They'll bloody well have to! Come on, let's go and play the wicked landlord.'

'Roger,' Jane said when they were once more in the car, 'How will I ever get to know all this – this folklore?'

He gave a short laugh as he slammed the car into gear and reversed out of the gateway.

'You'll be all right, in many ways you're better off without it.'

Dick Perret was standing in his farmyard watching their approach, a short, stocky figure with a wide leather belt, shirtsleeves rolled above the elbows and mouth turned down in permanent disapproval. Nearby stood a heavy truck, painted dark blue and with the words 'Royal Navy' in white lettering. High above them, from the rocky summit of Bittern Hill, three men in overalls looked down on the farm buildings.

Roger cursed under his breath. 'They've beaten us to it. Stay in the car while I speak to old Dick.'

Jane could not hear the exchange of words but, from the attitudes of the two men – squared up, feet apart, hands on hips – clearly they were getting nowhere near any sort of agreement. Dick Perret turned on his heel and stomped off towards his farmhouse. Roger called after him but his pace did not falter.

'There is nobody,' Roger fumed as the Humber rocked and bumped down the lane, 'more pig-headed and bloody infuriating than the traditional Devon farmer.'

The traditional Devon landlord comes a close second, Jane thought. She asked, 'What did he say?'

'He says he's not budging one inch.'

'Poor man, it is his home. He'll have to move out, will he?'

'He will and he knows it. He's just going to make things as difficult as he possibly can, obstinate old fool.'

'How old is he?'

'Only about forty. Looks more.'

'And his brother?'

'Couple of years older, I think. Why?'

'I'm not sure,' Jane said thoughtfully. 'What's Betty like?'

'Oh now, Betty,' he grinned, 'she's a fine girl, worth the two brothers put together. Must weigh 16 stone at least.'

'Do you think they are still feuding over her?'

He shook his head. 'Not after all this time. Each probably waiting for the other to extend the hand of friendship, which is what they ought to be doing right now. Farming families in the face of adversity should be helping one another, shouldn't they?'

'Could Will be persuaded to do that, to invite his brother to come down the hill?'

Roger drew in a long breath. 'Very slim chance.'

'But Betty might?'

He brought the car to a standstill, turned to face her. 'Jane, what are you saying?'

'I am saying that if Betty was courted by both the Perret boys, she may still have some feelings for Dick, if only sympathy. And if she has any influence over her husband, then...'

'Influence!' Roger began to laugh. 'I'll say she's got influence. Come on, let's go and talk to Betty.'

Jane would ever remember her first visit to Lower Weeke, the limewashed, newly thatched farmhouse, and the archetypal countrywoman who came out to see what vehicle had dared disturb the peace in her yard. Betty Perret had brown hair, rosy-apple cheeks and a waist apron tied around where once her waist had been, and forearms like a wrestler.

Before they left the car, Jane said, 'When you have told her what it's about, do you think you could make an excuse, leave us alone for a while?'

Roger looked at her suspiciously. 'Women talk, eh?'

'Something like that.'

—⌇⌇⌇—

It was not until early evening that Jane's heart-to-heart with Betty brought a solution to Dick Perret's problems, and a smile of wonderment to Roger's face.

'I don't know how you did it but they've come to terms,' he said, returning from the telephone in the hall. Sadly, her small achievement was overshadowed by Marie's announcement at the dinner table that she had no intention of sitting out another war at Cranmere. She would go to live with her sister Annette in Falmouth.

'There's no need for you to leave, Mother,' Roger exclaimed. 'You'll be safer here than anywhere. Even Falmouth could be bombed.'

'Maybe you are right,' she said gravely, 'but the war will come to Cranmere in one way or another, just as it did last time, of that you may be sure. In those days I was young and strong, that is no longer so.'

'You're not old, Mother.'

She gave him a thin smile. 'I am sixty-two and I feel unable to face that sort of thing for a second time.'

Jane was surprised; she had thought Marie to be at least ten years older, nearer to Bertie's age.

'Are you quite sure about this, Mother?' Roger asked, concerned.

'Quite sure, my mind is made up. Please do not try to dissuade me.'

'As if I could,' Roger said under his breath. 'When are you thinking of leaving us?'

'Within the next few days.' Marie rose gracefully from her chair, stood for a moment looking down on the upturned faces. 'It's better this way,' she said. 'You will have your hands full running Cranmere without an old woman to worry about.' This last was directed at Jane.

'Can't we worry about you in Falmouth?' Roger asked, a question that rang a little untrue. Both women knew that Roger worried about very little, least of all his own mother.

'Of course you may,' again the thin smile, 'if you wish.'

After she had left the room Roger sat staring moodily through the open window, seemingly more annoyed than saddened by his mother's leaving. Perhaps, Jane thought, it was considered 'bad form' to desert Cranmere in times of crisis. She remained silent, waiting for the quick smile that denoted the mood had passed.

'I thought she would be company for you while I'm away,' he said at length.

There it was again, 'while I am away'. It was taken for granted that she, at the age of twenty-three, would take charge of the Cranmere Estate, with a little – a lot! – of help and advice from Jim Sanders, the Home Farm manager. Would she be able to cope? She was left with little choice, it was expected of her. Just as it was expected that her husband would volunteer his services just as soon as war was declared, if not sooner. No Fulford, he said, had ever waited to be summoned to the flag. He would 'report for duty' when the time was right. These military turns of phrase, dredged up from the last war, were becoming more and more fashionable as the 'commencement of hostilities' drew closer. Whilst on the telephone to the grocer that morning, he had used the term 'as you were'. 'Are our quarters upstairs anything like ready?' Roger asked, adding yet another militarism to their vocabulary.

'Yes, ready to move in.' Jane had been longing for this day, postponed after Bertie's sudden demise when Roger, in a rare fit of thoughtfulness, had not felt it right to leave his mother on her own.

'Move in next week, shall we, after Mother's gone?'

'Yes, fine.' Our own home at last.

'That'll leave the ground floor free for whoever comes knocking at the door.'

'Who is that likely to be, do you think?'

'I don't know. More of the Royal Navy, I shouldn't wonder.'

Catching Jane's concerned expression, he reached out and placed a large hand over hers and said 'Don't worry, you'll be all right. And you still haven't told me what you said to Big Betty.'

'It wasn't much really.'

'No? You shifted an immovable object, that's all. However did you manage it?'

Jane toyed with her wine glass. 'I just enlarged a bit on what you had said. That the Admiralty only wanted Dick's farm buildings, not the land. Oh, and I said we would put up any additional sheds they needed at Lower Weeke to house the extra stock, and do up the empty cottage for Dick.' She glanced anxiously at her husband. 'That was all right, wasn't it?'

'Good heavens, yes. Whatever they need. But I still think you're a bloody marvel.'

She smiled sweetly. 'You always did have good taste, darling.' There was no need, she thought, to explain further how she had pointed out to Betty that if Dick became really difficult, gave up his tenancy and left the land, and if the age limit for conscription were raised, the he might become eligible for military service. She was learning fast.

—◦◦◦—

During the month of August the West Country sweltered in a heatwave. Day after day of glorious sunshine with holidaymakers driving up onto the moor or down to the coast, determined to enjoy themselves while they still could; even the crops ripening early in the fields around Cranmere as though they, too, had caught the sense of urgency. Farmers and their sons and workers toiled until dusk to get in the harvest before the impending storm.

Roger helped when he could, stripped to the waist, tossing the sheaves up onto the wagons with the best of them, joshing with the farmers' sons he had grown up with. Jane would remain at the side of the field in the shade with the farmers' wives, dishing out gallons of drinks – the older men swigging cider straight from wooden firkins – and pasties and thick-cut sandwiches and slabs of fruitcake. It was a good opportunity to get closer to the people who worked the Cranmere land, to listen to their gossip, learn their hopes and fears.

'My Peter's too young for call-up, isn't he, Mrs Fulford?'

'How old is he now, Mrs Brimblecombe?' Jane asked, not even sure which of the young, suntanned men was her Peter.

'Just gone seventeen.'

'I think he's safe for a while,' she said, remembering even as she spoke the stories of an uncle who had lied about his age and ended his short life at Passchendaele. Why ask her? She was no more privy to such information than anyone else. It seemed a lot was expected of a Fulford; with the name came responsibility and trust. She turned back to the Constable-like scene, men working in the late evening sun, throwing the sheaves high onto the overladen wagons, showing off in front of their womenfolk like roosters, Roger no better than any.

'Reckon he could be a bit of a handful at times,' said a voice by her side. Betty Perret was polishing an apple on her apron.

Jane laughed, 'Yes, he is, at times.'

'That's all right then.' Betty bit deep into her apple.

———

It was important, Roger said on the following morning, to get Cranmere onto a war footing and soon, because time was running out. No one but a dreamer or a maiden aunt could possibly believe that war was avoidable, not now. Although Jane was neither, she offered no argument even if, like millions of others, she still nursed hopes. But the daily papers told their own story despite last-minute pacts between countries under threat. Air-raid shelters were being dug or built in the towns and cities; thousands of galvanised iron Anderson shelters were being distributed to households, although none had appeared in West Devon yet. The war, the newspapers read, was to be conducted from the air by Hitler's mighty *Luftwaffe* (German for 'air weapon') and to combat them, ARP (Air Raid Precaution) wardens were being appointed. Jim Sanders was one: he was issued with a steel helmet which he never wore, and a whistle which he never blew. Mass evacuations from the major cities were planned. The WRVS (Women's Royal Voluntary Service) needed billeting officers – Jane's mother volunteered. Sandbags and further advice were available if required.

'I reckon we're quite capable of putting Cranmere into mothballs without anyone's advice,' Roger said as he and Jane began a survey of the house, she in her role as secretary with pad and pencil in hand. They started in the cellars which were dry and with domed ceilings, ideal, Roger said, for sheltering from bombs; the house could fall down but the cellars would remain intact. How could he possibly know that? Jane thought. 'I will inform the ARP warden exactly where you will be in case you get buried,' Roger said.

'Jim Sanders will know,' Jane pointed out.

'He might be off duty.' Roger took the cellar steps two at a time.

More than likely he'll be in the cellar with us, Jane thought. The simple truth was that no one really knew what to expect; so they would expect the worst. Only that morning the local paper had published a front page photograph of the PDSA reception centre in Exeter where the destruction of four-legged friends could be obtained free of charge. The sad little queue of owners with their pets, some on leads, some in cat baskets, stood waiting; the owners as unaware of their future as were their pets. But whatever lay in store, speed was essential.

As Roger strode through the ground-floor rooms – the great dining room, the salon, the ballroom – Jane had to run to keep up. 'We're going to need professional packers for this little lot,' he said. 'Try Yeoman's of Plymouth, they're a good old firm.' Jane made a hurried note.

Marie's final words of advice had been that Cranmere would be more vulnerable to damage from our own side than from the enemy. Pack everything away that is small or valuable or portable. In time of war no one was to be trusted, officers least of all.

'Where are we going to store it all once it's packed?' Jane asked.

'In here, I should think.' Roger was standing at one of the tall windows in the ballroom, unfolding the stout wooden shutters. 'Don't suppose we'll be needing it for a while.' Then, catching Jane's mood, he held out both arms and said, 'Shall we dance? *The Danube is blue, plink plink, plonk plonk'.* Three times they whirled around the empty ballroom, faster and faster, raising little clouds of old chalk dust from the polished floor until they stopped, breathless and laughing. Roger held her close. 'Don't worry, old girl, we'll put it all back together, after a while.'

Jane hoped he was right. The one time she had seen the ballroom put to proper use was at their engagement party, when little Archie Stannard had played the piano and given a brilliant Noel Coward impersonation – *The stately homes of England are beautiful, they stand, To prove the upper classes have still the upper hand.*

Her mother had been entranced.

Yeoman's van arrived with a mountain of packing cases and four men who worked with hardly a break, but it took them nearly three days to pack the china, glass, paintings and books and carry all but the largest pieces of furniture into the ballroom which was stacked to ceiling height. Whilst in the long gallery above, Mr Roland Wesson and his son Charles carefully and quietly dismantled the two cabinets that were the pride of the Cranmere collections. These were carried piece by piece out into the tythe barn and then carefully packed against a granite wall and a wooden frame built around them. Behind Cranmere the cavernous fuel stores were filled with split logs and coal, while Jane and Roger glued strips of brown paper to the windows of their new apartment as a protection against bomb blast. Whoever moved in downstairs, Roger said, could do their own damned windows.

Cranmere was ready for war. On the walls in the ground-floor rooms only the largest of paintings remained, portraits of long-gone Fulfords gazing balefully down on the emptiness, ready to receive their new tenants.

As August drew to a hot and dusty close, both Jane and Roger lived in a kind of limbo, Roger becoming more restless by the day. He kept a checklist on his desk. One by one he crossed off the jobs that needed to be done before... before what? Jane recalled the times when, as a child, she had counted off the last few hours of her school holidays, knowing that the awfulness of her boarding school drew nearer and there was not a thing she could do about it. Sometimes she would wish the hours away so that the inevitable could start. At least, then, she could start counting away the days to the end of term and make plans. In just the same way, there were few plans for the near future that could be made. Not yet.

They rode daily, each trying to pretend that this was their way of life forever, until they looked up to Bittern Hill now crowned with aerial masts and guy wires. Beneath the rocky outcrop Higher Weeke was enclosed behind a tall barbed-wire fence and patrolled by armed guards. Dick Perret's cattle stared in towards their old home, puzzled by their exclusion. It was on such a morning that they first saw the little aircraft high above them in a cloudless sky, unlike anything Jane had seen before, its underside painted in pale blue.

'What is that?' she asked.

Roger was already squinting against the bright sunlight, shielding his eyes with one hand. 'I think it's a Spitfire, a fighter.'

'A fighter,' Jane repeated, thinking how could a pretty aeroplane like that be a fighter? It looked friendly, not aggressive.

Even as they watched from the hillside, the Spitfire began to lose height. It flew the length of the Cranmere valley, turned in a tight circle and came back the other way, descending as it did so.

'Looks like he's going to land on our pasture.' Roger stood in his stirrups. 'Cheeky blighter!' Then a slow smile began to spread across his face. 'I'll lay odds that's little Archie. Come on, race you.'

They spurred their horses down the long grassy slope, both taking a five-bar gate in their stride. The Spitfire taxied towards the house and came to a halt, the propeller stopped turning and the quiet of the valley was restored. By the time they were close enough for recognition, the cockpit canopy had been slid back and Archie Stannard, ungainly in flying kit, stood proudly beside his aircraft. He held both hands high above his head calling, 'I surrender to the cavalry.'

They lunched out on the terrace, looking down on what Archie called his 'kite'. He could not bear, he said, to let her out of his sight for a minute, she was too precious.

'Sounds like you're in love,' Roger said.

'I am, utterly and completely,' Archie exclaimed, his schoolboy features shining with enthusiasm. 'What think you Jane?'

'She is very pretty.'

'Pretty!' he echoed. 'She is nothing short of – for a moment words failed him – wizard.'

'RAF slang,' Roger said unnecessarily.

Jane laughed, 'All right, she is a wizard kite.'

Archie beamed at her appreciatively. 'And I'll tell you something they don't know yet. She is faster and more manoeuvrable than anything the Krauts have got. They're going to be sorree.'

'Do you know anything we don't?' Roger asked.

'Shouldn't think to, except the balloon's going up any minute. I am training boys to fly, you may call me Squadron Leader, if you wish.'

Inevitably, the conversation turned to war talk – what else with a war plane sitting on the grass? Jane only half listened to terms such as 'air speed', 'rate of climb' and 'fire power'. Training boys? She thought Archie looked no more than a boy himself, although a year older than Roger – a boy with a new toy. But she heard very clearly when Archie asked the one question she had not dared to put into words.

'When are you off then, Roger?'

Roger glanced at her quickly and said, 'I don't know yet, waiting for a phone call. Soon after your balloon's gone up, I imagine'.

She felt a sharp stab of anxiety, almost *déjà vu*. How many young men, she wondered, had stood on this terrace and discussed an impending war? 'All over by Christmas,' they had said, and how dreadfully wrong they had been. 'What do you call her, Archie?' she asked in an effort to lighten the conversation.

'Hadn't really thought.' Then as though suddenly inspired he said, 'Would you mind if I were to call her Jane?'

'I would be flattered.'

'You will have to christen her,' he said solemnly.

'How do I do that?'

'Kiss her and say a few words.'

'Oh, which bit do I kiss?'

'The fuselage.'

'The what?'

Roger laughed, 'The body.'

They were treated to a tour of the Spitfire, walking around it, making

46

appreciative remarks, and were allowed to sit in the cockpit and play with the controls.

'Can you loop-the-loop?' Jane asked.

Archie gave her a withering look and said, 'Jane – *pulease* – that went out with crinolines and bonnets.'

They stood well back for the take-off, covering their ears against the noise of the exhaust. The little aircraft gathered speed across the smooth grass and then climbed up and up and up until it seemed tiny in the sky above them. Then, turning over, it performed not one but three perfect loops before coming out on a roll.

'Showing off,' Roger said.

'But wonderful,' Jane replied, knowing that this was for her benefit.

'Yes,' Roger agreed, 'and he's off the booze.'

The Spitfire flew past them once more, Archie waving from the cockpit, waggling his wings before banking and turning for home, due east.

They watched until he was out of sight.

Jane stared at the hole in the sky where the little Spitfire had been when, sadly, she realised that never again would it return to land on the smooth grass below Cranmere. With an effort, she dragged her mind forward to the present. More than fifty years had passed since she had kissed Archie's kite and wished her and all who flew in her God speed. For what good it had done. After a brief but dazzling career as a fighter pilot, Archie and his kite had gone down into the English Channel.

And now the sun was warm on her back, she had been sitting on the hard iron seat longer than intended and it was past time for one of those damned tablets – one every two hours – to ease the discomfort in her chest. Getting to her feet, she spoke to the dog, sitting obediently beside her.

'Come along, Tansy, time to go home.'

Instinctively the dog turned towards Cranmere. Jane called her back. 'This way, little one. It's the Dower House for you and me.'

—◦◦◦—

CHAPTER 6

Priestholm, the stone-built house facing directly onto the square in Lynchcombe, had been home to the Wesson family for generations; currently Henry and Annabel (Hal and Bella) Wesson and their small son Charles Edward. This, together with the adjoining workshop, constituted Hal's world, and he guarded them and those who dwelt therein with great care.

He parked his car in the cobbled courtyard behind the house, glanced quickly at his wristwatch and made for the back door. In the big kitchen Bella stood at the stove, stirring something in a little saucepan. She looked over her shoulder and said accusingly, 'You're late.' A heinous crime in the Wesson household. As a part-time working mother, her days were run to a strict timetable punctuated by meals.

Hal moved to her side, kissed the nape of her neck. 'And you are gorgeous. What's cooking?'

'Only a chicken casserole, and you won't get any if you don't let me get on'. She gave him a gentle push.

He sat at the far side of the table and watched her moving around, his wife for nearly three years and just as alluring as ever, even in old jeans and a shirt. Tall and slim, her fair hair was tied back revealing her profile as she worked, and a complexion Hal had been known to eulogise over. 'Is our son asleep?' he asked.

'Yes, and don't you go disturbing him.'

'Oh, all right. Sorry I'm a bit late.'

'Have you been talking to Dad all this time?

'Mmm, he does go on, doesn't he?'

'What about?'

'The Second World War.'

'No wonder you were late. And Mother was saying something about a vanishing cabinet.'

'That, too.'

As his meal was placed before him, he caught Bella around the waist and held her. 'Am I forgiven?' he asked, looking up at her.

She ruffled his hair. 'Yes, I suppose, as you were talking to Dad.'

'If you are nice to me,' he held her, 'I'll tell you about a girlfriend he's been running since 1938.'

'Who, Dad?' she pulled free. 'I don't believe it.'

'It's true, he told me so himself. Jane Fulford was something of a star in the showjumping world, pre-war. Your father was madly in love with her along with about ten thousand other blokes. Even had her picture on his wall.'

'Is that all?'

'No, it's not. He spoke to her on the telephone almost daily throughout the war years and on and off ever since. Quite a little flirtation, but they have never actually met. Can you credit it, he's been chatting her up for over fifty years and never actually set eyes on her?'

'I think that's sad, like *Brief Encounter*.'

'Yes, but they never did encounter, did they?'

'Do you think Mother knows?'

'Course she does,' Hal laughed. 'Probably pulls his leg about it.'

'I still think it's sad. What does she look like, do you know?'

'Tall, fair and very beautiful, according to your father. Must be pushing eighty by now.'

Bella brought her meal to the table, and sat opposite. 'So where does this vanishing cabinet come in?'

'That belonged to Jane and her husband.'

'And?'

'And it vanished.'

'Are you going to tell me or must I beg?'

'Oh, very well,' Hal relented. He should have learned by now not to tease his wife when she looked tired. 'Once upon a time there were these two cabinets...'

'Two cabinets?'

'Yes, two cabinets, please don't interrupt. We're talking big here, nearly ten foot wide and made by Ince and Mayhew, no less, one of the top cabinetmakers in London in the eighteenth century. They lived side by side in the long gallery at Cranmere in Devon, and the Wesson family have looked after them for over two hundred years.'

'Are you saying,' Bella said when Hal had reached the end of his story, 'that these people, the Fulfords, accused my Uncle Charles of stealing their beastly cabinet?'

'It sounds rather like it.'

'Bloody nerve.'

'That's exactly what I said.'

'They can't have known him very well,' Bella said sharply. 'Your father never stole anything in his life. He was a giver, not a taker.'

'Yes, he was,' Hal smiled at his wife's indignation. She had loved his father and he her. He had always thought it a crying shame that his father had not lived to see the union of the two families. But he consoled himself with the thought that both his parents would have thoroughly approved of Bella now running what was once their home, sharing what was once their bedroom, producing their grandchildren.

'So where do you figure in all this?' Bella asked. 'Knowing you, you're not going to just accept the accusation, are you?'

'No I'm not. I shall be driving down to Devon tomorrow morning to see the remaining Cranmere cabinet, and Mrs Jane Fulford.'

'Good. Give her an earful from me.'

'And then,' Hal said, 'I may be flying to the US of A, all expenses paid.'

'When?' Bella asked hopefully.

'Later this week if your dad can arrange it.'

Bella pouted. 'I can't get away, we're short staffed.' As a care assistant in a home for children with learning difficulties, stolen days off were not even in the frame.

'I'd love to take you, you know I that, but it's only a quick dash there and back. No time for sightseeing or shopping.'

'Well, bring me back something nice,' she said illogically.

'I will try,' Hal promised, adding, 'I am possibly flying supersonic.'

Bella's eyes widened, 'You mean Concord?'

'That's what we high flyers use.'

'Pig.'

CHAPTER 7

———⟋⟍⟍⟋⟍⟋———

In her little kitchen in the Dower House, still faintly smelling of fresh paint, Jane switched on the electric kettle – so much more convenient that dragging a heavy kettle onto a hotplate. The entire kitchen was convenient, carefully designed to be so by David and Catherine, cupboards and drawers set to minimise the need for stretching and stooping. Perhaps she should have expressed her gratitude rather more than she had. David understood how she disliked being fussed over; Catherine did not.

She fed the dog and carried her tea into the sitting room by a tortuous route, touching pieces of furniture as she went – like meeting old friends in unfamiliar surroundings – before settling in her wing chair by the window. From here she could see the entire front of Cranmere with its terrace and columns and pediment glowing faintly pink as the sun went down behind Sittaford Tor. It was ironic, she thought, that in all these years this was a view of the house she had rarely seen at this time of day. She would have been inside the house looking out; now she was outside looking in.

On a table beside her chair stood the silver-framed photographs of her family: Roger in his younger days in jodhpurs and highly polished boots; David at the age of twenty-one, similarly dressed; Richard and Thomas, self-conscious in school uniform. How very like their father they looked, and their grandfather. And in their history lessons they were studying, not the Kings and Queens of England, but the Second World War.

'What did you do in the war, Granny?' they had asked, saying it was part of a school project, inquisitive little toads. Did they really believe she was that senile? Soon they would be trying to teach her to suck eggs.

She leaned her head back amongst the soft cushions thinking, My God, what *didn't* I do?

———⟋⟍⟍⟋⟍⟋———

Her war had started in just the same way as it had for millions of others, sitting with her husband in front of the loudspeaker grille on the big wireless and listening to Neville Chamberlain's announcement at 11 o'clock on Sunday the third of September. '*I am speaking to you from the cabinet room...*' and she remembered thinking, why can't the silly man pronounce the word correctly? Cabinet is spelt with an 'a', not an 'e'... '*we are at war with Germany*'.

Apart from a news bulletin reporting a near panic in London when an air-raid siren had been accidentally sounded soon after Mr Chamberlain's speech, nothing seemed any different. There were no swarms of hostile aircraft above. But in the estate office a mounting pile of forms and directives from the Ministry of Agriculture gave due warning of what to expect. Officials would be calling to assess the extent of productive land on the Cranmere Estate.

'We've got land in acres,' Roger said, 'but what about the men to work it?' The Women's Land Army had yet to be conceived.

Jane tried her best to keep Roger in the estate office – there were a hundred things she needed to know about the farms. But by now he was like a coiled spring, waiting for the impending phone call. He spent a morning cleaning and greasing his beloved Alvis before putting her up on blocks and tucking her down beneath sheets and blankets like a child. When the telephone rang he raced to it, only to find it was a Commander Dobson calling from Plymouth to say that the Royal Navy would be moving in on the following morning. They came in a convoy of cars and trucks and took over the entire ground floor with a constant stream of able seamen carrying grey, steel cupboards and filing cabinets, desks and trestle tables and folding chairs. When they wanted to make the entrance hall their own, Jane, her patience wearing thin, pointed out, 'Those stairs lead to my home, that door to the cellars and air-raid shelter, and that passage to the kitchen.'

All right, they conceded, the entrance hall would be common ground, but a sentry would be posted there day and night.

'And the terrace,' she said. 'We will need a bit of fresh air now and then.'

'Of course,' Commander Dobson smiled, 'but we will have a sentry out there, too.'

By nightfall the tramp of heavy feet had almost ceased. Jane lay awake beside her sleeping husband and listened for the occasional sounds from down below – a voice, a door closing, the scrape of the sentry's boots on flagstone – not intrusive but unfamiliar. And she thought, whilst Commander Dobson had been as diplomatic as he possibly could be,

Cranmere was no longer theirs. They were like tenants in their own home, to be tolerated. But far better, as Roger had said before falling into a heavy, whisky-induced sleep, than being filled up with flea-infested refugees. She recalled Marie's words, 'The war will come to Cranmere in one way or another, of that you can be sure', and thought what a pity it was that she had not stayed on with her cello. What would the Commander have made of that?

At last she slept, only to be wakened by the insistent ring of the telephone on Roger's side of the bed. It was barely daylight. Half awake, she listened to the brief, one-sided conversation and knew only too well what it meant.

'Yes, sir,' Roger called very few people 'sir'. 'Very good, sir.' He was being almost subservient. '… I'll be there.'

He replaced the receiver, turned and took her in his arms and held her for a long time.

'When do you have to go?' she asked at length.

'Sunday.'

Two more days together: that was all they had left. Married less than six months, their honeymoon hardly over. They made love, slowly and exquisitely, bathed and dressed in riding kit before taking the horses up onto the moor for what would possibly be their last opportunity to ride out together. In the hall the sentry stamped his feet as they passed. 'Please don't do that,' Jane said, 'I am not an officer.'

'Yes, ma'am,' he said. 'I mean no, ma'am' – a response that lightened their mood just a little. But even up on the high moor it seemed there was no escaping the war. Between Cranmere and Higher Weeke canvas-covered trucks plied back and forth, the roar of their engines and the sounds of men's voices carrying clearly in what once would have been still, morning air. Otherwise Dartmoor looked no different: the autumn colours were just beginning to show themselves in the bracken and heather and the little stunted hawthorn trees. A pair of buzzards wheeled high above but, like us, Jane thought, the moor was no longer their own. They, too, would have to share it with strangers – for the duration.

In the same afternoon a horsebox arrived to take Roger's two hunters to a livery stable some ten miles distant. Tight-lipped, he led them gently up the ramp and said his farewells in private. Jane held him as he watched, over her shoulder, the vehicle's careful progress all the way down the long drive until it was out of sight. 'It's for the best,' he said, clearly trying to convince himself. 'You won't have time to look after them, and young Harry's already gone to the recruiting office in Okehampton.' But Jane knew what this was costing her husband; had he been anything but a Fulford, he would have wept. She felt the muscles in his arms tighten around her like a steel band. 'Some bastard's going to pay for this,' he muttered – which was probably the right attitude. Alone in her loosebox, Rosie was heartbroken.

—◦◦◦—

Sunday evening came all too soon. Jane stood on the platform at Okehampton Station together with a small group of wives, girlfriends, parents, all gazing eastward as the last carriage of the Exeter train disappeared around the curve of the rails, leaving no more than a faint whisp of smoke hanging in the trees. Then, acknowledging one another as was the country custom, and thankful for the tacit support, the small gathering filed quietly through the station and dispersed. Their loved ones had gone to war, taking Roger with them. The first adjustment she had to make was to the car seat, set for Roger's long legs, and it brought home to her how many far greater adjustments there would have to be in her new way of life. She drove the big Humber, now sightless with black-painted masks fitted to its headlights, down the steep hill into a town busier than usual for a warm, Sunday evening. Dressed in their best, the locals were going to their places of worship. Should she join them, put in a prayer? No. She felt not in the least like chanting meaningless hymns and psalms. She felt – desolate.

Halfway up the Cranmere drive she pulled the car to a halt and gazed for a moment at the front of a house that had been designed to impress, or overawe approaching visitors. Well yes, she thought, she was impressed, always had been; overawed she was not. Roger had left her in charge with his inane 'Chin up, old thing. Keep the place ticking over.' So take charge she would. She dropped the clutch and drove straight up to the front door.

At her desk in the estate office she looked at Roger's vacant chair and decided that would not do at all. Bruin, a large and well-worn teddy bear, a relic from her husband's boyhood, soon occupied his seat at the desk. She found Bruin a comfort; she could talk to him. And if anyone wishing to sit in that chair should discard him they would receive short shrift. If they placed him carefully on the desk or, better still, nursed him, they would be made welcome. Bruin was to become both comrade and confidant.

Even now, though fifty years older and becoming fragile – much like herself – Bruin sat looking at her with his glassy stare, a bit patched and darned but still the same old brown-eyed Bruin. Her grandchildren had been taught to treat him with the greatest of respect. According to Christine he had achieved an antique value, but the value Jane placed upon Bruin was far more than monetary. He had shared her bed as well as her office, and had accompanied her down to the air-raid shelter to comfort countless children, especially young Billy, who had loved him dearly.

When was it the children came: was it '40 or '41? Annoyingly, her memory was not as precise as it once had been, the years merging. But there were some things she would never, ever forget – the sound, night after night, of many aircraft high above en route for Exeter, Bristol or Gloucester, after they had finished with Plymouth. The deep, menacing drone of their engines had filled the air with fear. And the children, hurried sleepily down to the cellars, Naval personnel always lending a helping hand – women and children first. The children had arrived in the spring, following a devastating raid on Plymouth. The previous night, standing on the terrace and wearing a tin hat, she had stared helplessly at the orange glow in the sky over the burning city, thirty miles distant, had heard the gunfire and dull explosions. And she recalled, as though yesterday, the sentry's stricken expression in the low light. His home was in Plymouth.

So the telephone call had been half expected.

'Mrs Fulford, we are going to need your help.' It was a Miss Pearson, headmistress of a small school and part-time WRVS billeting officer. She had looked, without enthusiasm, around the dusty rooms in the East Wing, last occupied in 1919, and had said at the time that they might be considered if things got desperate.

'How many did you say?' Jane asked in disbelief.

'Twenty-seven children and four staff.'

'Yes, that's what I thought you said.' Jane swallowed hard. 'Well, we've got the space, as you know, but it's very basic, just as you last saw it. I doubt the floors have been swept in twenty years.'

'That doesn't matter.' Miss Pearson's voice sounded dull with fatigue. 'All we need is shelter. We cannot spend another night in Plymouth.'

'You mean you want to come today!'

'If we could, please. We have beds and bedding and transport; but no roof over our heads.'

'What time will you arrive?' Jane heard herself saying.

'About three o'clock. Would that be all right?'

'We'll be expecting you,' she said, sounding, she thought afterwards, for all the world like an hotel receptionist. She caught a faint 'God bless you,' before the line went dead. 'God help me,' she said, holding her head in both hands, her eyes passing swiftly over the hastily scribbled 'Must Do' notes in her desk.

For the past nineteen months she had managed, somehow, to keep Cranmere on an even keel, although at times it had seemed like a balancing act. And now this! She had the Royal Navy in residence on the ground floor and up at Higher Weeke – their trucks and despatch riders up and down the drive almost continuously; a skeleton staff in the house, food and petrol rationing, blackout, air raids almost every night, quite apart from seven farms to administer and the Ministry of Agriculture snapping at her heels. A certain relief had come with the arrival of the newly formed Women's Land Army, a truckload of splendid Land Girls now spread around the farms – much to the delight of the sailors. So what possible difference could twenty-seven children make?

The telephone rang. Alan Drewe of Upcott Farm, a miserable old man with a permanent dewdrop on the end of his nose, wanted his weekly grizzle. 'Can't get on with they young maids,' he sniffed. ''Tis men's work on a farm. T'aint fitty.'

Jane drew a deep breath. 'Mr Drewe,' she said firmly, 'you know what the Ministry requires of you. If you are able to fill those quotas without the help of the Women's Land Army, all well and good. If not, I suggest you make more of an effort to get on with them. We are at war, you know.' She put down the receiver, hating herself for using one of those trite little sayings – 'Dig for Victory, Don't forget your gas mask, There's a war on' – but they came in handy now and then. And right now she had more important things to focus on – like twenty-seven children.

CHAPTER 8

Mrs Kerslake, universally addressed as 'Cook', was at the sink preparing to skin a rabbit, a sight that turned Jane's stomach. Several more furry bundles lay on the draining board awaiting their final indignity. Mrs Kerslake was a kindly soul provided the strict rules of her kitchen were observed. She was also inclined to expect the worst until told otherwise. 'Nothing wrong, is there?' she asked, rinsing her hands under the brass tap.

'Nothing at all,' Jane smiled at her. 'I need to talk to you.' Immediately she saw anxiety cloud the older woman's face. Since the outbreak of war, the number of mouths to be fed around her table had dwindled to a mere six, including two of the Home Farm workers. Redundancy loomed. Jane wasted no time in explaining what could, to a lesser woman than Mrs Kerslake, be a crisis.

'Children,' she said. 'I've never cooked for children.'

'I imagine it's the same as for adults, only smaller.'

'Yes, very likely.' Mrs Kerslake thought for a moment and then asked, 'Where'll we feed 'em?'

Jane loved her for that. There had been no hesitation, no excuses, just a quiet acceptance.

'I was thinking I could get the old staff dining room scrubbed out.'

'That should be all right, but I'll need some more help in here.'

'You shall have it,' Jane promised.

'An' some more rabbits.'

As she left the kitchen, Jane hoped that her next request would be met with the same acquiescence from Lieutenant Dando RN. She had crossed swords with him more than once, the last time over something quite petty – a pile of boxes left in the entrance hall. When she asked for their removal, clearly she had caught him at a bad moment.

'Mrs Fulford,' he had said in a tired voice, 'I would remind you that the Royal Navy is in possession here. We are not guests under your roof.'

'Nor ever likely to be,' Jane had countered, walking straight-backed up the wide staircase. And then, relenting, she had paused, flashed him a smile and said, 'Please move them.'

'Aye aye, Ma'am.'

Standing on the turn in the stairs, Millie Morrish had hugged herself in glee. And now she needed his help. Pride would have to be swallowed. The sentry announced her through the partly opened door.

'Is it urgent?' Lieutenant Dando's voice called.

'Yes, it is,' Jane said to the sentry.

'Yes, it is, sir,' the sentry repeated.

'Show her in.'

The room where the Fulford family had once taken most of their meals was barely recognisable, the wall hung with huge maps and charts; another spread across the centre table had wooden ships on it. The lieutenant and a chief petty officer sat behind a long trestle table strewn with papers and a number of telephones, one of them red.

'You are not really supposed to be in here,' the lieutenant said, now on his home ground.

'I have signed the Official Secrets Act,' Jane replied. 'And you invited me in, and I promise not to look at anything.'

Lieutenant Dando gave her a weak smile, offered a seat and asked, 'What is it that is so urgent?'

'I am looking for volunteers.' Jane remained standing.

The two men looked at each other, grinned and turned back to Jane. She explained as briefly as she could exactly what was needed.

'Twenty-seven children, you say?' The grins had faded.

'Yes,' she said, adding for good measure, 'Bombed out. Homeless.'

'Arriving at 1500 hours?'

'Yes, three o'clock. Possibly Millie and I could get one or two of the rooms ready in time, but I wouldn't want to sleep children in them as they are. And there are bathrooms and lavatories, but I'm not sure that everything works.' A little female helplessness, she thought, would do no harm.

'May we see these rooms?' Both men were already on their feet.

They walked – in line astern – along the length of the corridor, looking into empty rooms as they went, most of them still painted in institutional cream with brown linoleum on the floors; all of them festooned with cobwebs, thick in dust and grime.

'What do you think, chief?' Lieutenant Dando addressed the older man.

'I've seen worse, sir. An' we've got five hours.'

'Right. Take the truck up to Higher Weeke and get as many off-duty men as you can. Turn 'em out of bed if you have to. Bring buckets, brushes, mops, you know the drill.'

'Aye aye, sir.'

After the CPO had left, Lieutenant Dando asked, 'How are you going to heat the place? It's still quite nippy at night.'

'Coal fires, that's all we have in this part of the house.'

'When were the chimneys last swept?'

'I've no idea.'

'We'd better get those done, too. They're probably filled up with jackdaw nests.'

Jane thought for a moment about fledglings but said nothing. The children had to come first. She said, 'I am grateful, lieutenant, truly, I am.'

He did not reply at first, and then turning, he said. 'Mrs Fulford, do you think you could bring yourself to call me James?'

'Of course, James,' she said, surprised. 'I am Jane.' And smiled as she recalled a Tarzan film she had once seen containing a similar dialogue.

'Well then, Jane,' he was saying, 'it is I who should feel grateful. Many of my people are from Plymouth. Better that they should be doing something useful for their own, rather than sitting around and wondering if their homes are still standing. I don't think we'll be short of volunteers.'

When the truck returned it contained nine Ratings and three Wrens, all dressed in denim overalls and armed to the teeth with galvanised buckets, brushes and brooms. They pitched straight into their task without delay, opened long-jammed windows, chased out whole families of spiders, swept and scrubbed and polished for three hours without a break, except to pause for endless mugs of tea carried up from the kitchen (galley?). The boiler was stoked by a professional who said, 'We'll need a full head of steam for twenty-seven kiddies.' The huge bathtubs were scoured, their brass fittings polished to a gleam, while Jane and Millie raided cupboards for pairs of heavy curtains, and attics for nursery fire guards.

After a morning of crazy activity, the volunteers were sat on long benches to each side of the kitchen table and fed with liberal helpings of Mrs Kerslake's speciality – rabbit stew, resulting in a prompt offer of marriage from one of the older ratings. At the head of the table, Jane thought the situation almost surreal: an admix of determination to get the job done, together with a cheerful banter amongst the volunteers, cloaked an underlying sadness. She looked down the line of young faces, most of them around her own age, but tired and strained, as well they might be. Their normal duties were hunched over a powerful radio receiver, two hours on, four hours off, around the clock, headphones clamped tight as they strained their ears to detect the faintest of signals, enemy or friendly, so that Lieutenant Dando's model ships could be placed correctly on the chart. And intelligence sent up country to a place, Jane later learned, called Bletchley Park. So scrubbing up for a party of evacuees was probably a welcome break in routine. Ten minutes to three and the volunteers were still there putting the final touches to their handiwork, lighting fires, sticking tape to newly washed windows, when a shout went up.

'Stand by to receive boarders.'

An old motorcoach in faded yellow-and-blue livery and emblazoned with the words 'Sunshine Tours,' nosed its way slowly up the drive, followed by two camouflaged trucks. They came to a gentle halt, the passenger door on the coach slid open and Miss Pearson emerged backwards leading a small child by the hand, followed by another, and another, and another. It very soon became evident that the fast-growing, dejected little huddle beside their coach was not composed of happy, boisterous children. They were tired and confused, their pinched little faces streaked with dried tears. The reception party moved forward as one, each claiming a child and leading him or her by the sticky, little hand into the warmth of Mrs Kerlake's kitchen. Some tried the gentle approach, 'Hello, I'm Mary. What's your name?' Others tried to be hearty. *'The animals went in two by two, hurrah, hurrah…'* The response in either case was minimal.

Around the kitchen table where the volunteers had been shortly before, the children sat quietly; one or two snivelled. Most had wet themselves at some time during their long night and day; the smell of ammonia was strong. Jane and Millie tried to tempt them with Mrs Kerslake's offerings – toast, baked beans, boiled eggs, freshly made cakes – but none was accepted with the eagerness expected, just a quiet thank you. Mrs Kerslake turned back to her stove, dabbing at her eyes with a small handkerchief.

On the upper deck (as the first floor was now called) the volunteers hurriedly assembled little beds unloaded from the trucks, made them up with sheets and blankets – rubber sheets first – and sent a message down to the galley. In small groups the children were led upstairs, undressed and dunked in the big baths, three at a time, rub a dub dub. But even at a time like this, propriety demanded that sailors were not allowed to bathe little girls; so they bathed little boys instead.

That night, for some unaccountable reason, perhaps the hand of God, a thick fog settled over the English Channel and the north coast of France, grounding the German bombers. And the children of Cranmere slept peacefully.

—❦—

Jane took out her handkerchief, surprised to find that even now, in age, she could still be moved to tears by memories of the children's arrival and how it had changed their lives. The mountains of washing – nineteen pairs of wet sheets on the first morning – all to be done by hand; no automatic devices in those days. And the bundles of ration books to be dealt with by the patient manager in Collins the grocers, when she drove down to the village for supplies. And yet the Cranmere children were the lucky ones; the stories coming out of Plymouth were horrific. It was the washing lines that remained firmly in her memory, strung in rows across the grass in front of Cranmere, and how the numbers of little sheets had diminished daily as the children began to come out from wherever they had been hiding, little faces opening like flowers to the sun.

Especially Billy Cann, a frightened little boy who had spent three days buried under the rubble of his home before rescue came. But Billy was a survivor, with black hair and dark brown eyes and an impish grin – and a malformed arm that hung uselessly at his side (not that it appeared to worry him a great deal). When he had first arrived at Cranmere Billy had been a deeply disturbed little boy, a sleepwalker. On a number of occasions Jane had found him on the landing and gently guided him to her room – until he had started to walk in unbidden – where he had spent the rest of the night in her bed. Jane smiled to herself. Even to this day she had not been able to decide whether Billy was all that disturbed, or a six-year-old smooth operator.

Of the other children – middle-aged now – some faces she could recall quite clearly, others were blurred, but the overriding feeling had been one of collective happiness. Even Roger, on one of his infrequent leaves, had spent hours leading Rosie, three children up, round and around the field, running beside them until he was near breathless. 'Ironic,' he had said, 'how all it takes is a few children to bring adults to their senses.'

—〜〜—

An unfamiliar warbling sound from her new telephone brought Jane back to the present. It was Edward Channon to say that his son-in-law, Henry Wesson, would call on her tomorrow about mid morning. 'Would that be convenient, Jane?'

'Yes, I will look forward to meeting him, and that's the second time you have phoned me today, Edward. People will talk, you know.'

'I hope they do,' he laughed. 'Goodnight, Jane.'

'Goodnight, Edward.'

She sat quite still, pondering on the wisdom of allowing a Wesson to set foot on Cranmere soil again. Could she have refused (she was no longer lady of the house)? Possibly, but on what grounds? That was what Edward would be asking, had she done so, especially as he was attempting to do her a kindness. But then Edward Channon, brilliant intelligence officer though he may once have been, could not possibly understand how this investigation – if that was the correct term – was sure to revive memories that were best left undisturbed. And while her most precious memories of the wartime years with the children – the dawn chorus of little voices – had remained fresh in her mind, there were others, pushed back into dark recesses, she had hoped would stay there for all time. As far as the missing cabinet was concerned, she had no strong feelings about it one way or another; in fact she doubted there was anyone on the Cranmere Estate who could remember seeing the two cabinets side by side. She could barely remember them herself. But perhaps she should make this last effort for Cranmere – the story of her life – and in Roger's memory, and for Edward, and of course, for the Wessons.

—〜〜—

CHAPTER 9

—⟨∿⟩—

Hal Wesson set out for Devon on a fine spring morning, joined the M5 motorway near Cheltenham, pointed the car towards the west and put his foot down. By mid-morning he had skirted around Exeter and was on the dual carriageway to Okehampton – still a fast road – until he saw the peaks of Dartmoor to his left, the signal to slow down. At Whiddon Down he left the main road and very soon found himself in narrow lanes with high banks and hedges to either side, with occasional snapshots of stunning scenery through the gateways. This, he thought, might have been the route his father had taken during the war, except that neither the motorway nor the dual carriageway were built then; or he may have come down via Bath and Shepton Mallet. Whichever way, it would have taken him five or six hours on a rackety old motorbike, frozen stiff by the time he arrived. But these narrow lanes would not have changed, not in centuries, nor the unfamiliar names – Chagford, Moretonhampstead, Gooseford and finally Cranmere. Except of course in his father's time, in the war years, there would have been no signposts either. But he must have passed this way.

'Cranmere 1 Mile' the last sign had read, although he seemed to have travelled a good bit more since then and the road was narrower, too narrow for two cars to pass and overhung with ancient oaks with sunlight filtering through, lending an air of mystery. He recalled a children's story that he sometimes read to Charles Edward, of a magic path through the forest which became progressively narrower, and the people on it smaller, until they could enter the fairy kingdom.

The high banks soon gave way to unfenced road with trees of considerable age, some hollow, and huge granite boulders embedded amongst the ferns. A primeval place untouched by man, scattered with wild flowers. The woodland continued on either side up a very steep hill until the road passed between two more massive boulders and the ground flattened out to form a plateau in brilliant sunlight. Hal drew the car to a halt and through the open window caught his first sight of Cranmere slumbering in its valley, a wide building in local granite relieved with sandstone around the windows and quoins, a large central section with wings built symmetrically to either side. The front was treated with four, slender Doric columns supporting a classical pediment and set back behind a terrace with wide steps leading down to the gravelled drive. And at some distance, in a turn in the long drive, was a much scaled-down version of the same building – the Dower House. He restarted the car and moved on. In time-honoured tradition, a Wesson was about to call to sort out the Cranmere cabinets.

—⁓—

Jane heard the sound of the car pulling in, a sound she had been listening for for the past half hour – perhaps a lot longer – and felt her heart begin to race. How pathetic, she told herself, act your age. But one quick glimpse of her visitor as he got out of his car was almost too much. She leaned on the table top for support, took a deep breath, and another. She had been expecting a similarity, naturally, but not quite so close a resemblance. When the bell rang she waited for just a little longer before putting on her no-nonsense face and going to the door.

'Mrs Fulford?' he said. 'I am Henry Wesson.'

'Yes, I can see you are,' she replied. 'Do come in.'

As they entered the sitting room she bombarded him with questions – 'How was your journey? Was the traffic bad? Did you have any difficulty finding us? Would you like coffee?'

'Coffee would be great,' he smiled, seeming not to have heard the previous torrent of enquiries.

'Out on the terrace?' she suggested as she made to leave the room.

'Better still.'

In her kitchen she could buy a little time, collect her wits. Henry Wesson seemed a charming young man, similar to, but not as like his father as she had first thought – her imagination was working overtime. And she was old enough to be his mother. So bear that in mind, Jane Fulford, she told herself severely. This is not the man you once loved but his son, and there is no harm in his being here. Even so, she would feel a lot more comfortable seated beside him on the terrace than facing him across the hearth. She busied herself with the everyday task of making coffee, preparing a tray – milk, sugar, cups and saucers, spoons – and felt calmer.

'Can I be of any help?' he called through the open doorway, startling her.

'Oh, how thoughtful,' she said, recovering rapidly, 'If you could

64

carry the tray.' Following him through the sitting room and the open French window, Jane was able to draw a comparison, at least from the rear view. He was not as tall as his father had been, but broader across the shoulders and with fairer hair growing thickly down to his collar, an improvement on the unflattering short-back-and-sides of the war years. And his offer of help, a simple enough gesture, but in its own way meaning so much – that he had inherited Charles' kindness and consideration for others. She felt a lot easier now that the initial tension had begun to fade and, in all probability like most young people these days, he would be anxious to keep another appointment, be gone within the hour. Yes, she felt she would be able to cope with Henry Wesson without too much effort, or pain.

She had been right about the terrace. No one came out here for the first time without either exclaiming at the outlook or standing in silence for a moment before speaking. Henry Wesson came into the second category, as she had expected. She watched him, still standing, taking in the scene, a panoramic view of Dartmoor from the valley floor right up to the peaks of Bittern Hill to the east and Sittaford Tor to the west. And in the middle ground Cranmere merged into the landscape almost like something grown organically, not made by man.

'When was the house first built?' he asked at length.

'Around 1100, I understand. It was a monastic house then. What you see now is mostly Queen Anne.'

Hal took the chair beside her, continuing to gaze at Cranmere. 'Well,' he said, 'full marks to the monks, they certainly knew how to site a house.' And turning to her he asked, 'Do you go out much?'

'Not a great deal.' Jane was surprised at the question.

'I don't blame you,' he smiled. 'I could sit and look at that all day.'

She poured the coffee, placing the cup and saucer on the table between them. 'I was so very sorry to hear about your father, Mr Wesson,' she said, thinking she should make some mention.

'Thank you, he said. 'And please call me Hal, everyone else does.'

'How old were you, Hal?'

'I was nineteen.'

'Is your mother still living?'

He turned to look directly at her, the wide-set grey eyes all too familiar. 'She was with him,' he said simply.

Jane closed her eyes for a moment, appalled at her blunder. Edward had not said that Hal's mother had died, too. 'My dear, how awful for you,' she said softly. 'Nineteen is not a good age to lose both your parents.'

'I'm not sure there is a good age,' Hal said. 'But I was very fortunate. Uncle Ted – Edward Channon – and Winnie took care of me.'

'Yes, Edward would be supportive at a time like that. Is he keeping well? He says so on the phone but you know what people are like.'

'I can promise you, 'Hal smiled 'that my Uncle Ted is in fine condition.'

'Good. And now he tells me he may have found our missing cabinet in New York. Is that right?'

'Well, we won't know for a day or two.'

'Until you have seen them both?'

'Yes.'

'What happens then?'

'If they are a match, that will be something for Sir Edward to unravel. I can't say I envy him. I suppose he'll have to trace the cabinet right back to the time it left Cranmere. There was some – er – misunderstanding about that, wasn't there?'

'Ah, you've heard about that. I imagine your father told you.'

'Well yes, but I'd forgotten about it until Uncle Ted brought up the subject – only yesterday, as a matter of fact.'

'Misunderstanding?' Jane repeated, pursing her lips. 'Yes, I suppose that is the best way to describe it. Although from what I heard, it was more like a slanging match. I was not here at the time.'

I was not here, she thought, because I felt unable to face Charles Wesson again without making a complete fool of myself, the more so with my husband present. I have never been much good at hiding my true feelings, at deception. So I went out for the day to see my recently widowed mother in East Budleigh, and took my little boy with me.

'Your father and my husband,' she said, 'were both men who held strong opinions and were not afraid to voice them. Roger had spent most of the war years in the company of resistance fighters and partisans, and all manner of thieves and cut-throats. The war had brutalised him. He had the greatest difficulty in settling down. Unlike most people who are prepared to think the best of others, until proved wrong, he was inclined to think the worst, to suspect. That was where the trouble lay.

But for Roger to suggest that your father had anything to do with the cabinet's disappearance was simply unforgivable. And I told him so.'

'He was very upset,' Hal said.

'I'm quite sure he was, and so was I!' Jane said. 'I thought at the time of writing to him to apologise, but that would have been disloyal to my husband. So, regrettably, I did nothing. But as they are no longer with us, I can at least apologise to you, if it is not too late.'

She was surprised at the suddenness and brilliance of Hal's smile, although she needn't have been; she had seen it many times before. 'Of course it is not too late,' he said. 'On Father's behalf your apology is accepted, and thank you.'

'Well then,' she said, greatly relieved, 'If you have finished your coffee, why don't we go and look at this wonderful piece of furniture?'

'Yes, why don't we.'

—◦◦◦—

Before they met, Hal had envisaged a sweet old dear who still carried the traces of once having been pretty, possibly now with a stick or Zimmer frame. But here was a tall, slim, straight-backed woman – something to do with all that riding? – dressed in trousers and a high-necked sweater and with the self-assurance of one who has been blessed from birth with the classic jawline and high cheekbones that marked her down as a beauty; and had won the hearts of many, his Uncle Ted included. A quick look at one of the silver-framed photographs, while Jane was out of the room, had confirmed this. Even now, though grey-haired and with crow's feet lines around her eyes, she was a handsome woman with a sense of humour, and the grace to offer an unasked-for apology for the injustice to his father all those years ago.

For all that, he got the distinct impression that Jane was not quite as hale and hearty as she would have wished, or tried to appear. She seemed to have difficulty with her breathing, and the whites of her eyes were not a good colour. This, Hal thought, was what comes from being married to a nurse. Bella would have diagnosed instantly. And it was for this reason that, having driven her the short distance from the Dower House to Cranmere and parked at the foot of the steps, he held open the car door and offered Jane his arm.

'Good heavens, I can walk up a few steps without assistance, thank you,' she said.

'I'm sure you can, Hal smiled. 'I was trying to be a gentleman, that's all.'

'Oh well, in that case,' she laughed and took his arm. And leaned on it quite heavily as they made their way up to the massive front door.

Once past the classical façade it became obvious that they were in a house of great antiquity. The hall floor was laid in worn flagstones and there were unexplained Gothic arches set into the walls, and old weapons left over from long-ago conflicts, and an oak staircase that was Elizabethan or even earlier. It was not a grand house when compared with some he knew up in Gloucestershire, but informal and welcoming, a family home with simple flower arrangements set on the polished side tables and coffers.

The long gallery led off the first floor landing and ran forty feet or more along the west front of the house, tall sash windows to one side, painted pine panelling to the other. And in the centre of this back wall stood the china display cabinet built by Ince and Mayhew in 1759; and rebuilt by Charles Wesson 200 years later.

—◦◦◦—

CHAPTER 10

Hal stood quite still, and from the far side of the room allowed his gaze to travel from one end of the huge cabinet to the other, and back again. And then from top to bottom, taking in every detail from the delicate tracery, the shaped canopy roofs relieved with light gilding, the tiny carved figures, the fine glazing bars in the doors, right down to the panelled doors beneath, each enclosing either a stack of graduated drawers or vertical divisions for large folios. He'd seen a few in the great houses in Gloucestershire, but nowhere near as fine as this. The Cranmere cabinet was nothing short of magnificent. He approached the cabinet slowly, with the reverence of a communicant to the altar, reached out one hand and ran his fingertips gently over the carved fret – and felt his father's work. Of that he was in no doubt. It was something known only to craftsmen of the highest standard, this ability to recognise a friend's work, his handwriting; the one way in which the eighteenth-century carvers – many of them illiterate – could express themselves. And this piece of blind fret carving he was touching had been done by his father, who was far from illiterate. He could go on – this piece here, and here, and this carved wood Chinaman, all bore the stamp of Charles Wesson. As did the entire cabinet. In fact, the almost seamless reconstruction – resurrection? – of the Cranmere cabinet was very probably the best thing his father had ever done.

He felt her eyes on his back and, turning, saw Jane sitting on one of the upholstered windowseats behind him with a curious little smile on her face

'I have been watching you,' she said. 'You've been in another world, haven't you?'

'Mmm. Sorry if I neglected you.'

'Not at all. Your father once told me that a good craftsman puts a little of himself into his work. Do you think that is so?'

'Yes, I do.'

'And if you hadn't known, would you have been able to tell that your father had worked on our cabinet?'

'Yes,' Hal said without hesitation. 'His footprints are all over it.'

'Good. Then it is a fitting memorial. I remember Edward saying that he knew of no one else who would have taken on the job. It had been blown to bits.'

Jane got to her feet and stood looking out of the window, frowning at a truck that had pulled in at the far end of the terrace, laden with scaffolding poles. 'The German plane came straight up the drive,' she said. 'It was very low; I could see the faces of the men inside and the bombs falling out. One of them fell in the woods down by the Lodge, another in the pasture where you can see the bed of daffodils – that was a bomb crater. The third fell just about where your car is now, and didn't go off, and the fourth fell in the stableyard behind the house. That was the one that did the damage.'

'I wonder why?' Hal tried to imagine the terrifying scene, without much success.

'Why what?'

'Well, why you were bombed at all.'

'Oh that's simple,' she said in a matter-of-fact voice. 'Someone left all the lights on. This room had a glazed roof like Paddington Station, it must have shone like a beacon.'

'That was careless.'

'Yes, I suppose so. He was a little boy who was afraid of the dark.'

So, Hal thought, there was the answer to one at least of Uncle Ted's queries. No leaked intelligence, spies or fifth columnists; no more than a frightened little boy. He should have asked Jane.

—⁂—

They left Cranmere under a darkening sky with heavy clouds rolling into the valley from the west, and arrived at the Dower House just as the first raindrops splashed on the paving stones – and the heavens opened.

'You will stay to lunch, won't you?' Jane asked (the traditional offer of sustenance to travellers from those who lived in big country houses).

'That's kind of you, but there's really no need.'

'A glass of beer and a sandwich then,' she said, looking out through the kitchen window. 'You cannot possibly set out in this.' It was put in such a way that a refusal would have been almost rude.

He was in the sitting room admiring some of Jane's antique furniture while she made sandwiches out in the kitchen, when the car pulled onto the gravel outside. He heard the back door open and a man's voice cursing the rain.

'David,' Jane said. 'We weren't expecting you until tomorrow.'

'And I wasn't expecting you to move out while I was away,' he said accusingly. 'Catherine told me on the car phone. Are you all right, Mother?'

'Yes, of course I am.'

'Quite sure? Got everything you need?'

It was the voice that stirred something in Hal's memory. Not the smooth, easy drawl known only to the very rich, but the pitch and natural modulation of a voice once known to him. He moved to the doorway from where he could see straight across the little hall and kitchen, to the back door. David Fulford stood beneath the porch, drying his glasses on a pocket handkerchief.

'Are you coming in?' Jane was saying.

'No, I can't stop, Mother. Bit of a flap on with Catherine's builders but I couldn't just pass by. You know how I don't like the idea of you being here on your own.'

'Please don't fuss, David, I am quite content here, and I am not on my own, I have a visitor.'

'Oh, well then, I'll cut along. Call back late this afternoon, if that's all right.' And seeing Hal in the doorway, he raised one hand and smiled. And in that instant, the crazy thought that had flashed across Hal's mind, to be quickly rejected, became a near reality. He was across the kitchen in two strides and peering through the rain-streaked windows as David Fulford ran to his car and drove off.

'Who was that?' he asked, almost in a whisper.

Jane, standing behind him answered, 'That was my son David.'

'Yes, I've no doubt,' Hal said. 'But who was the father?' He was already turning towards her as he asked this last question so that the word 'father' was flung straight at her. Jane had stepped back to the wall behind her, one hand clutching at the neck of her sweater, her breath coming in short gasps.

'Christ!' Hal said, appalled at his own crass stupidity. 'I'm sorry, I shouldn't have said that. You're not well, are you?' And, taking her very gently by the shoulders, he guided her to a chair in the sitting room and sat her down carefully. 'Can I get you something?' He felt totally inadequate. 'A glass of water?'

'Water,' she said between gasps.

He fetched the water and knelt by her chair holding the glass in both hands like an offering as she tipped two tiny tablets from a plastic container into her palm. He watched closely as she placed the life-saving tablets in her mouth, accepted the glass of water, also in both hands, and drank.

'What is it?' he asked, 'Asthma?'

'No,' she shook her head.

'Should I call someone?'

'No.' Very firmly.

'Are you going to be all right?'

'In a minute or two.'

'Cup of hot tea, then?'

Again the faint nod.' Thank you.'

In the kitchen he found tea bags, electric kettle, milk. He doubted she would want sugar. God, how he wished Bella was here, she would know what to do. What the hell was the matter with him? One minute he'd been talking to a lovely old lady, next minute he'd bloody near killed her! Waiting for the kettle to come to the boil, he kept glancing in through the doorway to make sure she hadn't collapsed. In which event, what should he do? Call David? That was something he didn't want to do; nor even think about David. Placing the teacup on her side table, he dropped to one knee again to look at her closely – or in supplication. Her breathing had improved.

'Feeling a bit better?'

'Thank you, yes.'

'Jane,' he said in an effort to make some sort of reparation, 'please forgive me. I feel deeply ashamed. I had no right to speak to you as I did.'

She gave him a brave little smile. 'I would say... of all people.... you had every right.' The answer to another question, a question he had not even dared to ask himself, nor think about with any clarity of mind. Until now. 'You had every right.' That's what she'd said. Almost an admission from her own lips, that the crazy thought he had refused to entertain, that had grown into a strong possibility when David smiled at him, had now been all but confirmed by Jane.

That David Fulford was his brother.

He stood looking gloomily out of the wide window as great curtains of rain gusted in from the west and down the length of the valley. Jane, who seemed to have recovered, had gone to her room to freshen up, saying, 'Help yourself to tea, or there's whisky on the side table if you prefer.'

Hal preferred whisky.

Just what had gone on here forty-odd years ago? It was fairly obvious, wasn't it? His mood surged through disbelief, to anger, to sadness and then back to near disbelief. Christ! No wonder his father and Roger Fulford had nearly come to blows. And yet, it was completely out of character; his father had been an honourable man. Sure, he'd put it about a bit, by all accounts, when young and unattached. Nothing wrong in that. But if he had got a girl into trouble, he would have stood by her, 'done the decent thing' as they said in those days. No way would he have cleared off and left her holding the baby; except that Jane was already married with a husband away at the war – fair game for a wandering Lothario? There were a malicious few still living in Lynchcombe who would just love to hear this, enlarge on it if they could. He had never paid any attention to tittle-tattle, had dismissed it as coming from ugly old women who had once been ugly young women and missed out on a few basic pleasures. But this was something different.

Through the driving rain the outline of Cranmere stood dark and uncompromising, as if to say – *So what's new? These things have been happening for centuries, even in the best of families.*

Not in my family, they haven't, Hal argued, feeling his anger rise again. In that house over there he had an elder brother – well, half-brother – a sister-in-law and two nephews, none of whom he had known about until just now and, unless he had read the situation wrongly, would not be given the chance to meet.

Christ!

But – doubts had already begun to creep in – was he absolutely sure? From the little he had seen of David, his impression had been of a middle-aged man of about his own build and colouring, who wore rimless glasses and was concerned for his mother's well-being. What else, a family likeness? Perhaps, but not immediately obvious. It was the voice that had aroused dormant memories, that and the quick smile like his father's – like his own! But, setting aside for a moment Jane's assurance that he had 'every right', could he be wrong? Could he be guilty of having made the biggest, the most God-awful gaffe of all time, firing from the hip as he had?

Only one person could answer that question.

CHAPTER 11

—◈—

Sitting at her dressing table, Jane looked for a moment at her reflection in the mirror, then lowered her eyes, unable to meet her own accusatory stare. She was calmer now the pounding in her chest had subsided, but it had been a near thing. 'Softly softly,' Doctor McMasters had advised. 'Try not to get over-excited, Jane.' How could she not when the secret she had guarded, the lie she had lived for over forty years was laid bare – and in such forthright terms?

She should have listened to her own warning against allowing a Wesson to visit Cranmere again, should have continued to hide behind that ridiculous – but oh so convenient – dispute between Roger and Charles. But if she were to be honest with herself – and not before time – she would have to admit that it was curiosity that had decided her. And had David not come home a day earlier than expected, all would be well. Even now, she was certain that her son had not noticed anything about her visitor that struck any sort of chord. Why should he? He had never set eyes on his natural father. Neither was he as perceptive as his – no, she could not bring herself to think the word – as Hal Wesson. There was very little she would be able to conceal from Charles' son who, it seemed, had inherited his father's steady gaze, which had read her innermost thoughts. Neither did she want to. Her only recourse now was complete honesty, to tell all and then throw herself on his mercy. If he was the man she judged him to be, he would treat her kindly.

His eyes were on her just as soon as she entered the room, following her until she sat opposite him with her back to the window, and to Cranmere. She felt more confident now that she had changed, washed her face in cold water, done a few running repairs; a little more poised. Was she nervous? Oh yes.

They sat in silence until Hal asked, 'Are you fully recovered?'

'Yes, thank you. And you?'

His answer was the minimal shrug that the young seemed to use these days when unable to think of a suitable reply.

'I am sorry if I gave you a fright,' she said.

'That's my line in the script, isn't it?'

She smiled, 'No, Hal, I don't think it is. And I have some explaining to do.'

'Only if you want to,' he said quietly. So like his father: he looked vulnerable, hurt, and it was her doing.

'I do want to. For your sake, for my own and for your father's. I don't want you leaving here thinking any less of him. That would be both unfair and untrue.'

Hal said nothing, looking steadily at her with his father's eyes.

There was no easy way to say her piece. She had to come straight out with it, put it into words for the very first time. Then offer explanations. 'During the war your father and I were lovers, and David was the result. You had already decided that, I think, but what I want you to know is...' Here she faltered, this was not easy...' the circumstances, how this came about. We were not casual lovers enjoying a wartime fling; we both fell deeply in love. And whilst I am aware that may sound an inadequate excuse, and that young people today have relationships, we fell hopelessly and gloriously in love and there was little we could do about it. 'How long have you been married Hal?' It was an appeal for help.

'Coming up to three years.'

'And when you were first married, did you experience that head-in-the-clouds, walking-on-air sensation when nothing mattered but you and Bella?'

Hal smiled, 'Yes, all of those things and more. Still do, some of the time.'

'Then I am happy for you both. The difference was, in our case, we had a few days together and then it had to end. If Charles had asked me to leave with him I would have thought about it very carefully, and probably refused; there were too many people dependent on me at the time. Had there not been, I would have gone with him to the ends of the earth. And I promise you, Hal, I promise you, that I have not for one minute regretted our love. We were two damaged souls living through a difficult time and in need of support. That is what we gave to one another, the will to keep going.'

Jane looked down at her hands, twisting and untwisting a tiny handkerchief. They had always betrayed her at times like this.

'Would you like one of these?' Hal was asking, holding up his whisky tumbler.

'Thank you, I think I would. Lots of water.' And a chance to think before saying any more, though she had never dreamed she would admit David's parentage to anyone. Why then to this young man, a stranger until this morning? Because he had already worked it out for himself, and more than that, she felt she could trust him. He was standing by her chair offering a glass of whisky diluted to the colour of pale straw. She would have liked it stronger.

'That looks just right,' she said.

Hal returned to his seat, looked at her solemnly and said, 'Jane, you don't have to go on with this. I do understand.'

'Thank you, but with respect, I don't think you do understand, not fully. I would like the chance to explain, if you will allow?'

'Of course.'

'Then you may judge me as you wish.'

———✷———

The rain had eased to a gentle drizzle, shafts of sunlight breaking through the clouds with the promise of a rainbow – which did not appear. Jane sipped her drink, put it down carefully and turned to face Hal.

'I am sure you have heard all sorts of stories about the war, seen the films, read the books; but what very few of them convey – why should they, they are for our entertainment? – is the drudgery and deprivation, and the hopelessness we felt in the early years. There was no good news. Even after the Battle of Britain we still feared invasion.

'In the spring of 1942 I was twenty-five years old and in charge of the Cranmere Estate and that house over there.' She made an elegant gesture with one hand vaguely in the right direction. 'I had very little experience of estate management, had been thrown in at the deep end, so to speak. My husband was away and, because of the nature of his work, we were unable to contact one another.

'I was very much on my own. Everything was in short supply; food, clothing, fuel, even soap. That was one of the worst things: can you imagine how demoralising it was to be short of soap with twenty-seven children and their washing?'

Hal did not answer.

'During the blitz, nearly every night the enemy aircraft were overhead. At first it was Plymouth they were after: they would come inland and turn around over Cranmere before going back to bomb Plymouth from the landward side. After they had destroyed Plymouth, they simply flew straight over us on their way upcountry to Bristol or Gloucester or the Midlands. Apparently we were on the flight path from their base in Brittany. It meant that for months on end the siren would sound at around midnight and all the children would be hurried down to the cellars; and back to their beds after the 'All Clear'. We were short of sleep, tired and irritable, but we didn't feel under any great threat from the bombers; what could they want with us? Until the third of May 1942. It was what they called a Baedeker raid, a spiteful tit-for-tat policy aimed at Cathedral cities. The RAF had bombed Lubeck a few nights previously. Now it was Exeter's turn.' Jane paused, her eyes focused on something on the far side of the room. She had reached a point when to continue would mean to recall in detail, and recount, all that had occurred on that long-ago May night, and in the following days and nights, memories she had tried to suppress. But if Charles' son was to be made aware of the circumstances surrounding David's conception, then she would have no choice but to revisit and relive the scene, no matter how great her reluctance.

When she spoke it was in a quieter voice than before and, it seemed to her, almost as though someone else was speaking on her behalf. For had she been asked, afterwards, exactly what she had said, she would have had only a vague recollection.

—=෮෮෮=—

Ten minutes past midnight and she was standing at the tall window on the landing, the children all safely in the cellar long before the air-raid siren had sounded down in the village. One of the advantages in having the Royal Navy on board was the early warning of approaching aircraft.

'Looks like Exeter,' Lieutenant Dando had said. 'One formation going up the estuary, another coming this way.'

Fifteen minutes had passed and still no sign of enemy aircraft. They would come. She and the staff had endured so many raids (or, rather, the passage of aircraft overhead to bomb someone else) they had become almost indifferent, except where the children were concerned; they were kept safe. And often she and Millie Morrish had stood on the terrace and counted the bombers as they went over, high in the sky, and the stragglers returning, Millie always insisting that there were fewer of them. But not tonight: this was the closest the war had come to Cranmere and already there was a dull red glow in the sky over Exeter, sixteen miles distant as the crow flies. Jane offered up a silent prayer for the city where she had spent much of her childhood, and for its people and her parents on the far side of the estuary. But even as she did so she heard the low growl and saw the formations, black against a moonlit sky.

They were lower than she had seen them before and banking in a slow turn to the east when one of them became detached from the rest and seemed to be heading in a long dive directly towards Cranmere. Like a fool, she stood transfixed as the Junkers made its run, bomb doors open, and for a brief moment saw the black crosses on its underside and the dark shapes falling from its belly like the obscene eggs of a huge insect. There came a bright flash and loud explosion somewhere in the woods south of the Lodge, another even closer in the pasture. She threw herself flat as a third bomb came straight for the house, covered her head with both arms and waited for the detonation – which for some reason never came. And she was conscious of someone running past and Millie's voice, shrill and urgent, calling, 'Billy, Billy Cann, where are you? Did you turn all these lights on, you daft little bugger? You'll have us all blown to kingdom come!' Jane scrambled to her feet and ran after her into the long gallery, ablaze with lights from end to end, and heard Millie's scream.

'BILLY!'

Billy whimpered and showed himself.

Millie was a well-built young woman from a moorland farm. She scooped him up, held him to her bosom and ran the length of the room with Jane hard on her heels, switching out lights as they went, and through the doorway onto the staircase. No sooner had they left, an explosion shook Cranmere to its foundations and with the sound of shattering glass, the roof over the long gallery crashed down onto the polished floor. They ran down the stairs together and in the hall, where Millie paused to catch her breath. Billy's thin little arm was clasped around her neck as though his very life depended on her – which it did. 'There now, don't 'ee fret, my little one,' she said softly. 'You'm with Millie now.' Another screech and detonation from somewhere at the rear of the house sent them scuttling down the cellar steps to the door marked 'Air Raid Shelter'. Miss Pearson stood in the doorway. She took one look at Billy and said, 'William! Just what did you think you...' The question was cut short as a purposeful Millie pushed her rudely to one side saying, 'Leave him be. Poor little mite's terrified' and, taking up a blanket, walked to a quiet corner of the room where she and Jane wrapped him like a cocoon and held him close.

In the low-ceilinged room the air was warm and stale though poor ventilation. After a while, Jane detached herself from a sleeping Billy and a dozing Millie and began what she thought of as her Florence Nightingale number, moving quietly from one makeshift bed to another. Most of the children were sound asleep, some were not, peering at her over their blankets with anxious eyes. Bridget was eight years old with an oval face and dark fringe. One day she would be beautiful, if God and the Germans allowed. 'Have they gone, Jane?' she asked in a tiny voice.

'Yes, they've gone.' Jane crouched by her bedside, smiled down at her, smoothed her cheek.

'They won't come back, will they?'

'No, they won't come back.'

'You promise?'

'I promise.'

Bridget's dark eyes searched her face. 'I love you, Jane,' she said.

'And I love you, Bridget. Try to sleep now.' Jane turned away, unable to deal with such trust.

Another voice was calling to her from the half open door. Jim Sanders, the Home Farm manager. She sensed trouble. 'What is it, Jim?'

'You'd better come, ma'am. It's your little mare, 'er's down, cast in 'er box.'

Please God, NO! Jane prayed as she picked her way between sleeping children. Cast in her box meant she had been flailing around violently, probably in blind panic when the bomb fell behind the house. 'Is she hurt, Jim?'

'Foreleg, I reckon. I managed to get the workhorses out, they'm running in the field.' Jane was already running across the stable yard. She could hear Rosie screaming in pain and fear, and called out to her as she struggled with the stiff latch, 'It's all right, Rosie, I'm here.'

'I'm not sure as I'd go in, ma'am.' Jim Sanders had just caught up with her. 'When an animal's hurt you can never be sure...'

Jane was already in the loosebox. Rosie lay on her side, drenched in sweat. She lifted her head as Jane entered then sank back onto the soft straw, her eyes glazed. Jane dropped to her knees by the mare's head, stroked her neck, spoke softly in her ear, soothed her. But even in the low light she could see all she needed to: the offside foreleg was shattered, white bone showing through. There was no possible remedy, only one answer. Jane had friends who had been through having to come to terms with this, and very quickly, and had prayed that it would never be a decision she would have to make. 'Have you phoned the vet, Jim?' she called.

Jim stood outside the box, keeping his distance. 'Phone's dead, ma'am. Reckon the line's down.'

At a time like this? she thought. Thanks very much, God. And to Rosie she said, 'Just lie still, my little one. I'll be back.'

She ran towards the house. In the estate office she tried the telephone in the vain hope that the newer instrument might be more effective that the one in Jim's farmhouse, or that someone somewhere might have repaired the broken wire.

Silence.

Pale faced, she took the key from the centre drawer in her desk and unlocked the mahogany cupboard immediately behind her. From the top shelf she lifted down the service revolver, still in its leather holster, one of Bertie's souvenirs from the 'last show' but always kept in perfect order. And a box of bullets. She checked the heavy revolver carefully. She knew how to work it; Roger had taught her how to shoot in case of invasion, or for moments like this. One by one she placed the brass cartridges in the chambers – though one would suffice – closed the gun, put on the safety catch and walked out into the night.

Standing by the stable door, Jim Sanders held out one hand for the revolver. 'Let me have that.'

'No,' Jane said. 'I'll do it.'

'But you can't ma'am!' In the semi-darkness Jim's voice carried a mixture of disbelief and affronted male pride.

'Yes, I can, Jim. I've seen it done. I know what to do.'

'But it ain't fitty for a young maid.' In his indignation Jim had overlooked their social differences.

'Possibly not,' Jane said firmly, 'but if anyone is going to do it, it will be me.'

'I'll be just outside then,' Jim mumbled, clearly knowing better than to argue with a young maid holding a loaded pistol.

Rosie had not moved. Placing the revolver on the floor beside her, Jane knelt by the mare's head and spoke quietly into her ear for a few minutes. Then with one finger she traced an imaginary line from Rosie's right ear to her left eye, and again from her left ear to her right eye; where those two lines crossed, that was the spot. She made a little mark in the stiff hair, leaned forward and planted a gentle kiss on the same place. Then moving back a little, she took up the revolver, slipped off the safety catch, cocked it, placed the muzzle to Rosie's forehead and squeezed the trigger.

The sound was louder than she had expected, a sharp CRACK! The mare's head came up and she shivered from head to foot until, with a deep intake and then expellation of breath, like a sigh, she subsided onto the clean straw. Jane moved forward, buried her face in Rosie's mane and stayed there.

—⁓⁓—

CHAPTER 12

A pre-dawn mist hung over the Cranmere valley. At a slightly higher level on the terrace, Jane stood immobile. She was not sure how long she had been there, had hazy recollections of Jim Sanders' rough voice as he had helped her to her feet, and drinking a mug of hot tea in his farmhouse, and of helping to herd the children back to their beds. Otherwise nothing. At sometime someone, probably Millie, had come out and placed a blanket around her shoulders. She pulled it close to her neck to keep out the morning chill. On the horizon to the east where the sun would first show itself over Mardon Hill a pulsating red glow lit the sky as Exeter burned. So there would be no proper sunrise this morning. Nor any morning. How could there be when her truest friend, who had carried her flying over the moor to see so many dawns, lay dead? Killed by her own hand. And in that moment, with that pistol shot, something in her had died just as surely as if the bullet had entered her own brain. She would remember always Rosie's trusting brown eyes as she had put the gun to her head, just like Bridget's as she had lied to her earlier. So what now? Oh she would help with the children, although not strictly her responsibility, and sort out the staff's and farmers' problems, and order up supplies and argue for extra rations, function as normal. But at arm's length. They must learn not to trust her. She lied and betrayed and killed.

Daylight came and the fiery glow over Exeter dimmed, to be replaced by a pall of smoke rising high into a summer morning sky. And with the dawn, Jane began to make a mental list of things that would need to be done soonest. What damage had Cranmere suffered during the night? The roof over the long gallery was the first priority; the children would not be able to use it as they had on a daily basis. And that bomb crater now visible in the pasture would have to be filled in before a grazing animal fell down it in the dark; and the washing line, essential for the children's daily needs, lay in the grass at the foot of the terrace steps. Oddly, and completely illogically, it was this minor damage that tried her patience more than anything else just at that moment. The roof was one thing, the washing line entirely different.

Shrugging off the blanket, she walked quickly down the wide steps to the grass and turned to her right – and stopped dead in her tracks. The thing half buried in the soft earth was dull black, like a huge, crudely made iron boiler with fins attached to one end and words stencilled around its fat belly – in German. In her still semi-comatose state, it was a few seconds before she understood just how threatening, and repulsive, and evil, an unexploded bomb could appear.

———*∿∿∿*———

She startled Lieutenant Dando. It was the first time she had burst into his top-secret world unannounced. He was unshaven, tieless, tired. 'James, can you come quickly?'

'What is it?' he asked, rising from his desk. The two Wrens sitting to his left exchanged glances, raised eyebrows.

'Best you see for yourself.' Jane waited by the door. A shamefaced sentry peered past her into the room. At the foot of the steps she pointed, 'There.'

'Oh Jesus!' Lieutenant Dando approached with cautious tread, crouched and placed an ear to the black monster and hurried back to where Jane waited. 'We must clear the building immediately.'

'But the children...' Jane began.

'Especially the children. You go and rouse them, my people will help.' The lieutenant was at battle stations. 'I've a truck outside, we'll get another sent down.'

'Where will we go?' Jane had to run to keep up with him.

'Anywhere away from here. We'll pack 'em in the farmhouse somehow.' In the doorway to his office he bellowed, 'We have a UXB. Lock files and top-secret material in the safe. All hands to assist with evacuation. We haven't much time.'

'What will you do?' Jane asked, bewildered at the speed and urgency.

'Call up the Royal Engineers. Bomb Disposal.'

'But the phone lines are down,' she wailed.

He put a hand on each of her shoulders, gave a quick smile. 'We have radio. Now please, Jane, the children.'

They were brought down for a second time, carried in their blankets, most of them sound asleep and clutching precious teddies, to be handed up carefully into the backs of canvas-covered trucks. Due to the quiet efficiency of the staff and Naval personnel, the evacuation was completed in fourteen minutes – including Billy Cann. Remaining behind in the comparative safety of the stableyard were Lieutenant Dando who, as officer on watch, was to meet and liaise with the Royal Engineers; Jim Sanders who was halfway through morning milking and buggered if his girls were going to be inconvenienced by any German bomb; and Jane, who could not face the thought of being crammed into a small farmhouse with so many well-meaning people. Already Lieutenant Dando, on seeing her wistful gaze across the stableyard at the bolted door, had laid a hand on her arm and said, 'I am so sorry, Jane.'

'Thank you,' she nodded, but she knew what they would be thinking. There were human lives at risk, children's – Rosie was only a horse. Why did she have such difficulty in accepting this?

She never had been much good at waiting around for something to happen – like her turn in the showjumping arena in a previous life. Then, success or failure had been in her own hands. Now, it was not. It depended on how soon the Royal Engineers would arrive or, at what time the bomb, which could reduce her home to rubble, had been set to go off. According to Lieutenant Dando the delay could be timed for anything up to twenty-four hours, but probably less. She did a quick calculation – if the clock had been set before the aircraft took off, say two hours before it was delivered at around midnight, and it was now ten minutes past seven, then over nine hours had already been used up and time was ticking by – literally! There was nothing she could do but wait. She was not even allowed back into her home to fetch a few things. She sat perched on the edge of a stone drinking trough, her back to the stables, blanking out in her only semi-functional mind what lay behind one of those doors. The sun was warm and the air still with scarcely a sound to be heard but birdsong, the cooing of the doves nesting in the gable end of the barn, and Jim Sanders banging about with galvanised buckets; a peaceful, pastoral morning. Had it not been for Lieutenant Dando rushing around making hurried arrangements, no one would have guessed that Cranmere was under threat.

She got stiffly to her feet, light-headed through lack of sleep, and walked across the yard to see why the tithe barn doors had been left wide open. Standing on the threshold, she peered into the dark interior, sensing immediately that something was not as it should be. As her eyes adjusted to the gloom, she saw the piles of twisted and splintered wood, broken glass and fragment of carvings from what had been the pride of her husband's collection. The Cranmere cabinets were smashed to a thousand pieces scattered across the barn floor. Pushing the heavy doors to, she secured them with the broken hasp as best she could. Just at that moment, the Cranmere cabinets did not seem terribly important.

—◦◦◦—

At last the Royal Engineers arrived in a convoy of two heavy trucks, one with a crane attached and a sign that read DANGER UNEXPLODED BOMB. They were led by a smaller vehicle which drove up into the stableyard where they were standing. A young captain jumped out and threw up a smart salute to his Naval counterpart. He wore brown leather gloves.

Side by side the two officers walked calmly through the house and down the terrace steps. Jane trailed after them, listening to their man talk.

'Oh, it's one of those, is it?'

'You've seen them before?'

'Yes, we're old friends. Ticking, is she?'

'Yes.'

'We'll soon put a stop to that. Where will you be?'

Lieutenant Dando pointed, 'Up there on the hillside, out of your way.'

'Right. Don't worry about security, no one's coming near while we're about.' He gave a short laugh, 'They'd be fucking idiots if they did.' And noticing Jane nearby, the captain blushed and smiled shyly. 'Beg pardon, ma'am.'

Jane thought he looked almost too young to be in uniform, and maybe fearful beneath his glib humour.

—◦◦◦—

Except from the air Higher Weeke bore little resemblance to the farm it once was. Vehicles were kept strictly undercover in the open-fronted implement sheds; doorways into barns and linhays and the newly erected Nissan huts identified by blue-and-white painted signs in the abbreviated terms known only to service men and women. A fire point with painted buckets and polished axe stood next to the antique iron pump.

Behind the farmhouse on an area of grass kept tidy by off-duty sailors, groups of children – still clad in their night clothes – sat in circles around their teachers and storytellers in the warm sun. They were not in the least concerned; this was good, a break in routine, no proper lessons today! One or two sent Jane a sad little smile or a subdued wave of the hand, not the boisterous welcome she had feared – because they had been told, and would understand better than adults. The exception was Billy, who came running to her demanding a hug. He looked up at her with his melancholy brown eyes. 'I'm sorry, Jane,' he said before breaking away and running back to his group. She was left wondering if this was sympathy for her loss, or an apology for leaving the lights on. It was hard to tell with Billy. The children had been breakfasted and most held mugs of milk or orange squash, by courtesy of the Wrens and sailors who also enjoyed a break in routine. Jane added a mental note to her list – reimburse the RN with sugar, butter, milk, cornflakes and so on, provided her house and larder were not blown to bits like Roger's cabinets.

A rustic table and bench stood at one end of the grassed area, shaded by a hawthorn tree in full bloom. From here she could see down the Cranmere valley to where tiny figures were moving busily around carrying lengths of cable and tools. She prayed they would beat the clock for their own sakes – another hour had slipped by. If they failed, her home would be gone and right now she wanted nothing more than a hot bath and change of clothes, and to curl up in bed for a week. Nearby, a bearded sailor was reading a fairy story – with voices – to a group of spellbound children. She listened for a while then turned away, rested her elbows on the table, covered her ears with both hands and watched the Royal Engineers at work half a mile distant. What would happen, she wondered dispassionately, if the bomb went off? Would she see Cranmere sink gracefully into a pile of rubble and hear the bang seconds later? And if so, would Roger rebuild it? And how could anyone be brave enough, or foolish enough, to go anywhere near that dreadful thing? The men had removed their shirts and seemed to be climbing all over it. 'God be with them,' she breathed. She could do nothing but wait, and pray.

Lieutenant Dando returned carrying a pair of binoculars. He had shaved and put on a clean shirt, but was unable to hide the strain that showed in his face and around the eyes.

'It's going well,' he said brightly.

'How do you know?' Jane had been catnapping, but suspected she was being fobbed off with platitudes.

'Because,' he smiled as he sat beside her, 'I have just received a report over the radio.'

'Oh.' She shook her head, and brushed her hair back with one hand. 'Sorry, I was miles away.'

'Did you get any sleep last night, Jane?'

'Not much. Did you?'

'We could find you an empty bunk in the house,' he suggested. 'Call you when things start to happen.'

'Thank you, but no. What I would appreciate is, if you could tell me what is going on down there.'

He offered his binoculars. 'Try these.'

'No,' she waved them away, 'I never could get on with those things. Just tell me in words of one syllable, please, James.'

'Very well.' The opportunity to explain technicalities to a beautiful young woman was not to be missed. He moved closer. 'You see that thing they've put around the bomb like a motor tyre?'

'Yes.' She could feel his body heat.

'That is a powerful electro-magnet. When the current is switched on, with any luck, it will stop ticking.'

'And has it?'

'Yes, it has.'

'So it's safe?' She moved away.

'No, but we have bought a little more time. Captain Stewart will now attempt to defuse it. He has a microphone strapped to him and will give a running commentary on everything he does by telephone to his sergeant in the stableyard, who will take notes. That way, if things go wrong, they will know what not to do in future.'

'It sounds very risky.'

'It is. It's the moment of truth. Trouble is, the Germans are constantly dreaming up clever devices to prevent us defusing their bombs.'

After a moment's silence, Jane said, 'He seems very young to be a captain.'

Lieutenant Dando was focusing his binoculars. 'I believe promotion is fairly rapid in his outfit.'

The full significance of this last remark did not occur to Jane until later.

The moment of truth came at midday after a cryptic call from the Naval wireless operator sitting beside the Royal Engineers sergeant in the stableyard. Shielding her eyes against the bright sun, Jane watched, hardly daring to breathe. Lieutenant Dando stood glued to his binoculars while behind them a group of silent children looked anxiously down the valley. Captain Stewart was out of sight, deep in the hole dug beneath the bomb. A solitary, fair-haired man stood nearby, his torso showing white, ready to receive the fuse when passed up to him – and get rid of it.

Minutes passed.

'This looks like it,' Lieutenant Dando said.

The man stooped, and then he stood holding a slim silver tube about eighteen inches in length. He held it vertically like an altar boy with a precious chalice, turned and walked carefully towards the bomb crater further down the drive.

'They'll most probably let it off in there,' Lieutenant Dando muttered almost to himself. The man had almost reached the edge when he appeared to stumble. The silver tube flew in a high arc down into the crater and exploded with a tremendous BANG! Earth and rocks flew high into the sky together with the figure of a man turning over and over and encircled by a broad band of red, backlit by the sun. As though in slow motion, he fell down into the crater beneath a shower of earth and stones, and something white and spherical bounced once and then rolled in after him. Above, a colony of rooks cackled with indignation as men raced from their places of safety and slithered down into the crater.

'Dear God,' Lieutenant Dando said quietly. He lowered his glasses and crossed himself. Jane stood, incapable of any movement. Behind them children were crying and were being coaxed and herded to the far side of the garden.

It seemed a long time before the field ambulance arrived, drab green with red crosses painted on each side. A covered stretcher was lifted in gently through the open doors. During all this time Jane and Lieutenant Dando had exchanged not one word.

'Is it safe now?' she asked, breaking their silence.

'It will be very soon.'

Together they watched the finale, the bomb being craned into a waiting truck to be taken away to a disused quarry near Okehampton and destroyed.

'It's enormous!' Jane said.

'About as big as they come, so Captain Stewart was saying.'

'Do we know what time it was set for?'

'Sixteen hundred hours. Four o'clock.'

'Tea time,' Jane said and for the third time in a very long day felt a wave disbelief flood over her. 'How could anyone,' she demanded, 'set a device to blow up a houseful of children while they were at the tea table? Or is that something to do with Germanic humour?'

Lieutenant Dando looked at her in astonishment, then smiled. 'Jane,' he said, 'promise me you will never change.'

'I don't intend to.'

———

CHAPTER 13

Early evening in what Jane came to think of as the worst day of her life: the house quiet, exhausted children in their beds and the telephone dead. At her desk in the estate office she tried to restore some sort of order, on paper at least. The long gallery roof was now covered with tarpaulins but dangerous shards of glass were hanging, so no children could be allowed in. She must find the keys to both doors. An outhouse roof had been stripped of its tiles. The tithe barn doors were insecure and the Cranmere cabinets smashed. So the damage could have been a great deal worse – apart from that young man, only twenty-four years old. What else? Contact the knacker's yard.

She had soaked in her longed-for bath, changed her clothes, had rested but not slept, and now felt more or less able to cope – until Lieutenant Dando put his head around the door.

'Could we have a word, Jane?'

'Yes, come on in.' She quite liked James Dando but in small quantities, unlike today. Oh, she was grateful for his help with the children – above the line of duty – of course she was. But he so liked to be in charge, could at times be just a tad patronising. Now she was on her home ground, behind her big desk. 'Won't you sit down?'

He sat, or rather perched himself on the arm of the chair and looked at her. If anything he seemed ill at ease. Perhaps he was going to proposition her? 'What was it you wanted, James?'

'Well, er, it's not easy, this, Jane.'

It is a proposition!

'Actually, it's about your little mare. It wasn't my idea,' he hurried on, 'two of our people know about horses. As a matter of fact they were both big fans of yours when you were showjumping, and they suggested I should ask you if you would like us to bury her.'

'Bury her?' Rosie is dead, her showjumping days over.

'Yes, we have the necessary equipment, lifting gear and so on, and we just thought you might prefer to have her near you rather than the – alternative.'

'The knacker's yard.' It had to be faced.

'Well, yes.'

She was caught off balance. 'I'm not sure. Could you really do it, James?'

'Yes, otherwise I wouldn't have offered.'

'No, you wouldn't, would you? Where would you suggest?'

'Anywhere within reason, but I would suggest, as we have a large crater already provided that will need to be filled in, that would seem an obvious pace. That is, if you think it appropriate.'

'The children would see. And so would I.'

'Not if we do it at night while they're asleep.'

'What about the blackout?'

'There's an almost full moon tonight.'

'The sirens, then.'

'It's Saturday night, remember?' For the past three Saturday nights they had been undisturbed. It was popular belief that the German aircrews had the nights off to visit the local *bistro or bierkeller.*

'It's a very kind thought, James, but I'm not sure.'

'Perhaps you would like to think it over.'

The telephone suddenly burst into life with its harsh ring. Jane lifted the receiver, and signalled her visitor to remain. 'Is that you, Jane?' Her mother's voice.

'Hello, Mother. Are you all right?'

'Yes, thank you. Rushed off my feet as usual. I thought you might have phoned us before now,' she said reprovingly.

'I've been trying to, Mother, but our phone's been out of order.'

'*Ours* has been working. I have called you several times with no result.'

Jane raised her eyes to heaven. 'Like I said, we were cut off. How is Dad?'

'He's all right. Away at a confinement at Yettington. The poor girl's early. Hardly surprising after last night.'

'Did you get any bombs?'

'Not *our* side of the estuary.' As though that would have been a breach of etiquette. 'But Exeter, my dear, is simply *awful.*'

'You've been in, have you?'

'For most of the morning. We, that is the WVS, have set up a field kitchen in Southernhay. That took some organisation, I can tell you.'

'Yes, I'll bet it did,' Jane said, a clear picture of her mother in mind, squeezed into her flannel uniform, red in the face, felt hat crammed down like a school prefect. 'How bad is Exeter?'

'Destroyed! Not the Cathedral, thank God, only minor damage. But the Globe Hotel has gone, and Dellers Café, and the Seven Stars, and the City Library, and…' Jane held the receiver away from her ear as her mother listed her once-favourite shops and watering holes, making a helpless gesture to Lieutenant Dando who was smiling at his shoes.

'Hello, are you there?'

'I'm listening, Mother.'

'I was saying Pocombe's shop in Fore Street where we used to buy your school uniform, remember? Completely burnt out, a shell.'

'Oh, what a shame.' Jane remembered well the whiskery old man who had pawed her while fitting her school blazer.

'Hundreds killed or injured or made homeless.' Her mother's voice was rising to a higher octave. 'I shall have to go in again soon, do my shift. I'm really not sure that I can face up to it.'

'I expect you will, Mother.'

'It's all right for you out there on Dartmoor. I don't suppose the war makes all that much difference.'

Jane bit back a very rude reply, and contented herself with, 'We do have the children.' 'Yes, of course you do. Has Roger been home on leave?'

'Not since last time.'

'No. Out there doing his bit. Perhaps you ought to think about doing some voluntary work, Jane.'

Jane did not reply, closed her eyes, clenched her teeth as with near perfect timing the operator broke in with, 'Your time is up, caller.'

'If you can manage to get our way,' her mother screeched down the phone, 'some butter and eggs would be very welcome…'

The line went dead.

She replaced the receiver, counted up to ten and looked across the desk at a po-faced Lieutenant Dando. 'Sorry about that,' she said, with an effort dismissing her mother. 'James, would you tell your people I am grateful for their kind offer and would like to accept?'

'Good. Just one thing, I don't think you should be here. Is there somewhere you could stay tonight?'

'What about the children?'

'Jane,' he smiled, 'they have their teachers and Millie and us in the event of an air raid. The place isn't going to fall down just because you are not here for one night.'

It very nearly did today, she thought, but felt so tired she would have agreed to almost anything. 'I'll go down to Lower Weeke,' she said, 'if they'll have me.'

—◦∾◦—

Arriving at Lower Weeke in the late evening, Jane felt she could just about walk the distance from the car to the farmhouse door, where Betty Perret awaited her with outstretched arms. She vaguely remembered being helped to undress and rolling into a huge brass bed that sagged in the middle.

—◦∾◦—

She woke to the sound of cattle being driven beneath her bedroom window, and Will Perret's dark brown voice as he called to his dog. 'Git vore un, dug, git vore un. Yip yip yip.'

Opening her eyes, Jane took in her surroundings – the washstand with big jug and basin, the sloping ceilings, the floral wallpaper – and remembered as the horrors of yesterday came flooding back. Rosie, shot dead and now buried; that poor young man, killed, decapitated on Cranmere pasture in a beautiful summer's afternoon; Exeter destroyed; and of shouting hysterically at Edward over the telephone. She closed her eyes and snuggled down into the all-enveloping feather tie, wished she could stay there forever. Minutes later, a heavy tread on the stair stopped on the landing, the door opened a few inches and Betty's voice called, 'Are you awake, Mrs Fulford?'

'Yes, come in, Betty.'

Because of her girth and the narrowness of the old doorway, Betty entered with a practised sideways movement. In one hand she carried an enamel jug of hot water which she placed on the marble-topped wash stand, in the other she held a dainty cup and saucer which Jane recognised as from the best tea service always kept in the glazed dresser and rarely used – only when gentry called.

'You slept well,' Betty said.

'Yes, I think I must have.'

'Looked in on you once or twice.'

'Did you? Betty, you're an angel.'

'Ho yes,' she laughed, 'some angel!'

'What time is it?' Jane asked through a huge yawn.

''Tis about ten.'

'Ten? But I just heard Will bringing the cows in for milking.'

'He was drivin' them out after milkin'.'

'Good Lord, I must have nearly slept the clock round.'

'Won't do you no harm.' Betty spoke as though to one of her daughters. 'Take your time an' I'll cook you a bit o' breakfast, when you comes down.'

When she had gone, Jane scrambled regretfully out of the big bed, sat and drank her tea, looked around the room from the raftered ceiling to the crazily sloping, polished floor and envied Betty the simplicity of her life. It was Sunday morning. She missed the sound of church bells floating up from the village. If it did, then invaders would be on English soil. And she hadn't asked if there had been an air raid last night. She washed and dressed quickly, took one last look around the little bedroom and went carefully down the winding stairs.

'Bacon and eggs all right?' Betty called. A place had already been laid at the head of the long table, more best china; Jane was quite touched.

'I can't eat your rations, Betty.'

'Rations? What's that then?'

Jane laughed, 'Betty, I don't want to know so please don't tell me.' There had been rumours – very strong rumours – of the odd illicit pig living on the Cranmere Estate, or of the sudden and unexplained disappearance of one of a litter. Jane had been questioned, quite closely, by the Ministry Inspector but as she knew nothing, she could tell them nothing. And that was how she intended to keep it. The penalties were horrendous.

'All I'm sayin',' Betty said placing on the table a willow-patterned plate heaped with still-sizzling rashers of bacon and two eggs, 'is that Will never was much good at reckonin' up.' When she laughed, everything wobbled from her chins downward. And Jane, suddenly aware that she had eaten almost nothing in the past twenty-four hours, tucked in like a famished schoolgirl.

Betty brought fresh cups of tea, and sat in a creaking chair. 'I 'spect you're missing him, aren't you, Mrs Fulford?'

'Mmm,' Jane said, mopping up egg yolk. 'Betty, please call me Jane.'

'I couldn't.' The older woman looked quite shocked at the suggestion. 'T'wouldn't be right.'

'Why wouldn't it? Go on, say Jane.'

'Jane.'

'There, that didn't hurt, did it?'

Betty coloured. 'All right, but not if Will's here.' She slurped her tea. 'D'you hear from Master Roger, much?'

'No, not much. Only that he's safe.'

'Safe? Master Roger? Ho, I wouldn't worry on that score,' Betty smiled. 'I mind the time out there in the yard, he'd have been about nineteen. There was this boy up from the village, Billy Brend, big for his age and for his boots, an' he'd been givin' Master Roger a bit o' lip. Now I'm not sayin' Master Roger was stuck up, nothin' like that, but he was old Bertie's son an' there were limits. He just took off his coat, rolled up his sleeves an' didn't he give Billy a leatherin'? Then he shoved his head in the 'orse trough an' nearly drowned 'un. So no need to fret about Master Roger bein' safe, he can take good care of himself. I almost feel sorry for any o' they Germans he gets 'is 'ands on, they'll wish they'd never been born.'

Replete, Jane sat back in her chair. 'Thank you for that, Betty, and the bed and breakfast.'

'You'm lookin' a lot better.'

'I must come here more often.'

'You'll be welcome.'

———◦◦◦———

Betty held the gate open as Jane drove the Humber out of the yard. She slowed to a halt, lowered the window and called, 'I'll tell you something, Betty.'

'What's that then?'

'Angels come in all shapes and sizes.'

Betty's laughter followed her down the lane.

———◦◦◦———

From her sitting room window on the first floor, the freshly turned earth – gently domed within an almost perfect circle – was, to Jane, the most prominent feature in the Cranmere valley. In time, she supposed, as nature took its course it would become one with the rest of the pasture, and forgotten. By all but herself. That small patch of ground, insignificant in the vastness of the Cranmere acres, even when healed over with fresh grass, would be the first place her eyes would seek every morning. To the west the sky had darkened, and already a few drops of rain ran down the window pane like tears. Tears she was unable to share. Throughout her school days she had had dinned into her – one did not weep. Only cissies blubbed. One should pull oneself together, no matter what. So how did she feel right now? Remorse over what she had done? Sadness at her loss, and the death of the young soldier? Fury at Billy for leaving the lights on? No, none of these things: she had no feelings left, only a numbness. But her sense of duty – that wretched word again – remained. There were tasks to be carried out, people reliant on her, problems to be overcome – like where would the children play in wet weather now that the long gallery was out of commission? But the first and most important of all was to make her peace with Edward, her lifeline to Roger. She sat by the telephone, and dialled the magic number.

'Edward, this is Jane.'

'Jane, this is Edward. How are you feeling today?'

'Ashamed,' she said. 'I think I might have been very rude to you last night, but I'm not sure what I said. If I was, I apologise.'

'There is no need, Jane,' he replied with a hint of suppressed laughter in his voice. 'Mind you, I was surprised that a nicely brought up young lady would even know such words.'

'I wasn't that bad, was I?' A small but potent vocabulary ran quickly through her mind.

'No, of course you weren't. And it does no harm to let off steam now and then.'

'Yes, but not at you, Edward. It was just that we'd had a bad day, an unexploded bomb and...'

'I know what happened down there, Jane.' The laughter had gone. 'It must have been dreadful, try to put it behind you.'

'You knew? How could you possibly?'

'Don't ask.'

'Oh, like that, is it?' They were all in cahoots she had long suspected.

A freemasonry amongst the intelligence people, boys only. Was she being spied on in her own home – and if so, by whom? Lieutenant Dando? Or his rarely seen superior officer Commander Dobson?

'On the brighter side,' Edward was saying, 'I have a couple of bits of news to cheer you up.'

'My husband?' Always her husband, never Roger for security reasons.

'Yes, we are bringing him home.'

'You are? When?' She had a nasty suspicion that she had requested her husband's return quite forcefully – *'I don't care if he's in Le Havre or fucking Timbuctoo. Other husbands come home on leave, why not mine, for Christ's sake? It's been over twelve months, I've almost forgotten what he looks like!'*

'It may take a little while,' Edward said, 'two or three weeks, possibly more, but he'll be on his way home just as soon as he can.'

'Thank you for that, Edward. What was the other good news?'

'Oh yes, Charles Wesson will be with you some time tomorrow. Bit of luck, that, he's got some leave owing. Do you remember him?'

'I can't say I do, they were only here for the day. Is he in the services then?'

'The Auxiliary Fire Service.'

'Well I hope it won't be a wasted journey, the cabinets are in a terrible mess.'

'He may surprise you. Actually, Jane, Charles is a close friend of mine. He's had a difficult time over the past few weeks – you will look after him, won't you?'

'I will – and thank you, Edward.'

'Goodbye, Jane.'

———⟨∞⟩———

Jane heard the sound of the exhaust first and, turning in her chair, saw both man and machine from the window of the estate office, an almost comical figure on a motorcycle with silver, torpedo-shaped sidecar attached. He cut the engine and climbed stiffly from the saddle, stood with both hands in the small of his back and arched himself backwards. He wore an outmoded riding mackintosh down to his ankles, huge leather gauntlets and a flying helmet with goggles. These he removed one by one, first the gauntlets, then the flying helmet and finally the coat, folding it carefully and placing all in the sidecar. He was tall and slim and now dressed in a cream, cricket-type pullover, collar and neatly knotted tie and corduroy trousers. He ran both hands quickly through his fair hair, flattened by his leather helmet, before walking with a loose-limbed confidence toward the back door.

'Charles Wesson,' he said as she opened the door to him. 'I believe you were expecting me.'

Had she admitted him before the outbreak of war, which would have been unlikely in the days of domestic staff, Jane might have questioned in her mind should she direct him to the green baize door or to her drawing room. She felt he would be equally at home in either setting but, as he was a friend of Edward Channon, she had already decided on the latter. And the estate office offered neutral ground. She went through her usual routine, 'So good of you to come. How was your journey? You must be frozen to the marrow travelling all this way on a motorcycle. Would you like tea?'

'Thank you, tea would be most acceptable.'

'Do sit down, make yourself comfortable. I won't be long.' He picked up Bruin and nursed him.

Walking quickly down the passage to the kitchen, Jane wondered why she felt a slight unease in the presence of this tall, quietly spoken, grave-faced young man, and on so short acquaintance? At least, she understood him to be young, about her own age. It was hard to tell; he had the solemnity of an undertaker. She remembered him hardly at all from his previous visit; there had been too much going on at the time. But she could recall the elder Wesson quite clearly with his bushy white hair like the Angel Gabriel. Perhaps they were members of an obscure religious sect, and she had put him in the guest bedroom across the landing from her own! She could always turn the key in her door. Millie could show him up to his room; she would sort him out.

Which Millie did, reporting back that in her opinion Charles Wesson had loved and lost. But if he needed a bit of comforting, he had only to ask. As Millie's choice in reading was what her mother would term 'penny dreadfuls', Jane did not pay too much attention. They met again at the lunch table, having first stood to one side to allow a seemingly endless – but very orderly – line of children to file out past them. Charles Wesson watched until the last. It was the first time that Jane had seen him smile, and some of them, recognising an ally, had returned his smile. But not until they were on their second course – Mrs Kerslake's highly regarded bread-and-butter pudding – did Charles Wesson begin to emerge.

'This is good,' he said.

'I believe Mrs Kerslake's had offers of marriage over it,' Jane replied.

'That doesn't surprise me. Did she accept?'

'No, she did not,' Mrs Kerslake called from across the room. 'An' it was rabbit stew, an' a sailor.'

When he laughed, just for a brief moment Jane saw what she thought was the real Charles Wesson before he hurried back into his own private darkness. 'Is there much damage,' he asked, 'apart from the cabinets? Edward said you had more than one bomb.'

'No, not really, just a glass roof.' Jane very nearly added – and a young soldier and Rosie; but she doesn't count, she was only a horse.

'Glass roof?' He was staring at her intently almost as though she had blasphemed.

'Yes, a glass roof,' she repeated, a little surprised. 'In the long gallery where you dismantled the cabinets, remember?'

'Yes, I do. Was anyone hurt?'

'No, fortunately there was no one in there at the time.' She and Millie and Billy might have missed death or mutilation by a whisker, but nobody was going to rat on Billy Cann.

'Perhaps I could see it,' he said.

They stood in the doorway, Jane prevented from entering the room by a sturdy arm that barred her way and Charles Wesson's exhortation,

'Don't go any further.' He ran his eyes from one end to the other of what remained of the roof, taking in the splintered sheets of plate glass waiting for the smallest vibration that could bring them raining down like spears. He shuddered visibly and withdrew, locked the door and handed Jane the key. 'Is there a way up to the roof?' he asked.

Jane showed him the little staircase that led up onto the roof, known to generations of maintenance men for the servicing of parapets and gutters and, rumour had it, younger members of household staff. But having no head for heights, she remained within the protection of the exit door while Charles Wesson paced around the perimeter of the damaged roof.

After a while he called to her, 'Do you have any building materials in the estate yard, galvanised iron and timber?'

'I think we probably have, I'm not sure. Why?'

He stood, hands on hips, looking down the length of the tarpaulin-covered roof. 'If you have the materials,' he said slowly, 'and if I could borrow a couple of your sailors, we could soon put a tin roof on this.

'Could you, really?'

'Yes. Two or three days' work. It wouldn't look very pretty, but at least the children would have somewhere to run around.'

'What about the cabinets?'

'I think the roof should come first, don't you, Mrs Fulford?'

'Yes, I do,' she smiled. 'And please call me Jane.'

Over the following three days she saw little of him apart from the occasional meeting on the stairs – when as often as not he was carrying a length of timber – or at mealtimes. Meals were taken in the staff dining room, after the children, a communal affair with the strictures of social division long forgotten, except that Jane sat at the head of the table. (Just what Roger would have to say on the matter she shuddered to think, probably, 'I'm not bloody well dining in the servants' hall!' When he returned she would feed him in private from her own, rarely used kitchen. If he returned.)

She welcomed the increased activity about the house, the sounds of sawing and hammering and men's voices from the long gallery, and the children's voices from their schoolroom lifting to *Jesus loves me this*

I know/For the Bible tells me so'. She envied them their blind faith. And there seemed to be more despatch riders to-ing and fro-ing on their noisy motorcycles, keeping pace with 'A flap on in the North Atlantic' concerning supply ships and wolf packs of U-boats. And the ever-constant siren late at night with the consequential disturbance, kept her busy and involved, for which she was almost grateful. Because when left to her own thoughts, the awful, aching hollowness would return to remind her of her loss and guilt. So strongly did she feel this physical pain she had tried dosing herself with milk of magnesia, which helped not one bit. And underlying all was the undeniable fact that while thousands were mourning the loss of husbands, sons and daughters, her grief was for a horse, and this worried her. She began to feel that she must be unnatural, uncaring, unfeeling, but try as she might to overcome her misery, it still persisted and there seemed to be no escape. Early morning was the worst time when she first awoke and longed for her husband and her little mare, in which order she was not sure. Even if she walked on the moor or in the woods, it was along paths once travelled with Rosie and in the soft ground there were small hoofprints still to be seen. So she stayed indoors and in her few idle moments tried to read or listen to the wireless, only to find her mind drifting until she was compelled to face up to her problem before it got the better of her.

Her relationship with Rosie had been almost unique. She knew that and so had Tom Challacombe, her one-time trainer, who said he had heard of similar understandings between horse and rider but had no personal experience. It was, he believed, a form of mental telepathy and she should be very grateful. She was – had been.

This ability to communicate had not been immediate but had grown slowly over their seven years together. It was something that Jane was reluctant to discuss or even admit to, for fear of ridicule, and in any case it was something between Rosie and herself and no one else. Not even Roger. Neither would it have been easy to explain. She was not even sure how it worked except that on entering her stable, she had known instinctively and without question what mood Rosie was in, and the communication went both ways, all day long, and especially at showjumping events. They had been far more than horse and rider: they had been close friends and confidantes. But on the night she died – was shot – Jane was receiving no messages at all. It was almost as though

Rosie knew that in the final analysis humans could not be trusted, not entirely, and she had closed down. It was this exclusion, even more than her loss, than had hurt and left Jane in a morass of uncertainty. Her actions on that night, no matter how distasteful, had been swift and merciful; in the absence of the vet there had been no alternative. So why no muted message from Rosie, not even of her fear and pain? Why no understanding? Why no absolution?

The need to talk to someone – anyone who would listen and try to understand – became stronger. Tom Challacombe would have been the best but he had closed down his stables at the outbreak of war and joined the cavalry, and died in a tank somewhere in the Western Desert. Who, then – her father? No, he would be kind and sympathetic but unable to stretch his mind beyond the boundaries of conventional medicine and psychology. Mental telepathy even between humans would be met with raised eyebrows. Her mother? No! She would come out with something utterly crass, like, 'I'm sure Roger will buy you another horse once we've taught Herr Hitler a few manners.' There were plenty on the Cranmere Estate who were familiar with the husbandry of animals, but from a rather different viewpoint. Lieutenant Dando would no doubt smile indulgently and put it all down to stress and lack of sleep.

But perhaps there was someone nearby who would listen without treating her as though mildly deranged. There was a calm about Charles Wesson that she found attractive, and a thoughtfulness for others, especially the children. And – unlike Roger – she had never once heard him raise his voice. He spoke quietly with a faint Gloucestershire burr, but with the authority of a man who knew precisely what he was doing. The off-duty sailors who had decided – or been persuaded – that the tin roof was of maximum priority obeyed his quiet orders without question and addressed him as Mr Wesson or Sir, although Jane felt sure he had not asked for nor even expected the distinction. He had earned their respect. Yes, given the chance she would talk to him.

—⚬⚬⚬—

In the afternoon of the fourth day, with a gentle rain pattering on the new roof, the children were allowed back into the long gallery. They filed in, some of them shoving and giggling, and formed into three ragged ranks like little soldiers. Miss Pearson, who tried hard to maintain discipline, thought it right to say a little prayer – and blessings on the new roof. Charles Wesson stood and looked uncomfortable until the final 'Amen', and was clearly moved when Miss Pearson suggested that the children should thank him. They mobbed him, pulling him by both arms into the centre of the room insisting that he join them in their game of rounders. He turned in appeal to Jane who went laughingly to his aid and captained the opposing team – and won. But during all the noise and excitement, she noticed how Charles Wesson lobbed an easy catch to Billy Cann. They opted out of the relay race pleading age and infirmity, and sat in one of the windowseats. 'Charles,' she said, 'I feel I have been neglecting you. What are you doing with your evenings?'

'I walk, though not tonight,' he said, turning to glance out at the steady downpour, 'And I read and rest. And I don't feel in the least neglected.'

'I just thought you might like to come and talk to me in my sitting room, listen to the wireless. I think there's some whisky in the cupboard.' She hoped she hadn't sounded too eager, or put the invitation in a way where it would have seemed ungrateful to refuse.

'Thank you,' he smiled, 'I would like that very much.'

And that was another thing she had noticed about Charles Wesson: he never wasted a single word. None of this – 'Oh how frightfully kind of you…' Just the essentials – 'I would like that very much.'

'After supper then, about eight?'

'I will not be late.'

—⌇∿∿⌇—

Ten minutes to the hour and she was ready to receive her visitor, and still not sure that it had been a good idea. She had made an effort, changed, brushed her hair with more care than usual, and now sat by the empty hearth wishing she had remembered to change the flowers. But like so many things in the past few days she had let it slide. Wilting flowers in the hearth! Her mother would have thrown a fit before rushing around tidying the room until it looked unlived in. Looking around her at the scattered books and almost unread newspapers, she thought let him find me as I am, tired and old before my time. In any case, only women noticed these things, so why bother? She was not trying to attract a lover, she just wanted to talk to him – and wanted him to talk to her, if he would.

The gentle tap on the door came almost as a surprise. He, too, had changed. He wore a lightweight sports jacket over a cream shirt with dark, diagonally striped tie. It was the first time she had seen him in anything but shirtsleeves or overalls. He looked quite distinguished, a man who would be noticed. Was it that once clad in his tweed jacket he took on a different persona as some men did with their uniforms? She hoped not; she wanted Charles Wesson to be the same all the way through.

'Do sit down,' she said. 'I have found the whisky.' But her short journey to the drinks table was interrupted by the telephone. A man's voice, unfamiliar, authoritative.

'Wing Commander Beresford,' he said. 'Would it be possible to speak to Mr Roger Fulford?'

'No, I'm sorry, he's away. Mrs Fulford speaking, can I help?'

A short pause. 'It's about Squadron Leader Stannard.'

'Archie? Is he well?' Even as she uttered the words she realised their futility and felt something go cold deep within her. Wing commanders did not phone without good reason.

'I'm sorry, it's not good news, Mrs Fulford.'

'Is he…?

'His aircraft went down into the sea off Folkestone early this morning. He was not seen to bale out. We have to be prepared for the worst. He left your husband's telephone number with the request that he should be informed in the event of something like this.'

'Yes, he would,' Jane said, 'they were at school together. But are you sure, is there no chance? Couldn't he be in his dinghy or something? Are you searching for him?'

'We are searching, Mrs Fulford, and will continue to do so until nightfall. He was my friend, too.'

'Yes, of course he was. Thank you for phoning, wing commander, it was kind of you.' Archie was everybody's friend. Jane closed her eyes to see a vivid picture of Archie's smiling, schoolboy face framed in his flying helmet. Would it have been mercifully quick? Did Spitfires blow up when they hit the water or sink to the depths with the pilot struggling to free himself? She could not bear to think of Archie like that, shook her head and opened her eyes to dispel the picture. But all she saw was a circular patch of freshly dug earth to remind her of another dear friend lost forever. How many more?

Her knuckles showed white as she gripped the telephone receiver in her left hand, every muscle in her slim body tensed and hard. And she began to shake from head to foot. 'Charles,' she said, turning to see his anxious face looking up at her, 'would you hold me, please? I feel if someone doesn't hold me I will fall apart.'

He crossed the room in two strides. She felt his strong arms enfold her and he held her close.

—◦◦◦—

CHAPTER 15

She was a child again being comforted by her father after a tumble from her new bicycle, feeling the warmth of his body, the roughness of his tweed jacket against her cheek, his strong arms holding her until the crisis had passed. Taking her gently by the shoulders, Charles guided her to the settee, sat beside her and held her again. She rested her face against the smooth linen of his shirt front, listened to the rhythm of his breathing and for the first time in many months felt safe, shielded from all the hopelessness that surrounded her. She began to feel drowsy, just wanting to stay where she was for a long, long time.

'Feeling a bit better?' The deep voice seemed to come from his chest into her left ear.

'No,' she said and snuggled closer.

'Who was Archie, a close friend?'

'No, he was Roger's friend really, although I liked him a lot. He was fun. Came here and landed his Spitfire on the grass in front of the house. When he left he did a loop-the-loop just for me. And now he's gone,' she said miserably. 'Why is it always the nicest people?'

'I think it just seems that way,' Charles said quietly. 'But it's more than Archie, isn't it? You have been very tense these past few days.'

'Am I that obvious?'

'No, you're not, far from it.'

'I can't tell you, Charles, you would think I'm unhinged.'

'I very much doubt it. Why not try?'

She did not reply. On the far wall patterns made by the paper strips glued to the windows moved slowly upwards as the sun went down behind Sittaford Tor. And still she said nothing. Perversely, now that she had the chance she found it impossible to put into words the source of her unhappiness: it was too deep, too personal. And no matter how understanding Charles Wesson might be, she couldn't very well say 'My horse wouldn't talk to me', could she? So she said nothing.

'I know you lost your little mare last week,' Charles broke the extended silence.

'I didn't lose her, I shot her.'

'*You* shot her?'

'Yes. She was terribly injured. I put the gun to her head and I shot her.'

'Was there no one else?'

'Jim Sanders offered, but I wouldn't let him. She was my friend. It had to be me.'

'What a dreadful thing for you to have to do.' She felt his arm tighten around her. 'No wonder you're upset. Were you very fond of her?'

'Yes, I was. We had been together for seven years. But Charles,' she raised her head to look into his eyes, 'tell me, please, do you believe it is possible to communicate with an animal, to know what it is thinking or feeling?'

'Yes, I do, to a certain degree. Is that how it was?'

'With Rosie, yes. Don't ask me how it worked, I couldn't tell you. All I know is that she could tell if there was something troubling me and *vice versa*. Do you believe me, or are you just being kind?' Her eyes searched his face for the slightest hint of mirth. There was none. Had there been she might well have hit him.

'I do believe you,' he said, 'and I'll tell you why. There used to be an old fellow in our village, Harry Kent, who spent most of his working days in the company of Queenie, an enormous shire horse, ploughing or pulling a wagon or whatever. Harry and Queenie had something going, he would talk to her all day long. He claimed that she would reply and I saw no reason to disbelieve him. Sometimes in a summer's evening he would bring her down to the pub and buy her a pint of ale. She would perform little tricks, wink one eye, shake or nod her head, raise one hoof. Oh yes, and let out a great snickering laugh after one of Harry's terrible jokes. It was all done with kindness and close understanding; had to be, she was ten times Harry's size. Then one day Harry died, he was a good age. And Queenie followed him less than a month later, just wasted away. They said she died from a broken heart. So yes, I believe you, Jane, and I believe to share such a relationship with an animal is a privilege few of us enjoy.'

Her gaze had not left his face. And now she felt an overwhelming relief wash over her as though she had been released from a form of confinement within herself. Here was a fellow believer; she was no longer alone. 'You really do understand, don't you?'

He smiled, 'Not always, but I try.'

'There's more to it than that, Charles.' She thought now that she had come this far she might as well risk all. 'On the night that Rosie died I was getting no messages from her at all. Nothing. Not even that she was in pain. She had cut me off.'

'Fear might have had something to do with it,' he said.

'Fear? Rosie wasn't afraid of me. She knew I'd have done nothing to hurt her.'

'I'm sure she did, but as a bomb had exploded in the stableyard, she must have been terrified. And fear can be a powerful emotion. I've known men rooted to the ground with fear, unable to move or speak like a rabbit caught in car headlights. There's no way of telling, but I think it's possible Rosie was so frightened she was unable to make any sort of contact with you, no matter how much she wanted to.'

'And you think that's why?'

'I think it likely. Animals aren't so very different to us, except they have more sense.' His face was in shadow, backlit by the suffused pinks and oranges of a summer's sunset, giving him an almost saintly appearance. Over his left shoulder through the open sash Sittaford Tor stood outlined starkly on the near horizon. For a brief moment Jane felt the two images were synonymic: the grey, uncompromising granite outcrop of Sittaford and Charles Wesson's stern, almost haunted features – until he smiled, which was not often, but when he did she saw a young man of both humour and compassion. And then he was gone, as if suddenly remembering that the humour he had once known was no longer allowed. On an impulse she reached up and kissed him chastely on the lips and said, 'Thank you.' And was rewarded with just the outline of his smile in the fading light.

'Did you really mean that,' he asked, 'or were you just being kind?'

'Both,' she replied.

'Then it is I who should thank you,' he said and she knew he was going to return her kiss, and that was all right by her but for the warning bell that was ringing through the house summoning them to the air-raid shelter, and the distant siren in the village sounding its mournful wail through the open window.

'Don't say a word,' Charles smiled again.

—◦◦◦—

In the cellar they sat apart on a bench set along one wall, separated by Millie and Billy Cann who had wormed his way in next to his new 'uncle' and now watched, fascinated, as Charles idly whittled away with a pocket knife at a piece of wood that was slowly taking on the form of what – a duck, a rabbit, a squirrel? Resting her head against the stone wall, Jane also watched with half-closed eyes. Charles, she thought, had beautiful hands for a man. Not square, chunky, artisan's hands but strong and with long, slim fingers like a musician. What would it be like, she wondered, to feel the touch of those sensitive hands on her body (or would sensual be a better word)? For a few deliciously drowsy moments she allowed her thoughts to drift into uncharted waters and then brought them back with a sudden jolt, half expecting Charles to be looking directly at her; but he was not. He was talking quietly to Billy who hung onto his every word. Because he had no father? Possibly, but more likely that with a child's instinct he had recognised a friend who would not lie to him and could be trusted to keep his secrets. Just as she had.

It was a gift, she decided, this ability to instil confidence in others, and it was possible he did not even know he possessed it or was doing it, and might be surprised at the suggestion. But for her own part Jane could confirm that he had, through his homespun logic and knowledge of human – and animal – behaviour and his quiet manner of speech, made her feel a lot calmer, and had at least offered a plausible explanation for Rosie's silence where before there had been none. And for that she was very grateful. Just how grateful she might have been had the siren not sounded earlier than usual was something she did not care to dwell on. Charles was a very attractive man and, more than that, her woman's instinct told her that he was attracted to her.

They came face to face at about twenty past one in the morning after the 'All Clear' had sounded and the children – thumb-sucking and grizzling – had been conveyed back to their beds, a task that tested even the most patient. Their meeting was quite by chance. Or was it, Jane questioned in her mind later? Had either of them been asked, they would have hotly denied listening for the rattle of a door catch on the opposite side of the landing, and truthfully. So perhaps it was mental telepathy at work once more; or that during their spell in the air-raid shelter they had both been wondering what might have happened on her settee had the Luftwaffe not intervened; or simply a warm, balmy, moonlight night. It was not the first time they had encountered one another, each clad in dressing gown and slippers, carrying a sponge bag and towel and heading to or from the bathroom at the far end of the passage. Like guests in a country house hotel, they would exchange polite smiles and hurry toward their respective doors.

But not tonight.

They paused and faced each other, inches apart; neither spoke. And later, neither of them could have said with honesty who had made the first move. Has she leaned towards him before his arm went around her waist or after? Had one of them brushed accidentally against her bedroom door causing it to swing inwards? Had she led him across the threshold murmuring, 'I don't want to be alone?' He held her, which was what she wanted him to do, very close, drawing her into him while with his free hand the musician's fingertips ran gently over her face, tracing first her eyebrow, then her cheekbone, her ear, the line of her jaw until, lowering his head he kissed her, also very gently.

She had been right about his touch, so tender that she was barely aware of her night clothes being eased from her shoulders and falling softly to the floor. Then they were lying naked on the bed together, his one arm around her shoulders while the lead violinist's hand took her up the scale and then down again, always starting at her face before travelling gently down her throat and neck, her breast, her stomach, down the outside of her thigh and returning by way of the inside, until she could hardly bear the exquisite trembling of her body. He seemed to know all her tenderest places, covered her breasts with tiny kisses, dwelling just above her nipples, and long before he entered her she knew that this was to be like nothing she had experienced – or even imagined. All was done with such refinement and consideration, his lean, muscular body supported on his elbows, not crushing her, his movements inside her matched to her own in perfect rhythm, rising in tempo until they had reached an octave almost too high for the human ear – and beyond. He continued to hold her, to bring her down gently. Neither did he sleep or turn his back on her but held her until she slept.

She woke at dawn to see him smiling down at her in the half light. 'You slept well,' he said.

'Mmm,' she moved closer. 'How about you?'

'With you beside me? Not a chance.'

She reached up and placed a hand on the side of his face where she noticed a few grey hairs in his overnight beard. He responded, running his fingers lightly down her arm, continuing down to her flank, his touch becoming more urgent as they prepared themselves for the second movement – which was even better than the first.

And then he was gone, slipping quietly back to his room before the household stirred into life.

—⁓—

Alone in the estate office Jane gazed across the big desk to where her husband's teddy bear stared at her accusingly. Nothing had changed, she told herself. She felt – well, how did she feel? – better than she had for weeks. Complete. Free of the inhibitions and miseries that had haunted her, and able to face up to almost anything. Sadness at Rosie's demise? Yes, of course, not forgetting little Archie, but her sorrow seemed to be more contained, no longer all enveloping. Guilt? Mmm, well yes, her upbringing forbade infidelity. But she was able to console herself with a few of her father's well-chosen words. *'These people'* – he meant the upper classes – *'play to a different set of rules than us'* – the middle classes. *'They seem to regard a few little peccadilloes as quite acceptable. Just as long as you know what to expect.'* So maybe she had scored another first over Roger, although she doubted it. She was under no illusions about her husband's vow of chastity while away in France. Or maybe she was growing up; and anyway, she argued, she had been left alone too long. War or no war, women had their needs just the same as men. All would be well provided she was discreet.

She telephoned Edward for news of Roger's return. Be patient, she was told, he should be home in about three weeks, all being well. And how was Charles Wesson getting on, was he relaxing?

'Yes, he seems to be, the children adore him.'

'He's had a very bad time, Jane. Take good care of him, won't you?'

'I will,' she promised, smiling as she put down the receiver. And in which case, she thought, perhaps she ought to see how Charles was getting on in the tithe barn.

Work had already begun on the Cranmere cabinets. Two huge grey-painted Admiralty crates had been brought down from Higher Weeke. They stood against the back wall where the cabinets had once been, together with a small mountain of cardboard boxes. All the tiny fragments, Charles said (standing a lot closer to her than was necessary) had first to be identified and then packed in the small boxes before being placed in the appropriate crates. The larger pieces presented no problem. He had one small assistant, a bright-eyed Billy Cann who scuttled happily back and forth like a child on the seashore collecting shells. 'Shouldn't you be in lessons, Billy?' she asked.

'I'm doing war work,' he said proudly, at the same time casting an anxious glance at Charles.

'He has official leave of absence from Miss Pearson,' Charles explained, 'and he is a great help.'

'Oh well, that's all right then,' she grinned at the boy. But Billy's grin was wider as he hunted around in the straw for more fragments to be identified.

'My goodness me, Charles,' she glanced around her at the seemingly thousands of scattered bits of wood, 'how long is it going to take you?'

'Two, maybe three days.'

'Well don't rush things, take your time,' she said, to be rewarded with a full-scale Charles Wesson smile the like of which she had not seen before, which thrilled her in its suddenness. She felt that perhaps, just perhaps, she could help to free Charles from some of his inner demons, as he had with hers. She could try. She wanted to hold him, and her thoughts were compounded when he leaned close and, dropping his voice to a whisper, said, 'If you hang around here much longer, I cannot guarantee my good behaviour.'

—◦◦◦—

Mealtimes were the worst when she sat like a prefect at the head of the table, Charles immediately to her right, which was in itself a safeguard. That way there could be no lingering looks across the table. Jane hoped she was acting normally, not being any more authoritative than she need, but it was far from easy. Charles seemed to experience no difficulty at all, withdrawing into himself, rarely speaking unless spoken to, just as he had all along. When the sun went down they both came out to play, but even then were compelled to restrain themselves until, in Charles' words, Herr Goering did his worst while they sheltered in the cellar. And on one memorable night after the 'All Clear' had sounded their intentions were frustrated yet again by the sound of movements on the landing outside Jane's door. Charles dressed hurriedly and left Jane's bedroom by the door to her sitting room and thence to the landing. While Jane, a sheet drawn up to her chin, strained her ears for a tiny voice she had half expected before now.

'Billy?' Charles said, surprised. 'What are you doing here?'

Silence.

'I think Jane's asleep, old chap. We don't want to wake her now, do we?'

Silence.

'Tell you what, Billy, have you ever had a ride on a motorbike?'

No response.

'Well now, if you go back to bed, close your eyes tight and go to sleep, I will take you out on mine tomorrow.'

'Cor! Really?' Billy had found his voice.

'Yes, really.'

'You promise?'

'I promise.'

'Can I wear the goggles?'

'Yes,' Charles laughed, 'you can wear the goggles. Goodnight, Billy.'

'Goodnight, Uncle Charles.'

When he returned to her, Jane was convulsed with laughter. 'That was bribery,' she said.

'Yes, I'm afraid it was.'

'He'll hold you to it, you know. You promised.'

'I wouldn't lie to a child.'

'Would you lie to me, Charles?'

Taking the sheet from her hands, he uncovered her completely and stood looking down on her nakedness. He said quietly, but very seriously: 'No, Jane, I will never lie to you.'

———◦∿∿◦———

Moonlight woke her as it sometimes did, flooding in through the big west windows. Charles was awake, sitting propped against the headboard, eyes wide open, his features in sharp silhouette. He could have been any age from twenty-seven to seventy-seven. For a while she did not stir, but gazed up from her pillow and wondered what was going on inside that handsome head, behind the façade. For it was no more than that, she felt sure. She had seen the real Charles Wesson and knew him to be in essence a very kind man with a good sense of humour. So why had he locked himself away and put up this 'Keep Out' sign?

Sensing her eyes on him – more mental telepathy? – he turned towards her. She placed a hand on his chest. 'Penny for them?' she said.

His hand closed over hers. 'They're not worth it,' he replied in a near whisper.

'Who says they're not?'

'I do.' The stone wall again, solid and impenetrable.

Minutes passed. Jane tried a different approach. 'Charles, a little while ago you said you would never lie to me.'

'Yes?'

'So if I were to ask is there something troubling you, you would answer me truthfully. Yes?'

'What makes you think I am troubled?'

She moved herself into a sitting position so that she could look at him directly. 'Because every now and then you seem to disappear somewhere inside yourself and you look very sad. And,' she added, 'Edward said that you had been through a difficult time in Bristol and that I was to take good care of you.'

'Did he say that? He's a good friend, Edward, but I doubt he meant you to take him quite so literally.'

She gave his chest a playful slap. 'You are avoiding the question.'

'Yes, I am. Why do you want to know?'

'I don't, not if you don't want to tell me. I just thought it might help. You listened to my tale of woe and I feel better for it.'

'You do? I'm glad.'

'So tell me.'

'I don't know, Jane.'

'Try.'

———⟨∿∿⟩———

CHAPTER 16

'My father was in the last war, in France and Belgium. He never talks about it, ever.' Charles had not moved. He rested his head against the pillows, unfocused eyes staring blankly at the windows. Jane knelt by his side, facing him, willing him to talk to her. 'When he is with friends who were out there with him, perhaps, but they very seldom discuss it. Why should they? They've all seen the same horrors and if they tried to describe them we would not be able to comprehend, not really. So they have sealed it all within them. I believe the men who returned from the Somme, or wherever, are different to others. There is something about them, almost an aloofness – although that isn't the right word. I think it must be that whilst still in their teens they witnessed an awfulness we cannot begin to imagine, mankind at its very worst, and its very best; so there is nothing you can tell them that they have not already seen or heard of or experienced in one way or another.

'We, my little team and I in the AFS, have seen our share of human misery over the past twelve months or so, and in the same way I suppose we have become almost inured to it. Or so we thought until a couple of weeks ago.'

Jane had one of his hands in both of hers, holding it to her, kissing his strong fingers. 'Tell me,' she said softly, but was not sure that he had heard.

'There was this building,' he began, 'in Bristol, well, a mile or two out of the city. I suppose they thought they'd be safe there, well away from the docks. Children's home of some sort. Big place. Nice old house on three floors with a huge square hall and the staircase running around all four walls right up to the top. And a glass roof.' He stopped speaking, looked directly at her and then away as though unwilling to meet her eyes. He began to tremble.

'When the roof came down,' he said very quietly, 'the hall had been crowded with children waiting to file down into the cellars… You cannot imagine the terrible wounds that falling glass can inflict, especially on little children… What was I supposed to say to a little girl so badly injured that I knew she wasn't going to make it – and so did she? She smiled up at me but I think she'd died before I handed her over to the ambulance crew… Or to a little boy with one arm amputated?'

Tears were running unchecked down his cheeks, his voice unsteady. 'The building was burning around us but when we'd brought out the injured, we went back for the dead... So small and limp, still warm. And then,' he took his hand from hers and covered his face, 'Christ help me... we went back in, Jack and I, with a hessian sack and gathered up pieces of children. Like little broken dolls. The ceilings were coming down but there was no way we were going to return those children to their Maker... incomplete.'

Jane took him in her arms and held him while he cried, great deep shuddering sobs, smoothed his back with her hands. She had never seen a man cry until now. He was no different to the children, only larger. His head was on her shoulder, warm tears running down her breast. She held him, rocked him gently.

'Christ, Jane,' he said between gulps, 'what have we become? Every night I hear the aircraft going over – theirs or ours, it doesn't really matter – smashing, destroying, killing. I don't destroy things, I make them or mend them. I can mend roofs or bits of furniture or wagon wheels, but I cannot mend children. When I lie down and close my eyes I see them as clear as daylight. I haven't slept much since then.'

She held him for a long time until he was calmer, whispering to him like a mother soothing an upset child. He had told her, put his hidden thoughts into words and, she hoped, purged some of his nightmares. But it would be a very long time before a man like Charles Wesson had recovered from such an experience, years, perhaps never. She wanted to care for him, to heal him. He was a gentle, creative, thoughtful man, unlike her husband who would smash his enemies without a second thought. But any such comparisons could not be entertained, not for long. Soon Charles would be gone without ever having declared his love for her, neither would she for him. It was not allowed. He raised his head to look at her, his face wet with tears. Taking up the first thing to hand, which happened to be her discarded nightdress, she dried his eyes and kissed him gently. 'When I first came here,' he said, 'you were grieving over your little mare. And you were right. How dare we place ourselves above animals – it's supposed to be our sense of reasoning, isn't it? Well I don't see much reasoning going on out there right now, do you? Animals don't kill without good reason. To defend their young or feed their young, perhaps, but not wholesale slaughter. And the tragedy is that sooner or later we will have to come to terms with the enemy. How many little children will have to die before then?' Jane held his head in both hands for a moment without answering any of his questions. Then she pushed him gently back onto the pillows and spread herself over him. She could help him forget for a little while. Later, lying in each other's arms, she watched his eyelids droop. And he slept until dawn.

Saturday morning, when the estate office always seemed busier than during the week. Jane took a call from Dick Maddaford who farmed Thorn on the northern boundary of the estate. His water pump had broken down and he was having to draw every bucket from the well by hand. Could she help? Well, maybe she could. She happened to know that Alan Nosworthy, who had always manned the pumps and was now a proud corporal in the Devonshire Regiment, was presently home on leave. Another call from Anne Tozer, an old pal from her secretarial college who now worked for the Ministry of Agriculture in Tavistock. 'Jane,' she said quietly down the phone, 'you can expect an unexpected visit on Monday morning.' Which meant the Inspectors would be calling. So on Monday they would require her to guide them around the farms. What fun! But not before she had warned Betty Perret, who would make sure the news was spread far and wide. The Cranmere Estate had its own intelligence network.

And so the morning went on until Millie came bursting into the room with, 'Jane, quick! Come and take a look.'

'What ever is it, Millie?'

Millie was already halfway down the passage leading to the terrace. Jane ran after her; she had already heard increased motorcycle activity, but put it down to despatch riders. The reason was a shiny, motorcycle combination travelling sedately in a wide circle on the grass with Charles at the controls. Sitting in front of him on the petrol tank was a small boy, barely recognisable in goggles and flying helmet but for the wide smile that was unmistakably Billy Cann's. He held onto the handlebars with both hands, Charles assisting with the disabled arm, and leaned into the bends as they described a figure-of-eight and went in the opposite direction, tooting the horn when he saw Jane and Millie. 'Dear soul,' Millie said. 'You'd never believe he could be such a little bugger.' They waved as he passed. 'Just look at his little face, thinks he's in heaven.'

But Jane was looking at Charles' face, also with a wide smile that was almost carefree.

'Fair does your heart good to see 'em, doesn't it?' Mille said.

'Yes, it does,' Jane agreed. But in her heart she also knew that Charles would soon be leaving.

And she was right.

―◦◦◦―

'I can think of half a dozen good reasons why I must not stay any longer, Jane, and you come top of the list. You already know that, don't you?'

'Yes,' she said softly. It was the nearest he had come to telling her how he felt about her. It was early evening in the tithe barn where he had spent the past hour preparing his motorcycle, checking the tyres, brakes, oil, carburettor. The petrol tank was filled to brimming by courtesy of the Royal Navy. The Cranmere cabinets were each packed into their crates and the floor swept clean. Charles Wesson's work was complete. He stood close to her and she knew that but for his oily hands he would have held her, and perhaps rolled her onto those hay bales at the far end of the room, or onto the blankets which covered the Alvis. And she would have let him.

Their last night together went uninterrupted by the Luftwaffe. They talked about anything but their parting, their childhood homes and memories, their hopes for the future – but always the war got in the way.

'What you're doing here, Jane,' he said, 'is something pretty wonderful. Those children under your roof may have had a rough deal, but they're happy now, you can see it in their faces; and they'll be with you for a while yet. So what you are giving them is a happy childhood in a beautiful place, something they will never forget. And they will never forget you. Neither will I.'

They made love, slowly and beautifully, they dozed, talked again in a desultory way but made no promises. Finally they slept.

―◦◦◦―

Just before dawn Charles Wesson pushed his motorcycle combination out of the barn and into the keen morning air. He mounted and ran it noiselessly down the sloping drive before letting in the clutch when the powerful engine roared into life. Jane did not stir, but at an adjacent window a small boy with a malformed arm pressed his face to the glass and wept silent tears. In one hand he held a small rabbit, exquisitely carved in walnut. It went with him everywhere. Even on bath nights he would not be parted from it.

———∿∿∿———

PART 2

Why tell them all your secrets?
Who kissed there long ago?
Whispering grass, the trees don't need to know.

CHAPTER 17

—◦◦◦—

Hal walked, fast, uphill, because that is what he does when his mind is in turmoil: head for the highest hill. He had left the car in a small parking area at the foot of Nattadon Hill and walked along paths through waist-high bracken until he had reached the summit overlooking Chagford, the small market town that his father must once have known. To the north, rich pastureland stretched out until lost in the haze of a hot afternoon after heavy rain. In any other direction Dartmoor rolled up to the skyline in a series of hills in improbable shades of green and brown and mauve with splashes of yellow, like an amateur watercolour, except these colours were authentic even if they did change whenever a cloud passed over the sun. And somewhere down there in its secret valley lay Cranmere.

High above, a pair of buzzards wheeled slowly in the pale sky, wider and wider, calling to one another, ever searching. At least, he thought, they knew what they were searching for, unlike him. He had been up there for an hour; he was not sure why, except he had always found lonely hilltops were the best places to shuffle his thoughts into some sort of order. Apart from an overview of the countryside they had a diminishing effect, made a man realise just how insignificant he was in the scheme of things and how very small his problems.

Turning to the west, he gazed towards where he knew Cranmere to be hidden. He had spent the best part of the day down there with a rather wonderful old lady, who had been his father's lover. No, more than that, with whom his father had been in love and she with him. It was her complete frankness in her account of their affair that he had found so moving, at times embarrassingly so.

And she had borne him a son! On her own admission! David, his elder brother by twenty years, a brother whose existence he had never even dreamed of, had been living here for forty-odd years – and no one had thought to tell him! And more than that – a brother he was not to be allowed to meet, leastways not as a brother. Christ! He felt cheated. In a single day, it seemed, he had both gained and lost a brother. What right had anyone to disallow or even discourage a man from meeting his own brother? In fact there was nothing to prevent him from going down there and hammering on the door at Cranmere and saying, 'Hi, David, I'm your kid brother,' and right now he felt like doing just that. But they wouldn't believe him, would probably set the dogs on him. Or, if he could prove his claim by blood tests or whatever, how would it profit him? Not at all. He could hardly expect David to extend a hand of brotherly love after causing all that family upheaval and embarrassment, could he? As for Jane, the shock would probably finish her off for good. And there was something else that prevented him from any such headlong action, something Jane had said. Sweet old dear she might be, but she was a clever and determined old dear, too. He would remember her words – *'I am entirely in your hands, Hal. But as you are your father's son, I feel sure that you will be discreet. As he would have wished.'*

That last sentence had to be conjecture on her part because, as Jane had been at pains to point out, Charles Wesson had had no knowledge of his son, nor had he ever returned to Cranmere except on that one occasion after the war when he had very nearly come to blows with Roger Fulford. Over what? A mahogany cabinet, for Christ's sake! All the same, Hal had to agree with Jane. Were his father here today, he would be dreadfully hurt; but discreet. So what now? What should he do? Go to New York and examine the supposed Cranmere cabinet and make his report. And hold his hand out for the cheque.

Otherwise, do nothing, tell no one, not even Bella.

Forget it.

Just like that? How could he possibly? He would have stayed longer talking to – listening to – Jane, but for the unexpected return of David. So for Jane's sake he had scuttled away like a brother who dared not speak his name. For all that, he had liked Jane a lot, for her courage and her straight-from-the-shoulder honesty, and for the way she had helped his father, just as he had helped her during the dark days of the war. Would he ever return to Cranmere to talk to her again? Probably not, but he had her phone number and would write to thank her for her hospitality when he got home; a lady of her generation would appreciate that.

———∽∼∽———

Driving up the motorway on automatic pilot, Hal's thoughts were not so much of Jane, nor his father, but of Sir Edward Channon. Much as he loved his Uncle Ted, he knew him to be a cunning old fox and couldn't help wondering if he'd had an ulterior motive in sending him down to Cranmere. Because even though he had never visited Cranmere nor met Jane Fulford, if there had been even the faintest of rumours buzzing around concerning David's parentage, he would have heard them; sure to have. So, Hal questioned, was this a backhanded way of confirming or denying any such rumours? Never! His Uncle Ted wouldn't do that, would he? No, of course he wouldn't… would he?

The car phone buzzed. It was Bella, Sir Edward Channon's daughter. 'Hal, darling, where are you?'

'Just past Bristol.'

'Still?'

'It took a bit longer than expected.'

'Yes, it must have. What was she like then, Dad's old girlfriend?'

'She was very nice, your father has excellent taste,' he laughed. 'Oh, and she apologised on her late husband's behalf.

'I should think so, too. Have you eaten?'

'Yes, I got something on the motorway.'

'Sounds dangerous.'

'It was. Greasy cutlery, rubber eggs and I'm not sure what the other thing was meant to be.'

'Yuk! When will you be home?'

'In about an hour.'

'Drive carefully. Mum and Dad are here.'

She meant: I am not alone in the house so there is no need to rush. Neither was there any significance, Hal told himself, in his in-laws being there. They often came over to spoil their grandson rotten, but more often than not just Winnie on her own. So why Uncle Ted tonight? Was it that he couldn't wait until morning for news of Cranmere? Could be.

———∽∼∽———

Entering the sitting room, Hal found it just as it had always been, heavily beamed ceiling, table lamps, polished oak furniture and pewter, and in the open hearth that he had dug out so laboriously when they were first married, a log fire smouldered. Nothing had changed.

Why should it have? For a while down there in Devon his world seemed to have tilted, but now it had righted itself and he was home and dry. Around the hearth in a ragged semi-circle of armchairs sat his family. Winnie nursing her sleeping grandson who had insisted in staying up until Daddy came back, but not quite able to make it. Bella, who must have been out in the sun judging by the freckles on her nose which he loved but she hated. And Uncle Ted who would, no doubt, wait patiently until they were alone before asking a single question. Hal stifled a yawn, but as always when he had been out driving he was fully alert and ready for that one probing question, no matter how well wrapped up, that would tell him whether or not Sir Edward Channon was privy to the truth about David Fulford. And for a brief moment he is once more with Jane in her neat little sitting room.

'You and I, Hal, are the only people who know the truth. Others may have suspected but, Betty Perret died years ago and Millie married her American soldier and now lives in California. And she would never breathe a word.'

'How about Edward Channon?'

'Good heavens, no. I've never even met Edward.'

Which didn't mean a thing.

And he had the advantage of being on his home ground, his Uncle Ted semi-submerged in his armchair, drinking his whisky. The question, when it came, would probably be sandwiched between less important items. There were times, Hal thought, when Sir Edward Channon seemed to forget that both his son-in-law and his own son Toby had been almost weaned on this sort of thing.

'Well then, Hal,' while the sleeping Charles Edward was being quietly put to bed, 'What did you make of Jane Fulford?'

'She's a lovely lady,' he replied. 'We had a long chat and she apologised most eloquently for her husband's treatment of my father.'

'Did she now? Pity that couldn't have been forthcoming sooner. Is she well?

'Not as well as she would have one think. But I suppose that's to be expected at her age.'

'Mm, very likely.' Sir Edward was a few years older than Jane. 'And did you meet David Fulford?'

Here it was, although Hal had not expected it quite so soon. The question was put casually, so he answered it equally casually. 'Yes, only briefly. Seems a nice enough chap, for an old Etonian.' And then out of devilment he added, 'Oh, and I managed to clear up a couple of outstanding queries.'

'You have?' Sir Edward's bushy eyebrows rose almost imperceptibly.

'Yes, as you said, the cabinets were packed into two crates that Father had begged from the Royal Navy, painted in grey and with Admiralty markings. Jane said that was almost certainly how the missing cabinet left and she was surprised they weren't both carted off.'

'We thought it was probably something like that,' Sir Edward said. 'What was the other thing?'

'Other thing?' Hal was enjoying this.

'Yes, you said a couple of queries.'

'Oh that, yes. The reason Cranmere was bombed was because a small boy who was afraid of the dark turned on all the lights in the long gallery, which as you may know had a glazed roof. Must have shone like a beacon. In fact Jane saw the enemy aircraft peel off from its formation and make straight for them.'

'Good Lord, is that all it was. We were very concerned at the time. Why didn't Jane tell us?'

'I think she was trying to protect the boy,' Hal said. 'It must have been a difficult time for her.'

'Yes, no doubt. Anything else?'

'No, I don't think so.' What else could there be? 'Oh, I managed to get you some photographs of the Cranmere cabinets.'

'How did you manage that?'

'Nothing simpler. I asked Jane and she said if she turned her back and looked out of the window, she wouldn't know what I was up to.'

'Better let me have the film, I'll get our people to rush it. There's a flight for you tomorrow at midday Not Concord, I'm afraid. That's not too soon, is it?'

'No, fine by me, but I won't be needing any photographs to refer to.'

Sir Edward smiled his secret smile. 'No, I didn't think you would.'

Later, standing with Bella on the doorstep, it was Hal's turn to smile as the big car pulled away. He was thinking – *'He knows that I know. And I know that he knows that I know that he knows'* – or something like that. But neither of us had dropped so much as a hint. And that is the way it must stay.

———

And still later, in the oak tester bed in which generations of Wessons had been begat and born, Bella sought reassurance of her husband. 'Hal, this trip to New York. You promise me it's not one of Toby's schemes?'

Toby: Bella's elder brother and Hal's childhood companion and comrade in a host of youthful escapades. At school they had been described by a patient science master as reasonable young men provided they were kept apart, but allow them to combine at your peril. It was Toby in his capacity as an insurance fraud sleuth, who had, some three years ago, recruited Hal onto his team investigating art theft on an international scale, resulting in Hal's abduction, imprisonment and very nearly much worse. And he had promised Bella, faithfully, that never again would he become embroiled in her big brother's activities, a promise he fully intended to keep.

She was rested on one elbow leaning over him, her shape silhouetted against the low light from the street lamp outside their window. Looking up at his young wife, Hal thought that right at this moment he would promise her anything she could possibly want and more besides.

He said, 'I'm not sure that Toby even knows about it. This is entirely between your father and me. He is tying up a few loose ends, wants to close the file.' He began to caress her.

'But what will happen if the cabinet in New York does turn out to be the missing one?'

'I really don't know. I imagine it will be the start of a long, legal process where the only winners are the lawyers.' He ran his long, musician's fingers down her back. She squirmed beneath his touch.

'That's all right then.'

———

CHAPTER 18

———

So smooth was the touchdown at JFK Airport that Hal was unaware that contact had been made with Mother Earth, until he opened his eyes and saw a blur of sunlit grass flashing past the window, and felt the deceleration; only then did he expel the deep breath he had been holding. He hated the whole concept of air travel – locked in a metal tube with two hundred fellow passengers while the shining monster dragged its heavy belly off the ground and remained airborne for eight interminable hours. It was against the laws of nature. And he disliked being barely able to move and the way the regular travellers knew where everything was, the names of the cabin crew – 'Hi, Angie' – and especially the overweight man in the adjoining seat who had snored his way across the Atlantic.

Taking up his one piece of permitted hand luggage, he followed the slow moving queue to the open door, thanked the pretty cabin crew and made his way down the metal steps in blazing sunshine; and set foot on American soil – tarmac. He had already adjusted his wristwatch – in London it was seven in the evening, here it was two in the afternoon – but made a mental note to keep hold of those five additional hours – and reality.

———

'Mr Hal Wesson, sir?'

The voice came from a tall, dark-haired young man standing near the exit. He wore a lightweight business suit and a welcoming smile. They all smiled; even through Customs and Immigration where, in addition, they had told him to 'Have a nice day' and 'Enjoy your visit, Mr Wesson, sir.'

Mike Monahan was from the Channon Grieves New York Office, and had an ID card to prove it.

He had been detailed, he said, 'To hold your hand and see no harm comes to you in this big city of ours, sir.' His handshake was firm and he looked well able to carry out his duties. Hal took an instant liking to him.

'Is that right you are related to our Chairman, Sir Edward Channon, sir?'

'Well, I'm married to his daughter.'

'Same thing, sir.'

'Mike, please drop the "sir", and I am able to carry my own bag, thank you all the same.' They were walking along a brilliantly lit subterranean corridor with turnings and steps leading up to daylight every twenty yards or so, heading for the parking lot which, when Mike had located it, seemed to extend to acres of almost identical vehicles, just like Heathrow except everything was larger. Mike could do voices. He came from much further south than New York and occasionally lapsed into an outmoded almost hayseed speak, just for the hell of it. His antecedents had come from Kilarney. He had strongly arched eyebrows giving him a look of permanent enquiry which, Hal thought, could be an asset in Insurance Investigation.

'I guess you will be acquainted with Toby Channon,' Mike said as he slid the big car neatly into a line of slow moving traffic.

'Acquainted? I was more or less raised with him,' Hal replied, pleased with his own Americanism. 'You've met, have you?'

'Well yes. He and I have enjoyed a pleasant evening or two visiting the more colourful watering holes in our fine city.'

'Don't tell me,' Hal laughed, 'the girls just rolled over for him.'

'Sir, I would say that is very near the truth.'

'Makes you sick, doesn't it?'

Mike grinned, 'It surely does.'

They crossed a long bridge over the East River and were soon in a jungle network of streets overshadowed by buildings so tall that it seemed sunlight could rarely visit their ground-floor windows. They were in a gorge with only a thin strip of sky way above them, not that anyone looked up: this was New York, The Big Apple.

'Your first visit?' Mike asked.

'Yes, it is,' Hal admitted.

Mike obligingly pointed out a few landmarks. 'To your left is Bloomingdales, a dee-partment store like your Harrods only larger and less expensive. Women have been known to disappear into that place never to be seen again. Well-adjusted guys like you and me suffer panic attacks and get carried out.'

From the exterior the hotel could have been a nineteenth-century civic building except it was fourteen storeys high. The interior, stylishly done in polished wood, deep-buttoned upholstery and leather and brass, boasted 170 rooms each with TV movie channels, air-conditioning and hair dryer, and just about anything the management could dream up to further their guests' comfort, plus a roof top terrace bar with a view of the Empire State Building. And it was there, the receptionist said, that a visitor awaited Mr Wesson's arrival.

'Are you sure?' Hal asked, puzzled. 'Did he give you a name?'

'Yes, sir,' she glanced at her notepad, 'a Mr Ralph Carrington.'

Hal cursed the man. There was very little time before Mike would return to take him to see the cabinet. He felt crumpled and travel-worn and a quick shower and change of shirt would do no harm at all. Sotheby's Head of Furniture Dept, New York, would have to wait. He pressed the button for the twelfth floor on one of three lifts – elevators – and waited while the doors closed softly with all the urgency of a museum. Fourteen minutes later, refreshed, he walked out onto the terrace and saw the dignified form of the Empire State Building much closer than expected. There were only three people present apart from the bartender, a middle-aged couple who seemed to be arguing, possibly over something they had seen in Bloomingdales, and – without doubt – Mr Ralph Carrington. He was tall and slim and beautifully suited, and there was something about his posture that marked him down as an Englishman. Had the terrace been crowded, Hal would have known him.

'Mr Wesson? Ralph Carrington.' The arm was extended – elbow outwards – salesman's smile in place. 'How was your flight, not too taxing, one hopes?' All this before Hal had identified himself.

Introductions over, they sat facing each other across a circular table beneath a sun umbrella, Hal nursing an iced mineral water which was all he would allow himself at three thirty in the afternoon in this heat, when it was really eight thirty at night. He gazed over Carrington's shoulder at the Empire State Building – sadly without King Kong – and waited for the sales pitch or whatever, aware that he was in the presence of a grade one English smart-arse – had to be to have got where he was – and mildly annoyed at being hustled along like this. He would have liked a little more time to unwind after his long journey. But Carrington was in no hurry. He turned and followed Hal's gaze, raised his eyebrows slightly and asked, 'Your first time?'

'Do you know,' Hal said, 'whenever I see that building I think of hot rivets.'

'Rivets?'

'Yes, when they were building it they would lob them from one to another, red hot. And it was finished ahead of schedule, or should I say "skedule"?'

'Is that right?' Clearly, Carrington was disinterested in any risks the construction men had run. 'Talking of schedules, might I ask when you intend to view the Agnolli cabinet?'

'Agnolli?'

'The present owner,' Carrington said with the smooth smile Hal was beginning to find irritating.

Glancing at his watch, he said, 'I'm off in about twenty minutes.'

'So soon? I thought you might wait until morning, after your flight.'

'No, I return in the morning.'

'Concord?'

'Sadly, no.'

'Poor you. I do hope it's not a wasted journey.'

'Do you think that's likely?' Hal recalled his Uncle Ted's words, *I cannot pretend I liked him much, but I did respect his judgement of antique furniture.*

'Mixed feelings, to be frank.' Carrington turned in his chair, stretched out his long legs, crossed them at the ankles. 'Seven long years have passed since I visited Cranmere. I could be mistaken.'

'But do you think you are?' Hal persisted.

'Surely, that is why you are here, Mr Wesson.' He smiled again as he said this, a smile that he seemed to switch on and off at will, a smile that appeared far too frequently to be trusted. 'Naturally, if I can assist in any way,' he added.

'There is just one small point that you might be able to clarify.'

'Yes?'

'Is this Mr Agnolli aware that there is a question mark over the legality of his ownership?' Hal was quite pleased with his reply. It sounded a bit better than 'in possession of stolen property'.

'No, he is not,' Carrington said quickly. 'At least, no mention has been made. Well, he wouldn't, would he?' Again the smile. 'And he holds a receipt for the cabinet's purchase from Dino Brocatti, one of the leading dealers in Milan. At the same time,' he said slowly, 'I get the impression that Roberto Agnolli, the present owner, is not entirely confident in this area.'

'Despite the receipt?'

'Despite the receipt.' Another smile. 'Perhaps I should explain. Old Luigi Agnolli, who died recently, was the founder of the Agnolli Empire, a firm that imports Italian foodstuffs from the mother country in shiploads. They're big. I doubt you could enter a supermarket or restaurant without finding the name on something. By all accounts, Luigi was something of a firebrand in his early days, may have cut a few corners here and there, most of 'em did. But his son Roberto, now he's of a different cut, one of New York's top lawyers and has no connection with the family firm apart from being a major shareholder. He is also currently entering the world of politics, so it is important to ensure that any mention of his old man's excesses that may surface from time to time are kept to a minimum.'

'Sounds just like home.' Hal thought it was his turn to smile.

'If I may advise,' Carrington continued, 'you are viewing the cabinet simply as an expert in English furniture, which I am assured you are' – another smile – 'to authenticate, and also on behalf of a possible buyer who Sir Edward has waiting in the wings. Or so he says.'

'Why shouldn't he have?' Hal asked, even though the existence of a buyer was news to him.

'Well, let's face it, he's a wily old bird but a little over the hill, wouldn't you say?'

'No, I would not,' Hal replied firmly. 'And any man who underestimates him, does so at his peril.'

'Do you know him well?' Was Carrington's smile a little less confident? Perhaps so.

'I've known him all my life,' Hal said – smile – 'As a matter of fact, he's my father-in-law' – smile.

'Good God, is he? Then you must have married – what was her name? – Annabel. Pretty girl.'

'That's right.' Another smile.

'Well, congratulations, my dear chap. Smart move. Chairman's daughter and all that.'

If there was anything guaranteed to annoy Hal, it was this sort of comment. Although Carrington's recovery, he thought, was admirable.

He was rising from the table, offering a card from his top pocket. 'When you have examined the cabinet, Mr Wesson, perhaps you would be good enough to phone me. My mobile number is on this.'

'Certainly, provided Sir Edward agrees.'

'Yes, quite. Keep it in the family, you mean?'

'That's right.' Hal had the last smile. He watched the tall figure walk towards the exit with a casual flap of the hand to the bartender, and a single word came to mind – bullshit. For a while he sat motionless, stared at the empty chair where the Hon Ralph – Something – Something – hyphen – Carrington had parked his aristocratic rump, thinking, *mixed feelings?* He was the one with mixed feelings, unsure whether to be amused or annoyed at the way he had been patronised. Carrington was an expert in English period furniture, and currently top of Sotheby's heap in New York, and he had *mixed feelings* over the Agnolli cabinet. Could have been *mistaken?* Like hell he could! If the Agnolli cabinet was indeed the missing Cranmere cabinet – and it sounded more than likely – on first laying eyes on it any furniture man worth his salt would have turned a double somersault. It was nearly ten foot wide, for God's sake. It was the product of one of the leading cabinetmakers and designers of eighteenth-century London, Ince and Mayhew, whose style was unmistakably their own. And Carrington had already seen its sister cabinet! So who the hell did he think he was fooling with his 'mixed feelings'? And why were his feelings mixed? Because he found himself in an awkward situation, that's why. He had accepted a large and valuable collection of antique furniture for sale by Sotheby's – shiny catalogue, evening dress only, free Dom Perignon all round – only to discover the star lot was hooky! Oh dear.

So how had he reacted, bearing in mind Agnolli was an influential man and pillar of society? On this one lot he had stalled, needed to call in a second opinion while he attempted to cut a deal with Channon Grieves, or anyone else with two-and-a-half million to spare, preferably in used notes. Because there was no way he could display an important lot like this in his saleroom without all the coloured photographs and pages of description – not to mention provenance – being sent far and wide. Someone would be sure to recognise it, despite the Fulfords' wish for privacy. But, on second thoughts, would they? Very few people had seen the cabinet in Cranmere, and how many were around today who even knew there had once been a pair, or had seen them together before the Second World War? Precious few. His Uncle Ted had never seen them, even Jane could scarcely recall them, and they were both in their seventies. Soon the pair of cabinets would be lost from living memory unless, of course, David Fulford were to see an illustration when something nasty really would hit the fan, an occurrence Carrington was anxious to avoid. In fact he, Carrington, was the only man who had laid eyes on both cabinets in recent years; and he was having kittens. Hardly surprising. Hal almost felt sorry for him. Oh yes, and one more thing. Two-and-a-half million dollars would be peanuts in today's market. The price tag was for a hooky lot and Carrington knew it, and so, more than likely, did Agnolli.

What was to be done? Nothing. Hal was mindful of his Uncle Ted's words. *Just examine the cabinet, Hal, and whatever your findings you report them to me. Leave any investigations to us. Understood?*

Whatever you say, Uncle, he thought as Mike Monahan made an entry onto the terrace. But he was looking forward to this appointment.

———ฒฒ̃ต̃———

New York was hot and noisy and congested, and becoming more so as they headed down town towards the Agnolli building. They could have walked the distance quicker than the traffic's slow progress except, Mike advised, no one walked the streets where they were going, not from choice. 'Best to keep your window rolled up and the door locked,' he added, 'or we may pick up an uninvited passenger.' He turned up the air-conditioning. Groups of young men of many nationalities lounged in doorways and watched the passing traffic, waiting for nightfall.

'Mike, tell me about the Agnolli family,' Hal said.

'There's a lot of 'em,' Mike replied as a black-and-white Police car cruised slowly past. 'Mostly they're in the family firm, but Roberto, or Robert as he likes to be called these days,' the voice changed, 'Good ole Bob, a regular guy now he's a fat cat lawyer way up there in the Attorney General's Department. We won't be seeing him, he's far too grand to come down here.'

'How about his father, the late Luigi?'

'Back in the fifties,' Mike said, 'old man Luigi, according to my father, was one of the biggest fucking crooks in the whole of New York.'

'Your father had a way with words, did he, Mike?'

'Sure, he did,' Mike laughed. 'And he was in the Police Department, stayed on Luigi's tail for years and never got near him, nothing proven.

'They became quite fond of one another in later years.' They turned into a wide gateway in a concrete wall topped with razor wire. A huge, black security guard in Police-style uniform needed to phone and announce them before the steel doors could be electronically opened. They were met by a middle-aged man with greying hair and an air of authority about him. He wore gold-rimmed glasses and a spotless white overall with a plastic name tag pinned to his chest. He was Giorgio Linelli, *Diretore*, and very polite.

Everyone they met wore white overalls. This was a well-run food distribution warehouse, seven storeys high, the rear windows overlooking loading and unloading bays with refrigerator vehicles parked in line and attended by men with clipboards. Beyond, Manhattan Bridge stretched across the water into the distance. On the fifth floor, down a long white corridor with admin offices leading off, they were shown into a large room, also in white and with high windows. And it was here Hal let out a gasp of delight. Standing around the walls were examples of English antique furniture rarely seen today, not in England – they had been shipped over here before he was born. Queen Anne period chairs in sets of twelve stood next to desks, tables, tallboys and bureaux in walnut, mahogany, yew wood and mulberry, as in an English saleroom of seventy years ago, or so he'd heard. Finely carved and gilded mirrors, fitted to wooden frameworks for their safety, stood propped against the walls and so it went on until, at the far end of the room, tall and wide and proud like the Thoroughbred she was, stood the missing Cranmere cabinet.

—ᴡᴡ—

—✧✧✧—

How long had it taken the image in Hal's mind to superimpose itself on what he now saw – three seconds? Less? He had been more or less expecting this and now he was in no doubt: this was the missing cabinet. Although there was little need, he would examine it carefully to make 100 percent sure. Experience had also taught him that when a second opinion is called in, just as in the medical world, the patient or patron required his money's worth of expertise, needed to see the specialist examine and probe and frown and consider; only then would he be satisfied. Giorgio Linelli, the *Diretore*, sat beside Mike in one of a pair of leather-upholstered wing chairs. Both men were smoking beneath a sign that read *Vietato Fumare*, and watching him with interest. He would not disappoint them; they would both be able to report to their respective masters that the examination had been thorough. Diagnosis would come later.

Starting on the left of the cabinet he examined first the glazed doors. There were six, each with twenty-eight tiny panes of glass shaped into elaborate patterns. Many had been replaced, but with old glass and in the correct manner, and with infinite care. Hal continued the examination down to the panelled doors and drawers in the lower section, pressing lightly with his fingertips, discovering old scar tissue, neatly repaired and healed, and the more he saw the more his admiration grew for the man who had carried out this restoration; perhaps not quite as good as his father's work, but good. He called for a stepladder which arrived in double-quick time and was set up by another white-coated employee. Linelli and Mike now had a tray of coffee on a table between them.

'Take a break,' Mike called, pouring him a cup.

Linelli's dark, Italian eyes looked up at him. 'You are satisfied, Mr Wesson, that the cabinet is *autentico?*'

'Yes, I am,' Hal reassured him. 'About 1760 and very beautiful. Do you know where it came from?' It was worth a try.

'From Dino Brocatti in the Piazza del Duomo, Milan,' he replied proudly. 'Signor Luigi bought many fine pieces from him.'

'It's had quite a lot of restoration.'

'That is right. Signor Luigi told me how the cabinet was damaged during the war but was repaired by the very finest restauratore in Milan, Giovanni Spargo. You may have heard of him.'

If there was any change in Hal's expression on hearing the name, it went unnoticed by his two companions. But his mind was reeling – Giovanni Spargo? Vanni! How the hell had he got himself mixed up in this? Draining his coffee cup, he returned to the cabinet and resumed his examination, seeing nothing, his mind elsewhere.

Giovanni Spargo – could there be another of the same name? – had arrived in Lynchcombe as an Italian prisoner-of-war, a bewildered boy of eighteen. Prior to his conscription he had been apprenticed to his father, a cabinetmaker in Milan, so it was not surprising that this likeable young man (whose parents had been murdered by the *Fascisti*) should be drawn as if by magnetism into the Wesson workshop. When peace was declared, Giovanni had elected to stay on in Lynchcombe and Charles Wesson was only too pleased to employ him, saying that Vanni, as he was universally known, was the best apprentice (and later cabinetmaker) he had employed. Vanni married a local girl, and their daughter Gina was born in the same year as Hal. They had been playmates, had started school together until, at the age of eight, Hal was whisked away to boarding school. And Gina had left with her family for Milan, her father's birthplace. Hal's parting from his first girlfriend had been painful; he had shed bitter tears for her after lights-out in his cold dormitory. Vanni he remembered as an elder brother figure who would sing beautifully at Christmas concerts in Lynchcome Parish Hall and reduce the entire audience to tears.

But during his working hours Vanni must have assisted with the repair of the cabinet that had been returned to Cranmere in the forties. And later, it seemed, had worked on the second cabinet, the missing one – the stolen one? How had this come about? An amazing coincidence or something more contrived? The questions bombarded Hal as he opened doors and drawers, looking for answers. One thing he could see – and only too clearly – was how it would have looked to Roger Fulford, if he had lived. Charles Wesson and Giovanni Spargo had colluded, concealed the second cabinet until the heat had died down – *for forty years?* – and shipped it over to Milan and shared the proceeds. And if David Fulford cared to take up where his father had left off, how would a case like that stand up in court? And even though the cabinet was sold after Charles Wesson's demise, the original intent would still stand, wouldn't it?

With an effort, Hal dragged his mind forward to the job in hand, climbed the aluminium stepladder and made a show of his interest in the pagoda roofs to the cabinet and the tiny carved figures. But still his thoughts wandered. Hadn't he heard that Vanni had died some seven or eight years ago? If so, if he identified this piece as the missing Cranmere cabinet, and if Uncle Ted started up legal proceedings for its return, and if David Fulford was made aware of the connection between the Wessons and Vanni, then the whole can of worms would be opened up again – but with neither of the accused able to defend himself.

This could not be allowed to happen.

—⁓—

At seven o'clock in one of a choice of three restaurants in his hotel, Hal ate a light meal – by American standards – and left half of it on his plate. His body clock told him it was gone midnight, too late to eat a big meal and too late to phone Bella. He wanted to talk to her but, as she was staying overnight with her parents in Lynchcombe House, he could not contact her without talking to her father. And, disloyally, his Uncle Ted was one man he did not want to speak to, not yet. He needed time to think, to decide where his first loyalty lay. It would be so simple to deny the Agnolli cabinet, to say 'Yes, there is a similarity but they are not identical.' He could launder the cabinet so that Carrington could sell it to a private punter on Agnolli's behalf – he surely wouldn't be fool enough to offer it by public auction. Uncle Ted would accept his judgement even if unable to close his file, the memories of Vanni and his father would remain undisturbed – everyone taken care of.

He was tempted.

In the hotel reception area, the size of an aircraft hangar, a clutch of young women now dressed in evening livery were, Mike assured him, 'Just dying to help you in any way they can'. And he was right. Patti, a dark-haired lovely, scarcely batted a long eyelash at Hal's request for a Milan telephone directory. It was all on the computer – wouldn't it have to be? – but she could help him if he needed her.

He did.

'What name?' she asked, turning to her keyboard with a little smile.

'Giovanni Spargo.'

Many clicks later and the screen filled with small print. 'We have a G. Spargo listed,' Patti said and read out the address. 'Want me to write it down for you?'

'Yes, please.'

Again the little smile as she wrote, while Hal wondered did the 'G' stand for Giovanni or Gina?

'Is there anything else?' Patti was asking.

'Yes, there is as a matter of fact.'

'I thought there might be.'

Hal smiled. 'Is there a Milan trades directory in that machine of yours?'

'Sure. What trade?'

'Cabinetmaker or antiques restorer. I think the word is *Restauratore.*' More clicks until in the centre of the screen, prominent in bold type, were the words *Giovanni Spargo. Restauratore.* The address and telephone number were the same.

'Thank you, Patti, you have been most helpful.'

'We aim to please, sir.' '

'As I am sure you do.' Hal gave her his best smile.

'Are you flirting with me, sir?'

'Perhaps, just a little. Goodnight, Patti.'

'Goodnight, sir.'

———*∾*———

In his room Hal kicked off his shoes and sprawled on the bed. He'd had enough for one day. At least he'd made a bit of headway; the firm Giovanni Spargo existed, even if Vanni did not. And it seemed he had lived on the premises, so presumably his widow Elsie or his daughter Gina were still there. He would have telephoned, but in Milan it was about three in the morning. Tomorrow he might see things differently.

But the bedside telephone's subdued purr told him that today was not quite finished. He lifted the receiver expecting to hear Bella's voice, but it was Patti. 'Sorry to disturb you, Mr Wesson, but we have a visitor for you in reception.'

'I don't know anyone in New York,' Hal yawned. 'Who is he, Patti?'

'A Mr Moreno, he's a lawyer. Want me to send him up?'

'Hell no, I don't want a lawyer in my bedroom.'

'Me neither,' she laughed. 'I'll tell him you'll be down, yes?'

'Yes, give me a couple of minutes.'

———*∾*———

CHAPTER 20

—◦◦◦—

Carrying a slim briefcase, Moreno was short and thickset and dark, and might have originated on almost any Mediterranean shore. His smile revealed two rows of very even white teeth as he approached with the wide-legged gait more usually associated with a wrestler than a lawyer. Possibly, Hal thought, he was both. But his manners were impeccable: he grasped Hal's hand and apologised for disturbing him so late in the day. Hal found himself wrong-footed. All the way down in the lift he had been trying to puzzle out just where this lawyer might have sprung from; it had to be Channon Grieves or Carrington. It was neither. Moreno took charge, guiding him to a table in a quiet corner where palm trees flourished, at the same time summoning a waiter.

'What'll you have, Mr Wesson?' That was something Hal had always admired in Americans: they wouldn't ask would you like a drink, just assumed you would. While they were waiting for two cold beers, Moreno made his first pitch.

'I represent Roberto Agnolli, Mr Wesson. Not the company, but Roberto himself. And I understand that you have been taken to examine an antique cabinet, the property of my client, at the Agnolli Depot on Lower East Side. Is that right?'

'Yes that's right,' Hal replied, now fully alert. He admired Moreno's directness, and wondered what was coming next: a bribe, New York sinister-lawyer-style, like in the movies? That was all right; it had been tried before now and, as Moreno was about to find out, Hal Wesson could play the English innocent better than many. 'Nothing wrong, is there?' he asked innocently.

'Everything's just fine,' Moreno smiled, 'except...' He had to pause as two frosted glasses of American beer were placed on the table. Flipping a banknote from his top pocket, he told the waiter, 'Keep the change. Except,' he continued, 'I am told there may be some misunderstanding over the legal title of ownership of the cabinet.' He was choosing his words with great care. 'That there is an identical cabinet in a house in the south of England, and that this cabinet, Roberto Agnolli's, may have been removed from said house without the knowledge or consent of the owner. And that you, Mr Wesson, are over here in your capacity as an expert in such matters, to ascertain whether or not my client's cabinet is the missing one. Is that not so?'

Hal found himself with little room to manoeuvre. 'You seem to be very well informed, Mr Moreno.'

'I am a lawyer.'

'And you have been talking to Ralph Carrngton of Sotheby's?'

'We've met.'

Yes, I'll bet you have, Hal thought, and he's probably in your pocket – and Roberto's too. But he would have to concede. 'What can I say, Mr Moreno? You seem to know all about it.'

'Well now,' Moreno became a little more avuncular having scored the first few points, 'why don't we kick a few ideas around on this one, see if we can reach an understanding to our mutual benefit?'

'Why not?' Hal sipped his cold beer. He was tempted to ask, 'How much?' but that would have been crude; there was a ritual to be observed.

'Maybe we should start with your telling me the results of your examination.'

Hal registered mild surprise. 'Oh, now I don't think I should do that, Mr Moreno,' he said primly. 'I am retained by Channon Grieves, one of the oldest [true] and largest [untrue] insurance companies in London, as a matter of fact by their chairman Sir Edward Channon. And I would have thought such information was his property until he chooses to pass it on to you.'

'Sure, it's Sir Edward's property but if, as you say, he is going to pass the information on to us, what difference does it make except a day or two? Hell, it's Agnolli's cabinet, ain't it?'

'Well yes, I suppose you're right. I understand he holds a receipt for its purchase.'

'That's right, he does.' Moreno was already sliding a sheet of paper from his briefcase, passing it across the table, a photocopy of the original. Hal scanned it quickly. It confirmed that seven years previously Luigi Agnolli had purchased from Brocatti of Milano: *A fine quality display cabinet in mahogany. English C 1760.* The price paid – with many zeros – was in lire.

'How much is that in dollars?' Hal asked.

'Just over one million.'

'Not a bad investment then.' Hal passed the document back. 'But I really can't see why Mr Agnolli need worry. It all seems perfectly legal.'

'Sure it's legal.' Moreno let out a little sigh, probably in exasperation. 'It was as legal and watertight as a fish's ass until your Carrington comes along with you in his wake.'

'He's not mine,' Hal said quickly.

'No, but I doubt you realise just how important you are, Mr Wesson. One word from you could cause a lot of grief.'

'Surely not.'

'Listen.' Moreno lowered his voice, leaned across the table. 'If it could be proved after all this time that Brocatti in Milan bought this cabinet from an unreliable source, and it was the one missing from your house in the south of England, then my client could be compromised and involved in lengthy and very public court proceedings, and that's just what he doesn't need right now.'

'Because he's a public figure, you mean?' Hal sipped his beer, longing for a warm English pint.

'That is exactly what I do mean. Roberto Agnolli is running for high office and he'll be up against the Ivy League and the very best and brightest young men in the USA, so there's no way he can allow even the slightest ripple on the surface where his family's business dealings are concerned, no matter how long ago.'

'Sins of the fathers, you mean?'

'Did I say his father was a sinner?' Moreno snapped.

'No, you did not,' Hal said hurriedly.

'Old Luigi may have been a colourful character, and sure, he may have taken a few risks in his early days, who didn't? But he was a fine upstanding man, a deeply religious man. Mass every Sunday. Know what I mean?'

'Of course.'

'And Roberto, no matter how straight a guy he is, has to be seen to be beyond reproach like Nero's wife, because if the opposition media got their hands on any dirt like this, they would use it.'

Hal stifled a yawn. 'Surely it was Caesar's wife. Nero was on the fiddle, wasn't he?'

'He was what!' Quite suddenly Moreno's dark features relaxed into a broad grin and he laughed. 'Nero was on the fiddle! Hey, that's good, I like that.'

I thought you might, Hal thought, but said nothing. Moreno was sitting back in his chair still chuckling to himself. 'Do you know what I am thinking, Mr Wesson? I am thinking that you are a whole lot smarter than you let on.'

'Not really,' Hal said modestly. 'And I was thinking that I would hate to be the wrong side of you in a courtroom.'

'And you would be correct,' Moreno said, still smiling. 'That is not a nice place to be.' Especially, Hal thought, if you had learned of the connection between my father and Vanni.

'So why don't we talk business,' Moreno was saying. 'Are you going to tell me yes, Agnolli's cabinet is the missing one, or no, it ain't?'

'Before I answer that, may I ask you something?

'Sure, go ahead.'

'Why the urgency? You'll be hearing from Channon Grieves in ten days or so.'

'Because my client,' Moreno said, 'is a worrier. He worries about what time he gets up in the morning and goes to bed at night, and everything else in between. So when Carrington gives him the glad tidings on his father's cabinet he goes near ballistic. That is why I am here, to set his mind at rest so he can sleep nights.'

'He doesn't have to sell it, does he? He's not hard up. Why not live with it or he could just shove it in the garage and forget it?'

'Sure, he could. But that way he would worry about the possibility of being in wrongful possession. You don't know this guy, he's a valued client but Christ he gives me grey hairs. He's the kinda guy who gets out of the shower to piss. So are you going to help me put him out of his misery or not?'

Hal could no longer evade the question, so he sidestepped it. Rather neatly, or so he thought.

'D'you know,' he said, 'I think if I could I most probably would. But the truth is, I can't.'

'Can't or won't?'

'Can't,' Hal said. 'You see, I have yet to examine the other cabinet.'

'You ain't even seen it yet?'

'No I haven't. The family who own it were about to set off on holiday when I phoned. It was not convenient.'

'Not convenient? Holy Mary,' Moreno said under his breath.

'No, and I thought it doesn't really matter what order I see the cabinets in, does it?'

'No,' Moreno said resignedly. 'So when is this family returning from holiday?' The word sounded strange on an American tongue.

'As I said, in about ten days.'

'And then you will send your report to Sir Edward, that right?'

'That's right.'

'And he will accept your judgement without question?'

'Well, yes.' Question my judgement? The very idea! In the silence that followed, Hal realised that he had left himself wide open and Moreno was about to deliver his final pitch.

'It seems to me, Mr Wesson, that the ball is in your court. So let me spell it out for you. You tell Sir Edward yes, this is the missing cabinet – maybe it is, maybe it ain't,' he said with a massive shrug. 'Then we have to set up a full-scale inquiry, call in our own experts to examine both the cabinets, go back to Brocatti and this man Spargo and find out how this cabinet came into their hands and a lot more besides. Could take months, years even, but if Agnolli is put in a position where he has to prove his innocence, he will, no matter what cost. You better believe it.' For a brief moment Moreno glared at him, and then relaxed into a smile. 'On the other hand, if you were to tell Sir Edward no, this ain't the same cabinet, then who's to know? The original owners must have been paid off years ago and I can find a buyer for Agnolli's cabinet to ease his conscience. Nobody gets hurt, nobody loses and you, Mr Wesson, would gain.'

'I would?'

'Sure you would, what did you expect? Moreno smiled again. 'How does three grand sound?'

'Three thousand?' Hal was astonished, but recovered himself enough to ask, 'Er, is that dollars or pounds?'

'Well, all right, pounds sterling. What do you say?'

'I say that is a very generous offer, Mr Moreno. But I think I would rather like to sleep on it. Would you mind?'

Moreno let out an audible sigh. 'Sure, you sleep on it. Phone me in the morning, okay?

'Yes, of course.'

'I have enjoyed meeting you, Mr Wesson.' Moreno was already

standing. 'I feel sure you will make the right decision.'

'Yes, yes I most probably will,' Hal smiled. 'And if I do, how do I collect my er...'

'Your commission?' Moreno showed his teeth for the last time. 'Don't you worry about that, Mr Wesson, we got people in England. We know where you live.'

———∿∿∿———

Minutes had passed and Hal's gaze was still fixed on the doorway where Moreno had made his exit. He, too, had enjoyed their meeting, both playing hard to get and being bribed to the tune of three thousand quid into taking a course of action he was already considering. Right up to that very last sentence – *'We know where you live.'* Was that a simple statement or the stick that followed the carrot – a threat? If it was intended as a threat, it was badly timed and went a long way to undoing all Moreno's patient persuasion. It had found a chink in Hal's armour. Three years previously, his home had been violated when armed men had burst in and taken him hostage, and he remembered only too well how it was not the violence to his person that had offended him most, but to his home. His home was sacrosanct, and was now home to the two most precious people in his life, Bella and their boy. It had sounded very much like a threat and, if so, Moreno had made a big mistake and there was no way now that Hal was going along with his grubby little scheme, whatever the consequences: lawyers, investigators, bring 'em on. He wanted the truth.

Getting to his feet, he walked slowly into the reception area where Patti was still at her console. She looked up at him. 'Everything okay?'

'Never better,' he smiled at her. 'Patti, does that machine do air travel and flights and seats and all that sort of thing?'

'Sure. Where do you want to go?'

'Milan.'

———∿∿∿———

Midnight and Hal found himself once more in an aircraft seat. Less than ten hours had passed since his arrival in New York, a nine-hour flight stretched out ahead, and his body clock was telling him it was just before dawn in Lynchcombe while, perversely, he remained wide awake. Tomorrow, he thought, the telephone line to his hotel room would probably be jammed with calls from Carrington, Moreno, Mike Monahan and Uncle Ted. They would all have to wait. Tomorrow he would talk to Vanni or Gina. Tomorrow he would buy something nice for Bella – in Milan.

—*∿∿*—

CHAPTER 21

─⟋⟋⟍─

Jane Fulford lay propped up in her bed – breathing became more difficult when lying flat – and watched the early morning sun light up the Cranmere valley, bringing with it through the open window the sounds of Dartmoor awakening to birdsong, starting with a single chirrup and swelling to a full blown chorus as they welcomed the new day. She, too, had been unable to sleep but for a rather different reason. Old age, she would tell her friends, which was true, but only in part. Soon she would have to be more honest with them, especially David; and with herself. But not just yet, not today. As she had lain awake she had been thinking of the young man who had breezed into her life, just as his father had. And in so doing she had opened a Pandora's box of memories that she had managed to keep firmly closed – until now.

─⟋⟋⟍─

Charles Wesson had left no note or letter of farewell, but on her pillow she had found a little carving, exquisitely done in a beautiful wood (she thought it was yew). Two doves stood with their necks pressed close together in mute statement of the feelings they had shared for one another. She had treasured it just as Billy had his rabbit, but at the time it had seemed small recompense for the loss of her lover. But the show had to go on. Appearances had to be kept up; the mistress of Cranmere could not be seen gazing into space and sighing like a lovelorn lass. Charles Wesson had gone without trace.

Or maybe not.

It was three weeks after his departure when Jane received the first indication that she just might be pregnant. It was no more than that, like a gentle breeze stirring the leaves on the topmost branches of the Cranmere elms, which might or might not be prelude to a force nine gale roaring up the valley. She had missed her monthly period, that's all it was. Many women were experiencing similar problems due to anxiety, stress, poor diet or whatever – why should she be any different? Three mornings later she felt bilious, made it to the bathroom just in time, ran water into the basin and swilled her face before raising it to look in the mirror – it was then she knew. But refused to believe it.

She telephoned Edward. 'He's long overdue,' she complained. 'Are you sure he's all right?'

'He's all right, Jane, he's on his way, I promise you. And he knows of your plight.'

Does he? Jane thought. I don't know how, I don't even know myself.

Another four weeks passed and with them any hopes that this might have been a false alarm. At lunchtime when they listened to *Workers' Playtime* on the wireless, Mrs Kerslake remarked, 'Your appetite's improving, Ma'am.'

'It must be your cooking,' Jane said without thinking.

'What was wrong with it, then?' Mrs Kerslake could tolerate no criticism.

'Nothing at all,' Jane laughed, 'It just gets better by the day.' She must try not to appear too ravenous. But, on the other hand, perhaps she should. It would account for her gain in weight which would become apparent in a few short weeks; and for how long could she keep up the deception? At mealtimes after the children had left she was surrounded by women, some of them mothers; and Millie who came from a huge family where pregnancies were commonplace. Her ignorance appalled her and there was no one she could turn to for advice – most certainly not her mother!

Millie would be her first choice. Millie was a true friend, a rock, and with a countrywoman's earthy knowledge of such matters way beyond her years. But it would be unfair to place so heavy a burden on her young shoulders. Later, she might have no choice, but for the present she was alone.

She telephoned Edward again. 'Where is he?' she beseeched him.

'On his way, Jane, I promise you.'

'That's what you said last week.' 'Yes, I know. He'll be with you soon.'

'I hope you're right.'

—✿—

'You are looking bonnie Jane, if you don't mind my saying so?' It was Lieutenant Dando who had wandered into the estate office as he sometimes did mid-morning when there was coffee on the go, or when he had news.

'No, of course not, James, and thank you. I have been taking a bit more exercise,' she said by way of explanation. The weather, which had been unseasonably cold and wet, had now cleared and in the evenings she had been taking long walks by the river or up onto the moor, to be alone, to think. As far as she could tell she was six or seven weeks into pregnancy, but with little to show for it yet. Except James Dando had noticed a difference in her complexion – wasn't it Rembrandt who preferred his women sitters to be pregnant? And only that morning the zip on her skirt had been reluctant to close fully. So her waistline had begun to expand; not a lot, but enough. Of course it could have been because she was eating like a horse, and why? Not as a result of more exercise.

'And we've all been getting a bit more sleep,' Lieutenant Dando was saying.

'Yes, five nights in a row. That's a record, isn't it?

'Yes, it is.'

'Why, do you suppose, or is that not in the bailiwick of NAV INT?' Sometimes Jane would revert to service jargon, if only to demonstrate her familiarity with such things, no matter how childish they seemed.

'I would think it's more MIL INT that NAV INT,' Lieutenant Dando said with mock gravity.

'Don't NAV ever speak to MIL?'

'We acknowledge one another,' he said. 'But I have some comforting news for you, Jane. It's restricted at the moment but you will soon know.' He nodded to the Daily Telegraph lying on her desk, open at the War Page.

'Yes?' she said eagerly. News of Roger? Had a secret message been passed from MIL to NAV?

'The German airfield near St Malo which has been mainly responsible for our disturbed nights has suffered a severe setback,' he smiled grimly. 'From the reports we're getting, it seems the French Resistance managed to get in there and lay explosive charges. Fuel and ammunition dumps and aircraft blown sky high. They won't be troubling us for a while.'

'Well, whether it was the Resistance or MIL or NAV,' Jane said, 'we at Cranmere are grateful.' She should have known not to expect too much.

'Indeed we are. Any news of himself?'

'Only that he is supposed to be home any day now.' Jane pushed her hair back with one hand in a tired gesture. 'But they've been saying that for weeks.'

'I'm sure he will.'

How could he be sure? she questioned, clutching at straws. Or was that just a platitude? From the floor above a chorus of little voices sang, *'Jesus wants me for a sunbeam, to shine by night and day.'*

Lieutenant Dando looked up at the ceiling and smiled, 'Better than Vera Lynn, I'd say.'

'Far better,' Jane agreed.

He had a second bit of news, but was not sure whether Jane would regard it good or bad. 'Try me.' She thought that by now, after three long years of war, she was prepared for most things.

'The Yanks are coming,' he said without enthusiasm, and she recalled how last December when Pearl Harbor was bombed some of the naval personnel – who should have known better – were almost jubilant that America would now be spurred into action. Her thoughts, along with most of the womenfolk in Cranmere, had been for the children whose fathers would not be home for Christmas.

'Coming to Cranmere!' she said.

'Yes, but don't let it worry you, they will camp well away from the house. You'll probably hardly know they're here.'

'When can we expect them?'

'Oh, not for a while, probably six months or more. You will be getting a visit from the military first to spy out the land.'

'Thank you for warning me, James.'

'You're welcome. Sorry to bring such troubles to your door.'

Troubles? Jane thought after he had gone. James, if you only knew. Rising from her desk, she went to the window where a butterfly was trapped, raised the sash and watched it fly free. Out in the pasture cattle grazed quietly, while nearer to the house a group of children were holding some sort of noisy relay race, excited voices calling encouragement punctuated by a shrill whistle. Things had been running quite smoothly since the sirens had left them undisturbed, but soon it seemed, within six months, their lives were to be disrupted once more. An American camp right on their doorstep, and they would *hardly know it was there?* Not much, they wouldn't! Lieutenant Dando, in his disapproval, had not said how many – fifty, one hundred, five hundred? Jane smiled, what *would* her mother say? What would Millie say?

So, six short months by which time her secret would be known – she might even be a mother! But she didn't have six months, more like six weeks – because no matter how her appearance did or did not alter, there was the other end of the pregnancy to to consider, wasn't there? A premature birth at seven months was just about acceptable; less than that was highly questionable. If the worst happened and she had to confess her guilt to Roger, how would he react? He was not known for his forgiving nature. Would she be sent packing back to her mother, or allowed to stay on under sufferance as an unpaid governess – for the duration?

She needed Roger here with her, not blowing up St Malo. Leaning her forehead against the cool windowpane, she mouthed the words, 'Please come home, Roger. Please?'

—⁓—

Jane was not sure that it was a motorcycle that had disturbed her sleep; she may have been dreaming of Charles' return. But there was no mistaking the sentry's voice as it cut through the night air with his challenge, 'HALT. Who goes there?'

There came a muffled reply

'Advance and be recognised.'

She was at the bedroom window in time to see an odd figure, dressed in French peasants *blouson* and huge beret, as he walked slowly up the terrace steps into the light. Roger? Could it be? She was left in no doubt when she heard his voice clearly through the now open sash.

'I doubt you would recognise me, old chap, as we've probably never met,' he said wearily. 'But somebody must. I live here, d'you see? As a matter of fact I own the place.' And turning his face up to her window, he called, 'Jane, Jane, wake up, will you? Come on down and let me in, there's a good girl.'

Slipping into her silk dressing gown, she ran barefoot down the stairs and the length of the hall. On the threshold she paused for a brief moment then hurled herself at him.

'Roger! Is it really you?'

'Yes, it's me, old girl.' He enfolded her in his arms, held her close. He smelt awful. She struggled free. 'Let me look at you, you're so thin!' She took his arm. 'Come on in. Have you had anything to eat?'

'Mmm, left it behind in the Channel. All I need is a bed, then I shall sleep for a week. Could you arrange that?'

Holding onto the bannister rail, the other arm resting heavily on Jane's shoulder, he hauled himself up the stairs, pausing halfway to call to Lieutenant Dando who had come to see what all the noise was about. 'James,' he said, 'there's a motorbike outside, would you take charge of it, please? I borrowed it from the Army, they might be a bit upset.'

James Dando grinned, 'Aye aye, sir.'

—*∿∿*—

Watched over by Jane, Roger Fulford slept, sprawled diagonally across their bed. He was fully dressed apart from his boots and *blouson*. At first she had been a little afraid of this unkempt stranger who smelled stronger than the worst stable she had ever mucked out, and who had fallen into a deep sleep just as soon as his head touched the pillow. But standing by the bedside, she watched his features soften as the facial muscles relaxed and her warrior husband slipped deeper into an almost comatose slumber, the like of which he had probably not enjoyed for a very long time.

Through talking to others, she had a good idea of what kind of life he had been leading – dirty, dangerous, exciting, constantly pursued – and she also knew, because he was her husband, the ruthless energy and enthusiasm he would have brought to bear on any task he had encountered. Now he was exhausted. And she was proud of him. She examined him closely as he slept, his hands roughened like a labourer's, fingernails broken and blackened, grey hairs at his temples – he was only thirty – and the age lines in his face which had horrified her when she first saw him; most of them would come out in the wash. So the moment you wake up, Roger Fulford, she thought, it's straight into the bathtub with you. And then down to see Mrs Kerslake for a good square meal. And then, who knows?

Later, sitting by his bedside like an anxious mother, she was able to see through the grime and growth of beard the handsome man she had married. 'I have wronged you, Roger,' she said silently, 'and though I do not want to, I intend to deceive you, because I have no choice. In return I shall be anything you want me to be – wife, whore, nursemaid and companion. I will never hurt you.'

Then opening the window sashes a little wider for ventilation, she curled herself on the *chaise longue* for what remained of the night.

'Jane, this is Edward. May I speak to your husband?'

'Edward, this is Jane. No, my husband is sound asleep.'

'Is he all right?'

'He is exhausted.'

'We will need to speak to him soon.'

'Then someone must come here. He is *not* leaving Cranmere, not until he is rested and fully recovered.' She used her newfound authoritative voice.

'All right,' Edward laughed. 'Message received and understood.'

'Good. Goodbye, Edward.'

'Goodbye, Jane.'

CHAPTER 22

Hal Wesson also slept soundly in his reclining seat as he passed through five time zones and entered a sixth, and when he woke his body clock had more or less righted itself. When he landed it would be just gone six in the morning, local time, and as the airport was fifty kilometres from the city by the time he had travelled that distance he should arrive at the start of the working day. So, first he would visit Vanni or Gina, then do a bit of shopping and catch one of the many flights home. With luck he would be back well before midnight, the time of his expected time of arrival from New York. And Uncle Ted would have nothing to complain about. *With luck.*

Way below through wispy clouds, dawn was breaking over a mountain range and a series of lakes. Maggiore and Como were the names that immediately came to mind: and why? Because that was where his father and mother had been heading on a similar spring day nine years ago. He looked down through the aircraft window. Why, he had often wondered, of all the flights in and out of Milan, had the one his parents were on run into trouble? Atmospheric storm, they had said. An Act of God.

The old rector in Lynchcombe had tried his best with an angry and confused nineteen-year-old. Why, Hal raged, had this God of love and compassion wiped out the two people who meant more to him that anyone else, who had never done anyone any harm? Why treat them like that? Some Act! Some God! He'd had visions – nightmares – of his parents as the aircraft went down. Had they known ten seconds before impact and held onto one another in a last terrible embrace? Or was it instantaneous? There had been nothing left but wreckage spread over a burnt hillside, just a few pathetic possessions. His Uncle Ted had visited the scene – he couldn't face it – and brought back a small carton of symbolic ash which they had scattered in Lynchcombe churchyard. In nine years he had got over the worst, but deep down the questions still remained unanswered, and the anger still smouldered. And that, he thought, was probably the reason for his going to Milan, a decision that now, in the dawn of a new day, might have seemed a bit impulsive. He could have phoned from the comfort of his hotel room in New York, couldn't he? No. Better this way, to confront Vanni or Gina. He wanted the truth.

At Malpensa Airport, within sight of the Alps, he had an hour to wait before the next bus to Milan. He bought a guidebook, breakfasted off coffee and croissants, changed traveller's cheques into lire and made use of the well-appointed *gabietto* where he shaved, put on his last clean shirt and prepared himself to meet – after twenty-one years – Gina, the first girl he had ever kissed. He remembered her as a constantly laughing tomboy with hair cut in a straight fringe and huge dark eyes that, even then, had aroused in him thoughts he had not fully understood. What would she be like now: tall and lissome like some of the Italian girls to be seen stalking gazelle-like around the airport?

He would soon know.

The airport bus, only half full, remained steadfastly in the slow lane across a flat and featureless plain while the young executives of Milan belted past in their Alfa Romeos, bearing out what he had been reading in the guidebook: that in Milan *Time is money and the pace fast, and the work-ethic rules the lives of its power-dressed citizens.* It sounded just liked home, Hal thought. What else? Oh yes, *Traffic is horrendous and the air so polluted that at times the Polizia wear masks.*

Stazione Centrale is a vast building originally commissioned by Mussolini, and is also the focal point for all forms of public transport. Hal stepped down from the bus into a Milanese-style rush hour. A press of humanity as dense as a football crowd pushed and shoved – 'Scusi Scusi' – towards the many exits. He took one look at the scramble for the Metro, decided against and headed for a taxi rank. 'Sure,' the driver knew the address in the Navigli quarter on the far side of the city. 'Sure,' he spoke English. The drive was memorable, and fast and noisy with the blare of horns. The gesticulations needed no translation. He rubbernecked as they flashed past architectural gems, graceful churches, the Scala Opera House and an Ionic gateway in the middle of a busy traffic island. Then they left the main road, slowed and entered a maze of older streets leading down to a canal. They ran beside a stone wall topped with clay tiles and pulled up opposite a pair of church-like doors. One of them bore a brass plate with the name in flamboyant script: *Enrico Spargo, Restauratore. Est 1907.*

There was an entry phone. Hal paid off the taxi and asked the driver to wait for a moment: there may be no one at home. A woman's voice answered in Italian.

'Do you speak English?' he asked.

'Yes, I speak English. Who is that?'

'Hal Wesson.' 'Who?'

'Hal Wesson from Lynchcombe.'

He heard a little squeak and the voice said *'Momento'*, followed by the sound of footsteps running across a stone floor. Bolts rattled and one of the big doors swung inwards. She was tall and brown, broad-shouldered and broad-hipped and pregnant. Her dark eyes were as he remembered but larger, and the wide smile.

'Hal!' She almost shrieked his name as she held out both arms to him. They hugged each other, separated then hugged again. Hal flapped a hand at the taxi driver who left with a yelp of tyres.

'Hal, what are you doing here?'

'I came to see you, Gina.'

'All the way from Lynchcombe?'

'From New York.'

She stood back to allow him to enter, closed the big door, shot the bolts. 'You live in New York?'

'No, it's a long story.'

She smiled, looked him up and down. 'You've grown since I last saw you.'

Hal laughed, 'So have you.'

She punched his arm playfully, but quite hard, and he remembered another thing about his first girlfriend: she could be violent.

They were in a courtyard paved in worn flagstones and surrounded on three sides by single-storey buildings with pantiled roofs extending to form a verandah supported by stone columns. The high wall that sheltered them from the street was covered in flowering clematis with fragments of ancient statuary peeping out from the foliage, the turmoil of the city barely audible.

Hal looked around him. 'Gina, this is beautiful.'

'It was Papa's old home.' She took his arm in a show of affection. 'He was born here. When we got the chance to buy it the whole place was a ruin. I helped rebuild it. You heard Papa died, I expect?'

'Yes, I did,' Hal replied, 'and I'm very sorry, he was a good friend to me when I was little.' At least he now knew for sure. It avoided any awkward questions. 'How long ago was it?'

'Seven years and I still miss him,' Gina said sadly. She was quiet for a moment, but the mood soon passed and her natural exuberance returned. 'Come on,' she said,'I want to show you everything.' And detaching herself from him, she ran light-footed towards an open doorway calling, 'Mother, look who's come to see us.'

Hal followed, recalling how in Lynchcombe the eight-year-old Gina had run everywhere, taking obstacles at full tilt, including the river. They entered a farmhouse kitchen, a huge room with white painted walls and dried herbs hanging from the beamed ceiling. At a pine table in the centre of the room two small boys sat side by side and looked up at him with interest. They each had jet-black hair cut in a straight fringe, and dark Italian eyes. 'This is Bepe,' Gina introduced them proudly, 'and this is Carlo.'

Hal grinned at them and said, *'Buon giorno, Bepe. Buon giorno Carlo'*, reducing both boys to gales of laughter. Behind them their grandmother stood with both hands pressed to her face, looking large-eyed at their visitor. 'Little Hal,' she said, coming around the table to greet him. 'For a moment I thought...' She hugged him as her daughter had. 'My goodness, boy, you're the image of your father.'

Chairs were hurriedly brought to the table, which was soon laden with coffee and a huge selection of little fancy cakes and pastries. Elsie Spargo, like her daughter, was a strong-minded Lynchcombe girl and there were twenty-one years to make up for before Hal could ask any questions.

To his surprise – and delight – at some time over the past twenty-one years his childhood sweetheart had served a long and exacting apprenticeship under her father who had, she said, taught her all he knew, and all his father and Hal's father has taught him.

'Then you must be good,' Hal said.

'She is,' Elsie said proudly. 'She is the best *restauratrice* in Milan.'

Gina, who was incapable of sitting still for more than five minutes, got to her feet. 'Come on,' she held out her hand to him. 'I want to show you our workshops and you must meet Poldi.'

'Who is Poldi?' Hal followed her across the courtyard, now baking hot in the morning sun.

'He is my husband,' she laughed over her shoulder. 'Where do you think my children came from?'

'I didn't like to ask.'

The workshop was large and light and air-conditioned. Gina and her father had rebuilt it almost single-handed, she said. She had mixed the cement. A glazed partition divided the huge room into two, his and hers. In the inner room, the door closed, Poldi was bent over his work. He wore an eyeshade like a Mississippi gambler and showed a bald patch on the back of his head. He was cutting marquetry into a large panel in the most intricate of designs.

'He doesn't like to be disturbed when he's working,' Gina whispered.

'I'm not surprised,' Hal replied. He had done some marquetry cutting, thought it a task sent straight from hell. Sensing spectators, Poldi looked up, sent them a faint smile and returned to his work.

They moved away from the window into what was Gina's workplace, the polishing shop. What Poldi produced, Gina polished, surrounded by her bottles and jars like a medieval alchemist, and the attendant smells of linseed, spirits, shellac and beeswax, a potent mixture. But while Hal was admiring her finished and unfinished work – and making the right noises – he was conscious that time was slipping by and this was not purely a social call. He had questions to ask. So it came as a relief as well as a surprise when Elsie appeared in the doorway and said he had a visitor.

'For me? But I don't know anyone in Milan,' he was saying while a strong sense of foreboding gripped him. Had Moreno tracked him down?

His visitor was a dark-haired young man, very polite and sorry to disturb him. He wore a lightweight business suit that seemed a bit familiar and held out an ID card that was very familiar – Channon Grieves. Would he please telephone Sir Edward as soon as possible? He held up his mobile, which meant – Now! 'For God's sake,' Hal said quietly, glancing at his wristwatch. It was about midday in London; he should have called in hours ago. This was exactly what he hadn't wanted, the long arm of Channon Grieves finding him where he was not supposed to be. Couldn't Uncle Ted trust him off the leash for half a day? Apparently not.

Ben Pavoni was the Milanese version of Mike Monahan and, Hal thought, probably knew Milan like the back of his hand. Could be useful, even if he had been instructed to nursemaid his charge to the nearest airport. They sat in the shade to one side of the courtyard, the temperature now climbing into the nineties. Ben pressed a long sequence of numbers on his mobile, listened for a moment and passed the tiny instrument to him. 'Lynchcombe House,' Sir Edward Channon's voice said as clear as though from five miles away.

'Hal, are you all right?'

'Yes thanks.'

'Why are you in Milan?'

'I am following up a lead.' He added quickly, 'I know we agreed that any inquiries were to be made by you, but this is personal. I'll explain when I get back.'

'I understand, Hal, and I know where you are. But when you have finished there I want you to come straight home. If there should be any further leads to be followed up in Milan, would you please leave them to Ben Pavoni?'

'Yes, all right, I won't muddy the waters. Oh, and the answer to the two-million-dollar question is yes, affirmative.'

'Thank you, Hal. No more on the telephone, please. I will meet you off the plane.'

He handed the mobile back to Ben who gave a sympathetic smile. 'Are you in trouble?'

'No, not really. At least, I don't think so.' Why should he be? He had spoken to no one since leaving New York, and he'd left them floundering. But the message had been clear enough, if a little terse. Sir Edward himself would be at the airport. Do not make any detours or any indiscreet inquiries in Milan. Do not collect 500 lire from the community chest. Come straight home.

'Do you know anything about this investigation?' Hal asked.

Ben spread both hands. 'All I know is you went to New York to identify a possibly stolen cabinet, and got a bit lost on the way home.'

'Yes, well I didn't get lost, Ben. As you say, I went to New York to confirm whether or not this was the cabinet stolen from a country house in England at the end of the last war. It is. I also learned that Gina's father did some restoration work on the cabinet about eight or ten years ago. That is why I am here. Giovanni Spargo has since died, but I need to ask Gina a few questions. As you are a Channon Grieves man, it might be helpful if you were present.'

'Sure. You knew Gina before, did you?'

'She was my first girlfriend.' Right on cue, Gina came out from the kitchen doorway and stood looking at them across the courtyard, her arms akimbo.

'She's a big girl,' Ben said appreciatively.

'We were only eight years old.'

'*Pranzo,*' Gina called to them.

'We are being invited to lunch,' Ben said.

'Lunch! Good God, she's been stuffing me with chocolate cakes for half the morning.' Ben smiled but said nothing.

The table was set for a banquet – flowers, bowls of fruit, cheeses and bottles of vino. Elsie sat to one end with a pile of dishes and a huge tureen. Poldi sat at the opposite end while Gina and her boys faced Hal and Ben across the table. 'It's only risotto,' Elsie said.

'Smells great.' Hal wondered how long all this was going to take, and when he would get a chance to talk to Gina. But as he might have expected, it was Gina who started the ball rolling.

'What were you doing in New York, Hal?'

'I went to see a cabinet, a big one, ten foot wide. I believe your father and probably you, did a lot of work on it.'

'Oh, that one.' Gina sprang from her chair and left the room, returning with a large photograph which she passed to him.

'That's the one,' he said through a mouthful of risotto.

'Did you look at the little carved figures around the top?'

'Yes, I did.'

'I made most of them,' Gina said proudly.

'They had me fooled.'

'So why did you go to see it?'

Just for a moment Hal hesitated. Later, he was to wonder why. This was what he had come to Milan for, wasn't it, to learn the truth? Or was it that the truth might best be left undisturbed?

'It seems,' he said slowly, 'that at some time in its long history, the cabinet may have been stolen.'

'Yes, well we knew that, didn't we?' Gina said, passing a dish to her younger son.

Hal looked at her across the table. 'Did we?'

———

CHAPTER 23

—◆◆◆—

Perhaps only seconds had passed since Gina dropped her bombshell, but Hal still gazed at her, blank-faced in astonishment.

It was Elsie who spoke first. 'Hal,' she said gently, 'Didn't your father tell you why he was coming to Milan?'

'I thought they were coming on holiday with you and Vanni.'

'Yes, so they were. We had friends who owned a pretty little *pensione* up near Lake Maggiore, they had the rooms all ready. Vanni wanted to repay your father and mother for the kindness they had shown him, and of course, he wanted to show off the Italian lakes in the spring. But he also wanted your father to see the cabinet, to identify it.'

'That thing was bad news right from the start, like there was a jinx on it,' Gina said bitterly. 'First your father and then mine, and now it's come back to haunt us, has it?'

'Where did it come from? Hal asked.

'From Dino Brocatti.' Gina made a face. 'He's a crook for a start.'

'Now, Gina, you don't know that,' Elsie said reprovingly.

'Don't I'? Gina said. 'He's a dirty old man, tried to put his hand up my skirt. I was only fourteen.'

Hal managed a smile. 'Did you hit him, Gina?'

'No, I didn't. Wish I had now. Anyway, Brocatti had owned the cabinet for four or five years before we agreed to take it on. Papa didn't want a big job like that and in any case we hadn't the workshop space. Then when I'd left school, we got the new workshop built and couldn't really refuse. Brocatti put a lot of work our way and I think he offered Papa more money, I'm not sure.' She broke off for a moment to supervise her boys' table manners. 'When the cabinet arrived,' she said, 'it was in a thousand pieces, all packed in a huge box. We got them spread out on the workshop floor and Papa became very excited; he said he was almost certain that this was the same as the cabinet he had worked on with your father in Lynchcombe, all those years ago. There was something odd about it, Gina's brow furrowed. 'It had been lost or stolen – I'm not sure what it was – but Papa said he thought your father would be very pleased. So he wrote and told him about it.'

'When was this?' Hal asked. 'Can you remember?'

'In the February,' Elsie said. 'I wrote the letter for Vanni, he wasn't too good at writing in English.' She paused for a moment, remembering. 'He was heartbroken when your father died, Hal. Wouldn't so much as look at that cabinet for six months or more.'

Gina was occupied mopping up sauce from Bepe's chin with a paper towel. 'And Brocatti kept nagging him all the while,' she said over her shoulder. 'So we made a start.' She turned to face him. 'It took us the best part of two years, off and on. Came out quite well, didn't you think?'

'Yes, I do,' Hal smiled.

'Brocatti was pleased with it,' Gina said. 'Paid Papa very well for the job, quite a lot in cash. And then...' Like her mother, Gina hesitated. 'Then about a week later he went out and bought this little sports car. Well, you know what Papa was like. He'd always wanted one, said if he didn't buy one now while he'd got the money, he'd be too old. Maybe he was, or maybe it was too powerful for him, but he took it up onto the *Autostrada* and had a bad smash. He died later that day.'

Hal looked first at Elsie and then at Gina. Until now he'd had no idea how Vanni died, and had assumed it was through illness or age – he must have been in his late sixties. But no, he had met a sudden and violent death – like Charles Wesson. 'I am so sorry,' he said.

'You see what I mean about a jinx,' Gina said. 'But for that beastly cabinet they might both be with us still. Who knows?'

Who knows? Hal repeated to himself. Or, more to the point, who knew, apart from Vanni, that the cabinet might have come off the back of a lorry? Looking directly at Gina, he asked, 'Did Vanni tell anyone else that the cabinet might have had a questionable past?'

'I don't think so, apart from Dino Brocatti. It was his property, after all. And Papa was very proud that Charles Wesson was coming from England to look at it. He thought there might be a reward.'

So, Hal thought, Brocatti knew and he also knew about the close association between Vanni Spargo and his father. And if anyone started asking too many questions, how long before Moreno and Agnolli knew, not forgetting the Honourable Ralph Carrington?

Christ, what a mess!

'What will happen now?' Elsie asked.

'I really don't know,' Hal said. 'I suppose there will be some sort of investigation of behalf of the rightful owners, although after all this time I can't see what good it would do.'

'Will we be involved?' she asked anxiously.

'No, why should you be? It seems to me that Brocatti's the man who needs to answer a few searching questions.'

'You won't get anything out of that creep,' Gina said.

Without warning, Poldi spoke up for the first time in a burst of rapid Italian. All heads turned his way. Gina translated.

'Poldi says we are not to upset Brocatti, he's a good client and has sent a lot of his friends to us. Personally, I think we could manage quite well without him and his friends.'

'Doesn't Poldi speak English?' Hal asked

'Not very well.'

'Well would you tell him that I have no intention of going anywhere near Brocatti. And also, any man who can produce fine quality marquetry like he does will never be short of a client.'

Poldi received the compliment with ill grace, forced a smile, raised his glass but did not drink.

'There's one thing that you might be able to help me with,' Hal said. 'Elsie, would you be prepared to put in writing what you just told me about writing to my father?'

'How would that help?'

'If Brocatti, or anyone else, tried to make out that the cabinet came from my father, your statement would prove them wrong, as he knew nothing of its whereabouts until you wrote and told him.'

'They wouldn't do that, would they?' Gina asked indignantly. 'They might. It would be a let-out for Brocatti to say that he'd bought it for cash from someone who'd since died.' He thought it best not to mention the possibility of Vanni also being implicated.

At the mention of Brocatti's name for a second time, Poldi broke in again even faster than before. Gina dismissed him with a gesture well known to Italian women, a backward swipe of the hand like brushing away a fly. Poldi stalked from the room muttering to himself, a sad little man. Hal felt quite sorry for him.

'Leave Poldi to me,' Gina said unnecessarily. 'You shall have your statement, Hal.

'Thank you, Gina. Let's hope it won't be needed.

The interior of Ben's car was like an oven as they bounced along the rough cobbled road towards modern Milan. Behind them Gina and her family – sans Poldi – waved until they were out of sight, Gina's last words still ringing in Hal's ears. *'Hal, just think what might have been.'*

He was still thinking.

At Ben Pavoni's suggestion, they were heading for the home of Isobella Tambrini, a one-time friend of Dino Brocatti. 'Bit of luck, that,' Ben said. 'My mother and Isobella used to go on shopping sprees when we lived in London.'

'Where did you live in London, Ben?'

'In Knightsbridge. My father was at the Embassy. I spent most of my time at boarding school.'

'You poor sod.'

'Yeah, that's what I thought at the time. But this was in the late seventies at about the time Brocatti got his hands on your missing cabinet. He would come over every six months or so, buying antiques, and he brought Isobella with him.'

'Was she in the business?'

'No, I believe the relationship was more of an amorous nature.'

'His *inamorata?*'

'Yeah, that'll do,' Ben laughed. 'I was going to say his "squeeze". But the point is, Hal, he dumped her. Italian women do not like that.' He negotiated a hair-raising traffic island and turned onto a ring road where the houses were tall and elegant and set well back behind dense foliage. 'So,' Ben said, 'if Isobella has anything on Dino Brocatti, it's ours for the asking. And she is expecting us.'

There was, Hal thought, a similarity in all Channon Grieves men, at least the few he had met. They were alert and resourceful and expected to work on their own initiative. Ben was no exception and, being a native, had a wide variety of contacts in both the lower and upper reaches of Milanese society. Hence Isobella.

'She's a tough old bird,' Ben warned. 'Better leave her to me.'

Isobella lived in a first-floor apartment in a classical town house overlooking beautiful gardens. She was tall and willowy and dressed in a loose-fitting caftan with full-length sleeves. She greeted Ben effusively in Italian, kissing both cheeks, took Hal's hand in hers and offered a thin smile before showing them into her drawing room. French windows were open onto a balcony at the rear of the house, the traffic's noise muted. Isobella had the grace of movement typical of Italian women of her generation, and had surrounded herself with beautiful objects, paintings, mirrors in gilded Florentine frames, Oriental rugs and antique furniture. She had herself once been beautiful and had both married and buried Giorgio Tambrini since her dalliance with Dino Brocatti. Now, wealthy and in her seventies, there was a hardness about her; she was no longer a woman to be trifled with.

They sat around a low table set well back from the open windows and direct sunlight. There was white wine for those who wanted it. Ben poured three glasses and handed them around.

'It's good of you to see us at such short notice,' Ben smiled. 'I wonder if you would mind answering a few questions about Dino Brocatti?'

Isobella frowned, 'If I must.'

Ben explained that we were on the trail of an antique cabinet that had been lost or mislaid or possibly stolen, and that at some time it had come into Brocatti's possession.' Isobella's pencil-thin eyebrows arched. 'That would not surprise me.'

'I was not suggesting that Brocatti was knowingly engaged in anything unlawful,' Ben added hastily, 'but it seems that the cabinet was shipped over from England during the late seventies, at a time when Brocatti was making regular buying trips, and when you accompanied him and visited my mother.'

'How is your mother, Ben? Is she well?'

'Yes, thank you.'

'Do please give her my best wishes. Tell her I will telephone.'

'Of course,' Ben said politely while Hal watched the exchange with interest. Here was a keen young man treading a perilous course between being patient with an old – and tetchy – friend of his mother's while at the same time questioning a possible witness. He wished him luck.

'What I was wondering,' Ben persisted, 'was if you could remember any of Brocatti's suppliers or business associates at that time?'

'Oh now I don't think so, Ben. It was rather a long time ago and I knew very little about Dino's business activities. Neither did I wish to.'

'It was a long time ago,' Ben agreed, 'But I was rather hoping you might recall something of where you went, or who Brocatti met on a regular basis.'

Isobella turned her head to gaze out of the window at something in the far distance. 'On a regular basis would be quite correct,' she said after a long silence. 'Dino was very much a creature of habit and our visits usually followed the same pattern. We would arrive at Heathrow on the Thursday, about mid-morning, and would travel by car to London where we stayed at the Dorchester. In the afternoon I would accompany Dino to the salerooms in Bond Street and St James's where we would view the auction sales to be held on the following day. And then in the evening we would take in a show, and possibly go on to a club if Dino was in a relaxed mood; but wait,' Isobella held up one slender finger, 'that is not quite right. After we had left the salerooms, Dino would call to see a man at an hotel in Russell Square. I never went in, I was left waiting in the car. But Dino would reappear carrying a small suitcase.' Isobella smiled unpleasantly at the memory.

'Do you know what was in the suitcase?' Ben asked.

'Oh yes, I knew. I was not supposed to but I caught Dino gloating over it on one occasion. It contained a great deal of money – in cash.'

'Did he offer any explanation?'

'No.' Isobella smiled indulgently at the question. 'Neither did I ask, although I must have wondered at the time. I had a feeling that Dino was up to something but,' she shrugged, 'it was no concern of mine.'

'Please go on.'

'Yes, let's see now.' As Ben had predicted, once into her narrative, Isobella was enjoying herself. 'On the Friday Dino would go off with his little suitcase to attend the sales and call on his other business contacts. I spent the day with your mother, Ben, in Harrods and Harvey Nicholls, spending some of Dino's money. Then on Saturday we would drive down to Brighton to see Mr duCann.'

'Mr duCann?'

'Yes, duCann was an old-established firm with a very beautiful shop in The Lanes, I think in Prince Albert Street. There was also a warehouse not far distant. I went there once or twice but it was a cold and draughty place. Usually, I spent the day looking around the shops. Then in the late afternoon we would drive to Heathrow for our return flight to Milan.'

Ben was quiet for a moment and then said, 'In this warehouse, Isobella, do you by any chance remember seeing a very large cabinet or a box that might have contained such a cabinet?'

'No, Ben, I do not.' Isobella's patience was running out. 'How could I? It was a huge place with cabinets and chests lined up like soldiers. But I do seem to recall duCann acted as an agent on Dino's behalf, so it would be more than likely that your missing cabinet was shipped through or by him. Is that of any help?'

'Thank you,' Ben said. 'I think it might be.'

'Good. Please can we talk about something else now?'

Linate Airport lies five kilometres to the west of Milan. Hal sat beside Ben Pavoni in the departure lounge. They sipped excellent Italian coffee from styrofoam cups. An hour had passed since they left Isobella's apartment, during which time they had visited a department store in the world-famous Duomo where Hal bought an outrageously expensive silk nightdress, described by the smiling assistant – who clearly doubted it was for his wife – as *molto provocante;* and a very large, stuffed toy lion with a comical expression and built-in growl. It sat beside him on the banquette. The flight to Heathrow had been delayed by forty minutes which suited Hal quite nicely, for during the past half hour all sort of ideas had been buzzing around in his mind and now was his chance to air them.

'Ben,' he asked, 'do you think Brocatti was involved with the Mafia?'

'Not to my knowledge. Why?'

'Because they had a racket running back in the seventies, or so I've heard. A dealer would come over from Italy, collect a sackful of cash from the local Godfather, buy a truckload of antiques and ship them back to Rome or Milan or wherever. That way he could launder the money and get it back home, *and* make a profit. I don't think they do it now, there aren't enough antiques left in Britain.'

'Could be.' Ben sat leaning forward, elbows resting on his knees, cradling his cup in both hands.

It was cooler in the big, high-ceilinged room with the air-conditioning going at full blast. 'I'd heard of that little scam, now you come to mention it,' he said. 'Long before my time. As for the Mafia,' Ben glanced around him to ensure no one was within earshot, 'most of the local boys are known to us, and the Brocattis have never been amongst them, but...' He broke off to watch through the observation window as a big Boeing made a perfect landing on the main runway. 'That doesn't mean a great deal. It could have happened like this, Hal. Brocatti receives a visit and they might have said, *"Hey, Dino, we want you to do a little job for us and you are on a percentage. If you don't agree, then maybe a four-ton truck will reverse through your nice shop window on a Saturday morning."* So he went along with it, and who could blame him?'

'Still illegal, though.'

'I'm not so sure,' Ben said. 'There is nothing illegal about buying antiques for cash. Granted, the cash was most likely acquired by unlawful means but Brocatti would have known better than to ask, and I'm sure there was a cover story that might have been difficult to disprove.'

There were times, Hal thought, when Ben spoke like a lawyer. It was not until later in the day that he discovered why.

'If I may advise, Hal, the way into this one is through your end.'

'DuCann, you mean?'

'Yes. If he was acting as Brocatti's shipping agent, then chances are the bulk of Brocatti's purchases passed through his hands, wouldn't you say?'

'Yes, I would.'

'Do you know anything about duCann?'

'Not yet,' Hal said quietly, but while Ben had been talking, his thoughts had been spiralling off in a rather different direction. 'Ben... if the Mafia were behind this, could they have been instrumental in preventing my father's arrival in Milan? Ben turned to look at him, both eyebrows raised in astonishment.

'If you are suggesting the aircraft may have been tampered with to cause the crash, then my answer is a resounding "No". It would be a very risky business to interfere with a civil aircraft – even the Mafia would think twice.'

'So you think it was just coincidence?'

'A very unfortunate coincidence, yes,' Ben said consolingly. 'Just ask yourself this question, Hal – how much was the cabinet worth?'

'It sold for a million dollars.'

'Well there's your answer. That would be small change to the people we are talking about.' Ben was speaking urgently, straight at him. 'I'm not saying they are incapable of such an act, but only if the stakes were high enough, and they were not.'

'Maybe not, but if my father had identified this cabinet it could have taken the lid off the whole racket, couldn't it?'

'Possibly,' Ben admitted, 'but we're still talking peanuts in an annual turnover of thirty billion or more. Hal, I think you should put that idea right out of your mind.'

'Well, what about Vanni Spargo?'

'What about him?'

'According to Gina, he died in a motor accident only a week after the cabinet left his workshop. In other words, they allowed him to finish the job before shunting him off the *Autostrada* to keep him quiet. Was that a coincidence, too?' Hal had spoken louder than he intended. One or two heads turned in their direction.

Ben raised one finger to his lips, looked around him. 'Yes, I think it was probably coincidental,' he said quietly. 'Gina may have put her finger on it, an elderly man in a powerful sports car.'

'Sorry, I didn't mean to yell at you, Ben. Perhaps Sir Edward forgot to tell you I'm a bit paranoid where my father is concerned. That's why I came to Milan. I'm not too concerned about the sodding cabinet, but there's no way I will allow my father to be used as a scapegoat by that bunch of creeps – nor Vanni for that matter. They may not be around to defend themselves, but I am.'

'Sure, I understand Hal.'

'I wonder if you do, Ben. How would you feel if this was your father?'

'Pretty much the same, I reckon.'

The departure lounge was filling rapidly with a party of over-excited schoolchildren who crowded the window like a flock of starlings while their guardians looked on anxiously.

'I still think you're wrong, Hal, but I'll make some inquiries if it would help.'

'Yes, it would. Thank you, Ben.'

'Can you give me any dates?' Ben took out a small notebook and a gold plated pen. 'My parents were on Flight 149 on the 17th of April 1983. Vanni died about two years later.'

Ben scribbled the details. 'I'll ask around, but I'll need to OK this with Sir Edward. Anything else?'

'There is one thing,' Hal said. 'Do you think you can forget the name duCann, if only for a while?'

Ben looked doubtful. 'I can't withhold information, Hal.'

'No, I suppose not.'

'Why do you ask?'

'It's just that I know my way around the antiques trade, talk the same language. I might possibly get a bit more out of him than others.'

'Twenty-four hours any good to you?'

'Twenty-four hours will do nicely, Ben.'

A voice over the tannoy, first in Italian and then in English, called for passengers to board the Heathrow flight.

'Be careful,' Ben warned.

'I will,' Hal promised. '*Arrivederci*, Ben.'

Ben grinned, 'Toodle-oo, old chap.'

—∿∿—

CHAPTER 24

—◦◦◦—

In an Exeter equally bathed in afternoon sunlight (if not as hot and humid as Milan) Jane Fulford sat and waited with commendable patience. Her surroundings were far removed from her comfortable home: a room furnished in shades of grey, the floor covering, the paintwork and melamine surfaces, all grey. Even Alec McMasters, a senior consultant at the Royal Devon and Exeter Hospital, whom she had once known as a red-headed and ambitious young man, had also turned grey. He was past retirement age but sorely needed by a hard-pressed National Health Service.

Jane watched as he glanced through the notes in the file on his desk, turning the pages quickly, the results of the latest series of tests. But because she had known this large, gentle man for so many years, she guessed – correctly – that what he sought was not on the printed page, but the words needed to express his – possibly final – prognosis. Was she frightened? No, not really; over the past months she had learned to accept the inevitable. He closed the file, rested his large hands flat on the cover as though to keep it closed, and raised his head. In his pale blue eyes she saw a deep sadness.

'How are you feeling now, Jane?' His voice still carried faint traces of a soft, west coast brogue, though not as pronounced as his father's had been.

'Tired,' she said.

'That'll be the tablets. You are taking them, I hope?'

'Of course.'

'You can increase the dose when you feel the need. But when you do, promise me you will hand your car keys over to David. Strictly speaking, you should not be driving now.'

'You're not going to scold me, are you, Alec?'

'Never,' he smiled. 'I take it you have told David?'

'Well, I er...'

'Jane, you *must*.' He looked pained. 'And you'll need someone with you. You cannot be alone.'

'I'll arrange for someone, nearer the time.'

He held her gaze for a moment, then lowered his eyes.

'How much time do I have, Alec?'

'I can't tell, Jane,' he said helplessly. 'All I can say is that you are no longer in remission.'

'The little cells are multiplying, is that it?'

'Exactly so. Will you not consider chemotherapy?'

She'd had a dear friend who had accepted this form of treatment, with the subsequent hair loss and nausea. That was not for her. 'Would it cure me, Alec?'

'No.'

'Then I would rather bow out with dignity.'

'That is something you have always had, Jane.'

She smiled. 'You're an old flatterer.'

'You know that's not true.'

'Yes, I do, Alec, forgive me. So what is it you are saying – six months? One month? Less?'

'Less.' The word was barely audible.

—◊◊◊—

He walked with her to the door of his consulting room, watching her until she had merged with the crowd in the main corridor. He had known and admired her for a very long time; had known, also, that her late husband, a man of remarkable physique before his final decline, had had such a low sperm count that it was highly unlikely he could have produced a son and heir. But then, as his father had so often said to him, *'Medicine is not an exact science.'*

—◊◊◊—

Leaving the city behind her, Jane drove carefully – much to the chagrin of other road users – her little Morris incapable of speed. As always, she avoided the dual carriageway and took the old road through Tedburn St Mary and Cheriton Bishop until, at the summit of a long hill, suddenly and without any warning she felt overwhelmingly tired. She pulled into a lay-by, lowered the car window, rested her head on the door pillar and looked out over the Devon hills folding one into another down towards Drewsteignton and the Teign valley. She breathed deeply. She had been thinking of Alec, such a kind man and so like his father Dr Douglas McMasters, who had examined her in her bedroom at Cranmere on a summer's morning in 1942. Then, the pronouncement had been of life, not death.

'I'm pleased to tell ye, Jane, that ye're about three months pregnant.'

'But that can't be right, Doctor, my husband came home only two months ago.'

'Aye, well, ye would know best. Medicine is not an exact science, ye ken?'

Yes, Doctor, she thought, I ken.

It was only three days since Roger had returned to his unit after eight weeks' leave in a glorious Devon summer. And during those weeks she had lavished all her care and attention on her husband. She had, initially, scrubbed him clean, shampooed his wiry hair, fed him ample portions of Mrs Kerslake's rabbit pie, and had loved him like never before; and watched the tension drain out of him while his weight increased. As did hers, but not noticeably so, not yet. And no matter how much she had wanted to tell Roger of her condition, she held back. Better to delay a little longer, she thought; the deception starts right here. Perhaps when he came home on leave in a few weeks' time. But he did not return.

He telephoned late one night. 'I'm off on my travels again, Jane.'

All right, she had been expecting this, but not quite so soon. 'When?' she asked anxiously.

'Well that's the trouble. Tomorrow night.'

'You mean you won't be coming home again?'

'No, not for a while. Bit of a facer, isn't it? Mind you, you've only yourself to blame; the MO took one look at me and pronounced me fighting fit. In fact he asked me could he send a few more patients down to Cranmere to convalesce?'

She knew he was trying to make light of it in his own way, in the fragile humour of wartime.

'But Roger, I had hoped…'

'Yes, so had I,' he interrupted her. 'I really am very sorry, it's a bit of a rush job. And there was something I wanted to say to you.'

'What was that?'

'Just that, well, the past few weeks with you have been so bloody wonderful. I know I'm not too good at this sort of thing, but I do admire the way you have kept Cranmere up and running despite everything, hoards of children, bombs, your little mare and Lord alone knows what else. I think what I'm trying to say is I'm proud of you, Jane.' He gave a

short laugh to hide his embarrassment. 'Proud of meself, too, for pickin'
the right gel.'

'Oh Roger,' she said helplessly. She was determined not to weep.

'Yes, I know, old gel.' Usually this would have been accompanied by
an arm around her shoulders and a squeeze. Now, she had to be content
with his conciliatory tone of voice.

'There's something I want to tell you, Roger.'

'Yes?'

The operator's voice cut in, thin and reedy, 'Your time is up, caller.'
She was about to pull the plug. 'For goodness sake,' Roger said, 'couldn't
you allow us another couple of minutes?'

'No, sorree, caller.'

'Roger, are you still there?' Jane called.

'Yes, I'm still here.'

'Take good care of yourself.'

'Yes, you too.'

'And always remember I love you,' she almost shouted. But the line
had gone dead.

Jane clutched the silent receiver to her, said, 'Fuck this bloody war,'
and dissolved into tears. She could have – would have – told him if that
operator had not been such an officious bitch. She could have spared them
another few minutes, surely. Now, she would have to send her most intimate
messages through Edward. She would write, she decided, in the hope that
they would be sent on, long and beautiful letters for Roger to carry in his
breast pocket until he returned to her. That he would return she never
doubted for one moment; he had self-confidence enough for a regiment
and had been told he was fighting fit. What a terrible term. There would
be no stopping Roger, not now. During his short leave he had brought
Cramnere back to life once more. On his first day – after the scrubbing –
he had hugged an astonished Mrs Kerslake and kissed her on both cheeks,
waltzed Millie around the kitchen and promised Jane, 'Your turn next.'
And during his second week he had called her out into the yard to meet
Flo, a little Welsh Cob harnessed into a highly polished trap.

'She's yours if you want her,' he said, looking at her anxiously. 'Wasn't
sure if you would, after Rosie, but she'd be handy around the estate.
That Humber's a heavy brute for you to handle and she drinks petrol.
What do you think?'

What did she think? She thought it was quite the nicest gift she'd ever been given; and more than that, far more, Roger's thoughtfulness, a quality seldom seen, was what decided her. She had thought, until now, that Rosie could never be replaced. And she was right. But one look at Flo's docile little face was enough. It was the first time she had been anywhere near a horse since the night Rosie died. Tentatively, she stroked Flo's forehead and ears, felt her warm silken muzzle, talked to her and made friends with a simple little soul who was quite content to pull a light trap rather than jump five-bar gates. And yes, she was going to be all right. And so was Flo.

Flo was exactly what she needed to partly fill the void left by Rosie, and as for being handy around the estate she was indispensable. Over the few precious weeks they had together, she and her husband travelled the length and breadth of the Cranmere land, visited every farm except Higher Weeke which was off-limits. They went at walking pace – 'Walk on, Flo' – sitting close, Roger's arm around her, halting to rest Flo and enjoy a leisurely picnic, or to make love in the heather. There were days when the war seemed a distant memory until an aircraft passed overhead when they would ask each other, 'Is it one of ours?'

But now, after that brief telephone conversation, Roger was gone again. Jane was not to know until much later that he had not been sent back into occupied France where he was very high on the Gestapo wanted list, but to Eastern Europe to help the partisans raise mayhem in Yugoslavia. Neither did she know that it would be three years before she saw her husband again.

———

'Edward, this is Jane.'

'Jane, this is Edward, and before you ask I heard from your husband only yesterday, and he is fit and well. How about you?'

'Oh, I'm in rude health, thank you. Which is why I called; I want you to pass on a message.'

'What, that you're in rude health?'

'No,' she laughed. 'Tell him that I am with child.'

'With what?' The line was bad.

'Pregnant.'

'Oh, my dear, how wonderful. Congratulations. That'll buck him up no end.'

'Does he need bucking up?'

'Indeed, no.'

'Are my letters getting through?' She had sent three since Roger left and still no reply. 'It takes time, Jane but he will get them, I promise you. Keep them coming.'

'I will.'

'When's it due?'

'When is what due?'

'The baby,' Edward laughed.

'Not until the new year. February or March, so I'm told.'

'What are you hoping for, boy or girl?'

'I really don't mind.'

'Your husband will.'

'Yes, I'm sure.'

—⁓—

An Indian summer continued through September and into the following month, the children sunburned brown as berries. It seemed, to Jane, that while Lieutenant Dando and his staff fought a grim battle with U-boats in the North Atlantic, on the civilian side of the house there was a marked improvement in morale. The immediate threat of invasion had passed and there was little aerial activity at night, and when there was it was usually the RAF going in the opposite direction.

And there was a subtle change in her perceived status. She was now the *pregnant* Mistress of Cranmere who carried the future within her, and was treated with a touching deference by all. But why was it, she questioned, that everyone – except Millie – assumed that the child would be male, and the new Master? Had the choice been hers, twin daughters would have been more than welcome. She found a quiet contentment in her early pregnancy, now that it was out in the open, watched over with care by Mrs Kerslake who kept a close eye on her diet and by Millie who was a mine of earthy information.

Her mother promised (threatened) that she would visit if she could scrounge a drop of petrol. Jane was sorry (she said) but she could not return the compliment as the Humber was laid up and she doubted Flo would make the distance. The children, naturally, were fascinated.

The highlight of the autumn came on 4th November when – in

peacetime – the children would be building a bonfire. Instead they all went out onto the terrace to listen to the sound of church bells down in the village. It was not a warning of invasion, but in celebration of a British victory at a place called El Alamein. On the wireless Mr Churchill told them that *'This is not the end. It is not even the beginning of the end. But it is, perhaps, the end of the beginning,'* which made Christmas 1942 a far more joyful time than the previous year. *'Peace on Earth'* was wholeheartedly wished for, although where *'Goodwill to all men'* had gone was anybody's guess. It was on Christmas Eve that one of the little girls asked her shyly, 'Jane, are you great with child?'

'Yes, Susan,' she laughed, 'I am *enormous* with child.'

But right at the tail end of the year, on 30th December, as though to warn them that the end was not yet in sight, the *Luftwaffe* mounted a daylight raid on Exeter. Eighteen people were killed and ninety-seven, including an old school friend of Jane's, were injured.

—◦◦◦—

Jane woke to a curious knocking noise, and opened her eyes to see a very young policeman looking at her curiously through the open car window.

'Are you all right, ma'am?'

'Yes, thank you, perfectly all right.' She sat up straight. 'I must have dozed off. What time is it?'

'Just gone six.'

'Good heavens, I must make haste. Tansy will be wondering where I've got to.'

'Have you far to go?'

'No, only two or three miles. Just the other side of Whiddon Down.'

He looked at her little Morris admiringly. 'Nice little car,' he said. 'Have you had her since new?'

'Yes, since she was a pup.'

His smile was indulgent. 'Sure you're all right?'

'Quite sure. Thank you for your concern.'

She set off towards home, travelling at her customary snail's pace. The police car followed at a respectful distance – something she found very off-putting – until she had negotiated the busy junction at Whiddon Down and taken the turning to Chagford and Cranmere.

Arriving home, she was surprised to see David's car in the drive. He came out to meet her.

'Where have you been, Mother?' He looked as concerned as the young policeman.

'Only into Exeter,' she said brightly.

'I could have driven you in, if you'd asked.'

'Well perhaps next time. I'm glad you're here, David, I need to talk to you.'

CHAPTER 25

—◦◦◦—

'I expect you're glad to be home, aren't you, Hal?'

They were sitting in surprisingly comfortable plastic chairs in the beer garden of a small pub near Cricklade. On the far side of a stream that bordered the garden fruit trees were in blossom and a blackbird sang its evening song to its mate – or prospective mate. Hal had read somewhere that in Italy they shot and ate songbirds.

'It's great to be back, Uncle, they don't brew ale like this in Milan, nor New York.' He held up his glass, studying the golden liquid with a practised eye.

True to his word, Sir Edward had been waiting at Heathrow with the firm's Jaguar and driver in the VIP car park. And it had been at his suggestion that they turned off the main road for a quiet pint which meant, also, a quiet debriefing.

'Unless you would rather wait until tomorrow, Hal? You must be tired.'

Yes, he was tired, hadn't had a night's sleep since leaving, longed for his comfortable bed and Bella – in or out of her black silk *camicia da notte*. But like one of Captain Edward Channon's wartime agents returning from the field, he would be required to answer a few searching questions, after which the intelligence gleaned would be shuffled into some sort of order. And he would sooner get it out of the way tonight while it was fresh in his mind, not, he suspected, that there would be a great deal he could tell Sir Edward that was not already known to him. And he was right.

Sir Edward waited until they were both settled. 'I have spoken to Mike Monahan in New York, and Ben Pavoni in Milan,' he said. 'And I think I have the picture, Hal, but what I am not quite clear on is why you suddenly took off for Milan. It all seemed quite straightforward until then.'

'Mmm,' Hal nodded. 'Sorry if I made a dog's breakfast of it.'

'I didn't say that.'

'No, I know you didn't. Thank you,' Hal smiled, perhaps a little sheepishly. 'Well let's start right from the beginning in New York. The cabinet at present in Agnolli's possession is, without any doubt, the pair to the Cranmere cabinet. I am sure Carrington already knows this, and has done since he first set eyes on it. But he's waiting to see which way the cat jumps before showing his hand. I would think he's made himself fairly unpopular by getting in touch with you, but as I see it he had very little choice.'

Sir Edward nodded his agreement.

'Although I never met Agnolli, I would imagine he suspects the cabinet he inherited from his father might be stolen property. Hence all the fuss.'

'Not necessarily stolen, Hal.'

'No,' Hal conceded. 'Well let's say from a dubious source. In the same evening I met Mr Moreno, Agnolli's lawyer. He came to visit me at my hotel.'

'Yes, so Mike Monahan told me.'

'How did he know? He'd already left by the time Moreno turned up.'

'I think he charmed the receptionist.'

'That wouldn't surprise me,' Hal smiled. 'But Moreno was a shifty little devil. He spent a long time telling me how Agnolli was as straight as a die and how his father wasn't nearly as dishonest as some people seemed to think. Then he asked me were the two cabinets a match.'

'Did you tell him, Hal?'

'No, I said I had yet to see the cabinet at Cranmere.'

'Do you think he believed you?'

'I doubt it, but short of calling me a bloody liar there wasn't much he could say. So he tried to bribe me, offered £3000 if I would report that the cabinets were not a pair.'

'Did he, now?' Sir Edward's bushy eyebrows rose a fraction. 'What did you say to that?'

'I said I'd have to think about it.'

'And have you?'

'Oh yes. Three thousand's a lot on money, especially when at first it was in dollars. He converted it quickly when he thought I might accept.' Hal thought it prudent not to mention that for a while he had considered going along with Moreno's little scheme. 'But surely,' he said, 'to offer me anything is an admission of guilt, or knowledge at the very least?'

'But deniable,' Sir Edward said dryly.

'Yes, I've no doubt, but then he went on to say that if his client were in any way involved or embarrassed, he would put a full-scale investigation under way, and he mentioned Vanni Spargo. And that was where I felt a bit unsure of myself. I don't *think* he knows about Vanni's association with my father – probably not, otherwise he'd have said. But if and when he does, it's fairly obvious where the accusations are going to be directed. That was why I flew to Milan, Uncle. My father was accused once, it's *not* going to happen a second time.'

'No, it is not,' Sir Edward said quietly.

'After all,' Hal was getting into his stride, 'our objective, or at least one of them, is to clear Father's name for good and all. Isn't that what you said?'

'That is precisely what I said, and nothing has changed.'

'And I'm not sure,' Hal continued, 'that Moreno didn't try to threaten me.'

'Threaten you! In what way?'

'Oh, it was a sort of parting shot. When I asked how I would collect my commission if I agreed with his ideas, he said, "We know where you live, Mr Wesson." It sounded a bit sinister at the time, might have meant nothing, of course.' Hal found his voice had trailed away. In the peace of a Gloucestershire garden somehow the statement had lost its menace.

Suddenly they were disturbed as coloured lanterns, strung along the walls and in the trees, lit up and a noisy party of young folk came out into the garden and took over the neighbouring tables. It was somebody's birthday.

'Let's walk.' Sir Edward tilted his head to one side. There was a path running along the bank of the stream to a children's play area with seats for grown-ups. Sir Edward lowered himself into one of these and looked up to the topmost branches of a pear tree to where the blackbird still sang in the failing light. Then he turned to Hal, now sitting opposite, and began. 'From what Mike Monahan was telling me, Moreno is a small fish in a very large pond, and neither he nor Agnolli is in a position to threaten us, rather the reverse. As for their making any inquiries, I think that unlikely, they might well discover something they'd rather not know. So take it from me, Hal, that so-called threat was no more than a piece of theatre.'

'I suppose it could have been,' Hal agreed. Perhaps he'd been overtired or jetlagged at the time.

'Listen, Hal,' Sir Edward sat forward in his seat, 'Since your identification of the cabinet, the position has become really very simple.

Agnolli is in possession of something that does not legally belong to him. As you said, he already *suspects* that this could be the case; but we *know*. And we can prove it. It was removed from Cranmere without the owner's knowledge or consent and no matter how it came into Agnolli's possession, under international law it is ours and we want it back. I really don't see why we should be expected to pay for it, do you?'

'No,' Hal,' said. 'Put like that, as you say, it seems very simple.'

'So, far from making a dog's breakfast of it, Hal, I think you have done rather well. We now know a great deal more and you told them nothing.'

'Thank you,' Hal said, relieved.

'The only danger is that in order to preserve his reputation Agnolli might consider cutting his losses and destroying the evidence.'

'He wouldn't do that, surely!'

'It has been known and has been done. Bearing in mind the huge sums of money the Americans pay out on their election campaigns, two million dollars might not seem too high a price.'

'But that would be nothing short of...'

'Criminal? Yes, it would, but we have a safeguard in Mike Monahan or, more accurately, his father's exhaustive notes on the late Luigi Agnolli. In young Mike's words, "It's a dossier thicker than a family Bible, chapter and verse." Now that could come in handy.' Sir Edward's face was faintly outlined by a green-tinted lantern which hung from the tree above him, and for a moment, in that light, Hal saw an expression far more menacing that anything Moreno had to offer. 'When the time is right,' Sir Edward said carefully, 'we will let Agnolli know that should he not come around to our way of thinking, or if he should be rash enough to direct any wild accusations against Charles Wesson or Giovanni Spargo, then we shall have no option but to instruct one of our writers to put together a biography, probably in serial form in the New York Sunday papers, on the life and times of Luigi Agnolli.'

'But didn't Mike say nothing was ever proven?'

'There would be no need. It would be mostly innuendo or alleged, but by the time our people had finished with him, Agnolli Junior could forget any ambitions he might have had about becoming a US senator – in fact he'd be damned lucky if he didn't have his US citizenship revoked.'

'Now that really *is* criminal!' Hal said admiringly.

'Expedient is a word I would prefer,' Sir Edward smiled in the dark. 'Let's hope it won't come to that. Feel better now, Hal?'

'Mmm, sort of.'

Perhaps it was because his Uncle Ted had always been around, a direct link with his childhood, that Hal found such reassurance in his bulky presence; or because he knew that beneath the jovial exterior there lived a good man with a core of high-tensile steel which showed itself rarely, but was there for his family and friends. What was it that bloody fool Carrington had said of him –'*A wily old bird but a bit over the hill*'? Well yes, a wily old bird certainly, but also a tough old bird who could – and would – destroy Agnolli and Carrington, too, if he thought it expedient. And in the past twenty minutes, he had put the New York scene into perspective. As he now did with Milan.

'I understand that since her father's death young Gina has been running the family business,' he said. 'Hard to imagine that; she was such a pretty child scampering around the place.'

'She's a big girl now, taller than me.'

'And she, or her parents, wrote to your father when they thought they had recognised one of the Cranmere cabinets?'

'Yes, that's what they said.'

'You must believe me, Hal, when I tell you I knew nothing about such a letter.'

'Neither did I.' They both remained silent for a moment, remembering a very private man.

Sir Edward continued, 'As I see it, your concern is that with a possible Mafia interest, however tenuous, you think your father might have been deliberately prevented from identifying the missing Cranmere cabinet. Is that right?'

'Well, taking Vanni Spargo's sudden death into account, yes, that's right. I've been thinking of nothing else since I spoke to Gina and Elsie. I am *trying* to be objective. One coincidence I could possibly accept, but not two, especially when you look at the timing of the separate accidents. Can you blame me? I mean, do you think I am being unreasonable?'

'No, I don't, Hal. I hear what you are saying.'

'Yes, but what do you *think*?'

Sir Edward thought. 'Hal, I think I agree with Ben Pavoni. I doubt the amount of money involved would have justified such drastic action unless, of course, there was someone else on that aircraft who was of interest to the Mafia. But I agree with you that it needs looking into, so I have given Ben a free hand to investigate both accidents. And he is very thorough.'

'Thank you, I liked Ben.'

'He's one of our best. Got himself a First in law at Cambridge and he's been with us ever since.

'He has a lot of contacts in Milan including, he was telling me, a woman who at one time was close to Brocatti. He will be talking to her in the next day or two. If there's anything there, Ben will ferret it out, after which we may be able to make a few inquiries of our own.'

So, Hal thought, Ben was as good as his word. He had allowed him his twenty-four hours.

———*𝒏𝒏𝒏*———

Hal had been home for half an hour before he could slip away into his little office beside the workshop, and then only because Bella was preparing a sumptuous, welcome home, meal. Her present, not to be opened until they went up to bed, lay in its expensive wrapping on the dresser. He had forbidden her to peek – knowing full well that she would.

In the *Antiques Yearbook* under a section devoted entirely to Brighton he found what he was looking for. A half-page advertisement, complete with a line drawing of an elegant Regency shopfront, announced to the world that William duCann sold English and Continental furniture and clocks, and that he was a member of the British Antique Dealers' Association and the Guild of Master Craftsmen. A little further down the page, in a more modest entry, was a name known to him. He smiled as he dialled the number.

'Solly?'

'Who want's to know?' A voice asked tetchily.

'Hal Wesson.'

'Hal Wesson! Haven't seen you around for a while. How are you keeping, my boy?'

'I'm well, thank you, Solly. And you?'

'Not so bad. Now why are you disturbing an old man in the middle of *Eastenders*?'

'Sorry about that, Solly. I need some information.'

'Oh yes?'

'Wiliam duCann. Is he all right?'

'How would I know?'

'Well, I thought you might.' There was a brotherhood within the antiques trade. Hal was admitted by association.

'Listen, Hal. If you are asking can you do business with Billy, then yes, he's a good Jewish boy.'

'Thank you, Solly,' Hal said, thinking he wasn't going to get much more out of the old fellow. But he was wrong; Solly gave him gold.

'You're welcome. Just don't get smart with him.'

'Why?'

'Couple of years back a pair of young schmucks tried to mug Billy in a back street. He put one of them in intensive care, the other ran off empty-handed. Not bad for an old man with one arm.'

'I'll remember to be polite.'

'Sure. Be lucky, Hal.'

'You too, Solly.'

Hal sat back in his chair, that name running rapidly through his mind. Billy with one arm? Perhaps not William duCann, nor Billy duCann, but Billy Cann. He felt the hairs rise on the back of his neck. Billy Cann the frightened boy with the malformed arm who had slept in Jane's bed at Cranmere during the war? The boy who had helped his Uncle Charles gather up pieces of a damaged cabinet, and then later became Brocatti's agent? Could they possibly be one and the same, or was this yet another scarcely believable coincidence?

'Billy Cann,' Hal said softly, 'It is high time we met.'

———

It was a hopeful Hal who sat on the end of the bed waiting for his wife to emerge from the bathroom in her silk *camicia da notte*. And like most husbands and lovers, he hoped and prayed that he'd bought the right size, because there was no way he could take it back to change it, not in Milan, not in that no-man's-land of a lingerie department – *Dipartmento di Biancheria Intima*, it sounded so much better in Italian – that he would not have dared to enter without Ben at his side.

'Does it fit?' he called out.

'Yes, just right,' came the muffled reply.

'Do you like it?'

'It's lovely.'

'Come on out, then.'

'I don't want to,' Bella said in a small voice.

'Why ever not?'

'I'm shy.'

Hal laughed, very softly. Bella was a fair-haired, peaches-and-cream-complexioned English girl and naturally shy. Equally natural was a sexuality that needed no embellishment. He could only guess at how she would look in her *molto provocante* nightdress.

'How about if I turn the lights down?'

'Yes, all right.'

Hal went around the room turning out lights until only a subdued glow from the bedside light remained, then resumed his seat. 'Ready,' he called.

The door catch rattled and Bella stepped out, backlit by the bathroom light. For a moment Hal said nothing, incapable of speech.

'Well, what do you think?' Bella stood barefoot, her arms to her sides like a schoolgirl. 'It's beautiful,' Hal said huskily, *'molto provocante,'* and reaching out he drew her down onto his lap and held her. She wriggled, 'It makes me feel... slinky.'

'Funny that, it has the same effect on me.'

'You tried it on, then?

'Actually, no.'

She snuggled into him.' It must have cost the earth, Hal. Where did you find it?'

'In the best shop in the Piazza del Duomo, Milan.'

'Milan? I thought you were going to New York.'

'I was, I did, then I went on to Milan.'

'Why?'

He wanted to say, 'To buy you a pretty nightdress,' but wisely held himself in check; any flippancy might have spoiled a beautiful moment. 'There was a man I needed to see,' he said, 'Giovanni Spargo, used to work for my father. Remember him?'

'Not very well.' Bella was three years younger than her husband. 'Why did you need to see him?'

'Because he was the man who helped put the first of the Cranmere cabinets together; and then the second one.'

He felt her tense. Involuntarily perhaps, but it was there without question, the female of the species' anxiety for her mate. And he knew what to expect.

'Hal, you're not getting into anything like that last time, are you?'

'Absolutely not.'

'You promise me?'

'I promise you.' He began to caress her flank.

'Don't you think you should tell me about it?'

'Yes, I will… later.'

'Oh, all right.'

—◊◊◊—

Later, the black silk nightdress discarded, Hal found himself recounting his traveller's tale once again, omitting almost nothing, including his hopes and fears.

Bella did not interrupt, but when he had come to the end she propped herself on one elbow and looked down on him, one small hand on his bare chest. 'Hal,' she said tenderly, 'your father was a dear man, but he died. I thought you had come to terms with that long ago.'

'Yes, I had, but this seems to have stirred it all up somehow. I have to know the truth.'

'Well… if you should find that there was something suspicious about his death, what will you do?'

For a moment Hal sought the answer to a question he had not faced until now, and he answered it honestly, 'I really don't know.'

—◊◊◊—

And later still, as sleep began to envelope him, Hal's thoughts were of the following day. With a little luck, by this time tomorrow he would have made his own inquiries of Willam duCann, or Billy Cann. And if his luck held, would have discovered the truths he sought, and maybe decided what was to be done.

By this time tomorrow...

—◊◊◊—

186

CHAPTER 26

In her bedroom in the Dower House, bathed in moonlight, Jane reclined against the soft pillows and thought of tomorrow. But unlike Hal she remained wide awake and with little prospect of sleep, tired though she was. Not just tired but exhausted, emotionally drained after her long conversation with David. It had been all that she had feared, and made worse by a strong feeling of guilt for her failure to tell him the whole truth – until this evening. Was it a sin, she questioned, to shield her most precious loved one from distress, as she had done on another matter over the years? If so, then she had sinned. David had known something of her condition because she had told him, telling him also that with the guidance of Alec McMasters – provided she took her medication and called in to see him regularly – then all was under control. Which it was until this afternoon. But no: that was not quite true. She had suspected over the past two weeks that the remission she had been granted might have been withdrawn – her breathing at times more difficult, and this constant lassitude. But to hear it put into words, no matter how kindly, was like a sentence – which is exactly what it was. She had been compelled to tell David, and if she now felt weighed down by wretched remorse she had no one but herself to blame. She had been wrong, but for the right reasons. Small comfort for David. And he, poor boy, had tried to share the blame for not paying closer attention to his mother over the past few weeks.

After his initial distress, David had taken charge. Like his father he could be firm, not unkind or unthinking like Roger, but very sure of what was required of him. Together they had phoned Anne Perret, one of Betty's many daughters, now a highly qualified nurse. Luckily, she was free and could move in early next week. So, Jane thought, her freedom was at an end, she was grounded. But David, knowing how she valued her independence, had made a thoughtful gesture in allowing her to keep her car keys, at the same time extracting a promise that she would not go out unaccompanied. The difference was subtle, but it meant a lot to her and her thoughts remained with David.

His very first night had been blessed with bright moonlight such as this. He lay beside her in his little crib while Millie slept in the neighbouring bed. Dear, dependable Millie, whose hand she had gripped throughout the long afternoon as she yelled and cursed and railed against her Maker, and fought to bring her child into the world.

'Millie, I've no more strength left in me.'

'You're nearly there, Jane.' Millie pressed a damp flannel to her brow. 'Next time, you'll see.'

'Millie!!'

'Go on, Jane, pu-u-u-sh.'

'Wha-a-a-a-a!'

Through the pain and confusion she heard another sound, her child's tiny voice for the first time, and Millie calling 'Tis all over, Jane. You've got a beautiful little boy.'

Later, when the circus had left – doctor, midwife and a very young surgeon lieutenant – she nursed her infant son and looked down in wonder at the tiny rosebud mouth encircling her nipple, and the perfectly formed hands with their long, musician's fingers. And she thanked God – if He was still listening to her after this afternoon – that she had always been attracted to fair-haired men.

In the days that followed, despite her protests, she was confined to her room (if not her bed) and plied with all sorts of nourishing soups and broths, their recipes handed down from mother to daughter since – the seventeenth century? Most were beef-based, some delicious, others tipped discreetly down the lavatory. Millie remained in close attendance.

'He's the image of his dad,' she said more than once.

Anyone but Millie and Jane would have been immediately on her guard, bearing in mind the old wives' tail about a newborn baby bearing a close resemblance to its father. And she had been there at the birth. But there was no malice in Millie, none at all, and even if little David's features had momentarily resembled his natural father, and even if Millie nursed any suspicions about her relationship with Charles Wesson (which was likely) she never once so much as dropped a hint. In fact, Jane thought, she might have approved.

On the fourth day she'd had quite enough of being treated like a semi-invalid, whatever nurse Millie had to say. As it turned out it was Millie who provided the catalyst, coming into the room with a big smile,

'Guess what, Jane?'

'What?' She had David over one shoulder, bringing up wind after his feed.

'The Yanks are coming.'

'I've heard that one before,' Jane said. 'When?'

'This afternoon, Lieutenant Dando said.'

'In that case I am coming down.'

Millie looked uncertain. 'Bit early, isn't it?'

'Nonsense, I'm as fit as a flea.' Jane rocked the infant gently, patting his back with one hand.

'Well,' Millie frowned…'Not until after lunch. I'll get the fire built up. Can't have Master David coming down into a cold room.'

'Oh all right,' Jane conceded. 'I'll just lounge around and listen to Glen Miller on the wireless.' It was not until Millie had left that she realised just what had been said: 'Master David.' That's what this tiny scrap was, Master David, heir to the Cranmere Estate.

'What do you think of that, little one?'

David burped and dribbled on her shoulder

—◦◦◦—

The Yanks arrived at two o'clock not – Jane insisted – 1400 hours or so many bells, but two in the afternoon; and with their arrival life at Cranmere was to undergo another change. They came first in an open vehicle which she later learned was called a Jeep and usually driven at breakneck speed, and then a covered troop carrier. It was as they approached up the long drive that she realised that she had never, ever met an American, nor yet a Yank. She had seen them in numerous films in the tin-roofed cinema down in the village, and had always supposed that they were much the same as us. They were not. In the weeks that followed she discovered an open, almost childlike frankness about them that set them apart from their British counterparts. And there were differences in posture, and the way they talked and walked or marched – usually at the double, clad in battledress (combat fatigues) carrying their rifles (carbines) – and the sound of their rubber-soled boots on a hard surface. They were friendly and uninhibited and at the drop of a hat would produce photographs of their 'folks back home'. The children, many of whom could barely recall chocolate, and certainly not candy or gum, adored them from the start. And so did Millie.

It was Millie who ushered Captain Lester J. Vanstone and Lieutenant (Lootenant) Donovan O'Neill into the estate office and remained because, she insisted, no young mother could be unchaperoned. They were very smart and when they each gave a snappy, John-Wayne-style salute, Millie clasped her hands together in near ecstasy. The captain was tall and slim and darkly handsome, his companion shorter but more heavily built and with the sandy hair and pale green eyes of his forebears. They were the advance party, Captain Vanstone explained. He and his men would mark out the site; engineers would be following.

'This is where we intend to pitch camp.' He took a map from his briefcase and placed it before her on the desk. 'If that's OK, ma'am.'

Jane took one look and said, 'There's a larger one on the wall behind you.'

He turned and walked across the room to where a yellowing map of the Cranmere Estate had hung since Queen Victoria was a child, peered at it closely and said, 'Abbot's Meadow. Is that right?'

'That's right.'

'Why is it so called?'

'I really don't know, I imagine abbots used to stroll around there at one time, so you had better tell your men to watch their language.'

'I can't guarantee that.' He had a nice smile, lots of even white teeth. 'But look, we'll need to put in a road branching off your drive, about here.' He indicated the place on the wall map 'If that's OK by you, ma'am?'

'Do as you must, captain, there is no need to ask my permission.'

'Sure, but, y' know.'

'Yes, I do know,' Jane smiled up at him. 'But thank you for asking, it was kind of you.' The captain looked a little embarrassed.

'You haven't chosen the most sheltered of places.' Jane recalled past winters when Abbot's Meadow had been the first to catch a hard frost.

'Reckon we can take care of ourselves, ma'am. We're US Fourth Cavalry.' This last was said with an almost discernible stiffening of the back, squaring of the shoulders.

Jane knew better than to inquire after their horses. She asked, 'How many will you be?'

'About one fifty, maybe two hundred when we're up to full strength.'

David protested in his crib beside Jane's chair.

'Well, what have we here?' Lieutenant O'Neill spoke for the first time.

'This is David, my son,' Jane said with as much pride as if he had been a Trooper in the US Fourth Cavalry.

'How old is he, ma'am?'

'Four days.'

Both men dug deep into their pockets and produced a silver coin which they placed solemnly on the blanket out of David's reach. They were the first dollars Jane and Millie had seen.

———∞∞———

The engineers came at first light in a convoy of heavy trucks and bulldozers. Without ceremony, a section of centuries-old stone wall was scooped up and laid to one side, then a carpet of daffodils and two sturdy oaks before the marauders were lost from sight in the spinney that led to Abbot's Meadow some half a mile distant. Jane watched sadly from her window, thankful for Captain Vanstone's words, 'We'll preserve as many trees as possible, ma'am, we need 'em for air cover.'

The drone of machinery went on for three weeks as tons of hard core and concrete were laid and the new road surfaced with asphalt. When, at last, the engineers had gone, they left behind them an army camp without stables but complete with rows of Nissen huts, neatly spaced and painted in camouflage, a flagpole and a barbed wire perimeter fence. And silence, as the Cranmere valley held its breath and awaited the new arrivals – any day now.

———∞∞———

'Jane, this is Edward.'

'Edward, this is Jane. Does my husband know he is a father yet?'

'He does and he is delighted. He says to be sure to put his name down for his old school. And he would have preferred Rupert, but David will do.'

She felt a bit disappointed at this response. Rupert, indeed! No child of hers was going to be named after a teddy bear. 'Is that all he had to say?'

'I think he said, "Well done".'

'Are my letters getting through?'

'He has them all, Jane, and there's one here from him to you.'

'Only one?'

Edward laughed, 'He is quite busy.'

'So are we.'

'Yes, I'm sure. How are your guests settling in?'

'Guests?'

'Come on, Jane.'

'Oh them! We don't see much of them. They seem to spend most of their time up on the moor.'

———

Two weeks had passed since the US Cavalry had taken up residence, and apart from a distant bugle sounding 'Reveille' or a plaintive 'Last Post' at the beginning and end of each day, very little had been seen of them, hidden as they were behind their screen of carefully preserved trees. But they had been observed – of course they had – through pairs of antique binoculars and the odd telescope, as they scampered up the rocky slopes behind their camp, and the sound of small-arms fire had been heard and duly reported around the farms and cottages in the Cranmere valley. But thus far – apart from a courtesy visit when Captain Vanstone had introduced his commanding officer, Major Stubbs – contact had yet to be made between the cavalry and the natives. There were those amongst the younger, female inhabitants of the valley – Wrens, Land Girls and Millie – who found the waiting almost unbearable. All were agreed, however, that when they did show themselves the visitors should be made to feel welcome. The Yanks had brought with them – like a breath of fresh air after over three years of the monotony of wartime life – hope.

Apart from the victory at El Alamein and the more recent news that the Germans had been booted out of North Africa, there had been little to raise the spirits in a remote valley on the eastern slopes of Dartmoor. On the wireless, Mr Churchill's cautious assurances that things were beginning to go our way were more than gratefully received. But now something was happening, and was seen to be happening. Morale in the Cranmere valley soared, and soared higher still when on the Saturday, after two gruelling weeks of training in all weathers up on Dartmoor, the US Cavalry were coming out to play.

Jane was first made aware of this by Millie asking could she have the evening off to go down to the village. There was a dance at the Jubilee Hall.

'Have you got transport?' Jane asked.

'Oh yes,' Millie replied, perhaps a little too casually. 'There's a truck laid on for anyone who wants to go.'

'An *American* truck?' Jane sounded like Lady Bracknell.

'Yes.'

'Just *you* and a truck full of *cavalry*?' Even more like Lady Bracknell.

'No,' Millie laughed happily. 'What do you take me for? There's a whole crowd of us going.'

Suckling her newborn child, Jane moved him from one breast to the other, looked up and smiled, 'Sorry, Millie. Have a good time.'

'I will.'

'And take care.'

'Don't you worry 'bout me.'

Despite her assurances, Jane was anxious for Millie and thought about her a lot during the long evening. She was not Millie's mother, she told herself, but she was her friend; and was relieved when an unscathed Millie returned with a highly detailed account of her evening, and how the US Cavalry were, without doubt, the best dancers she had ever met. Stories were rife about how, upcountry, there had been pitched battles between American servicemen and our own, sparked off, no doubt, by jealousy over local girls. 'Over sexed, over paid and over 'ere' was often quoted. Also, 'Wham! Bam! Thank you, Ma'am.'

'They're not a bit like that, Millie protested.

'They are US Cavalry and highly disciplined.' So, Jane thought, some of their pride had rubbed off on Millie in one way or another.'

'And anyway,' Millie said, 'the Snowdrops keep them in order.'

'Snowdrops?'

'Yes, their police. They wear white hats.'

In an odd sort of way Jane found that encouraging. In the many Westerns she and Millie had watched at the local cinema it was the 'good guys' who wore white hats. After their introduction on the Saturday night, it was not very long before 182 cavalrymen had been assimilated into the extended Cranmere family. During their off-duty hours they were to be seen teaching the children how to play baseball, or driving Jeep-loads of them – shrieking with delight – around the Cranmere lanes. But the high point of the summer came on 4th July when all were invited to a surprise party at the US camp, where many of the children tasted ice cream and Coca Cola for the very first time. For adults there was a dance laid on in the evening with a genuine American swing band. Even Lieutenant Dando managed to overcome his abhorrence at being addressed as *Lootenant* and showed the Yanks a thing or two when it came to Scottish dancing. But because she was the Lady of Cranmere and a nursing mother, and therefore expected to conduct herself with decorum, apart from a few stately waltzes with the officers – Captain Vanstone, as she had suspected, was a superb dancer – Jane was not able to join the madding crowd. But she looked on with a mixture of amazement and envy at Millie's expert gymnastics in something new – the Jitterbug.

—⁓⁓—

'*Pennsylvania Six Five, Oh, Oh, Oh,*' Millie sang and waggled her hips as she guided the big hoover around the landings, until asked could she please change the tune? 'All right,' she grinned, '*The stars at night are big and bright – deep in the heart of Texas.*'

By the end of September, the Italians had surrendered and Jane, contrary to the advice of some of the older matrons, had weaned little David – no longer little – onto bottles of National Dried Milk. And Millie had fallen deeply in love.

The first sign – apart from the off-key singing – was the constant repetition of a name, usually after one of the Saturday night dances which had by now become a regular fixture. 'Luke said' or 'I said to Luke' or 'Luke and I walked all the way back from the village by moonlight', quite often followed by a soft sigh and a lingering gaze at a blank wall, until Jane could stand it no longer.

'Bring him down to the house, Millie, we would all like to meet this Luke of yours.'

He was tall, a good head and shoulders above Millie, loose-limbed and wiry. His home was in Colorado Springs and he spoke almost lyrically of the Rockies. Luke, Jane decided, was the archetypal cowboy and she feared for Millie; and she was wrong. Luke and Millie became a couple, often to be seen walking hand in hand by the river or later, when the weather began to turn, side by side on the big settle by the kitchen grate – the warmest place in the house during a hard winter. Jane wished them every happiness, but soon Luke would be leaving to go to war, and she feared for them both.

CHAPTER 27

—⚬⚬⚬—

Jane swung her feet off the bed, put them into her slippers, went out into her little kitchen and switched on the electric kettle. She would not sleep, not for a long time yet. And indeed, she thought, if her end was nigh, why waste what little time she had in sleep? She did not turn the lights on, preferring the soft moonlight, but sat by the window looking out onto where a near-perfect disc of yellow daffodils showed clearly out in the pasture – Rosie's resting place. The animals grazing, both sheep and cattle, had never once intruded onto nor trampled the daffodils. She liked to think that this was out of respect for a fellow creature buried there – or for the young soldier killed while defusing a bomb in the summer of 1942 – or for the US Cavalry who had so cheerfully planted the bulbs gathered in the woods around their camp. Over the years the daffodils had multiplied and spread, unlike all too many of the young men – some no more than boys – who had died bravely on Utah beach during the Normandy landings.

The Americans stayed at Cranmere for just over a year, from one spring to the next, during which time they had endeared themselves to most. Even Lieutenant Dando, who had been a bit sniffy at first until his battle in the Atlantic began to show dividends, had learned to love them. How could he not when he and his crew were invited to share all their celebrations – Independence Day, Thanksgiving Day, Christmas and then their final send-off?

For weeks there had been talk of the impending invasion of Fortress Europe – one of the worst-kept military secrets of all time. In Plymouth, harbours were said to be filled with warships and landing craft – waiting. British and American troops were massed in southern England – waiting. Aircraft were fuelled and armed – waiting. It's tomorrow, or the day after, or next week. Tension was almost tangible, not least among the US Cavalry, itching to 'teach Adolf who's boss'.

Rumours began to harden when Captain Vanstone called in to see Jane. She and her people were invited to view a passing-out parade, he said, and a little get-together afterwards.

'And the children?'

'Especially the children,' he smiled. 'And there's something else, Jane.

Would you inspect the troops with me?'

'Inspect them? I've never inspected anything more than children's teeth and ears.'

He laughed, 'That should do it.'

'But why me?'

'Because you're our mascot. Surely you knew?'

'Yes, I think I did.' Jane gave a wry smile. There was a cartoon strip currently popular in the national press in which a tall, leggy blonde, also Jane, appeared daily usually in a state of undress.

'What do I wear?'

Oh, you know best, just a summer dress, I guess.'

'And a hat?'

'A hat would be nice.'

'Well, if you really think so,' she said, still unsure.

'I do. It would mean a lot to the men, Jane.'

———

The following day dawned humid and airless, a Dartmoor day that encouraged lethargy in both humans and animals in the Cranmere valley; except, that is, in the US Cavalry who were drawn up in ranks on the parade ground in the full glare of the afternoon sun, every man ramrod straight. Trying to recall newsreels at the local cinema where she had seen troops being reviewed, Jane prayed that she would be able to carry off her duties with dignity, not trip and fall flat on her face. She and Millie had spent some time pressing the pleats in one of the few presentable dresses she owned after four years' abstinence.

'You don't think this is a bit too revealing, do you Millie?' Jane looked at herself in the wardrobe mirror.

'No. You're their mascot, remember?'

'Oh, all right then, if you're sure.'

And they had found a matching blue band for her wide-brimmed straw hat and stitched some flowers onto it. The result was quite pleasing.

When Lieutenant O'Neill approached them, smartly to attention, saluted and said, 'Ready for inspection, sir,' she knew she was on. And as when she entered the show ring – a lifetime ago – she felt her initial nervousness dissolve and her confidence return. She took Captain Vanstone's offered arm as the band struck up with what she thought was the Missouri waltz.

196

Many of the faces were familiar, some more than others, but these men were different from their off-duty persona. They seemed larger, dressed in battle order – combat boots laced halfway up the calf, webbing belts and ammunition pouches, steel helmets, rifles with fixed bayonets. No longer were they the young recruits who had first arrived at Cranmere; these were warriors and God help the enemy. But unlike the British – in the cinema – they smiled as she passed by, one or two of them dropping a sly wink. If they wanted her as their mascot, why not? Leaning forward, she felt the sharp tip of a bayonet with her free hand which was probably quite the wrong thing to do, but if Captain Vanstone had noticed he made no comment. The owner of the bayonet was delighted! Then came the march past, expertly synchronised to the band's steady beat, when a gentle breeze obligingly stirred the American flag into life – which was, perhaps, a good omen. Captain Vanstone stood on the raised platform and took the salute – 'Eyes right!' Standing beside him, Jane raised one hand and gently waggled her fingers at the broadly smiling faces. All Americans, she decided, had beautiful teeth.

Later, seated at the high table in the mess hall during what Jane thought of as the last supper, Captain Vanstone took his revenge for her afternoon's levity. 'Ah, Jane, I wonder if you would be good enough to say a few words to the men?' He asked with a wicked smile.

'Who, me!' she said, horrified. 'What would I say?'

'Oh you'll think of something. Tell 'em your thoughts and prayers go with them. You know the sort of thing.'

Jane found herself standing alone apart from a microphone and nearly two hundred upturned faces awaiting words of wisdom from the Lady of Cranmere. Help! Her mouth had gone dry, her tongue withered. She felt like a school prefect at the end of term and determined not to sound like the Princess Elizabeth. 'Men of the US 4th Cavalry – friends,' she began. 'I wonder if anyone thought to thank you for coming here to help us defeat the Nazis. In case they didn't – thank you.'

A rousing cheer.

She rambled on about thoughts and prayers, and extended an invitation to any of them who found themselves in England after we had won the war.

Another rousing cheer.

It was then her scattered thoughts came into some sort of order.

Afterwards, she was to marvel at it. 'As most of you will know,' she said, 'my husband is a soldier and at present abroad.' They all knew that well enough. Although supposedly secret, the exploits of Roger Fulford behind enemy lines had been told and retold and exaggerated to very nearly *Boys' Own* status. 'Who knows?' she said, 'some of you may meet up with him – in Berlin.'

An even louder rousing cheer.

'But if he were here now,' she continued when she could make herself heard, 'I think I know what he would say' – pause – 'that he would be proud to serve with you.' The response was immediate and deafening. They were on their feet, whistling and cheering like schoolboys after winning a goal. Jane sat down quickly, visibly moved by her own rhetoric.

Captain Vanstone placed a hand over hers. 'That was just great,' he smiled. 'I guess you missed your vocation.'

At precisely the right moment Major Stubbs made his entry. He had been away all day attending a last-minute briefing. The clamour subsided and he faced an almost silent room.

'Men,' he said. 'You are confined to camp.'

Groan.

'You have tomorrow to prepare yourselves. We move out at first light on the following day.'

The roar of approval was subtly different to the acclaim that Jane had received, more like a war cry. And for a moment it chilled her.

—⁓—

'Jane, are you awake?'

'Yes, Millie,' she said drowsily. She had been awake off and on all night with David cutting yet another tooth.

Millie's wakefulness had been for another reason. Throughout the previous day she had been consumed with anxiety for Luke. Three times she had gone on foot to the American camp, only to find her entrance barred by the Snowdrops. 'Sorry, Millie, no one comes in or out without a pass. You ain't got a pass, have you?'

On her fourth attempt, later in the evening, she had managed a clandestine meeting with Luke when they held hands and exchanged chaste kisses through the barbed wire. But now, as the sky lightened in the east over Mardon Down and the sound of revving engines disturbed the pre-dawn hush, the time had come to part.

Jane slipped out of bed and padded barefoot into the dressing room where David now slept soundly, his fair hair tousled on the pillow. Then returning to the bedroom, she drew back the curtains and turned on the lights – bugger the blackout – took Millie by the hand and led her out through the French door onto the little balcony just as the first truck turned onto the drive.

'Give them a wave, Millie.'

The catcalls and whistles carried clearly in the thin morning air – 'S'long, Jane, s'long, Millie' – and again as the following vehicle turned the corner and the occupants caught sight of two shapely young women in their flimsy nightclothes, silhouetted against the light – 'S'long, Millie, s'long, Jane, yahoo!' And then Luke's voice, clear and strong. 'Bye, Millie.. I'll be back.'

They watched until the last of the tail lights had disappeared over the final hill and out of sight. Silence returned to the Cranmere valley except for the birdsong heralding a new day.

—∿∿—

'It's been three days,' Millie complained. 'You'd have thought he might have written. He promised.'

'He's probably not allowed to,' Jane replied, with a clear vision of Luke in her mind, crowded with his comrades aboard a landing craft, trying to keep dry. There had been a force nine gale blowing up the English Channel and the Cranmere valley for the past twenty-four hours.

'I don't even know where he is,' Millie said helplessly, and then, remembering, 'Oh, I'm sorry, Jane. Here's me moaning about three days an' your man's been away for three months an' more. Do you know where *he* is?'

'No, not really.' Jane shook her head. She had received a letter – three letters together – the latest one already six weeks out of date. All were written in pencil on lined paper torn from a school exercise book, and concise, almost curt, with several passages scored out in blue by the censors. She had tried holding them up to a bright light but could make no sense of the obliterated words.

He was in the mountains, very cold at night. He had a fur coat, very stylish. Things were going quite well. He was all right. She was not to worry. A big hug for little David and for her, too. She hoped that Luke would prove to be a more gifted scribe than her husband.

They huddled around the wireless in the kitchen – Millie appearing as if by magic when a news bulletin was due – but little was said about the coming invasion. *Everybody* knew about it, even the *enemy*, but it was still supposed to be secret.

Until Tuesday 6th June.

The sun rose on a near perfect day in the Cranmere valley, and after the recent storm it seemed very calm. Equally calm was the familiar voice of Alvar Lidell on the early morning news when he announced to the world that Operation Neptune had begun. A more excited voice – from an aircraft? – told them that the English Channel was packed with warships of all descriptions and all going one way. Even as he spoke, Allied battleships and cruisers were pounding the Normandy coast with their big guns while huge formations of Allied aircraft flew overhead. At the breakfast table in Cranmere the children were unaware of the unfolding drama, except for Billy Cann who tried to imitate an aircraft – with one wing. Millie dropped a pile of plates and burst into tears.

D Day, as it was now called, was unlike any day Jane had known or was ever likely to know. After years of preparation and training, it was really happening, the largest invasion force in the history of warfare: thousands of men were crossing the English Channel to meet up with God alone (and the Nazis) knew what. Whilst at Cranmere nothing had changed. Why should it? Cranmere had been silent witness to man's folly for centuries.

Only the people had changed, each going about their daily tasks, tight-lipped, barely speaking to one another, locked in their own thoughts. The was no one – household staff, teachers, Royal Navy personnel – who did not know someone involved – husbands, brothers, fiancés or simply friends. Paradoxically, Jane was the one exception; her husband was taking no part in the D Day landings. In Lieutenant Dando's words, he would be 'going in by the back door'. That did not stop her thinking of those eager young American faces turned up to hers in the mess hall, many of them too nice natured to ever be the killers they thought themselves. 'May God watch over them,' she whispered more than once during the long day.

Even the children had become subdued. With their super-sensitive understanding of tension amongst the grown-ups, they seemed to have made a collective decision to toe the line. Something was up and it was best not to make waves. Newspapers had been kept from them for obvious reasons, but that did not stop Billy Cann from getting hold of back numbers which he read carefully, tracing the words with one finger. He became better informed on the progress of the war than many adults and was told sternly – by those same adults – to keep quiet. But for Millie there was no let-up: Luke and her entire future were at risk. She dusted and polished with a frenetic energy, ironed a huge mound of sheets and children's clothing and stacked them in the linen cupboards, only breaking off to catch the hourly news bulletins. But they left her not much wiser than before. 'Beach heads have been established,' the voice said, 'along the coast of Normandy at Sword, Juno, Gold, Omaha and Utah.'

In the afternoon Jane took her down to the village in the Humber to collect supplies, but even in Collins the grocers there was no respite. A big wooden wireless sat squarely on the counter, crackling out, '*Sword, Juno, Gold...*'

While they were carrying a large box of groceries to the car, a passer-by remarked, 'It's all right for some.'

Millie turned on her, told her to fuck off and mind her own business.

By nightfall it seemed that the Normandy landings had been a success, Lieutenant Dando adding a little to the official BBC announcements. But there was no news yet of those who had been killed or wounded on the beaches – memories of Dunkirk were still fresh in the minds of civilians. At last Cranmere slept, except Millie; for news of Luke she would have to wait until morning.

—◆◆◆—

Major Stubbs sat in one of the leather chairs in the estate office. He looked very tired. Jane poured coffee and sat opposite. He and a skeleton staff had remained behind for communications purposes and to finally close down the camp. Now he was leaving – his staff car stood outside in the yard – but not before saying his farewells to Jane and bringing her what he termed 'an update' on the news from France. In civilian life he had been a lawyer and spoke with a slightly outmoded courtesy. 'The day went well,' he said, unconsciously quoting. In fifteen hours they had landed nearly twenty thousand men and unloaded twelve hundred vehicles on Utah beach. Far better than expected. Their losses had been comparatively light.

'How light?' Jane hardly dared to ask.

'Fourteen,' he said quietly, 'and twenty-three injured.'

'Fourteen!' Jane said, appalled. 'That's far too many. I am so sorry.'

'One is too many, Jane, but thank you for that. I have a list,' he patted his top pocket, 'if you…'

'No,' Jane shook her head, thinking of those young faces, 'I'd rather not know.'

'Militarily,' he said, 'we did well. They had a bad time on Omaha.'

'Militarily,' Jane repeated to herself, and for no particular reason suddenly realised that she had never learned Major Stubbs' first name. 'You knew them all, didn't you?'

'Pretty much, yes. I've been up half the night writing letters. God-awful job.'

She was about to ask if Luke's name appeared on this list when she noticed Millie who had slipped quietly into the room. She stood near the door, both arms by her sides, simply staring at the visitor. There were dark smudges under her eyes: she looked wretched.

'Ah Millie,' Major Stubbs saw her standing there, he smiled up at her. 'I have to tell you that your Luke is okay. Right now he's most likely tucking into a double ration of pork and beans.'

Millie stood uncomprehending for a moment, then covered her face with both hands and wept uncontrollably. The major moved quickly across the room, took Millie in a fatherly embrace and held her until the worst was over. 'C'mon now, Millie,' he said, 'this isn't like you.' And fumbling for a khaki handkerchief, handed it to her. She dabbed at her eyes, blew her nose noisily and passed it back to him. Manfully, he returned it to his trouser pocket then, holding her away from him, he said, 'Now you listen to me, Millie, Luke is the very least of my worries. That young man is a survivor. Right?'

'Right,' Millie said with a brave little smile.

Major Stubbs performed another act of kindness before he left, although Jane was not to fully appreciate it until later. He placed a handful of keys on her desk. 'You have yourself one US Army camp, hardly used. Maybe you and Roger can start up a pig farm or holiday camp when all this is over. Oh, and the second hut contains all that is left of the stores. You'll find a few crates of food in there, you are welcome to them. And don't you go all British on me and say you couldn't possibly accept them,' he smiled. 'They're for the kids. Right?'

'Right.'

It was not until late in the afternoon that Jane and a now almost fully recovered Millie went up to the camp to claim their booty. In the stores they were faced with row upon row of steel shelves sagging under the weight of crates of canned food – fruit, meat, sausages, pork and beans. They ran down the length of the building like children let loose in a toyshop. Millie wept again, and so did Jane. There was enough to feed a regiment – or a houseful of healthy children (kids) – for a very long time. Possibly until the end of the war.

—ᴥᴥᴥ—

But hostilities did not end quite as quickly as some optimists had predicted. Jane bought a war map, something she had sworn never to do, and she and Billy Cann – now co-opted as in-house expert – moved the front line forward daily. Slowly at first; it was not until August that Paris was liberated, by which time Millie was receiving weekly letters from Luke, some of them, judging by her blushes, explicit (which made Jane quite envious). With the aid of map pins and coloured ribbons, and under Lieutenant Dando's guidance, Billy established his front lines in France, northern Italy and Yugoslavia (where Roger was) and Poland in the east. He did this with a grim determination disturbing to see in so young a boy. No less determined, judging by the news bulletins, was the population of London as Hitler played his last card in the form of *Vergeltungswaffe* (Revenge weapons Mk1 and Mk2) – flying bombs and rockets – which did nothing but strengthen their resolve.

Then after a bitterly cold winter, General Patton and the Third Army, aided and abetted by Luke, crossed the Rhine. An ecstatic Billy withdrew his map pins and moved his front lines until in April they had converged on Berlin. Suddenly Adolf Hitler lay dead beneath the ruins of his Chancellery.

It was over.

Victory came almost as an anti-climax. Church bells rang down in the village, Mr Churchill growled at them on the wireless and glasses were charged. But any jubilation was tinged with great sadness; most of them had lost someone. They all wept a bit, even Lieutenant Dando. He and Jane wandered out onto the terrace, listened to the church bells and watched some of the children playing. David, who was by now walking sturdily, was being mothered by the older girls.

'What will you do now, James, stay on in the Royal Navy?'

'Good Lord, no. I think I might look for a bit of land near Inverness, start a smallholding.' He did nothing of the kind, she learned later. He took a postgraduate course at Edinburgh University and became a maths master in an English public school.

'How about you, Jane,' he asked, looking up at the front of Cranmere, 'what will you do with this great place when we've all gone?'

She followed his gaze. 'Do you know, James, I haven't given it a thought.'

—◦◦◦—

CHAPTER 28

———

Brighton sea front on a warm summer's morning was becoming crowded: deck chairs were out (and the tide) and ice-cream vendors doing a brisk trade. Hal leaned on the railings with the holidaymakers and looked towards the distant sea. There was no bracing breeze, any trace of ozone masked by exhaust fumes from the busy road behind him. But he was in no mood to sample what Brighton had to offer, a town that he – and much of the antiques trade – thought of as where stolen antiques got themselves recycled. And he had an appointment with a one-armed bandit.

Crossing the Kings Road, he turned into Black Lion Street which led right into the heart of the district known as The Lanes where nearly every other shop sold antiques of one sort or another. Here he found Prince Albert Street, and the Regency shop front as depicted in the advertisement stood facing him on the opposite pavement. Over the doorway, between two bow windows painted in National Trust green, a shaped signboard proudly bore the name 'William duCann' in gold lettering. Hal crossed the road and walked straight in.

Like churches, antique furniture shops have their own distinctive smell, a mixture of Rentokil, wax polish and old dust, and sometimes – but not in this case – burning joss sticks. And their proprietors have their own methods of approach; they will either pounce just as soon as a prospective buyer gets in the door, or allow him to browse for a while before making an entrance. The duCann establishment, as Hal suspected, fell into the second category, except he was quite sure he was being observed. He had time to admire a fine pair of satinwood armchairs (no price tag) and a walnut bureau cabinet (also no price tag) before a quiet voice asked, 'Can I help you?'

She was tall and slim with dark hair and brown eyes, the product, he guessed, of one of the expensive girls' schools in the Brighton area. A pair of granny glasses swung from a gold chain around her slender neck.

'I have an appointment with Mr duCann,' Hal smiled. 'I telephoned.'

'Are you Mr Wainwright?'

'Yes, I am.'

'Just one moment, Mr Wainwright, I know he's expecting you.'

He was on his own again, the sound of her footsteps retreating to some inner part of the building. He was Mr Wainwright because: when he telephoned for an appointment it was the first name that came to mind. He was Mr Wainwright because: if he had said Wesson and William duCann and Billy Cann were one and the same, and had been guilty of anything underhand, he might have been refused admission. So he was Mr Wainwright with valuable antique furniture for disposal. If this was Billy Cann, then he would have to admit the deception and apologise – perhaps. If not, well he would think of something. In any case it was a bit late now: the dark-haired lovely was returning.

'Mr duCann will see you now, Mr Wainwright.'

She walked with him down a long passage toward a half-open door – an imagined book still balanced on her head – and ushered him in. The room was long and narrow, carved brutally out of the original drawing room. At the far end two open sash windows gave onto a small courtyard. At the opposite end where the light was not so good, William duCann sat behind a large mahogany desk in his shirtsleeves, a racing paper spread out before him together with a pen and notepad. On one corner of the desk a portable TV displayed the runners at Kempton Park. This he extinguished as Hal entered the room, half rose from his seat and indicated one of the chairs facing him.

Hal's first impression, which remained with him, was of contained energy. DuCann was not tall but he was powerfully built with a pugilist's broad shoulders and neck and barrel chest, and a full head of dark hair, and more dark hair sprouting from his open-necked shirt and one cuff. He seemed to have a lot of gold about him – pen, wristwatch, rings and half-sovereign cuff links, almost gypsy-like. He was looking at his visitor intently, a puzzled frown across his dark features.

'We've met before, haven't we, Mr Wainwright?' The voice was deep and gravelly, like that of a heavy smoker.'

'No, I don't think so.'

'You quite sure?' The frown deepened and Hal recalled old Solly's advice, '*Just don't get smart with him.*' But was this the opening he had been looking for – so soon? He took a chance.

'I think,' he said, 'you may have known my father, Charles Wesson.'

'You're Charles Wesson's son?' The frown changed to a look of surprise. 'He's not with you, is he?'

'No, he died.'

'I'm sorry to hear that.' DuCann reached out and turned the desk light onto Hal, leaning across for a closer look. Hal allowed himself to be examined. He had found Billy Cann.

'I can see the likeness,' duCann said. 'It was one hell of a long time ago but I never forget a face. So why are you calling yourself Mr Wainwright?' The question was rapped out fast.

'I thought you might not see me.'

'So what is your name?'

'Hal, Hal Wesson.'

'Well, Hal Wesson, I'll tell you this for nothing. I'd have been a lot more likely to see you if I had known. He was like an elder brother and a father rolled into one. Did he tell you about me?'

'No, it was Jane Fulford at Cranmere.'

'Jane! For God's sake!' DuCann's face seemed to light up. 'You've seen her recently?'

'About a week ago.'

'And how is the lovely Jane?'

'Not all that well, she's an old lady.'

'Yes, I suppose she must be.' The smiled faded and then returned. 'But she remembered me?'

'Oh yes, I think you made quite an impression.'

'She was a beautiful woman,' duCann said. 'Gorgeous. 'I've often thought about her. So what did she say?'

'She said,' Hal had to think for a moment, 'she said she was not sure if you were all that traumatised or just a smooth operator.'

The big laugh started somewhere deep in duCann before it came bubbling to the surface. 'Did she? Did she say that, really?'

Hal grinned, 'Yes, she did.'

DuCann leaned back in his chair, still chuckling to himself. But the mirth subsided just as quickly as it had risen. 'I'm not sure what to make of you, Hal Wesson. You come in here and throw a couple of names at me and they're the two people I'm least likely to forget – ever. So if you're not Mr Wainwright, I don't suppose you are trying to sell me a roomful of antique furniture, are you?'

'No,' Hal shook his head. 'Sorry.'

'Then why are you here?'

It was a reasonable question and Hal chose his words with care. His answer had to be the right one otherwise he would get nothing more from Mr duCann, nor even Billy Cann, a man he judged – correctly – to be of quick intelligence. So recalling Solly's advice for a second time, he said, simply, 'I thought you might be able to help me.'

'Help you?' duCann looked surprised. 'It's not often anyone asks for my help, unless they're on the scrounge. You're not, are you?'

'No, I'm not.'

'What then?' DuCann leaned one forearm on the desk, looking at Hal from under heavy eyebrows.

In answer, Hal took a photograph from his inner pocket and slid it across the polished surface. DuCann glanced at it, then looked closer, and then took up a large magnifying glass and looked closer still. 'Now that,' he said after a prolonged silence, 'is a very nice cabinet, very nice indeed.' He kept it in focus. 'Is it period?'

'Yes, it is.'

'Is it for sale?'

'I suppose it is, in a way.'

DuCann raised his head slowly. 'As you were telling me you visited Cranmere recently, I assume this could be one of theirs. Am I right?'

'Yes.'

'Who put it together, your father?'

'Yes, I'm told it took him a couple of years.'

'I don't doubt it.' DuCann continued to stare at the photograph. 'I wouldn't have thought it possible from what I can remember. He was bloody good, wasn't he?'

'Yes, he was the best.'

'Did you follow him into the same trade?'

'Yes,' Hal said. 'Served my time.'

'So what's the problem?'

'It's quite a long story, I don't know if you've…'

'I'd like to hear it,' DuCann cut him short, reached for the telephone, pressed a key and said, 'Jess, no calls for a while… You deal with him, sweetheart. You're better with the gentry than I am.' He put down the receiver. 'Now then, Hal.'

'The problem is,' Hal began, 'there were two cabinets like that one in the photograph.'

'I know, I was there, remember?'

'One of them went missing after the war,' Hal said, adding quickly, 'It was thought that it was probably removed in error when the Royal Navy were clearing out.'

'That wouldn't surprise me,' duCann said, 'the place was a shambles for a while. Hey, I hope you're not accusing me, I was only a kid?'

'No, of course not,' Hal smiled. 'But now it's turned up.'

'It has? Restored like this one?'

'Oh yes.'

'Where?'

'New York.'

'Are you sure it's the same one?'

'Yes, I was over there the day before yesterday, and I promise you there is no doubt at all.'

DuCann glanced up at the wall clock. 'Just hold on a minute, would you?' he said and leaning across the desk, switched on the TV. He swivelled it so that Hal could see the screen. Under an overcast sky at Kempton Park the runners were in the final straight, three out in front, the rest of the field bunched together, the commentator's voice in overdrive as they neared the finish.

'Idle bloody mare,' duCann muttered.

'Did you back one?' Hal asked innocently.

'Christ, no.' DuCann stared at the little screen. 'I've got better ways of throwing my money away. I am an owner.'

'Which one?'

'Number nine with the orange colours, just coming in now.'

Hal watched the tall, leggy chestnut slow to a leisurely canter as she passed the camera. 'She's beautiful,' he said.

'Oh sure, she's beautiful, and not a bit of use if she isn't even placed. She'll be dog meat at the rate she's going.'

'You wouldn't!'

DuCann smiled. 'No I wouldn't, but I'll sell her if she doesn't move a bit quicker.'

'What's her name?'

'You'll see in a minute, she came fifth.' The frontrunners' names appeared against a background of blue to one side of the screen. Number five was named Cranmere. 'There you are,' duCann switched off the TV, 'make what you will of that.'

Which was exactly what Hal was doing even as he spoke. In the past few minutes he had revised his opinion of duCann, a little to the good. He now had him down as a hard-nosed dealer with a slightly soft centre, and a man who held memories of his father and of Cranmere in affection. A man he could reason with… but just how reasonable would he be on hearing the name Brocatti?

DuCann was speaking. 'All right, Hal, so you went to New York to take a look at the cabinet. Would you mind telling me, what is your interest?'

'We want to find out how it got there and hopefully get it back.'

'Just a minute.' The suspicious scowl had returned, 'Who's *we*?'

'Ah yes, perhaps I should have said.' Yes, he should, that wasn't very clever. 'I do a few odd jobs for Channon Grieves, the insurers and art recovery people. You may have heard of them but, I am here more for personal reasons.'

'Sure, I've heard of Channon Grieves.' Clearly, duCann was unimpressed. 'But didn't you say you were a cabinetmaker?'

'Yes, I am, most of the time. But you see, the chairman, Sir Edward Channon is my father-in-law and he consults me every now and then.' Hal felt he was losing ground rapidly, but no, duCann's scowl had relaxed once more to be replaced with a smile of almost impish glee.

'Your father-in-law! I might have guessed Charles Wesson's son would have landed on both feet. Married the chairman's daughter, eh?'

Hal gritted his teeth, he loathed this sort of remark. 'No,' he said, 'it wasn't like that. We'd known each other since childhood.'

'Sure you had,' duCann was enjoying this, 'and is Sir Edward's daughter beautiful as well as rich?'

'Yes, she is.' Hal kept himself in check.

DuCann relented. 'Good for you, Hal. Any children?'

'Yes, we have a son – named Charles.'

DuCann closed his eyes, moved his head slowly from side to side. 'Another Charles Wesson,' he said. 'That's the best bit of news I've heard all day. But you were saying you had a personal reason for all this. May I ask what it is?'

'My father was accused of stealing the cabinet, and I believe Jane was implicated by association.' He was not sure of this last statement but thought it might help. And it did.

'Who by, for God's sake?'

'By Roger Fulford.'

'Oh him. He was an arrogant sod, a right bonehead. He didn't like us kids and we kept well out of his way. And I didn't like the way he treated Jane, she deserved better than that.' DuCann muttered this last sentence. 'But what possible reason could he have had for fingering your father?'

'As I understand it,' Hal said, 'it was when my father returned the restored cabinet to Cranmere, Fulford suggested that as he was one of the few men capable of such work, and as he'd had the opportunity, logically he was the most likely culprit. Mind you,' Hal added, 'from what I've heard, his nerves were pretty well shot, he'd had a rough time during the war.'

'Didn't we all! That's no reason to blame your father, of all people. So, apart from getting the cabinet returned to where it belongs, you are out to clear his name. Is that it?'

'Yes.'

'I don't blame you. Is Fulford still around?'

'No, he died some years ago.'

'Can't say I'm sorry,' duCann said. 'But there is something I'm curious to know, Hal. Why did you come to see me? Apart from Cranmere, what's the connection?'

This was the big one and there was no way he could avoid it, so he went straight in. 'The present owner of the cabinet bought it from a dealer in Milan named Brocatti.'

'Dino Brocatti? Don't tell me you've been talking to him.'

'No, although I did go to Milan. It seems that Brocatti is retired, but I spoke to a woman who used to travel around with him.'

'Not Isobella?'

'Yes, that's right,' Hal kept going, 'and she said she thought you used to act as Brocatti's shipping agent, so it was possible the cabinet was shipped through you. I just thought I'd ask.'

DuCann covered his face with one large hand in a theatrical gesture, peered at Hal through splayed fingers. Removing it he said, 'Look, if you're going to dig up any more names from the past, perhaps you would warn me first.'

Hal smiled, relieved there had been no detonation. 'I think that's about all.'

'Thank God for that!'

The silence that followed was disturbed by the noise of squabbling seagulls outside the open windows. DuCann crossed the room, put his head out and shouted 'Fuck off out of it!'

The seagulls obliged.

Returning to his chair, he sat and looked at Hal for a long moment before speaking. Hal waited; there was little more he could say. He had voiced the name Brocatti without any violent reaction; in fact duCann had as good as admitted that he had known Brocatti. So he waited for duCann to come to him.

Finally, duCann said, 'I'm glad you came to see me, Hal. And yes, I believe I can help you. In any case I owe it to your father.'

'Thank you,' Hal said. 'Though I doubt he felt he was owed anything.'

'Maybe not, but I owe him, believe me. And no one ever accused me of not paying my debts. Not to my face, anyway.'

DuCann began to fidget with things on his desk – pens, a calculator – the first time he had appeared anything but completely at ease. 'When I was a small boy,' he said, 'I lived in Plymouth. One night during the blitz our house was hit, went down like a pack of cards. I was trapped in the cellar with my mother. She was dead, although I didn't know it at the time, kept trying to wake her. So I stood in the dark and yelled blue murder. Nobody came. I reckon I'd be down there still if it hadn't been for a little dog I used to play with. She heard me and started digging, like they do. When the rescue people got us out we'd been down there for three days and three nights in total darkness. I don't know about being traumatised, it wasn't a word we used in those days, but I was bloody scared of the dark. I still sleep with the curtains drawn back and a bedside light.' DuCan looked up from his desk toys. 'None of this goes any further than these four walls,' he warned.

'No, of course not,' Hal assured him.

'A few days later I fetched up at Cranmere with a busload of other kids. Cranmere was all right, they were nice people. I used to have a nightlight in a saucer by my bed, only some of the older boys thought it funny to creep over and blow it out. That was when I started to wander out of the room onto the landing where there was a low light, and that was where I met Jane one night. She took me to her room and cuddled me. I used to get a lot of cuddles in those days,' he smiled, 'from Jane and the Wrens and a girl called Millie who I liked. I suppose they felt sorry for a kid with no parents and a dud arm. This one's plastic, in case you were wondering.' He tapped his left arm with his pen. It gave off a hollow sound.

'Smothering a boy like that is all very nice, I've never objected to being cuddled, but it wasn't doing me a lot of good. That was when your father came on the scene. He never cuddled me, treated me just the same as the other kids. I helped him pick up all the pieces of that cabinet.' DuCann pointed to the photograph still lying on his desk. 'Kept me hard at it. "Come on young Billy," he would say. "No standing around, all those bits over there. Jump to it." And I did, worked like a little beaver. I'd have done anything he asked. Then when we'd finished for the day, he would sit me on the petrol tank of his motorbike and we'd go on the grass or around the lanes. Those were the only times he would make any concession for my dud arm. He would lift my hand onto the handlebars and hold it there so that I could drive. That was pure magic. He knew how to treat a boy. He would work me hard and then reward me. I dare say you had some of the same.'

There was a sadness in Hal's smile. 'Sounds familiar,' he said.

'In the short time I knew him,' duCann said, 'what your father gave me, or returned to me, was my self-confidence. Dodgy arm? So what? There was nothing the other kids could do that I couldn't do just as well – better. Since then I've never looked back nor felt sorry for myself. That's why I owe him, Hal. Now do you understand?'

'Yes,' Hal said. 'Thank you for telling me.'

'And to convince you I mean what I say about helping you, I can clear up the mystery of how the cabinet came into Brocatti's hands. Isobella was quite right – I sent it.'

'You did?'

'Sure, but it's quite a long story.' He looked at his watch, worn on the right wrist. 'What are you doing for lunch, Hal?'

'Nothing special.'

'Good.' DuCann was already on his feet, slipping into his jacket with a well-practised ease, first the dud arm and then the good one. 'Come on, let's go find a trough.'

—⊷⊷⊶—

At the rear of the duCann premises a flight of concrete steps led down into a courtyard where an open-topped Mercedes waited in the shade.

'You don't mind being driven by a one-armed man, do you?' duCann called over his shoulder.

'I'm game if you are,' Hal replied. What else could he say?

The car was beautiful in Italian racing red, because keeping a low profile was of no interest to Billy Cann. Gold-rimmed sunglasses added the final touch – a one-armed hit man, perhaps? Everything was done – necessarily – with his right hand, his seat belt fastened like sheathing a sword, the engine started up, the gearshift flicked into drive and the hand brake released. On the leather-covered steering wheel a polished steel handle enabled him to swing the big car out onto the road, edging forward to join the stream of traffic. His only disconcerting movement was when he let go the wheel to acknowledge an acquaintance – and he seemed to have many. He was not showing off, Hal decided. He had no need. Possibly he was showing the other kids there was nothing he couldn't do just as well.

They pulled up at a set of traffic lights. 'I should have driven up to see your father. Could have done,' duCann said reflectively. 'But you know how it is, you get in a rut, don't you? I very rarely leave the coast, never go any further north than London these days. I mean, how many people do you know in Brighton?'

'Only Solly Wiseman.'

'Everyone knows Solly. Did he tell you I was a good Jewish boy?'

'Yes he did, as a matter of fact.'

'Then I'll tell you something, Hal. I don't even know that I am Jewish. My father went down with his ship in the early years of the war. Trouble was, he and my mother never got around to tying the knot. He might have been Isaacs or Smith or Jones, for all I know.' He lifted both shoulders in a huge shrug. 'Does it really matter?'

Hal did not reply, but he thought perhaps it mattered rather more than Billy Cann was willing to admit.

The lights changed to green and they roared up the steep hill out of the town heading east, a wide expanse of English Channel to their right, and then down an even steeper hill towards the sea. A couple of miles flashed past before duCann slowed and swung the wheel over to enter a tunnel of trees. They reached a pair of steel gates which slid noiselessly apart on their approach. A Jack Russell terrier appeared from nowhere and ran beside the car barking happily. Her name, predictably, was Becky.

'Do you own a dog, Hal?'

'No, not at present.'

'You should, a guard dog is tax deductible.' He smiled fondly at Becky.

The house stood well back behind a gravelled turning circle, 1920s' stockbroker-style in mellow brick and timber, straight out of a *Country Life* advert. They entered through a side door, but not before duCann had pressed the correct sequence of buttons on a security plate. Becky led the way into a square hall panelled in oak with an oak staircase running up two walls. The doors, architraves and skirtings were also in oak; this was a quality house, the one-time home of successful stockbrokers – and now Billy Cann. Hal had years of experience of wealthy clients wanting to show off their beautiful homes and their treasures to him (which was the very last thing he needed right now). He wanted to hear about Brocatti.

On the south side of the house three intercommunicating reception rooms faced onto a stone-flagged terrace and thence a perfect lawn and the sea. The drawing room was deeply carpeted and furnished in mostly English period satinwood and mahogany, the spoils of duCann's forays into the salerooms. Each well-selected piece was carefully positioned and in mint condition, with the exception of the cabinet that disguised a fridge. DuCann took out two bottles of beer and handed them to Hal together with glasses and an opener. Which, Hal thought, was his way of saying there are one or two simple tasks that I can't manage quite as well as the other kids, like pouring a beer. They sat out on the terrace in film director's canvas chairs beneath a sun umbrella, removed their jackets, stretched out their legs and sipped cool beer. DuCann's housekeeper, a middle-aged woman addressed as 'Mrs P', was preparing a selection of sandwiches.

'My wife's away,' duCann said, staring out to sea. 'She left two years ago, haven't seen her since. Haven't missed her, either.' Again the deep chuckle. On the horizon in one of the world's busiest shipping lanes, tankers and cargo ships shimmered in the haze, and for a moment they sat in silence.

'I could sit here all day,' duCann said contentedly. 'Don't know why I bother to go into the shop, don't need to.' The sandwiches arrived – chicken, cheese, smoked salmon but no ham – all neatly cut into triangles and served with lettuce, tomatoes and cress. 'Where had I got to?' duCann said, seemingly coming back to life. He piled up his plate.

'You were going to tell me about Brocatti,' Hal said.

'Brocatti, yes, we'll come to him later.' He devoured a sandwich in two bites. 'When I left Cranmere,' he said, 'I was sent to a God-awful children's hostel in Plymouth. I teamed up with a lad a couple of years older than me called Dicky Cunliffe. One night we decided we'd had enough so we went over the wall. We lived pretty rough for a while holed up in bombed buildings. Lived on our wits, odd jobs, bit of thieving, bit of dealing. Then we got better at it, the dealing, that was. You could sell anything in those days, building materials were in demand. We'd take windowframes and floorboards out of bombsites, cleaned up old bricks and slates and sold them by the load – we had a handcart. Then we rented a yard with a tin shed – which was home. Boots were a pretty good line, everyone needed boots. We'd buy them at the Admiralty surplus sales in lots of ten pairs for about a quid, polish them up and sell them at five bob a pair.

'After about twelve months we rented a shop down on the Barbican. We were really flying now, into secondhand furniture and antiques. We bought an old van, painted it green like Harrods and put our names on the side. *Cunliffe and Cann. Dealers in Antiques and Works of Art.*'

DuCann got up from his chair to fetch two more beers from the Geo 111 fridge, handing them both to Hal. 'One afternoon,' he said, 'I drove all the way up to Cranmere. I'd put on my best suit – my only suit! – to visit Jane. But I met Mr Fulford on the back doorstep with his dogs and his tweed hat, looking like the lord of the manor, which I suppose he was. I was very polite, explained how I'd been here during the war and please could I see Mrs Fulford? He looked me up and down like I was something the dogs had left on his carpet. He said Mrs Fulford was not at home and even if she was she would not want to see the likes of me. It may have been the wording on the van that riled him, or me in my sharp suit. Probably thought I was a spiv on the knocker. He told me, amongst a lot of other things, to clear off and not come back or he'd set the dogs on me. I think he meant it. I've never been back.'

Hal poured the beer and passed a glass to him. 'That must have been very upsetting after you'd been there all those years.'

'Upsetting? It was, I was gutted. But one thing I've learned, Hal, is that it's no use trying to get back at a man like that. Just bide your time and your opportunity will come. And it did, sooner than I'd expected. No more than twelve months later we had the chance to buy the contents of a store down on the waterfront, from the Admiralty. We had a Chief Petty Officer in tow who would push things in our direction – for a backhander. The place was stacked from floor to ceiling with steel lockers, cooking pots, iron beds...'

'Boots?' Hal suggested.

'Yes, boots and webbing haversacks and stoves and brooms, you name it. We hauled the whole lot out into the yard, stuck lot numbers on everything and I was the auctioneer. And I was mustard, we had a bloody good day.' He smiled at the memory. 'Then right at the back of the shed we found these big crates under a huge pile of blankets and duffle coats and... well, you've already guessed, one of them contained the wrecked cabinet.'

'What an amazing coincidence,' Hal said.

'Well I'm not so sure. At that time there were stores and warehouses all over Plymouth crammed with surplus kit. You were probably right, Hal, the box was carted away by a squad of demob-happy matelots who just wanted to get the job finished and go home.'

'No, I meant it was a coincidence that you should find it.'

'Yes, I think I stood with my mouth wide open for a while. But coincidences do happen, don't you find?'

'Yes, I suppose. Did you never think of returning it to Cranmere? There might have been a reward.'

'Sure, I did,' duCann gave a wolfish grin, 'for about thirty seconds. And then I thought – screw you, Fulford. This box of tricks is my property, bought and paid for and with a receipt from the Admiralty, no less. As for a reward, ha! Can you imagine the reception if I'd turned up at Cranmere with that thing? He'd have called the cops. I toyed with the idea of offering it to him anonymously, through a lawyer. But just suppose he'd discovered my identity, and he probably could have with the help of a high-powered barrister. I wouldn't have stood a cat's chance and I was not prepared to take the risk. Not with him. I didn't tell you what he called me, Hal, it had to do with my physical shortcomings, race, religion and parentage, all of which may have been true but I didn't need to be reminded by a schmuck like Fulford. So I hung onto the box and I gloated over it. And that did me the power of good. You tell me,' duCann turned in his seat to look directly at Hal, 'What would you have done in my position?'

Hal was taken aback by the suddenness of the question. 'I don't know,' he said, 'pretty much the same, I think.'

'Course you would.' Becky looked up adoringly as her master fed her bits of chicken.

'Dicky and I went up to London soon after, reckoned we'd outgrown the West Country. I didn't care for London much, needed to be near the sea, so I came down here and brought the box with me. I suppose you could say I was being dog in the manger; the cabinet was of no value to anyone except Fulford, and he wasn't getting it. So there it sat gathering dust in my warehouse, until Dino Brocatti came along.'

Brocatti at last! Hal breathed an inward sigh. Perhaps now he would begin to learn something; he was rapidly tiring of duCann's potted life story, colourful though it was. And looking at the man, now well into his fifties, his face tinted an odd colour by sunlight filtered through green canvas, he found it hard to visualise the boy, Billy Cann with the cheeky grin, who had beguiled both Jane and his father. No doubt his father had recognised a latent determination in the boy and encouraged him to grow into a forceful – if slightly unscrupulous – man. A man who remembered Charles Wesson with affection and felt in his debt. Maybe he was, and maybe that was Hal's trump card.

'I liked little Dino,' duCann was saying. 'He would come over two, maybe three times a year. Good buyer if I'd got the sort of goods he wanted. Spent like a sailor on shore leave.'

'And all in cash, or so I've heard,' Hal said.

'Isobella tell you that?'

'Yes.'

'She would.'

'Do you think he was into some sort of racket?' Hal asked innocently.

DuCann laughed, 'Sure, he was. No man runs around with a bag of money like that unless he's up to something. But sure as hell I wasn't going to ask. None of my business. What do you do if someone wants to pay you in cash?'

'Hold my hand out,' Hal said.

'Course you do, and why not? Anyway, it must have been one of the last times Dino came over. He'd had a duff run around the London rooms and I hadn't managed to find a great deal of what he was after, marquetry and the like. Good antiques were becoming harder to find. So I showed him the damaged cabinet. He liked it, said he'd just taken on a new restorer, and he bought it. I didn't charge him a lot. Few hundred. And that was the last I'd heard about it until today. So you see, Hal, no crime was committed, not technically. Morally perhaps, but I gave up on morality years ago. And it gets your father off the hook, doesn't it?'

'Only partly,' Hal said.

'How do you mean?'

'Well, you said you thought Brocatti was up to something. Do you think he could have been mixed up with the Mafia?'

'Who, Dino? Never! He was a funny little man, sweated a lot I seem to remember. Not the type at all, believe me.'

'I wasn't suggesting he was *that* involved, but do you think it possible his paymasters might have been?'

DuCann thought for a moment. 'In hindsight, I suppose they could have been. Someone was backing him for sure, and I heard about the Mafia interest in antiques but not until after Dino stopped calling. Why, does it matter?'

Hal evaded the question. 'Does the name Giovanni Spargo mean anything to you?'

'Not a thing.'

'He was a cabinetmaker,' Hal said. 'Originally an Italian POW who worked for my father for several years, and helped him rebuild the Cranmere cabinet. Then he married and moved back to his home town, Milan. He was a very good craftsman and may well have been the man Brocatti was referring to when he bought the cabinet.'

'You see what I mean about coincidences, Hal?'

'Yes, but again, maybe not all that coincidental. As I said, Spargo was a highly skilled man so it was on the cards that he and Brocatti would meet up before long. At first, Spargo wouldn't take on the cabinet, it was too big a job. When he finally agreed – it was now 1983 – just as soon as he got the cabinet spread out in his workshop he recognised it. So he wrote to my father.'

'Go on.' DuCann was leaning forward in his chair, almost as though he anticipated the tragic news to come. Possibly, Hal, grave-faced like his father, had been giving off silent messages.

'My father and mother arranged to go over and stay with Giovanni Spargo and his wife, partly on holiday and partly so that Father could identify the cabinet. Only they never made it. Their plane went down in the Alps just north of Milan.'

DuCann was staring at him. 'Christ, I'm sorry, Hal. How old were you?'

'I was nineteen at the time,' Hal said, and kept going before duCann could add any further commiseration. 'There is a question that's been going around in my head and it's this – was my father deliberately prevented from identifying the cabinet? You see, Spargo was an excitable sort of man, and he was sure to have told Brocatti that he had assisted in the restoration of an identical cabinet that was lost just after the war, and thought that this was the pair to it. And in case there was any doubt, Charles Wesson was coming to identify it. So, if Brocatti had any connection with the Mafia, however tenuous, could they have been responsible for my father's death?'

'No, Hal. No!' DuCann almost shouted, his expression a mixture of horror and astonishment. 'Where did you get that idea? I know they are capable of most things but they're not stupid. They would never run the risk for a cabinet worth a few hundred, or thousands for that matter. Never! And if they did, not in their own back yard.'

Hal persisted. 'Well, how about if it lifted the lid on some grander scheme?' he asked with a strong sense of *déjà vu*. He had put the same question to Ben Pavoni and his Uncle Ted.

'It never was all that grand a scheme,' duCann said. 'And it was over by 1983. They'd found something more profitable than antiques.'

'What if there was someone else on the aircraft they wanted out of the way?'

'That's a remote possibility. But the Mafia must have fifty simpler ways of silencing their rivals. I think you're way off beam there.'

Hal had put the same questions and received the same answers. No one could see what seemed to him fairly obvious. 'There's a bit more,' he said.

'There is?'

'Yes. A week after Spargo had completed the second cabinet and returned it to Brocatti, he was killed in a traffic accident on the *Autostrada*. So the doors were slammed at both ends. Or is that two more of your coincidences?'

'I don't know,' duCann said thoughtfully.

'And another door opened in New York.'

'Go on, Hal, I'm listening.'

'The present owner of the cabinet in New York, Roberto Agnolli, is a wealthy man who is trying to get into politics, so he has to keep his nose clean. He employs a lawyer, Moreno, to protect him. Moreno is bent – he's already offered me money not to identify the cabinet.'

'That's a good sign,' duCann said. 'He's on the back foot isn't he?'

'Yes, maybe, but he said if his client is accused, or even suspected of being in possession of stolen property, he will start up a full investigation to clear his name. If he does that and discovers the relationship between my father and Spargo, he'll put two and two together and make five. And we might have a hard time proving otherwise unless, of course, you were prepared to testify.'

'What does Sir Edward Channon have to say about this?'

'He says he thinks Moreno's bluffing.'

'I think he's right, Hal.'

'He also said that if we don't move quickly, there's a chance Moreno might cut his losses and destroy the evidence.'

'How long before they get their chainsaws out?'

'I'm not sure, weeks not months at a guess.'

'It's a mess isn't it?'

'Yes, it is.'

'I'd like to think about this for a while, Hal. Do you swim?'

'Do I what? Er, yes, why?'

'Let's go and cool off.'

—◦◦◦—

Late afternoon and a thoughtful Hal Wesson sat in a window seat in a crowded commuter train heading for Cirencester, thankful that he had chosen this form of transport rather than face the long drive home – and to reality. He was tired. Not physically tired, even after trying to keep up with a one-armed man swimming lengths of his king-sized pool. DuCann had moved through the water like an otter using a curious overarm stroke of his own, and fast, because he was better than the other kids. Hal was mentally tired – exhausted – through spending the day in the presence of a man of such dynamic energy and drive, Billy Cann, the boy who once sold boots for five shillings a pair.

It was as they sat on the edge of the pool, their feet in the water, that Billy – for Hal could think of him now by no other name – had astounded him yet again. 'I'll get Jane's cabinet back for her,' he said. 'It's high time I took another trip to New York.

Hal turned to look at him, but duCann was watching Becky as she splashed happily in the shallow water. 'I'd like to meet this Moreno character,' he said. From what you were telling me he sounds like a man who'd talk business. It's knowing *how* to talk to these people, Hal. D'you think he might offer me a bribe?

'He might,' Hal said when he had overcome his astonishment, a vivid mental picture of duCann and Moreno head to head, in mind. 'Are you serious?'

'Sure. You asked for my help, didn't you?'

'Yes, but I didn't mean…'

'Listen, Hal. None of this would have happened but for me. I was the kid who switched all the lights on, or didn't Jane tell you?'

'Yes, she did.'

'And she never grassed me up, not once. Isn't that a good enough reason?'

'Well yes, I suppose, but....'

'Hal, trust me. You do trust me, don't you?'

'Yes,' Hal said. What else could he say?'

'Good.' DuCann smiled in a way that could have been interpreted as anything but trustworthy. 'And tonight,' he said, 'I'll call up a man I know in Naples. He owes me a favour and he can talk direct to the families in Milan.'

'You mean he's one of them?' Hal was no longer sure where to place his trust.

'I don't know what he is and I don't ask. He's not the sort of guy you'd want your sister to meet but, like I said, he can talk to the families and he will tell me if there was any interest in either your father's accident or Spargo's. Straight from the horse's mouth.'

'Thank you.'

'Save your thanks till later.' DuCann was deadly serious. 'There is one condition, Hal. You and me, we never met. And if anyone from Channon Grieves should come around asking questions, I've never heard of Wesson nor Cranmere nor Billy Cann. I am William duCann of Brighton. Is that clear?'

'Yes.'

'Have we got a deal?'

'Yes.'

DuCann held out his hand and gripped Hal's to seal their agreement.

———⌇⌇———

The carriage was hot and airless. Hal shifted in his seat, his back tingling where he had caught the afternoon sun. Had he done the right thing, or had he buggered up all his Uncle Ted's careful planning? He hadn't done anything, not really; the decision to go to New York had been Billy's, and no power on earth was going to stop him now he'd set his mind to it. The same could be said of his own decision to visit duCann in the first place. Had he set a thief to catch a thief? No, Billy was not dishonest, just had a slightly different slant on things than others. Like Uncle Ted? One thing Hal felt sure of, having shaken on a deal, Billy would never break his word. So he could be trusted. Just how he thought he could persuade Moreno to return the cabinet remained to be seen.

———⌇⌇———

CHAPTER 30

—◦◦◦—

Jane had been living with Anne Perret in the Dower House for ten days and already she was beginning to get on her nerves (through no fault of her own). She was a nice enough woman in her late forties with her mother's round face and dark, curling hair – although she would never be half the woman Big Betty had been. But she had this unfortunate habit of using the Royal 'we' – We don't want to get up yet, do we, Jane? We don't want to do this or that? – which irritated Jane almost beyond belief.

'I am going out for a walk,' Jane announced.

'Yes, all right, I won't be a minute.'

'I would like to be alone for a while, if I may?'

Anne looked doubtful.

'You see that seat halfway up the drive?' Jane said, pointing through the window. 'That is where I'll be, by the daffodils.'

'They're nearly over,' Anne said.

Yes, and so am I, Jane thought. She said, 'You can see me from the kitchen in case I should fall in a heap.'

'We musn't talk like that, Jane. Don't forget your stick.'

Jane bit back, no we mustn't forget our sodding stick, must we? Calling the dog, she set out up the gently sloping drive. The afternoon was warm with a gentle breeze straight off the moor, bringing with it the scents of gorse and heather and damp peat. She breathed deeply and for a moment imagined herself up there once more astride a good horse, heard the saddle's creak, the song of the skylark high above, felt the wind in her hair.

Reaching the seat – conscious of Anne's eyes following her slow progress – she was thankful to rest. Above her a beech spread its graceful branches, one of the same beeches that had been stripped of their new leaves by a violent explosion on a sunny afternoon fifty years ago almost to the day. The trees had recovered. Nothing had changed. To her left the south front of Cranmere basked in the sun. Neither would that change, protected now by an Act of Parliament. On the first floor the windows of what she had always thought of as the children's dormitories were open wide and the faint sound of hammering and sawing reached her. So yes, there would be changes made to the interior

– and not before time if Cranmere were to survive. The long gallery, the Victorian ballroom and the decorated ceiling in the salon – on which Roger had spent a ridiculous amount of money when they could least afford it – were also protected. Catherine had ideas of using them for lectures or conferences. And why not? When the lecture bored, the students could look up to watch satyrs and putti chasing bare-breasted maidens around the room. But for all Catherine's efforts – and the apartments were sure to be created very tastefully – Jane did not want to see them, preferring her memories.

She rarely thought of the immediate post-war years, a time of mixed emotions on whose memory she had slammed the door years ago. But today, possibly because she had left the house in such a foul mood, she opened the door just a little.

—◦◦◦◦—

Roger's return was not as she had expected. He was to arrive during the late afternoon by staff car driven down from Salisbury. He was now a colonel. She had spent the morning tidying the estate office and their rooms, arranging fresh flowers, trying to make his home welcoming. And she had taken more trouble than usual over her appearance, had dressed David in his best shorts and brushed his hair ready to meet his father for the first time. An anxious time for them both. She spared a thought for the many women whose husbands would return to meet an unexplained child. At least she would not have that to contend with, not in quite the same way.

When the telephone rang she remembered – much later – saying, 'What now?' As though the intrusive bell could only be the harbinger of bad news.

'Mrs Fulford?' a man's voice inquired.

'Yes?' It was bad news, she was sure of it.

'Sergeant Hunter, ma'am. Colonel Fulford's driver.' The sergeant spoke in short, military sentences. 'The colonel's unwell. I have taken him to the Royal Devon and Exeter Hospital. They have admitted him.'

She had almost expected something like this. 'What's wrong with him?' she asked.

'He seems to be running a fever, ma'am. He was all right when we left camp. I thought it best to bring him here.'

'Yes, thank you, sergeant. Give me the details would you, the ward and the doctor's name?'

She spoke to a Doctor Stanbury. 'May I come in to see him?'

'Best leave it for a while, Mrs Fulford. We'll keep him in overnight under observation. He's been abroad, I understand.'

'Yes.' She was about to say Yugoslavia but checked herself. No one had told her otherwise.

'I've put him in isolation to be on the safe side,' Doctor Stanbury was saying. 'If you can supply any more info it might help.'

'I'll try, Doctor.'

She dialled the magic number. 'Edward, this is Jane.'

'No need for that now, Jane. Not any more.' He listened to her for a moment. 'Jane,' he said, 'give me the hospital number, I'll get the MO to talk to them direct. And try not to worry, it's probably just a bug he's picked up.'

'Thank you, Edward.'

'I'm away at the end of the month,' he said.

'You mean I won't be able to call you?'

'No, sorry, I'll be a civilian. But we'll keep in touch.'

'Yes, we must,' Jane said, but she knew she was going to feel strangely alone without her lifeline to Edward Channon.

—◈—

The Royal Devon and Exeter Hospital in Southernhay was built in the 1750s to resemble a country house, which it did quite successfully, thus diverting the onlooker's thoughts from the awful practices once carried out behind its mellow brick façade. Southernhay was warm and sunlit when Jane parked the big Humber – washed that morning by Jim Sanders for the Master's return. A lorry was drawn up by the main entrance and a party of soldiers were busily removing sandbags put there for protection against bomb blast. The war was over.

When she had telephoned earlier in the day, Jane spoke to the sister-in-charge of Dunsford Ward.

'Yes, Mrs Fulford, the fever has left him, you can take him away,' she said, and Jane had sensed an abruptness in her voice almost as though she would be glad to see the back of Roger. Perhaps all sisters-in-charge were like that, she thought, or Roger had been rude to her. It had been known.

She was directed up a flight of stone stairs to the first landing where Doctor Stanbury awaited her. He was forty-ish, balding and dressed in the obligatory white coat with a stethoscope protruding from his pocket. There was a hesitancy in his manner as he ushered her into his office, offered her a seat and took his own behind a scratched oak desk. He would not meet her eye, almost as though he was embarrassed.

'Did my husband's medical officer get in touch with you?' Jane asked in an attempt to put him at his ease.

'Yes, yes, thank you. And we have run our own tests, of course.'

'What is wrong with my husband?' Jane asked. It seemed that directness would be the only way to get a straight answer.

But she did not get a straight answer. 'When did you last see him?'

'He's been abroad. I haven't set eyes on him for three years. Why?'

'Ah,' he said, 'that's good.'

'Why?' Jane raised her voice. 'What's good about it?'

'Mrs Fulford,' Doctor Stanbury said, 'Your husband has syphilis.'

Just how long she sat and stared at the white-coated man Jane never knew. She felt as though someone had emptied a bucket of cold water over her. Syphilis? She knew very little about it except it was awful, horrible – biblical! 'Can he be cured?' she asked at length.

'We've had some encouraging results with this new drug penicillin,' Doctor Stanbury said, a little more relaxed now that the word had been spoken. 'Usually when the infection is caught in its early stages.'

'And has it been?'

'No, but we live in hopes, Mrs Fulford.' She was to keep her husband in bed for a day or two. His GP, Doctor McMasters, would be in touch.

Roger was waiting for her on the landing. His tweed suit – the same he had worn when he left three years ago – hung on him loosely. He was hollow-cheeked. Without speaking, he enfolded her in his arms and held her.

'Come on,' she said, 'let's get you home.'

———⚬∾∾⚬———

She put Roger in the guest room – at his request. During what seemed like a long journey home they had hardly exchanged a word, most certainly not the 'S' word. He had lolled in his seat with his eyes half-closed, still running a mild temperature. She was confused and felt highly incensed at the off-hand treatment she had received in the hospital. They had discharged him early, and why? Because his illness was not just socially unacceptable, but frowned on by the medical profession, too. We'll soon see about that, Jane thought. Doc McMasters would sort it out, and get second and third opinions if he thought it necessary.

When she went into Roger's room he was already undressed and in bed. He looked awful; there was a yellowness about his eyes. 'Would you like some tea?' she asked. The English answer to any difficult situation.

'Thank you, that would be nice.' Even his voice had lost its strength.

She turned to leave the room. 'Jane,' he called her back. 'They told you, did they, in the hospital?'

'Yes,' she said.

'Do you know what it means?'

'Not really, they were a bit sniffy about it. Doc McMasters will be coming to see us tomorrow morning but… no more children, is that right?'

'Rather more than that, Jane.' He held out a hand to her.

She moved to his bedside, took his hand in hers. 'Then, tell me.'

He looked up at her from his pillow. 'There can be no more contact between us, other than this,' he gave her hand a gentle squeeze. 'No lovemaking, no kissing even. I am infectious, unclean like a leper. Better if I hadn't come home.' He turned his head away.

'Don't say that, Roger.'

'Listen, Jane,' he turned back to her. 'If you want to walk out on me, go right ahead. I'd be the last to blame you. Only, I hope you won't.'

—◈—

CHAPTER 31

—⁓—

The elderly Austin rocked to a halt in the cobbled yard behind Cranmere and Doctor Douglas McMasters stepped out. He was a tall man in his late forties with pepper-and-salt hair and a fine pair of eyebrows to match. And, it was said, a short fuse to match them both. A man of plain speaking which had not endeared him to some of his private patients but – and Jane placed great store by this – the children loved him, even after their inoculations. She could think of no one better to advise her.

She had spent a wretched night. Across the landing in the room once occupied by Charles Wesson she knew her husband had lain awake, just as she had, each agonising over their future – if they had a future together. His suggestion that she might walk out on him had been hurtful, if practical, and a dozen questions raced through her mind. If she were to leave Roger, where would she go? To Charles? She had heard nothing from him. Certainly not to her old home and her mother, she had travelled too far for that. She had no money of her own, and yet she was not yet thirty and reasonably presentable... she could start an entirely new life, couldn't she? But without little David – never! And there was no way she could imagine Roger allowing his son – his son? – to leave with her. David was heir to Cranmere, the only male Fulford and with no chance of any more. And Roger would need to be looked after, wouldn't he? There was also the small matter of the vow she had made to him on the night he had returned from France, near exhausted. *'I will be anything you want me to be, wife, whore, nursemaid and constant companion. I will never hurt you.'* That must count for something, surely? Roger needed her now as never before but, if she stayed with him, in effect she would be a war widow without the freedom allowed to widows. Until she had spoken to Doc McMasters she could make no decision.

McMasters reached into the car for his medical bag and, like many country doctors, walked straight in through the back door without knocking, to meet Jane waiting for him in the hall. Then, unlike many country doctors, he placed his bag on the floor, took Jane in his arms and gave her a hug before walking her gently up the stairs. He spent a long time in Roger's room, emerging only once to request the whisky decanter and two glasses, while Jane paced around her sitting room, sat and flicked through the pages of outdated magazines, got to her feet and paced again. When at last he reappeared, he smelt not of whisky but disinfectant.

He sat by the open window and watched the children playing on the grass below while Jane made coffee in her little kitchen. 'Is that young David down there?' he called. Jane came back into the room carrying a tray, she glanced out, 'Yes, that's David.'

'How old are the girls with him?'

'Mary is twelve and Olive just gone thirteen.'

'Does ye're heart good to see them, doesn't it?' he smiled. 'Little mothers in the making. They're our future, ye know, Jane.'

'Yes, I suppose they are,' she said.

'But it's Roger's future ye want to hear about, I'm thinking.'

'Yes.' She sat beside him.

McMasters sipped his coffee, then put down his cup and saucer carefully. 'We don't need to ask how ye're husband contracted syphilis, but ye'll not be holding that against him, will ye?'

'I think I'm a bit more adult than that,' Jane said.

'Aye, of course y'are,' he smiled. 'I shouldn't have asked. Well then, Jane,' he paused for a moment, pursed his lips. 'Syphilis is a nasty infection caused by a wee organism known as *Treponema pallidrum*, and it goes in three stages. If we catch it in its primary stage, nowadays we can finish it off quickly with penicillin. If not, we've a few problems.'

'What stage is Roger in?'

'Oh he's in the tertiary stage, it's been in his system for two years or more.'

'Why ever didn't he seek help before now?'

'He couldn't where he's been, hiding up in mountain caves and derelict buildings; I doubt they had so much as a packet of aspirin. Even if he could have reached a clinic, they wouldn't have had penicillin. He's been a very sick man, Jane, but there's more to it than that.'

'How do you mean, more?'

'I mean he's given everything he had to give and there's not a lot left, ye ken. Roger's the sort of man who puts one hundred per cent effort into anything he does, wouldn't ye agree?'

'Yes, I would.'

McMasters drained his coffee, and held out his cup for a refill. 'Did I ever tell you about my brother?'

'No, I don't think so.'

'Ye're husband reminds me of him in some ways. Jamie was a field surgeon in the First World War. Spent three years in a forward dressing station. When he came home I hardly recognised him. Like Roger, d'ye see, he'd done his best and more beside. He used to drink a drop, poor fellow. Died quite young.'

'Will Roger die young?'

'I'll not lie to ye, Jane, he's got an uphill struggle afore him, but there's no reason why he shouldn't lead a full and active life for another twenty or thirty years, given proper care and treatment.'

'And what is that?'

'The caring is where ye come in. At the present moment the poor man's lying there not knowing if ye're going to stay with him or not.'

'That was his suggestion, not mine.'

'Aye, well, it was for ye're benefit. I don't imagine he's the easiest of men to live with, but right now he's a remorseful man and deeply ashamed. Ye'll have to tread carefully. D'ye love him enough to cope with that?'

'Yes,' Jane nodded. 'What must I do?'

'First ye go in there and tell him; that should buck him up no end. After that, plenty o' rest, good food and fresh air and he'll be on his feet in no time.'

'But no physical contact, is that right?'

'None at all. D'ye think ye can keep ye're hands off him?'

'I'll have to, won't I?' Jane felt herself colouring.

'Aye, ye will. Ye can take a lover if you feel the need.'

She smiled faintly. 'Is that medical advice, Doctor?'

'Maybe it is, but don't quote me. And it's Douglas, please. As for treatment, I'll be in every week and I'll pack him so full o' penicillin the wee beasties in his bloodstream won't have room to breathe. And I'll be taking samples from ye as well to be on the safe side. Before very long ye'll both be sick o' the sight o' me.'

'I don't think we will, Douglas.'

'Aye, well we'll see.'

'Later on,' Jane asked, 'will it affect his mind? I've read somewhere...'

McMasters shook his head. 'Not necessarily, Jane, and let's take our fences as we come to them. In any case I'll be keeping an eye on him. Ye can call me any time. And let's hope that before long medical science will have come up with another wonder drug.' He looked at her appraisingly. 'I'll not pretend it'll be easy but ye're a strong woman, more than able.'

'I wish I had your confidence.'

'Confidence! Jane, I was there at the County Show when a brave young lassie knocked her future husband into second place. Damn nearly yelled meself hoarse.'

'That was a long time ago.'

'Aye,' he smiled, 'all of seven years. But if ye want any more proof of what ye can achieve, just take a look at those children running around down there.'

'What about them?'

'Jane, please,' He looked pained. 'Accept a little praise where it's due. I mind the time I examined those bairns when they first came here. Some were in a sorry state, and now will ye just look at them?'

'Not all down to me,' she said, 'Not by a long chalk.'

'D'ye know when their birthdays are?'

'Yes, of course I do.'

'And who is it sees they get a birthday card and a present, and a little party?'

'Well, yes, all right but...'

'No buts, Jane. D'ye not see, ye're their mother figure? Ye've given them nearly five years o' happiness, and that's half a childhood. So then ye're feeling a bit low, think on them, because ye can be damned sure they'll be thinking of ye.'

Jane did not reply for a moment, then she smiled and said, 'Douglas, when you come to visit, will you promise to say nice things to me?'

'Aye, I will.'

—⁕—

Jane shifted her position on the iron seat. She must return soon or Anne would be fussing around her, but not just yet. There were some memories of the post-war years that she did not wish to recall; Douglas, the dear man, had been right when he said it would not be easy. She thought of those years as a series of peaks and troughs. A deep, deep trough when the children finally left in a flurry of hugs and tears and promises. An equally deep trough when she drove Millie down to Plymouth to board a ship laden with GI brides heading for an uncertain future in the USA. And an even deeper trough when David left for his first boarding school, dressed in his little cap and grey flannel suit. He was eight years old.

And troughs in varying degrees as Roger, now as fit as he would ever be, became obsessed with the restoration of Cranmere and flew into a rage with anything or anyone who thwarted his plans. Like old Mr Yeoman whose family firm had so carefully packed the Cranmere treasures in 1939. His firm had not survived the war, neither had his warehouse nor his only son. But that did not prevent Roger from tearing strips off him. Like Charles Wesson, accused of making off with one of the Cranmere cabinets; even she had been blamed for being so careless in losing a thing of that size.

The height of his imprudence had been when he called in experts to restore the painted ceiling in the salon, which they had done most beautifully, but at such a cost that one of the Cranmere farms had to be sold off to foot the bill. Thereafter, Roger confined his efforts to money-making schemes, but because of his inability so settle into them for very long none had made any money. He tried pig farming, poultry farming, pony trekking and even house guests. This last was doomed to failure right from the start; Roger's abrupt manner had soon frightened any guests off.

For all that, there were peaks. When she and Roger had spent a day out in the Alvis – now lovingly refurbished – and had toured all their pre-war haunts along the north coast, and reached a magical 100mph on the long straight between Bude and Holsworthy. Another peak when David went up to Oxford to read law, another when he came down with his degree and commenced a career with a firm in the City. And a peak of stupendous height when he telephoned late one evening.

'Mother, I am coming home.'

'Oh, lovely! Do you want to be met at the station?'

'No, I mean home for good, if I may?' A few years in the City and he'd had enough, was more than ready to change direction and cities. He would be taking up a partnership in Exeter.

'Of course you may, David. But are you sure?'

'Quite sure, Mother. London's not for me, and I'll be able to help you run the estate.' Music to her ears: she had been running the show almost single-handed since the outbreak of war. Roger no longer took any interest, spent most of his time closeted in his study writing his memoirs. She had sneaked a look while he was out one day – and closed the book hurriedly.

'I can think of nothing I'd like better, David, so long as you know what you're doing.'

'I do, Mother. Trust me.'

Jane put down the receiver and wept for pure joy. Not just because her son was coming home, but because he had turned out to be such a kind and thoughtful young man. Her happiness, however, was tempered with the knowledge that David and her husband had not always seen eye to eye, and Roger might not take too kindly to what he saw as interference. There could be a few problems.

There were none.

Three days before David's return and, looking out of the window, Jane noticed Roger's hunter grazing in the pasture – fully saddled? She ran out, caught the horse and mounted, pausing only to shorten stirrups, and cantered off in the direction Roger always took. He had been gone for well over an hour and would never have left his horse unattended if he had returned. She called out to him, looking to each side of the track in case he had taken a fall and was lying injured. Roger did not fall! Despite his erratic behaviour of late he was a superb horseman. After half an hour of frantic calling and searching she found him, lying in the centre of the track beneath the overhanging limb of a mighty oak. They had ducked under it enough times, lying flat along their horses' withers; but Roger hadn't ducked soon enough. His forehead was discoloured with a terrible bruise; his neck was broken. She knelt beside him for a while, dry-eyed, then she got to her feet and walked slowly back to the house, leading her late husband's hunter behind her.

—◆◆◆—

Beneath a photograph of Roger as a young man, the *Western Morning News* ran the announcement.

Roger Bertrand Carew Fulford of Cranmere, 52, one of the unsung heroes of the last war, and well known in the show-jumping world in pre-war days, died in a riding accident on the Cranmere Estate yesterday afternoon. He leaves a widow and one son.

At the funeral service in Chagford Parish Church, Roger's coffin lay draped in the Union flag but unadorned with medals. Jane recalled his words, 'They don't hand out gongs in my outfit.' But an elderly brigadier who claimed to have known Roger well gave a moving address when he spoke of valour and dedication and leadership, and how his widow and son could be justifiably proud of the late Colonel Fulford. The manner of his death had never been held in question except by two people in the congregation, both of whom had known Roger very well indeed. Jane, who felt sure – well, almost sure – that Roger would never have made such a stupid error of judgement; and an elderly Doctor Douglas McMasters kept his inner thoughts very much to himself.

Later, at a formal gathering in the salon at Cranmere – the ceiling much admired – one of the male guests, the worse for drink, remarked in a loud voice and with monumental insensitivity, that 'Old Roger met his death as he had life – head on. What?'

David stood with Jane on the terrace as they watched the last of the guests depart. He put a comforting arm around her shoulders and said, 'Just you and me now, Mother.'

—◦◦◦—

'Mother? Mother?'

Jane looked up from the iron seat to see David smiling down at her. 'Are you all right?' he asked.

'Yes, of course I am.' She had not heard the car pull up. 'I was just dreaming. That's what we old biddies do, you know.' She cocked one eyebrow at him, 'I hope you are not going to say you were just passing.'

'I wouldn't dare lie to you,' he grinned.

'Did Anne Perret phone you?'

'Yes, she did. She thought you might like a lift home.'

'Hmm, she would.'

'If you can't get on with her we'll get someone else.'

'No, Anne's all right. I am just a crotchety old woman. You will have to help me to my feet, David, I think my bones have set.'

—◦◦◦—

—∿∿—

'You have made your contribution, Hal, leave the rest to us. I will let you know just as soon as we hear anything from them,' Sir Edward Channon had said.

'Stay at your bench and make something beautiful, Hal. Don't call me, I'll call you,' Billy Cann had said.

He had been at his bench for days working patiently on a carved wood mirror frame which reminded him of Gina and her workshop in Milan. He tried hard to concentrate; he didn't want to think about Gina, or Moreno, or Billy Cann, not even his Uncle Ted. Especially not Uncle Ted! For the past week he had been privy to the story of the missing cabinet from the time it left Cranmere right up to the present day; and he had withheld that information because of his vow of silence. In hindsight it seemed ill advised, except that he knew, without any doubt, that once a man like Billy Cann had given his word – sealed with a firm handshake – he would never, ever break it; so neither would he. But he was a cabinetmaker, for God's sake, not a dealer, or a smooth operator, or any kind of an investigator. And hadn't they told him to go back to his bench and leave the rest to them? That was what he intended to do. All the same, he thought he might have heard something by now; time was slipping by. The days extended to ten and then eleven, and on the twelfth day the telephone rang. He recognised Billy Cann's gravelly voice instantly.

'Meet me for lunch, Hal. Basil Hotel, Basil Street, just behind Harrods. D'you know it?'

'No, but I can find it. When?'

'Tomorrow. Midday suit you?'

'Yes, all right. Do you have some news, then?'

'Tell you tomorrow. Oh, and Hal?'

'Yes?' 'You're paying. *Ciaow.*' His laugh sounded deeper over the telephone.

A sixth sense – or common sense – prompted Hal to travel up to London by rail. Lunch with Billy Cann was sure to be a liquid affair and the very last thing he needed was to get himself breathalysed on the way home. A similar sense, or reasoning, told him that if Billy were inviting him to an expensive lunch – no matter who paid – then it was on the cards that he had some good news, something to celebrate even.

—◈◈◈—

Basil Street is a quiet tributary off seething Sloane Street in the very heart of Knightsbridge, and the Basil Hotel a welcome beach. Somehow the management has preserved an atmosphere of calm and good taste, making it a place where country parsons might meet their wives and daughters. Not the sort of establishment that Hal would have immediately associated with Billy Cann, but then, on second thoughts, why not? Hadn't he spent five of his formative years at Cranmere? And didn't he look entirely at home standing at the bar in a room painted in pastel shades and hung with framed prints? Billy was the only customer – the parsons and wives yet to congregate for their preprandial sweet sherries – and deep in discussion with the barman. Which was what Hal might have expected. A gregarious man like Billy would engage in conversation with anyone from baron to bootboy; not for him sitting alone over his beer.

His greeting, 'Hal! Come on in, what'll you have?' Was almost too hearty for his surroundings. Today he wore dark pinstripes with highly polished black shoes, and a pale blue shirt with neatly knotted tie, very much the city gent; but his broad smile was indicative of his genuine pleasure at their meeting.

'You're looking well, Hal.'

'So are you.'

'Yes, well I've been abroad where the sun shines.' Billy glanced out of the window to where the first heavy raindrops were raising little dust clouds on the pavements.

'In New York?'

'That's right. Looked up a few old friends, saw the sights.'

'Did you see a cabinet?'

Billy smiled mysteriously, 'Later, Hal.'

Anton, the seven-foot head waiter, had appeared silently in the doorway to inform Mr duCann that his table was ready when he was. He deferred to Mr duCann. Billy confided that he and Anton – whose real name was 'Arry – had always looked after one another. They sat in a corner, at Mr duCann's usual table, and looked at huge menus.

Billy put his down and asked, 'What do you recommend, Anton?'

'Knowing your tastes, Mr duCann, the salmon followed by the beef.'

When Billy's salmon was placed before him it had been taken off the bone and the new potatoes sliced to bite-size. A one-armed man eats with his fork.

'Now then,' Billy said, spearing his salmon, 'Your father.'

'Yes?'

Billy glanced around the rapidly filling dining room. 'I can promise you, Hal, that the people we were talking about had no interest in your father, or in the aircraft he was travelling in, or Giovanni Spargo. None at all.'

'You spoke to your friend in Naples, then?'

'I did, though I wouldn't call him a friend. He also made inquiries of the people who deal with these incidents and some of the men who were at the scene. They recovered the flight recorder and their findings were that this was nothing more than the result of an electrical storm which threw the instruments out. A God-awful accident when we are told that air travel is safer than crossing the road. I can't tell you how sorry I am, Hal.'

'Thank you,' Hal said quietly.

Billy was looking at him closely. 'Can you accept that?'

After a long pause, Hal said, 'Yes, I can. I've given it a lot of thought and perhaps I was a bit over the top. It seemed to me that there were too many coincidences, but if your man says no, plus the evidence from the flight recorder, then yes, I can accept it and I'm very grateful for all your trouble.'

'No trouble at all, Hal, and as much for my own sake as yours. But I think we must also accept it was just a coincidence that your father was going to see Giovanni Spargo at the time.'

'Yes, I suppose we must.'

'Friend of yours, was he, *Giovanni*?'

'Yes, he was, some years ago.'

'Then you may have known he was a bit overfond of the vino.'

'I didn't, though it doesn't surprise me.'

'Giovanni bought himself an Alfa Romeo Spyder. That's a very fast car; I should know, I owned one. He didn't even get onto the Autostrada; he lost control on a bend in one of the feeder roads, went over the top.

There was no other vehicle involved.' Billy stabbed at an infant potato with his fork. 'At the autopsy they found he was three times over the Italian limit. Let's face it, Hal, there was no mystery, no bogeyman, he was pissed out of his mind. Which was a damned shame, he was a fine craftsman.'

'Yes, he was,' Hal said. 'So you did see the cabinet.'

'Oh yes,' Billy smiled, 'I saw the cabinet, and I met our friend Moreno.'

'No friend of mine,' Hal said. 'What did you make of it, the cabinet?'

'I have to tell you that I was sorely tempted; I've a couple of clients looking for something like that. But then, knowing its history I was able to restrain myself.'

'You mean Moreno offered to sell it to you?'

'I think that was on his mind.'

'The cunning little sod. You'd have thought he might have waited for the Channon Grieves report.'

'He had no need,' Billy said. 'I told him I'd seen the Cranmere cabinet, which was true, even if it was in bits and I was only a kid at the time. And I confirmed that this was the pair to it.'

'You mean you *told* him!' Hal said, horrified.

'Sure, why not?'

'What did he say?'

'Not very much, I think he already knew. So I pointed out to him that now Channon Grieves were onto it there was no way he could sell the cabinet legitimately, and more than likely it would be illustrated in every coffee-table book on English furniture for years to come. And I suggested that Mr Agnolli's best move might be to hand it back to where it belongs and make a bit of political mileage out of it at the same time. He seemed to like the idea, a future senator being all heart, cementing Anglo/US relations and so on.'

Hal did not share Billy's confidence. The Channon Grieves report was due to land on Moreno's desk any day now, with a possible follow-up containing veiled threats from Mike Monahan about adverse publicity, and now Billy had gone in like a bull at a gate. He had visions of his part in all this going horribly wrong. 'He might destroy it,' he said.

'He won't do that, Hal.' Billy sat back in his chair and smiled at the younger man like a benevolent – if slightly wicked – uncle.

'No? Moreno's a crafty little bugger, there's no knowing what he might do to protect his boss.'

'Moreno's all right, I quite liked him. We ate a nice meal together.'

'I'm pleased to hear it,' Hal said, anything but pleased. 'But what guarantee do we have that he's not putting a match to the cabinet right now?'

'This might help.' Billy was holding out a long white envelope. 'You'd better take a look.'

Hal withdrew an official looking document headed 'Bill of Lading'.

'I expect you've seen one of those before, haven't you?'

'Yes,' Hal nodded. He was already reading – Bill of Lading aboard the *SS Manitoba NY*. The *Consignor* was a firm of New York Lawyers, Moreno and Heinmann Inc, of East 42nd Street. The *Consignee* – via a firm of London lawyers, Harding and Willis of Cheapside – was Channon Grieves of Moorgate EC2. The *Consignment – A large antique cabinet in mahogany. English circa 1760. Customs cleared by the Antiques Association of America. Due arrival at Southampton 17th August 1992.* He read it through quickly, then again very slowly and felt his hands begin to tremble. 'I don't believe this,' he said almost to himself.

'You are holding the proof in your hands,' Billy said. 'I know it's only a photocopy but you can take it from me it's kosher.'

'It's coming back?' Hal looked up slowly from the printed page.

'That's right,' Billy grinned. 'All the way back to the long gallery at Cranmere where I used to play football.'

'But how on earth did you...?'

Billy tapped the side of his nose then held up one finger that said, 'Don't ask.'

'This is unreal!' Hal looked again at the document still held in both hands, shook his head in near disbelief. 'I don't know what to say.'

'How about, thank you, Billy.'

'Well yes,' he began to laugh, 'Thank you, Billy.'

'And how about, can I buy you a drink, Billy?'

'Can I buy you a drink, Billy?'

'Sure, you can.' Billy signalled to Anton waiting in the wings and suddenly they were surrounded by a flurry of waiters as dishes were removed, their next course placed before them and vegetables served, while Anton supervised the ice bucket and removed the cork from a vintage bottle with a discreet pop. Other diners looked at their watches and muttered.

Hal, still slightly dazed at the news Billy had brought him, looked on in admiration at what was clearly a bit of stage management. And why not? Billy had succeeded in his mission and this was his moment of triumph.

But Billy had become serious. 'Let's drink to your father, Hal.' He raised his glass, 'To Charles Wesson'

'To Charles Wesson,' Hal repeated.

'And Giovanni.'

'And Giovanni.'

'And to Billy Cann,' Hal said before he could object.

'Oh, all right.' Billy drained his glass before refilling them both. 'We mustn't forget Jane.'

'No, that would never do. What am I going to tell her?'

Billy put his glass down. 'You tell her nothing. You agreed, remember?'

'Of course I remember, but she's bound to ask, I'll have to tell her something.'

'Tell her from an old admirer.'

'All right, to Jane from an old admirer.'

'I've another reason to celebrate, Hal.'

'What's that then?'

'My little filly Cranmere was first past the post at Sandown.'

'Great! Here's to Cranmere, saved from the knackers. Do you think one bottle will be enough?'

'Wouldn't have thought so. You're paying.'

'My pleasure, drink up.'

—◦◦◦—

Later, and after a pot of strong coffee, Hal climbed unsteadily into a black cab. Before closing the door, Billy grasped his hand. 'Remember, Hal, we never met, okay?'

'Never, ever,' Hal said solemnly.

'But if you should find yourself in Brighton, be sure to look me up.'

'I promise, Billy.'

'And bring Bella with you.'

'No bloody fear.'

Billy Cann stood laughing on the wet pavement as the cab drew away.

———∞———

In an almost empty carriage on the mid-afternoon train to Cirencester, Hal sprawled in his seat and watched the rain-sodden fields flash by. Occasionally he smiled as he recalled snatches of his conversation with Billy – to the consternation of a middle-aged woman sitting nearby – and reached into his inner pocket to make sure the Bill of Lading really did exist. It did. And his smile grew wider as he considered how he would break the news to his Uncle Ted. Would he commence – 'Oh, by the way…?' No, he would not! All the same, it was so nice, so very sweet to savour the thought that he was ahead of the field, just this once. Uncle Ted might hit the roof, tear him off a strip for meddling, or for withholding information. No he wouldn't. How could he when presented with this *fait accompli*? For the present moment he would revel in his secret knowledge before passing it over. He smiled again.

As for Billy – without doubt one of the most charismatic characters he had ever (never) met – why all the secrecy? Because he had knowingly held onto the cabinet and then sold it to Brocatti? Hardly an indictable offence as he was the legal owner at the time. And surely his crossing the Atlantic to get it back – and just how he had achieved that was beyond Hal's comprehension – had more than expunged what little guilt he might once have felt? Or secrecy because in his world of hard dealing it might have been seen as a sign of weakness to perform an act of kindness? Or because Billy Cann always pays his debts? Whatever the reason, Hal felt deeply grateful for Billy's help in clearing up any questions over his father's death and would forever be in *his* debt, not the other way around. Thinking of debts, he wondered what Uncle Ted would have to say when he claimed the costs of two lunches swilled down with vintage champagne – just behind Harrods – on expenses.

'What the hell!' Hal smiled again.

———∞———

It was an odd sensation, a bit like a man who had won the lottery but was unable to tell anyone. He had driven – very carefully – from the station, showered, changed, read Charles Edward his bedtime story, walked across to the workshop to see what had or had not been done during his absence, and now sat in his office while Bella watched *Casualty* on TV. He could not even confide in Bella, much as he wanted to, not yet. In a day or two perhaps, when the dust had settled. Nor could he speak to his Uncle Ted who was dining out. Tomorrow then. In the meantime there was one person he could talk to and that was Jane.

When he dialled her number a woman's voice answered, a Miss Perret. And no, he could not speak to Mrs Fulford, she was sleeping at present.

'Are you a relative, Mr Wesson?'

'No, just a friend.'

'Perhaps you were unaware that Mrs Fulford is seriously ill.'

Seriously ill? Miss Perret sounded like a professional, and they never said seriously ill unless the patient was – well, seriously ill. 'I knew she wasn't too well,' he said 'but...'

'I am sorry, Mr Wesson. I can take a message if you wish.'

'Yes, if you would. The message is – the missing cabinet will be returned to Cranmere by the end of August.' He waited while she repeated the message slowly as she wrote it down. In the circumstances it seemed trivial. 'She will be pleased with the news,' he added.

'Thank you, I'll make sure she gets it when she wakes. Is that all?'

'Just give her my love.'

'Goodbye, Mr Wesson.'

'Goodbye, Miss Perret.'

There was nothing more he could do.

—◦◦◦—

CHAPTER 33

—◦◦◦◦◦—

Jane had spent the day in bed – for the first time since when? When David was born? She could not remember, neither did she have any choice; she felt so weak and so very, very tired. Was she dying? Well maybe she was, and if so it was not an unpleasant experience, not really. They had stepped up her medication, she felt sure of it. She felt, if anything, slightly squiffy like that time in Totnes when she had drunk too much gin.

Alec McMasters had been in to see her during the afternoon. She had mistaken him for his father and called him Douglas until corrected.

'Well, you are very like him,' she said. 'He was a dear friend. I remember him telling me about his elder brother.'

'Ye must be thinking of someone else, Jane, my father was an only child.'

'I was not thinking of someone else, Alec,' she smiled drowsily. 'He was a very dear friend.'

From her high-ended bed she had watched the sun going down over Sittaford and now the moon was up, flooding the room with its pale light. David was sound asleep in the wing chair; he had been with her all evening and insisted he would stay the night. She had not protested too strongly, she loved having him there. He had been reading to her, *Lorna Doone*, one of her childhood favourites. She had listened with her eyes closed.

'Mother, are you listening?'

'I haven't missed a word, my dear,' she had replied although, in truth, she was not sure if Jan Ridd had climbed up the waterfall or fallen down it. It was the sound of her son's voice she loved, especially when he tried to put on a West Country brogue, not very well – but when he did he sounded very much like Charles.

In his sleep David looked half his age, more like the young man who had returned to take Cranmere in hand, had battled with the Inland Revenue over near devastating death duties and found a publisher for Roger's memoirs which had been made into a film and saved them from the bailiffs. And had made the estate into a limited company to protect it from future predatory governments. Cranmere was safe in David's hands; and so was the Fulford name, if not the bloodline. The days were long gone since she had felt any guilt over her deceit. To the contrary, with two grandsons the Fulfords would be secure, and strengthened by their Wesson genes. As she gazed at David his features seemed to dissolve and change a little to become Charles, soon to be replaced with Charles' other son, Hal. How very kind of Hal to send her that message. Although she had only known him for that one afternoon, she had felt sure that he would succeed in his mission. And now the cabinet would at last be returned to the long gallery. David would be pleased, Catherine even more so.

Jane slept, and as she did so a succession of images passed through her mind's eye, faces from the past in soft focus and blurred around the edges like old photographs. Faces of people she had known, some recent, some from long ago and in haphazard order. Children, American soldiers, Lieutenant Dando, faces once familiar to her, their names long forgotten. Then old Bertie Fulford, Doris, a stable girl she had once known, and little Billy Cann, and Millie, dear, sweet Millie, now a mother several times over; and Charles. Then the images faded and there was nothing.

When she awoke the moon had gone leaving the room in total darkness, no chink of light and no sound. But a familiar smell reached her – horse? Could she smell horse? Yes, she could, and she could feel the warmth of a horse nearby.

And she understood.

'Rosie?' she whispered, 'Is that you?'

'Yes.' The voice was soft and low as she had always known it would be.

'Is it time, Rosie?'

'Yes, you must come with me now.'

'I am ready...'

—⁓⁓—

CHAPTER 34

—◦◦◦—

Hal was shaving when the telephone rang. Bella answered it and called up the stairs, 'Dad wants to know if you can drop in to see him this morning?'

'Yes, in about an hour,' he called back and heard Bella ring off. 'What's it about?'

'He didn't say.'

'He didn't need to,' Hal muttered to the shaving mirror, wiped off the condensation. 'The old buzzard already knows,' he said to his reflection, 'I'd put money on it.' And this was to have been *his* moment, *his* denouement. He might have guessed. There was no way he was going to steal a march on his Uncle Ted.

—◦◦◦—

The minute he walked into the room Hal knew that something was wrong. Sir Edward sat at his desk in his study and smiled in greeting, but there was a sadness about him; his shoulders sagged and his eyes were moist almost as though he had been weeping.

'I have some very sad news,' he said before Hal could ask. 'Jane Fulford died during the early hours of this morning.'

Hal sat in the chair facing the desk, his previous night's brief conversation with Miss Perret still fresh in his mind, so it was not unexpected. 'I am sorry, Uncle. You were fond of her weren't you?'

'Yes, I was. We went back a long way.'

'I liked her,' Hal said.

'Of course, you met her, didn't you? I never had the pleasure, spoke to her on the telephone often enough during the war. I should have gone down to see her. Too late now.'

For a moment they fell silent, Hal wondering if Jane had received his message and thinking, how bloody ironic that this should happen right now with the return of the missing cabinet almost in sight. But his sympathies were mostly for his Uncle Ted; he was at an age when his contemporaries were dying off apace. And no doubt he'd be castigating himself for not driving down to see Jane, just as Billy Cann was over his father.

'She died peacefully in her sleep,' Sir Edward was saying. 'Her son was with her.' He turned in his chair to gaze out through the open French window for a moment before returning to his desk and the thick folder before him. 'Well then,' he said, once more the chairman. 'Thank you for coming, Hal. I now have all the reports and we can finalise this one, if you have the time?'

'Yes, of course I have.'

'Good.' He put on his reading glasses, opened the file and began, 'Ben Pavoni has been very thorough. Don't ask me how, but he is able to communicate with some of the lower echelons of Milanese society, even to the extent of a side door into local organised crime communities. Which is one of the many reasons why he is so useful to us; he's a first-class fieldman.'

Hal smiled at the flowery description of Ben's talents. 'I think the word is "streetwise", isn't it?'

'Yes, very likely.' He turned the first of a five-page report. 'He assures me,' Sir Edward looked at Hal over the top of his glasses, 'that the Mafia had no interest in your father, nor in anyone travelling on the same aircraft, nor Spargo, nor the missing cabinet.'

Hal half-listened to an almost identical report to Billy Cann's version of the disaster in which both of his parents had died, including flight recorders, interviews with officials and those working at the scene. But while Sir Edward read from the close-typed page, he found his thoughts wandering to an afternoon in the Dower House at Cranmere when he had been so brutally tactless, and hoped he had not hastened Jane Fulford's end.

'Ben also remarks,' Sir Edward was saying, 'that he got the impression that someone else had been making similar inquiries quite recently. You wouldn't know anything about that, would you?'

Hal shook his head. 'No, not a thing.'

Giovanni was dealt with almost cursorily. An elderly man, a known alcoholic, had bought himself a powerful sports car and found he was unable to handle it. The best that could be said was that he probably died happy. Summing up, Ben Pavoni said that he had found no connection between the two accidents and nothing suspect about either. He hoped that this would help to set Hal's mind at rest.

'Does it, Hal?' Sir Edward removed his glasses.

'Yes, it does.'

'Are you quite sure, because I know this has been worrying you?'

'Yes,' Hal said. His mind had been pretty much at rest since yesterday lunchtime, although he wouldn't say so; but this clinched it. 'Yes, I'm quite sure, Uncle, and would you pass on my thanks to Ben for all his trouble?'

'I'll be pleased to,' Sir Edward smiled. 'And now on a happier note, the Cranmere cabinet.'

'Yes?' Hal felt apprehensive. Did Uncle Ted know, and if so, how much did he know? He was soon to find out.

'You will, no doubt, be gratified to hear that the cabinet is on its way home to Cranmere.'

'Yes.' There was no point in even trying; Uncle Ted knew, and knew that he knew.'

'But you're not surprised?'

'Well no, I learned yesterday afternoon. I phoned as soon as I got back but you were out.'

'Well I'm here now.' Sir Edward sat back in his chair and waited, a faint smile around his lips.

Hal shifted uncomfortably. He had thought a lot about this, had to offer some sort of explanation – but there was no way he was going to grass on Billy. 'It's difficult for me, Uncle. You see, the man responsible insists on remaining anonymous, and I gave him my solemn word I would not so much as breathe his name.'

'There is mention in a letter I have from a firm of London lawyers of an old admirer,' Sir Edward said. 'I imagine Jane would have had many, so why don't we call him Mr Jones?'

'Yes, all right,' Hal agreed. 'Well, Mr Jones was an evacuee at Cranmere during the war years. He first arrived there at the age of six or seven having just been dug out of a bombed building where he had been buried for three days. His parents were both dead and to add to his difficulties he had a malformed arm. I believe both Jane and my father made a special effort on his behalf because he remembered them with great affection. Later, he made a success of his life, due largely, he said, to Jane's and Father's encouragement, and is now a very wealthy man.'

'Excuse me interrupting, Hal, but how did you get to hear of this Mr Jones?'

Hal was ready for that one. 'Jane first mentioned him, and

coincidentally as he is in the antiques trade I was able to trace him.'

'So you went to see him?'

'Yes, I did. I thought having been at Cranmere he might be of some help.'

'And was he?'

'Yes, he was. When I told him my father had been accused of stealing the cabinet and Jane also implicated, he became very annoyed. He remembered Roger Fulford with no affection at all, said he thought Jane was not treated at all well. He insisted on going to New York to try to get Jane's cabinet back. I didn't ask him, Uncle, I promise you. But I don't think I could have stopped him if I'd wanted to.'

'When was this, Hal?'

'Nearly two weeks ago. I'd heard nothing from him until the day before yesterday, almost given him up until he phoned. Then we met and he told me the news and gave me this.' Hal held out his precious Bill of Lading.

It was waved away with a, 'Thank you, I already have a copy,' and Hal waited for a minor eruption which never came. He was fully expecting a 'Just what did you think you were playing at?' It would have been well deserved. But no, Sir Edward sat like a great Buddha lost in thought.

After what seemed a very long silence he asked, 'How do you suppose your Mr Jones managed to persuade a tough nut like Moreno to hand over the Cranmere cabinet so willingly?'

'Well firstly,' Hal said, relieved at the lack of a detonation, 'he identified the cabinet as the missing one.'

'How could he do that? Had he been to Cranmere recently?'

'No, he was merely repeating what I'd told him. And then he told Moreno that now that Channon Grieves knew the truth, there was no way he could sell the cabinet legally, and it would probably appear in every illustrated book on English furniture for years to come.'

'Did he, now?' Sir Edward said appreciatively.

'Yes, he did. And then he went on to suggest that Agnolli would be well advised to make a gesture by returning the cabinet to its rightful owners and so gain some political Brownie points.'

'Your Mr Jones sounds to be a very astute man.'

'I think he must be to have talked Moreno around to his way of thinking,' Hal said. This was turning out easier than he'd dared to hope.

'Quite honestly, Uncle, I don't know how he managed it, unless there was something he wasn't telling me.'

'There was.' Sir Edward passed over a sheet of paper embossed with the name Moreno and Heinemann, Inc. It was a receipt in favour of Channon Grieves for *One Antique Mahogany Cabinet c 1760* in the sum of 1.2 million dollars.

Hal looked up into his Uncle Ted's broadly smiling face. 'You mean he *paid* for it?'

'It looks very much like it.'

Hal began to laugh. 'The old fraud!'

'Come now, Hal, I wouldn't call a man who pays out that sort of money a fraud, even if he did halve the asking price.'

'No, I beg his pardon.'

'I wonder what made him do it?' Sir Edward said reflectively. 'What was the motivation behind such generosity?'

Hal thought for a moment of Billy Cann sitting alone in his beautiful home in Millionaires' Row. 'It's in character, I suppose. He's a man who prides himself in paying his debts, and he felt indebted to Jane and my father. And, of course, he is very wealthy, even owns a racehorse.'

'In my experience of the very wealthy they are more inclined to be anything but generous.'

'There may have been an element of guilt,' Hal added.

'What did he have to feel guilty about?'

'Oh, didn't I say?' Hal smiled and offered up silent thanks for a flash of pure inspiration. 'He was the little boy who switched on all the lights on the night Cranmere was bombed. He was afraid of the dark, you see?'

And he had the satisfaction of seeing his Uncle Ted's look of astonishment. 'Well I'll be damned,' he said. 'Is that all it was? There had to be a reason why Cranmere was targeted.'

Hal felt a deep sense of relief. His explanations were at an end, and Billy was safe in his secrecy.

Sir Edward made to close the file, then hesitated. 'Hal,' he asked, 'during your travels did you ever come across a Mr duCann in Brighton?'

The smile left Hal's face very quickly. He looked his Uncle Ted straight in the eye and said, 'I never mentioned that name.'

'Nor you did, Hal.'

'Please don't disturb him.'

'I see no reason to, apart from a letter of thanks.'

'No!' Hal shook his head.

'Very well, I will ask the London lawyers to convey our thanks to the unknown admirer.'

He closed the file for the last time and, catching sight of the name printed on the cover, said, 'What a crying shame that Jane never knew.'

'She may have done, Uncle. I telephoned yesterday evening and left a message with her nurse.'

'Good. Let's hope she received it. The funeral will be sometime next week, I imagine.'

'Will you be going?' Hal asked.

'No, I don't think so. It wouldn't seem right as I never met her in life. How about you?'

'I don't know.'

'Well if you should decide, perhaps you would represent me?'

———∽∾∿———

On the following morning, Hal sat at the breakfast table going through his mail while Bella spooned baby food into Charles Edward in his high chair. She looked across at her husband, frowned and said, 'Hal? Is something wrong?'

He did not reply but stared at the letter in his hand, a modest thing handwritten on a single sheet of ruled paper torn from a pad.

She moved around the table to his side. 'What is it?'

'Take a look.'

———∽∾∿———

The Dower House
Cranmere
Devon

Dear Hal,
Just a line to thank you for the kindness and consideration that you have shown to me and my family. You are your father's son.
Affectionately,
Jane Fulford.

Dictated and signed by Mrs Fulford. Written by Miss A Perret SRN.
P.S. Mrs Fulford wished you to have the enclosed.

Bella leaned one arm on Hal's shoulder. 'So she did receive your message after all.'

'Yes, I think she must have.'

'What was enclosed?'

In reply Hal opened one hand and held out a tiny wood carving of two doves with their necks entwined. Bella took it from him, turned it over in her hands.

'It's beautiful,' she breathed. 'Is it your father's work?'

'Yes.'

'He must have loved her deeply.'

'Yes.' Hal looked up to his wife for guidance. 'Should I go to the funeral, do you think?'

'Yes, I think you should.' She leaned down and kissed him gently on the lips. From the far side of the table Charles Edward gurgled in glee.

———∽∽∽———

CHAPTER 35

A thin moorland mist swirled around the ancient granite tower of St Michael's Church, Chagford, giving an air of gloom appropriate for the occasion. The interior was packed to capacity, the congregation spilling out into the churchyard where they stood about self-consciously waiting for the service to begin. A tannoy system had been hastily installed with cables and loudspeakers slung in the trees to accommodate outsiders. Hal looked around him; this was an event and the County had turned out in force. Farmers trussed into their funeral suits, their wives in more sombre plumage than usual, mingled with tall – now stooped – military-looking men, Jane's admirers from years long gone, while above them the mist seemed to dull the deep sonorous note of the single bell.

At last the bell fell silent, hymn sheets were hurriedly passed around from one hand to another and the service began.

'I am the resurrection and the life.' The priest's voice sounded tinny over the tannoy. Standing next to Hal a tall man, deeply tanned and with a fine head of snow-white hair, kept one arm protectively around his diminutive wife who snuffled into a man-sized handkerchief. Judging by their dress, he thought they might be Americans and was proved right when the singing started.

'*The day thou gavest Lord is ended…*' He sang strongly and rolled the 'r' in 'Lord', while she mumbled into her handkerchief. Hal mouthed the words from the hymn sheet with the rest of the congregation but doubted they meant any more to them than they did to him. This was a ritual, he decided. How many of these people were regular churchgoers? Very few. Christmas, Easter and Harvest Festival and that would be about it, apart from the Americans who took their religion more seriously than did the English.

Why had he come? Funerals were for the living, not the departed, and yet he knew no one here. For Jane's sake? No, not really; although he had admired her he had only known her for that one afternoon. For his father's sake and Uncle Ted's? Yes, to a certain extent. For his own sake? If he were honest with himself, yes, and to get one last look at his half-brother and possibly his nephews. That was why he had come, and because Bella felt that he should – to lay the ghosts of whatever had been troubling him.

Over the tannoy the priest's thin voice rambled on about Jane's unstinting service to others during the war years, together with a number of stock phrases dusted off for the occasion. Hal wondered if they had ever met? At last the final hymn, *Abide with me fast falls the eventide.* Then the blessing.

In accordance with her wishes, the Fulford family vault was not prepared ready to receive Jane. Her mortal remains were to be taken to the Exeter crematorium, her ashes to be scattered on Dartmoor – from horseback. A big Daimler hearse waited at the gate not far from where Hal stood, another funeral limo parked at a respectful distance. 'They're coming out,' a voice whispered.

Six sturdy men from the Cranmere Estate carried Jane's coffin with pride and apparent ease as they walked slowly towards the gate, keeping in perfect step. The coffin was draped in a dark green cloth bearing the Fulford arms. Hal bowed his head respectfully as they passed, and then looked up straight into the grey eyes of his half-brother walking immediately behind. David held his gaze for a brief moment, then smiled in recognition.

'Thank you for coming,' he said quietly as they moved on.

Beside him a tall woman looked steadily ahead, her features classically beautiful – and hard as nails. Behind them the two boys, uncomfortable in their grey suits and black ties on a humid day. The younger boy, a fair-haired rebel, tugged at his collar. Hal smiled at him and he smiled in return. He wanted to call out, 'Hey, I'm your Uncle Hal,' but the moment had passed and the boys stood with their parents at the gate while their grandmother's coffin was loaded with great care into the waiting hearse.

'Who was that you spoke to?' Catherine demanded of her husband.

'No one you would know,' David replied in his lazy drawl. 'He's just a cabinetmaker.'

Car doors were closed, the cortège moved off and the crowd began to move forward. The tall American comforted his weeping wife. 'C'mon, Millie' he said. 'Let's get you back to the hotel.'

At the gate Hal was accosted by a cub reporter who needed names of mourners. 'I represent Sir Edward Channon,' he said and took care to spell out the name otherwise they'd be sure to get it wrong.

'And you, sir?'

Hal's face was expressionless as he said, 'Charles Wesson.'

He walked slowly and thoughtfully back up the hill to where he had parked his car and stood for a moment looking down into the churchyard where floral tributes were being admired — or criticised. When quite suddenly his face broke into a broad smile as he said, 'Well, yes, thank you for that, David. You are quite right. That's what I am, just a cabinetmaker.'

> *Don't tell them all the old things,*
> *They're buried under the snow,*
> *Whispering grass don't tell the trees,*
> *Cos the trees — don't — need — to — know.*